FROM SORROW'S HOLD

FROM SORROW'S HOLD

JONATHAN PEACE

This edition produced in Great Britain in 2022

by Hobeck Books Limited, Unit 14, Sugnall Business Centre, Sugnall, Stafford, Staffordshire, ST21 6NF

www.hobeck.net

A CIP catalogue for this book is available from the British Library.

ISBN 978-1-913-793-75-3 (pbk)

ISBN 978-1-913-793-74-6 (ebook)

Cover design by Jayne Mapp Design

Printed and bound in Great Britain

ARE YOU A THRILLER SEEKER?

Hobeck Books is an independent publisher of crime, thrillers and suspense fiction and we have one aim – to bring you the books you want to read.

For more details about our books, our authors and our plans, plus the chance to download free novellas, sign up for our newsletter at **www.hobeck.net**.

You can also find us on Twitter **@hobeckbooks** or on Facebook **www.facebook.com/hobeckbooks10**.

PRAISE FOR JONATHAN PEACE

DIRTY LITTLE SECRET

'A masterfully told thriller which mines the darkest corners of the 1980s as an experimental police unit race to save a young life from a sadistic killer.' *Graham Bartlett*

'My goodness what a novel!! This story was absolutely full of suspense, mystery, strong female characters, misogynistic males in roles of power and thrills. Honestly I devoured it as quickly as I could, I couldn't put it down!' *Bex Books and Stuff*

'This was well written, pacey, the plot was solid and the ending left you quite stunned and ready for more.' *Hanny May Reviews*

'Jonathan Peace did a fantastic job of expertly weaving story lines like spider's webs, interweaving them until you were so wrapped up, you forgot all notion of time.' *Books With Gina*

'Altogether an addictive and immersive read.' *Sharon Beyond The Books*

'There is a tautness to the storytelling, especially until the climax block, that keeps us hooked.' *Surjit Book Blog*

FROM SORROW'S HOLD

'An exciting read.' Carole Gourlay

'Another enjoyable read.' Sarah Leck

'One to look out for.' Pete Fleming

'Although I enjoyed the first book, I enjoyed this one more … An enthralling read throughout.' ThrillerMan

NOTE FROM THE AUTHOR

Writing a second book before the first was even accepted by a publisher was an interesting challenge. It was also very liberating; I wasn't writing to an already captive audience. In a way it was like writing for the very first time as there were no expectations – no one, not even my wife, had met these characters yet and so I was under no pressure to follow a particular path which some authors who have written long series have talked about. I could do what I like, go where I wanted, and I was very surprised by exactly where the story went.

I hope you will be too.

And this is the second book in what I hope will be a very long series, certainly at least twelve books with a long-term plan that I can't really talk about as it would spoil potential storylines. What I can say is that *Dirty Little Secret* began the series set in 1987; the final book would be set in 2023 – 41 books in total.

From Sorrow's Hold briefly touches the topic of teen suicide. Future books will go into the subjects of mental health, anxiety and depression, all contributing factors to the causes of suicide, and as a sufferer of anxiety and depression myself, I hope I've handled them with the respect they deserve.

If you are suffering in any way, there is always someone willing to listen.

UK

The Samaritans
www.samaritans.org
Call: 116 123
Email: jo@samaritans.org
Dial 999 in an emergency

US

National Suicide Prevention Lifeline (NIMH)
www.nimh.nih.gov
Call: 1-800-273-TALK (8255)
Text: text HELLO to 741741
Dial 911 in an emergency

You can always contact me to talk via social media or email me jonathanlpeace@gmail.com

For those who suffer in silence,
And for those who are left behind.

DECEMBER, 1988

No one ever told me that grief felt so like fear.
C.S. Lewis

PROLOGUE

SATURDAY, 10TH

The abandoned warehouses beside Holy Trinity Church were not ideal for business, but on a cold night such as this, and with nowhere else to go, it would have to make do.

Not that the punter was complaining; he was drunk enough to think a ten quid blow-job in a dirty, deserted warehouse on a cold December night was a good idea, and that was good enough for her.

Helen Williams had been doing this long enough to know he wouldn't last, probably wouldn't even be able to get it up – the easiest tenner she'd earned all week. Nearly the only money she'd earned. With only a couple of weeks till Christmas, money was tighter than usual, and with so many parties taking place there weren't that many marks around for her to ply her slick trade on. Even the Carps had been quiet tonight. Her brother, Pete, was hustling a couple of lads on the pool table for pints; he'd be as drunk as her mark by now.

She gave the rotten wooden door a yank, wincing at the loud screech it made as it pulled on rusted hinges. It stuck on something on the ground, a half-brick that she kicked aside. She had to give it two more pulls before she could squeeze inside. Her mark was no help; he was leaning against the wall, head down, trying not to be sick.

With any luck, while she was on her knees she'd be able to lift his wallet without him noticing and take whatever cash he had left. He'd been drinking shots in the Carps and bought everyone a round. He'd wake in the morning and think he'd spent his Christmas bonus on the booze. So would his wife. If he was lucky.

If he struggled, then she had other options.

Helen took him by the hand and led him into the warehouse. It was dark inside but there was enough light coming from the lampposts that ran along the inner wall of Holy Trinity Church just beside the building to see by. Dust, broken glass and litter were scattered over the floor, but Helen knew where to tread. This wasn't her first time here this week, and she had a spot perfect for her needs. Office doors were open either side of the corridor they walked down, but she ignored these. Most had been used by the others, the ones who came to shoot up the strong stuff.

Helen never touched that, though a lot of folks in town thought she did. The police, especially. They thought both her and her brother were strung out junkies, but it was just another act, just another game she played. Pete used, but she just pretended.

She smiled in the darkness. *Got the money for it though, don't I? Got it from that one in charge. Gullible, like all men, is Manby. Thinking that by throwing me a few quid for my fix I'm on his side.*

She was on no one's side but her own. Even Pete could take a flying fuck if she needed. There was only one person she could rely on and that was her.

Her mark stumbled in the dark and nearly fell. That wouldn't be good; there were used needles, broken bottles and God knew what else hidden amidst all the rubble. They'd started to knock the building down last year, but something had stopped them. *Some local politician's worry about causing damage to the listed wall of the churchyard,* she dimly remembered.

Whatever the reason, she was glad for it. She now had somewhere to bring her trade on these cold winter nights. Better than being bent over the bins behind the Carps, or twisted into a knot in a mark's car.

A sound echoed through the building, bringing Helen up short. She peered into the darkness but couldn't make anything out. It came again. Laughter. Kids laughing.

A bottle smashed.

Fuck! Someone's here.

'We gunna fuck, or wha'?' the man said, slumping back against the wall. His coat would be covered in lime dust and asbestos. Try explaining that one to the missus.

'Not here, love,' Helen whispered. 'We're not alone. Let's go back outside.'

'Let 'em watch,' he said, trying to tug at his zipper. He stared at its stubborn refusal to move.

Helen glanced back down the corridor. It had gone silent. Nothing moved. She looked back at the mark. He had a drunken grin on his face, a total contrast to his usual stern countenance. She needed the money she'd seen in his wallet – worth the risk.

'Look'it,' he said, proudly thrusting his fist towards her.

Sighing, Helen slipped on a smile and dropped to the floor, being careful not to kneel on any glass.

The kid in the Sisters of Mercy t-shirt and grey tracksuit took another long pull on the beer bottle and laughed as his friend with the buzz-cut popped another wheelie on the bike. They were in a large room broken with several pillars. A metal door filled one wall, its mechanism long since rusted. A chain hung down beside it, a smaller door set within the larger. This had once been a loading area but was now nothing more than forgotten rubble.

Buzz-Cut bounced three times on the rear tyre then dropped it to the ground, totally unconcerned about the glass that might shred his tyre.

'Nice bike,' Sisters said again.

'Wanna buy it?' His friend got off and rested the bike on the ground next to the small fire they'd lit. There were plenty of bricks lying around so they had been able to build a makeshift campfire. Wood from broken doors or desks had been the perfect fuel and bunches of stacked paper made great kindling. It had burned low now, their evening in the warehouse coming to an end.

'I've asked my parents for one for Christmas.'

'I doubt they're going to spend that on you.'

'They might,' Sisters said with a grin. 'I've been good this year so I'm on the nice list.'

That drew a laugh. 'You? Good? Give me a fucking break. You've been a depressed Goth all fucking year. Sullen and Moody – that's what everyone calls you and your bitch of a girl-friend. If they knew some of the crap you get up to they'd have a bloody heart attack.'

'You watch the fuck what you say about her!'

'Oh, come on,' Buzz-Cut said, grabbing the beer bottle. He wiped the top with his shirt sleeve before taking a sip. 'She's as depressed as you. I don't know which one's worse. All you do is mope in your bedroom and play that stupid game with her. Fucking idiots, the pair of you, and you think your parents are gonna get you a fucking bike as good as this one? Dream on.'

He was going to say more but a sudden sound brought him up short. 'What was that?'

They'd both heard it. A low sound, like a groan or a moan.

They got up and headed to where the corridor started towards the main entrance. Buzz-cut moved slowly, almost cat-like, across the rubble-strewn floor, barely making a sound. Sisters followed behind him.

Carefully, Buzz-Cut peeked around the corner.

A woman was on her knees giving a very enthusiastic blow-job to a punter who seemed to be asleep, leaning against the wall, his face lost in the shadows. Buzz-Cut stifled a laugh and nudged Sisters with the pointed jab of an elbow.

The woman gave another unenthusiastic moan as she worked the man faster with her mouth.

Her hands were in his pockets.

Buzz-Cut sniggered and gave Sisters another nudge as she lifted the man's wallet and took out several notes. These disappeared into the waistband of her skirt.

'She's fucking robbing him,' Sisters whispered.

Buzz-Cut said nothing. His eyes were locked on the woman.

A moment later she pulled her head back and spat on the floor.

'Guess they're done,' Buzz-Cut said. He stepped out into the corridor and started clapping. 'Bravo! Magnificent!'

The woman leapt to her feet as the man pushed himself off the wall, instantly sober, his face falling into a pool of light briefly.

Sisters of Mercy gasped. He moved behind Buzz-Cut. 'Ian,' he said. 'Look who it is. Let's go.'

'Nah... This is fun.' Buzz-Cut pointed at the man hurriedly trying to put his erection back inside his trousers. 'Who'd have guessed?'

'Fuck!' the man said. An instant later he was nothing but an echo as he stumbled in the dark in his haste to get away. They could hear the screech of the wooden door as he pummelled it open and then silence.

'Well thank you the fuck for nothing,' Helen said, wiping her mouth. 'What were you little pervs doing? Tugging each other off while you watched?'

'We saw what you did,' Buzz-Cut said. 'So... share the spoils.'

'Fuck off, kid,' Helen said. She wiped at her knees, scuffing away the dust. She'd gotten several notes from the man before he ran off so tonight wasn't a total waste, but this was shit she could do without. A moment later there was the sound of a car starting, tyres scrabbling and then silence once more as the engine faded. 'Now I've got to walk back. Run home to your mummy or Santa won't be coming this year, little boy.'

Buzz-Cut stepped forward. 'I'm not a little boy.'

His face was dark.

Sisters felt a thrill of fear skip along his spine and he shivered. 'Let's go,' he said, reaching out to take Buzz-Cut's arm.

'You're nothing but a wee baby,' Helen said, turning her back on them. 'What are you? Twelve? Thirteen?'

'I'm fifteen,' Buzz-Cut said angrily. Sisters could see the light in his friend's eyes darken.

Helen laughed, dismissing Buzz-Cut. 'Run along with your little friend back to mummy and daddy, and leave the grown-ups.'

Buzz-Cut bent down and picked up a brick, the slow scrape as he dragged it along the dust-laden floor loud in the midnight silence. His fingers whitened at the knuckles as they tightened around the brick. He took another step towards Helen who still had her back to him. She'd pulled the notes out from her waistband and was holding them up, twisting them to try and make out what they were in the half-light.

'My parents are dead,' he said in a voice as cold as the December night.

Helen's attention was all on the money. 'Not surprised they dumped you. You sound like a whiny brat.'

Was that a twenty?

She didn't see Buzz-Cut raise the brick high above his head.

'My new dad would understand,' he said.

Sisters' eyes widened.

She heard a shocked gasp and then rocked forward as Buzz-Cut brought the brick down onto the back of her head. She moaned in pain and fell to the floor. The money fluttered from her grasp.

'*What the fuck?*'

Sisters ran forward, pushing Buzz-Cut to one side. Blood ran from the large wound in her head.

'What did you fucking do?'

Buzz-Cut grinned and leaned down, stretching past his friend to snatch at the fallen notes. 'She's fine. Just a bump to the head. There's about fifty quid here.'

'She's bleeding, you idiot! We have to get her help.'

Sisters stood up.

Buzz-Cut stepped in front of him, stopping his friend from moving.

'No. No, we don't,' he said. 'She's a fucking whore. No one cares about her. She sucks cock and takes it up the arse for a bag of chips. No one gives a fuck about her. She's nothing. And besides,' he said, looking down at Helen, who moaned softly in the dirt, 'she's okay. She'll come round in a bit and think twice about being mean to kids.'

'She could bleed to death,' Sisters said. 'No. I'm getting her help.'

He moved around Buzz-Cut and started towards the main door.

Buzz-Cut picked up another brick.

'I can't let you do that...'

CHAPTER
ONE

SUNDAY, 11TH

The rain was cold and quickly turning to sleet. The ashen-grey sky had been filled with fluffy marshmallows, their edges wispy enough that the sun could streak through in long streamers, warming the ground below. But now it was one gigantic cloud; the threatened wintry storm had finally arrived. At first there had been hope that the forecasters were wrong, that the storm would pass them by and their journey to Edinburgh wouldn't be delayed.

They were wrong.

The roads were slick, at first with the sleet and now with ice as the temperatures fell. It made it all the harder to navigate the twisty back roads as the Miller family made their way north, heading from Ossett to the A1, avoiding the car park that the M1 had become thanks to the hazardous conditions. The plan was to get to Pontefract and from there head on up to Edinburgh.

Her father had planned six hours for the trip; this was why she had been pulled from bed at the extremely rude hour of five in the morning, but as soon as she saw the thick sleet falling from the sky, her excitement levels jumped through the roof.

Louise loved these trips up to Scotland; Edinburgh-Granny – her dad's mum – lived in a beautiful stone townhouse on the third floor with an impressive view across the Meadows, the lush green of the park dotted with tourists strolling along, taking pictures or simply sitting and enjoying the view. She could remember (I don't want to remember) a particularly fun afternoon in the park, skipping in front as her mum and dad sauntered behind, hand in hand and eating 99-cones of ice cream. A large bird, a magpie she thought, swooped low and fast and deposited a grey-white spatter that hit her dad's ice cream just as he was about to take a bite.

He didn't see, and she never told him.

And she would never get that chance; either to walk once more beneath the great shadowed boughs of the Meadows, or to tell him of the bird shit he ate in his ice-cream. Nor would he see her graduate from college and move to Manchester, because on that cold, wintry day in December of 1974, on that stretch of back road between Ossett and Pontefract, their car would meet another, headfirst on an icy blind-bend.

She could hear it now, hear its approach, and there was nothing she could do to stop it. Nothing she could do to prevent what was about to happen.

Louise Miller, now just fourteen years old and about to become an orphan, screamed silently at her parents to stop the car. They both turned to her, eyes sparkling in the early morning sun, smiles on their faces, but it wasn't the sun in their eyes, it was the headlights of the approaching car.

Why couldn't they see?

Why couldn't they hear her?

Louise screamed at them again, and this time they threw their heads back and laughed, but it wasn't the laughter that jolted their bodies, it was the crushing impact of the Ford Granada hitting their car at a combined speed of seventy miles an hour. Their heads now whipped forward, striking the windscreen, which was shattering into a million shiny stars of glass. The dashboard was eating them up, crumpling around their bodies as the front wheels whizzed towards their still laughing faces...

Louise woke from the nightmare in a cold jolt of terror, at first a little confused about the cold sensation that was gently tickling at her face, and then, when the faint scent of stale tuna broke through, amused.

There was a dull weight on her chest and what sounded like a misfiring engine purring in her ear. Slowly she opened one eye.

The Dude glared at her, his whiskered face so close to hers it became a fuzzy, out of focus, ball of fur.

'Well, good morning to you, too, Tom,' she said, her voice thick with sleep. He was her Dude, always would be, but standing on the doorstep late at night and calling out for Dude to come home was a bit embarrassing. Tom seemed just as good a name as any, and if he cared one bit what he was called, he didn't show it as long as he was fed.

His answer was a scratchy tongue-lick across her face, followed by one of his deep-throated pigeon-purrs that she loved so much. Pulling a hand from beneath the warm embrace of the blankets, she gave Tom a scratch behind his ear and along the side of his cheek.

Waking like this had become a habit, an early morning ritual and part of their daily routine now that he was officially *her cat*. Or more accurately, she was *his human*. Of that there was no doubt; she brought him his favourite food – luncheon meat scraps torn into a bowl and accompanied with full fat milk – and tickled behind his ear every time he gave one of his plaintive yowls. It was like a bizarre twist on Pavlov's conditioning theory, except that the practitioner of the experiment was now a cat and not a dog, and she was the one answering the purring call.

Tom gave another pigeon-purr growl and jumped down. He landed with such a thud Louise was worried he might have knocked some of the stored products in the stockroom beneath her flat off their shelves. She rented the one-bedroomed flat from the Wadees, who also owned and ran the shop below her. The soft lull of voices could be heard when customers were in the shop, along with the tinkle of the bell over the door as they entered or exited. On busy times it could get quite loud, and Vanita Wadee always apologised when Louise went in the next day for a bottle of milk or more cat food for Tom, even though she always said there was no need.

As though sensing her thoughts about his size, he paused at the door, turning to look at her, still tucked in bed.

'Well, you are a bit on the big side,' she said, pushing a hand through her hair. 'We might have to put a notice round the neighbourhood – *Don't feed me! I already have a home and steady meals every day*! Put a picture of you in the kitchen being fed, let people know you're well looked after. A community diet... What do you think?'

The purrs ended instantly. Turning back round, he – she didn't want to admit this, but it was the only way she could describe his side-to-side walk – waddled out of the room. A moment later his plaintive yowl sounded.

From the kitchen, of course, she thought with a smile.

Pulling back the blankets, she swung her legs round and sat up. The cold of the morning bit at her exposed skin and she shivered. Winter was taking hold early; it was not even two weeks into December and she was having to wear a couple of t-shirts beneath her dress-shirts at work. She was also seriously considering wearing thermals beneath her trousers, and had already sourced a pair in the Co-op. The only thing stopping her buying them was the fact that Karla would laugh at her the moment she found out.

The thought of Karla warmed her better than the first cup of coffee of the day. It had been a week since their last get-together, the psychologist joining her in Wakefield at the Lotus Chinese restaurant, where they discussed the complexities of interviewing people who suffered from mental disorders. To everyone around her their growing relationship was purely work-based; to the two women it was a date. They'd ended the night back at Louise's, the two falling onto the bed together.

Tom had *not* been impressed, letting them know his displeasure with a sharp growl and a haughty waddle. Another yowl came from the kitchen. *This bowl is not going to fill itself!*

Louise smiled and reached for the digital alarm radio at the side of her bed, wanting to switch it off before it began to warble at her to get up. The Sunday news would still be full of Edwina Currie and her egg debacle, she knew, and the last thing she needed to hear about this morning was eggs. They'd had quite a bit of wine last night and her tongue felt like a velvet carpet. Hopefully the horrible woman would resign soon and let that be an end to it all.

'And now I want fried eggs and bacon,' she said to the empty room. But her morning run was waiting; even on her days off she got up early to run, even Sundays.

That was when she saw the time: 05:15.

'Dude – you're killing me!'

CHAPTER
TWO

Wendy Jackson had managed to sneak out of the house before her dad had woken up, hungover and angry from last night's drinking session. The streets of the Broadowler estate on which she lived were empty, the houses shut against the rising sun. Somewhere in a back garden a forgotten dog barked to be let in. Smashed bottles lay on the pavement surrounded by the coffin-like wrappers holding the discarded remains of fish and chip suppers and the stubbed-out corpses of cigarettes. Wendy had heard them, shouting and swearing, drinking and dancing in the street long after midnight.

Just another Saturday night on Broadowler.

Wendy was excited to be seeing James; spending time with him always made her feel better, and it seemed to make him feel the same too. They both loved Dungeons & Dragons, the game they had been playing for well over two months now, and he was getting good at teaching her how to paint the little models they used. They also liked the same music, and they also had other things they shared.

She'd packed her bag, putting the little sweet tin wrapped with toilet tissue in last, making sure it and its precious cargo were safe. Wendy couldn't wait to show James what she'd done.

The little goblin he'd given her last week was all painted now. Not perfect, but she'd got the green skin in the right places and the sword looked especially dangerous with its purple-metallic sheen.

No one had woken as she crept through the house and out of the kitchen.

Skipping through town, she smiled as the snow began to fall. Christmas was only a few weeks away, and she was hoping the new Dungeons & Dragons set she'd asked for would be waiting under the tree come Christmas morning. It was only ten pounds, a lot cheaper than the bike James had asked for. There was no doubt he'd get it as well; his parents were extremely rich, at least compared to her own, and they lived in one of the posh houses on Healey Road, not in a council house on Broadowler estate like Wendy. None of that mattered though; getting the D&D set was also the perfect excuse to get James to come over to her house to play.

Thinking of James made her hurry her pace, being careful not to slip as Dale Street began its downward curve towards Dewsbury Road. She turned left, moving past the Red Lion where her dad had spent most of last night, throwing darts and downing pints. Probably chatting up the barmaid with whom he'd had that brief affair. Oh... Wendy knew all the secrets, keeping a few of her own from the Sunday club, the ones that were too dark to talk about.

But James knew. James shared her pain.

She couldn't wait to see him.

The Southern wall of Holy Trinity Church appeared, and she carefully opened the gate. It swung inwards with a metallic creak that made her shiver. The dark roadway, once used as the main entrance to the church but now abandoned and forgotten, led up towards the church, the trees that stood either side bending over to cover the path with a shadowed canopy. They stretched into the graveyard proper, hiding the stones within their shadows. Not much snow had fallen here, and she scuffed her shoes on the gravel once or twice.

She was still thinking how excited James would be when she showed him her painting when she saw him lying across the gravestone. Always with the jokes was James. At the Halloween party at North Ossett High School only a few short months ago, he had drooled tomato ketchup pretending to be a zombie, scaring Mrs Hollindrake to death. Everyone had laughed; everyone except Mrs Hollindrake and the headmaster, Mr Williams. And now here he was playing dead in a graveyard.

'You idiot!' she called out, laughing as she ran forward. 'You'll catch your death of cold, doing that.'

When she saw the knife in his hand, she stopped moving.

When she saw the blood on the ground, she started screaming.

CHAPTER
THREE

Louise was bored.

She stole a cheeky glance at her watch, the red LED numbers betraying the fact that she had only endured twenty minutes of the Sunday service and not the hoped-for hour which would signify that her torment was over and she could get out and get some fresh air, however bitingly cold it was. The heaters in Holy Trinity Church were great; she was thankful for the initial blast of warmth that had thawed her toes from the blocks of ice the walk up from her flat had turned them into, but sitting directly beneath one made her feel sleepy, enough so that she had slipped her coat off, bunching it up on her knees

Beside her, Aunt Fiona sang with gusto. The Psalm book barely looked at, she knew all the words to all the hymns in the same way Louise could recite the lyrics to all her Huey Lewis and The News albums.

But Louise was bored.

She'd agreed to come to church with her aunt, a chore she was happy to do if it fitted in with her work, but a chore, nevertheless. What made it worth the cold, and the awful singing, was the lunch that would follow down at The Lodge. Chef Pete made the best Yorkshire puddings, filled with minted gravy. Her stomach gave a low gurgle at the thought, drawing another disproving look from Aunt Fiona. She returned it with a lopsided grin and silently mouthed '*sorry*'.

Louise tapped at the small keyboard of her calculator watch with her nails, a *schnick-schnick* sound that her aunt immediately picked up on, thumping her leg in admonishment.

When she next tuned in, the singing was over. Reverend Dawson was in mid-flow up in the pulpit. Something about the love of man conquering all. Well, that was bullshit, and she knew it. She'd seen what man, or more accurately, men, could do to each other. Love wouldn't conquer the sight of a baby wrapped in a pillowcase floating on the canal. Love wouldn't conquer the smell of two-week decomposing flesh, stuffed behind the wardrobe and forgotten about. Love wouldn't conquer the junkie prostitute beaten and left for dead in a back alley, her face torn open by a pimp who thought she'd been holding out on him.

Love could do a lot, but it couldn't conquer that.

And it wasn't just men that carried out such acts of cruelty. Louise had seen first-hand the terrible consequences of motherly love-gone-wrong. In Manchester she had been the first on scene at a three-roomed flat on the outskirts of the city. The screams coming from within had frozen her colleagues, turning their fast response into slow indecision. When the baby's cry had sounded, that all vanished, but by then it had been too late. What she had seen in that bedroom on that dark night in 1983 would remain in her mind forever. It had also taught her not to hesitate; to think fast and act faster, but with cold logic, not hot emotion.

The sister jealous of her sibling; the wife who wanted the money, not the marriage. Louise knew only too well that women were just as susceptible to their darkest desires as men, and from her experience, they were more vindictive.

And imaginative, she added with a wry grin.

A sound came from behind as the door to the church swung open, pushed with enough force that it slammed into the small table on which the collection plate was kept. It rocked for a moment then crashed to the floor, the golden metal quivering in loud circles as it rolled and rocked. The clatter of coins sounded like hailstones striking tin on the marble floor, but they were drowned out by a sudden scream.

Louise turned and saw a young girl stagger in.

The front of her shirt was covered in blood. So were her hands, which she held out in front of her, disbelief in her fear-stretched eyes. She stumbled down the central aisle, ignoring or perhaps not even hearing the startled gasps of those she passed by. Without knowing she had risen, Louise was in the aisle, quickly joined by the vicar, his cassock floating behind him like a wraith.

'My Lord,' he said without apparent irony, his words catching in his throat. As he spoke, the girl grasped at his cassock as she fell forward, leaving bloody handprint streaks behind.

Louise was already running an objective eye over the girl, even as people began to crowd around them. Brunette hair; clean, brushed. Tracksuit shirt and trousers; blue with a white stripe down both sides, blood spattered. Grey trainers; muddied, perhaps blood. No jewellery that she could see... A robbery, perhaps? No visible marks to face or hands – no, wait. Can't make out the hands, too much blood. Dark blood, fresh but only barely. Hours old, maybe?

The girl was crying now, cradled by the vicar. Reverend Dawson seemed unphased by the blood that covered her hands and chest, and now him too.

Deliberate act? she thought. *Covering his own involvement?*

She silently cursed herself for thinking such things about a member of the clergy; what would Aunt Fiona say? Where was Aunt Fiona?

Louise turned to see her aunt still sat in the pew, her face frozen and pale. Louise offered a silent '*You okay?*' Aunt Fiona nodded once, and Louise turned back to the vicar and the girl.

'Sweetheart,' she began, kneeling down beside her, ignoring the sharp pain of the cold stone floor biting into her legs with its numbing touch. The carpet that ran down the nave was a dark maroon, now stained with the muddied footprints of the girl. Snow had settled in the vestiary before someone had thought to close the door. Another person had picked up the collection plate, settling it back in place. Already Louise was making a mental list of people she would need to talk to in any investigation that might result from whatever... this... was.

'Where are you hurt, darling?'

She reached out to stroke the girl's cheek, noting that her eyes were red from crying. Was it the tears or something else? Something more?

There were times Louise wished she could turn off her detective's mind; everything became a question; everything became a dark possibility of something more. Suspicion was her natural state, and there were times when it became exhausting, crippling even. It was a state she couldn't explain to anyone outside the force, certainly not her aunt or uncle. How could she explain to them the way she now saw the world? The things she had seen, even done, back on the Crescents in Manchester... How could she tell her aunt those things that now drove her? That one night in Manchester when she'd come face to face with a killer...

She couldn't, and more importantly, she wouldn't. Those were her experiences, her burdens that she would carry so others didn't have to.

The girl gave a whimper and tried to crawl into the vicar's chest, pushing her face into his cassock, despite the blood that now stained his clothes.

Blood put there by her.

'That's Wendy Jackson,' someone said behind her. The vicar nodded.

'She should be going to the Sunday Club,' he said to Louise's unspoken question. When she raised her eyes, he continued. 'We run a small club every week here at the church for a select group of kids. Teenagers for the most part. Kids like Wendy here.'

'Satan's minions, you mean.'

Louise looked up to see Catherine Hallum craning over the shoulders of some of the onlookers, her face crinkled in disgust. Catherine Hallum was a known force throughout Ossett and the surrounding boroughs of Horbury and Gawthorpe. Highly religious, vocally prolific; if there was a potentially controversial issue taking hold, Catherine Hallum and her Church of Divine Light followers would have something to say. That she came from old money was obvious; she wore the finest clothes, attended all the social parties, invited or not, and was a general pain in the backside of Prospect Road Police Station's Sergeant Harolds. If he didn't have a complaint from either Hallum or a member of her so-called 'church' then there was something wrong with the phone line.

Louise continued to stare at the woman. From this angle she looked like a bizarre U.F.O. *Especially with that hat*, Louise thought. It was wide and angled, and if a wrinkly looking E.T. stepped out from it, she wouldn't be surprised.

Catherine ignored the glares some of the others were throwing her way as she continued. 'Always in trouble, always causing trouble,' she said, as though that explained everything. Her face now crawled into a sneer. 'Always listening to the devil's music. Like that Holland girl, and her dead friend.'

The Jacobs case still reached into the community with cold fingers, but not as cold as Catherine Hallum's words. Before Louise could say anything harsh in reply, her aunt stepped forward.

'Why would you say such a hurtful thing, Mrs Hallum? Those are two young children. *Children!*'

'It's true though,' Catherine said, standing her ground and pouting. 'Nothing good ever comes out of Broadowler. It's the devil's home.'

'Those are children!' someone else repeated, the anger plain in their voice.

Catherine said nothing in response, her usual tactic when confronted with the facts.

Louise sighed. The recent court case of Terry Jacobs was still fresh in everyone's minds. His despicable acts might have taken place nearly twenty months ago, but the law moved slowly, and he had only been tried last month. Tried and found guilty on all counts, he had been given two life sentences with no chance of parole. Wakefield High Security Prison was now his permanent residence.

He might have been taken from Ossett, but the stain of his vile crime still remained.

As did the anger.

Towns turn bad, Louise thought. *Like a rotten tooth.*

They moved Wendy into one of the pews. Someone had fetched a glass of water, and Louise was glad to see that it had been her aunt. The pair exchanged a glance as she held the glass to the girl. Wendy didn't react, just continued to stare back to the main doors. Her body trembled, and Louise was certain it wasn't because of the cold.

'What happened?' Louise asked, putting a firm emphasis on each word. A little police verbal prodding, as DI Manby would say. She knelt before Wendy, holding her by both arms, gently but firmly. Certainly not hard enough to produce the wince that crumpled the girl's face, forcing her to pull back.

Louise let go instantly but kept her eyes locked on the girl. 'Wendy,' she said. 'Tell me what happened. Whose blood is this?'

Wendy tried to keep her eyes downcast, staring at the blood on her hands. Someone had handed her a handkerchief, which she used to wipe at her hands. Louise gently took it away from her, not wanting to remove any potential evidence.

And there it was: she was already considering what was evidence and what wasn't. That fathomless pit of anxiety had once again collapsed open deep within her, a pit that could only be filled by the steady examination of facts and evidence.

Louise didn't know – yet – what had happened here, but she

was certain it wasn't something that could be easily dismissed as an accident.

At first she didn't realise that Wendy had spoken, but when Louise didn't respond, Wendy leaned forward and repeated herself.

'He's out there,' she said, as though revealing some dark secret to a best friend. She pointed to the far end of the church, beyond the pulpit and past where the choir stood silently. One of the choir boys was whispering something to the Head of Choir, a large man with slick black hair and dark spectacles. Whatever was said, the Head of Choir gave a soft smile to the boy and patted his shoulder. His hand lingered, a second too long for Louise's comfort.

He caught Louise looking and turned away.

'Who's out there?' Louise asked, putting that thought aside. For now. 'The person who did this to you?'

Wendy shook her head. It looked like she wasn't going to reply, and Louise was just about to try another prompt when the girl whispered, 'James. James Willikar.'

'Is he hurt?' Wendy shook her head.

'No,' she said, her words wet with grief. 'He's dead.'

CHAPTER
FOUR

'Show me.'

Telling everyone to stay inside the church, Louise took Wendy and the vicar and went outside. Before they exited the warmth of the church into the bitter chill of the December storm, Reverend Dawson spoke briefly with the Head of Choir. That done, the vicar joined Louise and Wendy. Louise had put her jacket around the shoulders of the young girl, bravely doing her best to ignore the cold while they waited.

'Marcus will keep everyone inside,' Reverend Dawson said. He saw the quizzical look Louise gave him and continued. 'Marcus Riley. He's the Head of Choir and also runs the weekly group. Is that where you were going with James?' he asked Wendy.

She didn't say anything, just stood in the cold, her eyes staring off into the churchyard.

Towards her friend.

Towards the body.

'They're going to sing a few songs,' he continued, turning back to Louise when it was obvious there was no response coming from the girl. As he said this, the organ let out a discordant groan from within, the pipes wheezing back to life following the impromptu break.

Louise was perversely glad she wasn't inside.

'Right, Wendy... where're we going?'

Wendy led them around the side of the church, being careful as they went down the slight incline onto the lower level. Louise held her hand and could feel the girl trembling as they began to walk into the churchyard. There was no path for pedestrians to walk, just the gravelled roadway that led from the entrance to Holy Trinity Church, splitting in two, continuing either side of the building, the left staying level while the right-hand road dipped down. Once around the church the two roads met up again and continued down to the south exit. They were walking along the lower right-hand side, the vicar bunching his cassock in his arms to prevent it dragging along the muddied snow.

There were no footmarks that Louise could see, no tyre tracks either. 'You came back the other way, didn't you?' she asked. Wendy didn't say anything but nodded. The snow was falling heavily now, no longer sleet and when she looked back, Louise saw that their tracks were already starting to get covered over. *It's going to be a bugger to find anything in this give it an hour*, she thought, feeling the frustration already starting to build. She pulled her sweater tighter around her, wishing she had thought to ask someone inside to pass her coat before stepping out into this storm.

'He's over there,' Wendy said, pointing to a large clump of trees just off the main roadway.

Dark shadows rose from the white ground like the clutching fingers of some giant beast. The gravestones had been laid out in neat rows initially, but the passage of time, the inconsistencies of upkeep and the obvious presence of kids running havoc – troublemakers, as Catherine Hallum would undoubtedly call them – had resulted in the pathways between the graves becoming twisted and overgrown in places. Old grass poked out from the snow like aged feral animal pelts.

Louise made her way towards the group of trees that Wendy had pointed to, watching the ground carefully for any stray roots she might snag her shoe on and trip. Last thing she needed to do right now was go headfirst into a gravestone.

Is that what happened here?

She looked back at Wendy, who stayed on the main path with Reverend Dawson. He had his arms around her, protecting her from the worst of the snow as well as he could. Her shirt was covered in blood and Louise could see that some of it had got onto her jacket.

Definitely a possibility – a fall could easily result in a wound that weeps that much blood. Hopefully he wasn't dead, as Wendy had said; hopefully just a really bad wound that a few hours in Dewsbury Memorial Hospital would fix.

Moving carefully, Louise made her way through the trees. She could see a large, long grave, the kind that looked more like a tomb from which Dracula would rise. Rectangular in shape, made of grey marble, it stood about two feet in height, the top slightly angled like a house roof. A shape lay sprawled across it, and as she drew closer she could see it was the body of a young male. He wore a grey tracksuit, the front unzipped to show a snow-covered Sisters of Mercy t-shirt.

Another kid.

Around the grave the snow was stained red, with a few red indentations where drops had fallen. Two bags lay discarded nearby, both lightly covered in snow as well.

'Ms Miller?' Reverend Dawson called from behind her. 'Is he—?'

'Just a minute, please,' she replied.

The pit in her stomach widened as she stood beside the dead teenager. His body hung over the edge of the grave, his head craned forward. His eyes were open, though they were covered in a thin sheet of snow. That he was dead was obvious, even though she knew it wouldn't become official until the police surgeon arrived on scene to declare it.

She still had to check though, but before she did, she turned back to the vicar and Wendy. The girl was clutching the man tightly, her face pressed into his side. She didn't need to be here now; her job was done, and there was nothing constructive in keeping her out here in the cold with the body. That was Louise's job now.

'Mr Dawson, can you take Wendy back inside where it's warm? Perhaps get her a cup of tea. I'd also like you to call the police station and tell them what has happened. Tell them I'm here and securing the area.' Not taking her eyes from the unfortunate boy on the grave, she gave the direct number to the station. 'You'll no doubt be speaking with Sergeant Harolds. He can be a bit gruff and direct, but he'll get the job done. Tell him we have a fatality.'

Louise saw that Wendy winced at that; her eyes squeezed tight. It was unavoidable; the deed was done. Now it had to be sorted. Harolds would get everyone out here who needed to be here: the police surgeon to formally pronounce death, SOCO staff to secure and collate the scene.

'Have you got all that?' she asked.

The vicar replied that yes, he had, but she still asked him to recite it all back to her. She gave the number again and then suggested he get going. The sooner he called them, the sooner they would be out here.

'Quite so, quite so,' he replied. 'Come on, young one,' he said to Wendy, turning her and beginning to steer her back to the church entrance. She flinched at the touch to her arms, Louise noted. *Jumpy? Shock, or something else?*

Questions. Always questions.

'And get someone to bring me my coat back out when they arrive,' she called after the vicar.

'I'll send Marcus,' he replied with a wave of his hand.

Giving her arms a quick rub to get the circulation going, Louise turned back to the body on the gravestone.

He lay under the sprawl of a giant oak tree, its shape reminding Louise of the Fisher Price Family Treehouse she'd seen stacked in the window of Allwares. But there was no hidden magic lift to whisk her to the top, no bushy secret doghouse and certainly no jolly family living within its branches. Its twisted boughs stretched over the gravestone, casting it in shadow, the leaves long dead.

The boy, however, wasn't.

When she touched his neck, feeling for a pulse, she could feel a distant trace of warmth despite the chill that snapped at her fingers. She felt the unnatural stillness of waxy flesh and marvelled at how the warmth was being leached away, stolen by the obvious loss of blood, coupled with the cold temperature of exposure.

The blood hadn't fully frozen over either, also indicating that this horrendous act had only recently taken place; that was how Wendy had ended up covered in it.

And how had that happened, exactly? Had she stumbled across the boy sitting here, silently slitting his wrist, and struggled with him? Had she tried to stop him, or had she just found the body and grabbed at him?

Questions that needed asking. She made a mental note and carried on inspecting the body. He wore a tracksuit similar to the one Wendy wore, except his was grey with a red stripe. The sleeve of his left arm had been pushed up to the elbow. *To make it easier to cut the wrist?* The boy – *James, his name is James*, she reminded herself – had made sure the stroke of the knife did its job; the cut ran from his wrist straight up, almost to the elbow. Cutting across the wrist was the more common way to do it, the way it was always shown on TV or in books, but Louise knew only too well that the more practical method was the vertical slash, not the horizontal cut.

There was something off though about the cut, something she couldn't make out yet. It tickled at her in the same way a rogue hair tickled the inside of her throat. Frustrating and maddening all at the same time. It would hang about at the back of her mind until she figured it out. Best not to push. Not yet.

The knife in his hand was like no knife she had seen before. It lay in his open left hand, caught just between the crook of the thumb and forefinger. Black plastic handle, some lettering that she couldn't make out. The new SOCO team, run by Peter Danes, would take pictures, up close pictures full of details for her to explore further.

The last year had seen a lot of changes, including the dedicated SOCO team running out of Prospect Road Station. She also had a dedicated partner in Elizabeth Hines who recently had completed the detective's training.

Thinking of Hines made her smile, despite the gruesome nature of the moment. Surrounded as she was by death and blood, she pictured the reaction she knew Hines would be going through, right about now, if the vicar had done what Louise had asked.

In fact, if she strained hard enough, she could probably hear that reaction.

CHAPTER
FIVE

'You have *got* to be kidding!'

WDC Elizabeth Hines drew the phone receiver from her ear and stared at it as though the black plastic was personally responsible for the loss of her day off. In the bed beside her, Joe snored like a hippo, his naked body oblivious to the fact she had stolen the covers when she answered the phone. Putting the phone to her ear once more, she looked down on her bed guest, replaying the athletics they had indulged in only a few hours earlier. They had spent most of the night in the Carpenters; Joe had been working the bar, as usual, and so Hines had joined him, sitting at the end drinking Bacardi and Cokes and throwing flirty glances at him all night. They'd stayed for the traditional lock-in afterwards, getting home in the early hours where they continued with some sexy games of poker.

Today was supposed to be a day of lounging in bed, a late Sunday pint at the Red Lion, followed by more drinks at the Carps while Joe had his shift. Maybe some karaoke. Joe stirred, let out a long, high-pitched lager-fuelled fart, then rolled over.

'Good morning, soldier,' Hines said wistfully.

'What was that?' barked Sergeant Harolds on the other end of the phone.

Hines snapped back to the here and now.

'Nothing, Sergeant,' she said. 'I'll need twenty minutes.'

'Car's already on the way for you,' he said then hung up.

Hines put the phone down. 'Perfect,' she said, not meaning a word of it. Something in her stomach shifted, the room tilting violently for a split second. Her gorge rose, and she covered her mouth with her hand, desperately looking for something she could puke in. There was nothing nearby and she didn't think she'd make it to the bathroom in time. Just as she'd resigned herself to the fact she was about to be sick on the floor, her stomach shifted again, and the wave of nausea passed.

She looked around the room.

Bottles lay strewn everywhere. Most were empty, but some still held a little of the liquid inside. Wine, whisky, rum, even vodka. They'd had a little of everything; she couldn't remember drinking most of it. Couldn't remember much of anything they'd done other than go to the Carps, or the Horse & Jockey, or The Lodge for a meal. The one good meal of the week. Everything else was just snatched sandwiches, fish and chips or curries. Crumpled bags of crisps lay strewn about the flat as well as the bottles, and the smell of old ash hung like a veil.

Was this really what she wanted? She looked at the naked body beside her. Was he what she wanted? The sex was good... The sex was fantastic, to be honest. Athletic. Fast. Furious. But also clinical. By the numbers, an erotic step-by-step. Where was the passion? Where was the heat?

Lots of questions and no answers was a bad thing. Louise had told her that once when they were sitting in the Shop, working a stolen car case, one of the many unresolved ones that lay within its special folder with the equally special case name and stacked on the ever-growing pile of similar folders.

Sighing loudly, Hines rose from the bed.

Throwing the sheets onto the unconscious Joe, she started to get dressed.

CHAPTER
SIX

Louise had now walked all around the gravestone, looking at the body from every angle.

Thankfully, the snow had stopped, but it was still bitterly cold. Her breath came in short, ragged gasps, feeling as though it was being ripped from her lungs. Her fingertips were tingling with what felt like small bursts of electricity, as were her toes; heels and tights were not the best option for cold weather work. Hopefully the team would be here soon and she could be on her merry.

A flash of green caught her eye, partially hidden under a mound of snow. She was about to move towards it when she heard the approaching warble of sirens.

Smiling, she wrapped her arms about herself and waited for them to arrive.

The first to appear on the scene were Police Constable Dillon Smith and Detective Constable Tom Bailey. Bailey had joined the ranks of detectives operating out of Prospect Road CID and rumour had it he was being fast tracked for promotion. Louise doubted it; he had less experience than Hines and, while he was eager, he lacked some of the more fundamental skills, skills that Hines had as a natural talent. She was certain he had only been given the rank of Detective to counterbalance Hines' side-step, but this wouldn't be any different, would it? Promote from whom you know, not how good they were at the actual job. Until that changed, Louise was certain her own career would stall right where she was, and for now, she was okay with that.

They parked the Granada just to the right of the main entrance, the siren coming to a warbled silence, and got out. Bailey instantly slipped on ice and would have crashed to the ground if he hadn't grabbed hold of the door.

'Jesus-jumpin' Christ, Trips!' he yelled. ''Aven't they heard of salt?'

Constable Smith laughed at his colleague's misfortune but stepped with extreme care as they made their way to the church entrance. The last thing he needed was another week off with a thrown disc in his back, especially one caused by slipping on some ice. Last time he'd tripped and gone arse-over-elbow down the stairs from the interview rooms at the Shop, cups of cold tea smashing around him as he fell. 'Trippy' Smith was what they called him now, sometimes reduced to just 'Trips'.

Standing at the entrance was a bulk of a chorister. Broad shouldered with slick black hair and horn-rimmed glasses, he held a woman's jacket in his shovel-sized hands.

'Jesus, look at the size of that,' Bailey whispered. 'Brick shit house in a dress.'

Smith laughed again, barely hiding it behind his hand. He attempted to turn it into a cough but only succeeded in nearly choking to death, Bailey slapping him on the back.

Marcus Riley stepped down, ignoring the obvious amusement aimed at his expense.

'She's round the back,' he said, indicating that the officers were to follow him.

'Heard you had a bit of trouble,' Bailey said as they walked behind Marcus. 'Some lad topped himself?'

'She's just round here.'

Smith looked quizzically at Bailey. 'She? I thought it was a lad?'

Marcus didn't turn around as he walked down the steps to the lower level. 'Detective Miller is here,' he said simply. 'Waiting for you. And for this.' He gave the jacket a shake.

Bailey sighed.

'Course she is,' he said. 'Course she bloody is.'

Marcus walked ahead of them, his footing a lot surer than that of the two Police Constables. Several times they grabbed on to each other, their feet slipping out from beneath them. 'Ain't you heard of salt?' Bailey asked of the lead chorister, the third time he nearly went sprawling to the ground.

'No one comes round the graves on days like this,' was the reply.

'Someone bloody well did,' Smith replied under his breath, 'otherwise we wouldn't be here. Oh, look... there she is.' The disdain dripped from each word.

They rounded the corner of the grassy embankment to their left, its steep incline rising up to the church. It was little more than a snowy hillock now, patches of yellow-green grass sticking up like straw. The footprints of small animals could be seen in the snow, criss-crossing each other in frenzied patterns. Cats for the most part, but Smith could see that one or two of them were foxes. There had been several calls over the last couple of weeks about bins being disturbed, knocked over and in one case, completely torn open. That had been a strange one, but there were no lengths a hungry animal wouldn't go to in order to secure a meal.

Smith waved a hand as they came to a stop, just outside the perimeter of the grave garden.

'Cold 'un this morning,' Smith said to Louise in greeting. Despite the thick leather of his gloves, his fingers were bone cold.

'Cut diamonds on those or catch someone's eye out.' Louise didn't need to look down to know what he was referring to. It never changed, did it? Always reduced to breasts, arse or in this case, her very hard and cold nipples that poked against the fabric of her shirt.

'Give 'er the coat, numpty,' Smith said to Marcus. 'She looks frozen.' It came out *frozzun*, his Yorkshire accent crushing the word together like two icebergs grinding in the Arctic.

Marcus stood to the side, his eyes locked on the body of James Willikar sprawled across the top of the gravestone. Thankfully, from his perspective all he could see were the soles of the boy's trainers. 'He really is dead,' he said. It was a statement of fact, but the way his voice rose at the end suggested he was questioning what he was seeing.

'You knew him?' Louise asked, taking her jacket and pulling it on, thankful for another layer. She could feel the extra insulation starting to do its work already; tingles ran up her arms as the jacket began to warm her.

'James Willikar, yes. He comes to our Sunday Club here at the church every week. Sometimes the Wednesday one as well, but that's not as regular. The Sunday one he had to attend. Only been coming a few months though.'

He took his eyes from the body, turning to face Louise directly. She offered him a smile but he didn't return it. 'Can I go back inside? You don't need me for anything here, do you?'

'No. By all means, head back inside. No sense in us all freezing out here. We'll probably want to talk to you before you leave though – with everyone, to be honest. Just to get more of an idea of the young chap here.'

Marcus nodded and turned away. In four giant strides he'd reached the top of the embankment, great footprints left in his wake. He walked carefully to a set of steps that went down to the basement level of the church and disappeared. A moment later there was the sound of a heavy door opening and slamming shut and then silence once more.

The Police Constables had moved either side of the grave, Bailey standing closer than Smith, who had taken up a natural perimeter position, one ideal for keeping people away.

'Topped himself, eh?' Bailey said.

'Stupid lad. What did he go and do some'at like that for?' Smith answered.

''Specially this close to Christmas. Fucking kids,' Bailey replied. 'Don't know they're born, some of 'em.'

Louise didn't say anything.

She just looked at where Marcus Riley had disappeared back into the church and stayed quiet.

In less than thirty minutes from Reverend Dawson's phone call, Holy Trinity Churchyard was packed with three police cars, one ambulance and a slowly gathering circle of onlookers. Some had been inside the church when Wendy Jackson had come running in, the rest had turned up from the nearby houses when the sirens came rolling up Church Street.

Four more uniformed officers had arrived and were now on crowd control, keeping people back on the pavement outside the church grounds and either side of the entranceway to allow easy access for the vehicles.

Detective Inspector Bill Manby had arrived along with Sergeant Harolds and WDC Elizabeth Hines, pulling up in the DI's car. Parking outside, they walked to the church, stepping through the small crowd with muted hellos and good mornings to those they knew, and those they didn't, equally. Questions thrown at them were ignored with a smile and a nod of acknowledgement.

'Bit parky out, Bill,' Harolds said, stuffing his hands into his overcoat pockets with force. 'Going to be defrosting my fingers all day at this rate.'

Manby deciphered this as a heads up that his Sergeant was

going to be on a go-slow this afternoon. He was already nudging retirement age; would anybody notice the difference?

'Well, in that case, how about you check in with the uniforms and make sure we have a full list of names and addresses for everyone here and start divvying them up for later? Me and Beth here'll go round back and have a gander.'

'You got it, Bill,' Harolds said. Manby could tell he was pleased with the task. Of course he was; he'd have to go inside the church, where it was considerably warmer than out here.

If the cold bothered her, Hines didn't show it. She was wearing a thick coat and had the foresight to be wearing gloves. From what he could see of her legs beneath the long hem of her coat, she had also chosen to wear trousers and some good, strong shoes. Not that he was looking, mind; he was happily married and not one with a quick eye.

'Sixteen years we've been married,' he said, as they walked down the east side of the church. Hines smiled but said nothing.

To their left, gravestones ran in two long lines, a gravel pavement between them. On the right, the church. A small patch of grass between it and the road on which they walked, edged with a black chain that hung like daisy-chains between black metal spikes at regular intervals. The windows of the church were high up, a good seven or eight feet, but beneath those, just at ankle level, were another set, covered with metal mesh, that looked down into the basement rooms of the church. Manby could see movement inside, shadowed figures that stalked the length of the church.

'Sixteen years,' Manby said again, as though making sure Hines had heard him. 'Very happy for the most part as well, I'll have you know.'

'Erm... that's good, sir.'

'Yes. Yes, it is. Just wanted to make that clear.' Manby fell silent as they continued on, glad that it was all sorted. He knew how things were with the women officers. He knew they had it harder than the lads, had more to prove, had more to shoulder from fellow officers and those they had to deal with alike. But they handled themselves all right; certainly Miller and Hines did, Hines especially. It was why he'd put her on the detectives' track during the Jacobs case, and so far his decision had proven well.

She had investigated the stolen car ring in Horbury, a good way to ease into her new role following the Jacobs case, tracking them to a disused railway warehouse on the outskirts of Earl-sheaton. All four cars had been recovered along with a firearm and a stack of cash, the cars showing signs of tampering beyond the usual. Two arrests had been made and a third individual was being sought. Not bad for a first investigation.

'What, sir?' she asked, noticing his smile.

He waved her question away, ignoring her formal tone for now, as they rounded the corner of the church. She was still finding it hard to call him Bill, no matter how many times he asked her. Sir was what he called his superiors. He expected all his officers to call him by his God-given name, none of this tugging the forelock when he was around, but for someone as young as Hines was – she'd turned twenty-five this year and he still had nightmares about her birthday party in the Carps – she always referred to him with more respect than some of the older officers.

Police officers bustled around the area, some stringing police tape up between the trees and across the roadway that stretched down towards the south entrance and exit onto Dewsbury Road. He could see a couple of uniforms standing there, a car parked to one side, a small gathering of people clustered to the right of the gates, which were now shut.

Members of the SOCO team were spread around the grave-stone on which the body lay. Some were picking at the ground; others were crouched over checking the pathway that led to that particular cluster of graves moving in a slow line. Around them all, Officer Danes snapped photos, taking in every angle of the body. As he manoeuvred to a new position, the SOC officer closest to him took a polythene bag and wrapped it around the hand that held the knife the boy had used to cut his arm.

The SOCO paused. 'You got pictures of this, right, Peter?'

Danes peered from behind his camera. 'Course I did, Mike, you numpty. First thing I did. Who's handling all the evidence bags?'

'Connor,' the officer said, throwing a nod over to where another officer stood with several large boxes at his feet and a clipboard in his hand. As each piece of evidence was handed to him he noted the name of the officer handling the item, the date, time and location found, as well as making sure the evidence bag itself was properly marked. Only when he was satisfied that the chain of evidence had been met was the item deposited into the correct box, ready to be shipped back to the lab for inspection.

'Where's Louise?' he asked, looking around.

'Up top,' Danes said without turning. Looking up, Manby could see Louise sat on the slate ledge that ran the length of the church. She had her arms clasped about her and was stamping her feet on the ground. Her eyes never left the body, surrounded though it was now by the professional technicians collecting evidence samples.

'Beth, you stay with Peter. Take a look and see what you think,' Manby said, ignoring the look that passed between his officers. 'I'm going to have a chat with Louise and see what this is all about.'

CHAPTER
SEVEN

Louise watched Danes and his SOCO team taking samples and photos of the body and the localised area. Organised chaos was how someone had once described to her the workings of a crime scene. To Louise it felt like controlled free-fall, that she was hurtling faster and faster, carried along only by her training and experience, falling past each milestone with ever increasing speed. Area secure, localised people safe, headquarters informed and teams on the way, potential witnesses identified, details taken. The list went on and on, each stage a vital piece of the puzzle to come. Sometimes it was a thousand-piece beast, each small part nothing but white, almost impossible to put together. Other times, perhaps like today, it was a basic shape, nothing more than one or two pieces to slip together.

Perhaps.

Hines stood to the side, taking notes. She looked good, dressed casually, not her usual day time attire. *A date last night, perhaps?* Ended well, that was for certain. Louise hoped it wasn't with Joe again; there was something about him that rubbed her wrong. The fact he was in his mid-twenties and still lived with his parents was just the start. He was a bartender with no plans for the future, no drive to get out of his parents' home and strike out for himself, and she didn't want Hines to get infected with that malaise. He also had a temper, one that could boil over without any warning. She had seen it happen a couple of times now, never directed at Hines, though she was sometimes caught up in the fallout. Always in the Carps. Always with the guys who had drunk a little too much and were getting rowdy.

Louise didn't want Hines getting caught up in all that mess. So far the young woman had proven herself, just like she had, although the small market town of Ossett was a complete contrast to the rough streets of Manchester on which Louise had had her indoctrination into the world of criminal investigations. Stolen cars, fake tax discs and a spate of warehouse break-ins, the most recent being only a couple of days ago; Hines had proven herself time and time again, making herself indispensable, a vital part of the team.

And a good friend.

Manby came trudging up the hill, choosing the direct approach rather than the broken stone of the steps. Probably the best choice; she'd seen two uniforms nearly go arse-over-tit on them, the ice hidden beneath a layer of snow that was now melting and freezing back into black ice.

He gripped his left hip, each step forward bringing a tough grimace to his face. By the time he reached Louise, he was breathing hard and sweating despite the cold.

'You all right, Bill?' Louise asked, kicking herself off the ledge to stand before her boss. 'Looking a bit peaky there, if you don't mind me saying.'

'Cold always makes my joints freeze, pun very much fucking intended,' he said. 'You're all dressed up. Got dragged here with Fiona?'

Louise nodded. 'I'd planned on going with my aunt to The Lodge for lunch. Uncle Bernard's supposed to be picking us up.'

'Don't see why that should be a problem,' Manby said.

Louise gestured to the activity down below. 'Going to be here awhile talking to folk, and then there's the parents.'

Manby nodded, his face solemn. 'There is that, but you don't need to be doing it. Your day off and all that. I'll be in the Carps before two, and that's a fact. Tom and Steve can handle this, and Peter and his team have it under control on the evidence front.' He pointed back down to where Danes was finishing his last shots. 'And Beth seems more than capable, and I know she's eager to prove herself still, so she won't mind working her day off.' Two ambulance paramedics stood to the side, a stretcher waiting between them.

'I know,' Louise said, then seeing her DI's grim face added, 'I know, sir. Honest, I get it, but even so...' Her voice drifted away. First on the scene, she wanted to see this through. Didn't matter that she wasn't even officially on duty; she was here and that was it.

'No sense in wasting time passing things on?' Manby said. 'I can understand that. What do we have here so far?'

Louise glanced back down the small hill, then turned back. 'Still waiting on the police surgeon, but it looks like... it looks like a suicide.'

Manby gave her a stern look. He had heard it in her voice, the slight hesitation. The way her voice trailed away at the end. 'But you're not sure. Right?'

Her grimace was all the answer he needed.

He knew it would take the police surgeon to put an official interim assessment on record, one that would be confirmed back at the mortuary, but those police officers who had been around a while could tell. Even Louise, who he knew had experienced a couple of similar incidents in her time in Manchester. Hulme estate, locally known as The Crescents, a bedrock of crime for the region, crime that fostered a dark environment for all who lived and worked within its borders, an environment that could over-whelm in an instant, with only one choice left to escape its evil clutches.

Manby had read Louise Miller's file before she transferred back to his Shop, had read what she had endured in the last weeks of her time investigating the Hulme estate. Charlie Sharpe. That had been a tough one.

But Louise had been tougher.

'Okay... tell me what you really think happened here.'

Peter Danes, formerly a DC in the new Prospect Road CID branch but now head of the newly installed SOCO team at the station, finished taking photos and was putting the large camera back into its protective foam case when Hines gave him a nudge with her knee.

'You do portraits as well? I could do with a good 5 by 10 on my bedroom wall.'

Danes slid the foam lid over the camera and gently closed the lid before replying. After making sure the clasps were fastened securely, he stood with a groan. 'It'd certainly be better than that hideous mirror you have hanging there.'

'I moved that to the ceiling weeks ago. Gives a better view, but if I remember right,' she said, lowering her voice, 'you certainly enjoyed what you were seeing when it was on my wall and—'

Danes grabbed her arm and was about to pull her towards him when he saw the quizzical look one of the uniformed officers was giving him. He released her arm and took a step back. 'That was a onetime thing,' he whispered. His face had flushed, and his eyes darted around to see who, if anyone, was watching.

'Three times by my memory,' Hines replied with a grin, 'not that I'm complaining, mind.' She ran her eyes over him with a mischievous grin dancing at her lips. 'Not complaining at all.'

'What do you think of this?' he asked, desperate to change the subject. They'd had an athletic session across her bedroom, kitchen and living room, finally finishing on the garden patio table in the middle of a rainstorm. But that was in the past. She was with Joe now, and he was married.

'Fucking shame is what it is. A real fucking shame.'

He nodded, moving to his left, making room for Hines to come and stand beside him as soon as she'd finished slipping a protective suit over her clothes. He watched as she lifted another leg into the suit, remembering how it felt to hold her thigh as he slowly kissed his way up. She chose that moment to look up and caught his eye. Face reddening, he looked away as she finished getting dressed, a smile on her face.

The body of James Willikar had been covered with a plastic sheet. Tape had been strung from the large oak tree, across the southern leading roadway and around several smaller trees nearby, creating a square pocket around the grave on which James lay.

Now that Hines was properly dressed, Danes lifted a corner of the sheet to allow her to peek underneath.

She looked.

Danes half expected her to twist away, to recoil from the sight of the torn wrist and arm and the blood that now glistened in the morning sun, a deadly red lake of ice.

Instead of pulling back, she leaned in closer to look at the cut. She then looked down at the two bags stacked against the grave.

'The blue one's his,' Danes said. 'Name written in Tippex confirms it. The other belongs to the girl who found him. His girlfriend, I think.'

There was a police identification tag on both bags. Danes had scrawled the numbers that referenced the photos he'd taken. He gave a nod to signify it was okay to touch the bags. Hines lifted the blue one and tugged back the zipper.

Being extremely careful, she began to look inside.

Louise Miller was hesitant about telling her boss what she really thought about the body in the graveyard. It seemed most folk had already made their decisions – troubled lad, slit wrist. Suicide. Job done. But she wasn't so sure.

'I've seen a few suicides,' Louise began, deciding the best

thing to do was be honest. You didn't twist the evidence to fit your suspicions, not if you were doing your job right. You followed the evidence and drew logical conclusions from it. 'And they always left me feeling sad,' she continued. 'But this one... this makes me feel suspicious.'

Manby's brow furrowed but he didn't interrupt, letting his detective do what she was supposed to do. Question the evidence.

'For a start, the body looks posed to me. Displayed for maximum impact on whoever found him. Almost as if a message was being left.'

'Message? What's the message, then?'

Louise shook her head, pulling at her ponytail as it spilled over her shoulder. She could feel the cold inch back as her inquisitive fire began to smoulder. 'No idea. Yet. But there's a message here, that's for sure. But the most glaring hint that something's not right here is the knife. It's in his left hand.'

'So... he's left-handed. Not exactly a crime. Suicide isn't a crime either, not any more. Knowing someone was going to kill themselves and doing nothing to stop it... totally different. Is that what you're sensing here... the girl? Her complicity in the lad's death; was that the issue?'

'His left arm is cut, from the wrist up to the crook of his elbow. Not the right. How does he cut his left arm if he's holding the blade in his left hand?'

Manby opened his mouth to answer, realised he had nothing to say and closed it with an audible *pop*. Louise saw and smiled.

'See what I mean... He's not going to do it with his right and then put the knife into his left. There's something off with this, Bill. I feel it. I don't think it's a suicide. I think it's a murder.'

'I hate to disagree with you,' a voice sounded.

Hines stood at the lip of the embankment, a grim expression on her face.

'But it's a suicide.'

CHAPTER
EIGHT

'There's blood on the right wrist and what looks like the start of another entry wound,' Hines said, almost apologetically. Almost. She was pulling the glove from her hand, struggling as it caught on one of her rings, until she gave up all attempts at being careful and just ripped it free.

Danes, standing beside her, nodded in agreement.

'I'm thinking he cut his left arm first,' she continued, miming carrying out the act, 'then transferred the knife to his other hand but couldn't do it. Possibly due to blood loss. That's when he passed out and fell back into the position we found him in.'

Louise shook her head, not willing to accept that. 'It seems a little convenient, don't you think? And where's the suicide note?'

Hines shrugged. 'Is there a rule to say that you have to leave one?'

Manby looked to Louise. 'She's right, you know. I had a suicide a few years back – no note. Never found out why she did it. Had a few ideas. Nothing concrete though. It happens.'

'In his bag we found some game books, a few Iron Maiden cassettes and a couple of candles. Nothing else.'

That got Manby's attention. 'Heavy music, candles and a dead body in a graveyard; all the staples of devil worship gone wrong.' He let out a laugh then stopped when he saw the look on Louise's face. 'I'm joking, Louise. Lighten up.'

'You should have heard Catherine Hallum when the girl came into the church. Talked about the devil and his music. Kind of like what you were saying.'

'Hey! Don't go putting me in the same category as that nut job. She might come from money, but she's nutty as a fruitcake and twice as stale. But I take your point,' he added, seeing Louise drawing in another breath to argue.

'What do you want to do next?' he asked.

'I'd like to talk with Wendy. I've already got a modest connection to her, having been first on the scene with her. She's more likely to open up to me, don't you think?'

Manby had to agree that she was right. 'But don't take all day about it. Go and speak with her now before the ambulance takes her to get checked out. Someone from family liaison will be heading over as well, so don't go stepping on their toes. Let them do their job.'

Louise nodded. 'After that I think we,' she pointed first at herself, and then at Hines, 'should go inform James' parents.'

Hines went pale.

The dreaded doorstep knock – the death-knock. The last thing any officer wanted to do, and Louise knew that Hines had not had to do one yet. She'd not even accompanied another officer when it was their turn. But she would have heard the stories, seen the fallout, and definitely experienced the aftermath. For James Willikar's parents their worst day was heading towards them, an out-of-control nightmare that would never end. And there was nothing anyone could do about it.

It looked like Hines was trying to swallow and couldn't.

Manby was already shaking his head against the idea.

Louise noticed this and ploughed on regardless. 'Sir, I think two female officers might be better to soften the blow, so to speak. We can quickly talk with Wendy, and then head over to the Willikars. It won't take long, and I know you're concerned about me working my day off. Don't worry, I'm not going to be putting in any request for overtime; you're paying enough out as it is with Beth. I just want to see it through a little further. Hines can then drop me at The Lodge straight after. Sergeant Harolds has already organised a family liaison officer to meet us at the house for follow up.'

For a moment Manby said nothing, rolling the idea around.

'Does anyone get to ask me what I think about working my day off?' Hines asked. When no one answered, Hines stamped her feet on the ground to get some warmth back in them, her arms wrapped around her body as she continued to watch the white-suited SOC officers packing up their gear, their hushed whispers of occasional gallows humour drawing barks of nervous laughter from their colleagues. Such was the nature of the job.

Manby looked from Louise to Hines, who appeared to have gone a shade of green he recognised from his first ever death-knock. This would be good experience for a junior Detective. Hines could probably take lead on this short-lived investigation – no matter what Louise thought, he suspected this was just another suicide – and speaking to Wendy would have to be done at some point; sooner rather than later was probably best. A couple of days tops and this would become nothing but a paper-work exercise and another scar on a copper's memory.

He respected Louise and her point of view, but his experience was telling him that this was a one-and-done. Perhaps this would be a good learning experience for Louise as well as Hines.

'Fine.' With that sorted, he turned to Danes. 'Looks like you've got this all locked down pretty tight here, Peter, as usual. I'll head back to the Shop with Harolds and get the paperwork rolling. Beth, I'll leave the car here for you. Make sure you drop Louise off at The Lodge and then come back and we'll have a chat. I know this is your first suicide and it can be a little dicey, so we'll just make sure everything is covered.'

'Not a problem, sir,' Hines said, doing her best to keep her voice from wavering. She was going to be dropping the death-knock shortly. *Jesus, she needed a drink.*

'Bill. Will you ever call me Bill?' He laughed when she started to blush. 'And I do appreciate you taking your day off to handle this, Beth. How does an extra day off around Christmas grab you?'

'Nice one, boss,' she said. 'Thanks.'

Manby nodded down to where a tall man in a three-piece suit had appeared, the grey suit a stark contrast to the white around him. And the blood that covered the ground. 'Seems Davison has arrived.'

Charles Davison was the police surgeon, called to every crime scene where an injury or death was involved. It was his task to officially pronounce the body dead, even one as obvious as James Willikar. 'I'll pop down and stick my head in with the lads for a sec. A tough job well done by the looks of it.'

He turned back to Louise. 'Don't take forever on this. A chat with the parents to find out perhaps why he did this, and Hines can finish off the paperwork. Right … are we sorted then? Everyone know what they're doing?'

They all nodded.

'Good. Let's get to work.'

CHAPTER NINE

'You still don't think it's a suicide, do you?' Hines asked as the two detectives walked towards the church. Above them the large stained glass window gently rattled, its frame vibrating from the dull bass of the church organ that continued to play inside. There had been several fund-raising events held over the last year, a heroic effort to get ahead of the repairs the church so desperately needed, but one that looked doomed to fail.

'I honestly don't know,' Louise replied, 'but if it is, it's the strangest one I've ever seen.'

Hines gave a non-committal grunt as she gingerly began to take the steps down to the lower basement entrance. It was easier to get into the church here rather than fight their way past the SOCO teams and bystanders who would no doubt be crowding the main entrance. Also, it was slippery as hell on the roadway and neither of them wanted to risk falling.

Not that the steps down to the lower basement entrance were any better. She gripped the handrail and started down, the steps free from the snow, protected by the overhang of the back portion of the church, but she was wary of black ice. If anyone had thrown salt here, she couldn't tell. A fall here would spell disaster.

Aged crisp packets were scattered across the stairs along with several dead cigarettes, their tips stained with burnt ash. A few discarded cans of pop and beer lay crushed in the lower corner, right beside the thick wooden door. She walked down carefully, aware that this was an accident claim waiting to happen. The air however was crisp and cold, but an old scent lingered, like an unwelcome guest that wouldn't leave.

'Do you smell that?' Louise asked, a couple of steps above her.

Hines crinkled her nose. 'Old ash, you think? Fag ash, I mean.'

'You think someone was here? Maybe they saw what happened.'

'It's an obvious hangout,' Hines said, indicating all the rubbish around them, 'I remember sneaking down here for a few snatched puffs back in the day. But I doubt anyone was out here recently. Not in this cold.'

'Back in the day . . . You're only a couple of years younger than me, and I'm not that old,' Louise laughed.

Hines smiled. 'You know what I mean. Back in my teen years. This was our church, well, Mum and Dad's. Every Sunday we'd be here come rain or shine. No matter we had to bloody walk near on two miles from town to get here. Most times I'd be sat listening to that lot singing their hymns with soggy socks. What about you? You part of the gang?'

'No,' Louise said, all too aware of how firmly she denied the charge. 'This isn't my thing. My aunt's, yes, but not mine.'

I swore I'd never go back to church again, after.

And yet look where I am.

Her father's voice in her head startled Louise to the point that she missed the last step with her heel and stumbled forward. Hands first as she fell, Louise hit the door, hard enough that the pointed metal studs dug deep into the flesh of her palm. She cried out in pain and twisted, slamming her shoulder into the stone wall to her left. Hines reacted slowly but was able to stop Louise from falling to the floor by grabbing her arms.

'Jesus, Louise!' Hines cried out as she helped her friend and colleague gain her footing. 'Maybe next time get them to water it down some.'

'Bloody ice on the step,' Louise replied. The surprise and anger had quickly morphed into embarrassment. There was just enough space in the small opening at the bottom of the stairs for the two detectives to stand side by side, with Hines steadying Louise before letting go. After taking a moment to collect herself, Louise pushed open the door, and the two stepped inside.

Darkness stretched before them, broken only by the faint grey light that spilled in from the windows at ground level. The dirty beams were broken when someone passed by overhead, their footsteps heavy on the gravelled roadway outside. The throaty rumble of the ambulance as it drove past, no doubt bearing its new passenger to the first of its final resting places, drew a casual glance from Louise. They would need to be quick here; a more formal interview could take place later, one in the presence of the poor girl's parents.

Coming across such a gruesome find was going to have repercussions, nasty ones, for the girl for a long time to come. The insomnia would be first – not wanting to close her eyes for fear of seeing him again, of seeing his body lying across the gravestone atop a lake of his own blood like some horrific pirate on a stone cutlass. The night would stretch away from her, unable to be caught and claimed, a seemingly never-ending minute stretched out into forever. And when she was finally able to sleep, the nightmares would come.

The roar of an engine, close by. The screech of metal tearing metal becoming a feral scream, mixing with her own cries of terror.

'Jesus-damning-Christ!'

Louise tore herself from her thoughts to see Hines clutching her foot, half resting against a covered table with one hand as she examined the wounded foot with the other. 'Damn thing leapt out at me. Oh, that's going to leave a scar,' she added. Louise peered at where Hines was pointing.

'There's nothing there.'

'Not on the outside maybe, but inside... crushed bones, I'm telling you.'

Louise laughed. Hines slipped her shoe back on and tested her weight on her foot. 'I'll live,' she said. 'A right pair we make. You nearly breaking your hand, me my foot.'

Louise simply shook her head and walked away.

'What?' Hines asked as she hurried after, wincing only slightly at the dull throb in her foot.

They'd reached the other end of the basement, having navigated through the covered tables, stacked boxes and rows of folded chairs that were scattered about with no apparent thought of clinical organisation that Louise could see. A small rise of steps led to a closed door, under which a thin stream of light had been their guide across the dark room. From beyond came the hushed sound of voices and the occasional sob of a young girl. Wendy, no doubt.

'What was that earlier? With you and Peter?' Louise asked.

Hines stopped at the top of the steps, and turned to look back at Louise. 'What?'

'Something went between you and Peter. A look.'

'There was no look.'

'There was a look.'

Hines shook her head. 'You're imagining things.'

'I hope so,' Louise said, moving up behind her friend. 'He's married.'

Hines didn't answer. Instead, she gave a single rap on the door, and without waiting for an answer, opened it.

Light flooded across the two detectives as the inner office of Reverend Dawson was revealed. In a chair directly opposite them was Wendy, her face buried in her hands. Behind her stood the Head of Choir, Marcus Riley. The vicar was just to their left, sitting behind his desk.

'Ah, it seems the police are here, Wendy.'

Together, the two detectives stepped into the office and closed the door behind them.

CHAPTER
TEN

There wasn't much more they could get from Wendy. Not now. Not so close to the event. She huddled as deep into the large chair as she could, legs curled beneath her, arms clutched tightly about her body. Her head was down, face pressed into her forearms so that her hair fell around her like a protective veil.

Despite her best attempts, Louise couldn't coax more than muffled sobs from the girl. She knelt beside her, one hand on the chair arm, the other gently patting the girl's back. Beside the detective, the hulking form of the Head of Choir loomed, his shadow spilling over both of them.

'How is this helping?' Marcus asked. Louise looked up but the question hadn't been aimed at her. Reverend Dawson rubbed at his chin but said nothing. Neither did Louise; she was looking at Marcus, taking in his stubbled face, the double chins pushing out the ruffle at his neck in a weird pattern that made Louise think of a strutting peacock.

But one that has rolled in stale socks, she thought. The scent of unwashed body odour mixed with a strange spice filled the space between them. It wasn't ash they had smelled in the staircase leading to the basement; it was Marcus. He stood closer now, hands on Wendy's shoulders over the back of the chair. He was tall, taller than she had originally thought. Black boots poked out from beneath the white curtain of his cassock. Around his neck was a medallion, a gold star on a red cloth chain.

It was Hines who answered.

'It's awful what's happened, no lie to that, but we need to get a statement from Wendy as to exactly what happened. What she saw; when she saw it. We'll be as quick as we can, and then it'll be over.' She said it as softly as she could but everyone in the room knew her words held little weight. This wouldn't be over for Wendy for a long time, if ever.

'What good is that going to do?' Marcus asked. 'He killed himself, right? Slit his arm wide open...'

'Marcus!'

The vicar pushed his chair back and rose, his hands planted firmly on the desk in front of him. 'Think before you speak!'

And he was right.

Wendy had pulled her knees up further, her arms squeezing tighter as she began to rock back and forth.

Louise cursed silently. This was over before it had begun. There was no getting anything useful from the girl now; her sobs had become hard tears.

'Has someone called her mother?' Louise asked. Reverend Dawson nodded.

'I expect her to be here shortly. It's a bit of a walk from Broadowler under normal weather conditions. In this cold, with the ice, it could be some time.' He looked past Louise and Hines. 'Marcus, can you please go see if Mrs Jackson has arrived, and if so, bring her back here please.'

Marcus didn't move. His hands were still on Wendy's shoulders. 'I think I should stay with her. She is part of my group and needs a friendly face right now.'

'She has us, Mr... Riley, wasn't it?'

Hines stepped forward, one hand cupping beneath his elbow to gently steer him away from his position behind the chair and towards the door. The Head of Choir towered over the diminutive Hines, but if she felt any intimidation, she never showed it, continuing to lead him to the door.

'As soon as she arrives, please bring her straight back here if you would, Mr Riley. Thank you, very good of you,' she finished, opening the inner door to the office. The murmur of those gathered in the church drifted in. Thankfully the organ was silent now; if it had still been playing Louise knew it would have driven her mad.

Marcus stood in the doorway, filling it completely, as he struggled to find something to say that would stop his exit from the room. He glowered at the vicar, obviously expecting him to step in.

'Thank you, Marcus,' he said instead.

Hines smiled and, before the Head of Choir could say anything else, closed the door.

'Bit over-protective, that lad,' Hines said as she came back across the office. Her footsteps were muffled on the carpet. 'I say lad... He's big as a shed.'

'He takes his role as leader of the youth group very seriously,' Reverend Dawson replied. He had taken his seat once more. 'The whole initiative was his idea... He's very caring that way.'

'I suppose that's a good thing,' Hines said. 'What kind of club is it?'

'Just a Sunday club, usually held during the service for some of the more, shall we say, energetic youth of the area. Some, not all, I might add. Wendy is one of our longest members, as is—' his voice dropped to a whisper, '—as was James. Not that he was any trouble. He was a good lad, always willing to help out. Oh, dear. Such a sorry mess. A sorry mess, indeed.'

Hines perched on the edge of the desk. If the vicar objected he didn't say anything. 'And what do they do? Discuss the bible, study religious teachings?'

'There's a little of that,' the vicar said.

'We play games, mostly.'

Everyone turned to see Wendy sitting up in the chair. Louise noticed that she had straightened up, her legs sliding out from beneath her. Her head was still bowed, but she was looking up at them, her eyes red with her tears.

Louise took the girl's hands in hers. They were cold and shaking slightly, but there was something else. A clammy touch; cold sweat. 'That sounds like fun,' Louise said, trying to sound as cheerful as she could. It was stupid under the circumstances, but if she could do something to take away a little of the pain the girl was no doubt feeling, it might help.

Nothing's going to help here except maybe a few weeks of therapy, she thought. Perhaps she could talk to Karla about offering her services to the CID. It was something they had touched upon on one of their dinner dates over the last few months. Karla had a wealth of experience in dealing with those who had suffered some level of trauma; perhaps she could make this a permanent thing – she'd been talking about making a change in her professional career and this would be, could be, something that drew them even closer together.

Now who was being unrealistic?

There was a knock at the door and Marcus poked his head back in. He blanked the two detectives. 'Mrs Jackson is here, Reverend,' he said. Before he could say anything else, the door was pushed wide open and a woman barged past him, heading straight to the girl in the large chair.

'Wendy, my sweetheart!'

'Mum!'

As mother and daughter hugged, Louise gave Hines a nudge. 'We'll get going.'

Hines nodded and made for the door. 'Thank you, Reverend, for all your help.' She held her hand out. Reverend Dawson took it and they shook.

'I'm truly sorry for all this,' he said, his voice catching and his eyes never leaving Wendy and her mother. She was buried in her mother's chest, crushed into a strong embrace as she was gently rocked side to side. Both of them were crying, and seeing it brought a lump to Louise's throat.

She gave a low cough to hide and clear it. She turned to Mrs Jackson, who still had her arms right around her daughter. 'We'll pop by later for another chat, if that is all right with you, Mrs Jackson? Just to take Wendy's statement. It shouldn't take long.'

'And we can arrange for someone to talk to,' Hines said. 'This must have been a terrible shock for her.' Mrs Jackson said nothing but nodded. Her eyes were streaming and Louise thought she could see a bruise hidden beneath a heavy layer of foundation.

'Are you all right?' Louise asked, immediately concerned.

Another nod.

'It's all just so upsetting. What she must have seen...'

What has she seen? Louise thought.

Louise turned back to the vicar, who was standing close by, watching. 'If we have any further questions, we'll be in touch. Uniformed officers will be taking the names of everyone here for follow ups.'

The vicar nodded. 'No problem at all. Thank you. Give my best to your aunt. She did a cracking job looking after everyone.'

Of course she did, Louise thought with a smile.

Marcus was still standing in the doorway, his frame filling it once again. Hines looked up at him. 'Excuse me,' she said.

For a second he didn't move and then, with a twitch at the corner of his mouth, he stepped aside, leaving enough space for Louise and Hines to leave.

CHAPTER
ELEVEN

The drive to the Willikar residence started off in silence.

As they'd left the church Louise had spoken briefly with Aunt Fiona, promising to meet her at The Lodge for lunch as arranged. What they had to do wouldn't take too long, and worst-case scenario, Louise could leave Hines to sit and wait till the family liaison officer arrived. She knew Harolds would have already arranged for one to attend the family, but it could be some time before they arrived, shipping out of Wakefield Central where the unit was based.

Ossett Station was growing; *had grown*, Louise corrected herself, staring out of the window at the snow around them. It was nearly two years now since the CID branch in Ossett had been formed, the special detective branch the first in a series of trials amongst rural populations. Placed to improve response times to serious crimes and reduce some of the bureaucratic red tape that had been seen to hamper many of the more prominent cases. Louise scoffed at that thought – prominent meant visible; visible meant media and that meant political wranglings. This wasn't about serving the community; this was about serving someone's political aims. She hated that; everyone she worked with took the job seriously. Louise stole a glance at Hines, who was concentrating on navigating a particularly tight and slippery turn. Some could do with taking it a little more seriously, she thought as the car lurched to the left.

Hines grabbed the wheel tighter and corrected the car's course.

'Sorry 'bout that. Bit icier than I thought.'

'No worries,' Louise said, making sure her seat belt was secure.

If Ossett Station was a political ploy, did that mean her position was one too? Same with Hines; she'd been put on the detective training course shortly after the Jacobs case had finished. It had gone through smoothly considering some of the viewpoints of her colleagues. Some of them, again, not all of them. Manby was certainly in their corner.

The sudden rock of the car dragged her from her thoughts again as this time Hines slammed on the brakes to avoid a cat that had run out into the road.

'Black cat,' Hines said. 'Bad luck.'

Louise said nothing and pulled her seat belt even tighter.

They arrived at the Willikars without another incident. Located at the crest of Healey Road, the house was set back from the road at the far end of a long gravel driveway, the crisp crunch under the car's tyres heightened by the cold snap that had fallen. A few stray pebbles shot out from underneath to rocket into the high shrubbery that lined the driveway on both sides.

'Not bad,' Hines said as the car rolled forward. 'I bet this cost a penny or two.'

To the right beyond the shrubbery was a long lawn, its surface poking out from beneath the thin layer of snow. A stone bird bath dominated the centre of the lawn and a wooden swing seat stood at the head on a paved patio in front of double windows.

'Is that the mum?' Hines pointed to a woman who stood

inside the house staring at them as they approached. She held a cup and saucer in her hands and watched as they drove closer to the house. She then turned to one side and they could see her mouth move as though talking to someone they couldn't see.

A moment later the front door opened and a man stood there. He wore thick glasses and held a paper in his hand. On his feet were slippers that Louise saw were like the pair she'd bought her uncle for Christmas.

Hines brought the car to a stop a few feet away from a small van parked outside the garage. *Willikar's Windows* was stencilled on the side in bright red letters. Before she could get out, Louise placed a hand on her arm.

'This is your first time delivering the knock, isn't it?' she asked.

'Don't have to knock. They've opened the door already for us.'

Louise knew this was just nervous bravado, a way of putting off what was to come, but Hines had to walk a very fine line here. Very fine indeed.

'You know what I mean. We're about... You're about to devastate a family's lives. Change them forever. Shits and giggles is one thing in the Shop, where everyone else has the same sick jokey response to all the crap we see and hear every day, but right now is not the time. Right now you have to be...'

'Be what? I know what I'm doing,' Hines snapped back. 'I have had the training, you know.'

'Training is one thing... Saying the words to someone who is probably thinking about what they're going to have for their tea is one thing. Saying it to someone who is now scared to death about their loved one is a whole different experience.'

'I've had the training,' Hines repeated, apparently as much for her own benefit as for Louise. She got out of the car and slammed the door. Louise noticed that the man, Mr Willikar she presumed, jumped at the sound.

Oh... this is going to go well, she thought, following Hines as she stomped up the pathway to the house.

'Mr Willikar?' Hines asked as she reached the doorway. He nodded, still holding the paper in his hand. Hines looked behind her to make sure Louise had arrived and was rewarded by a single nod. 'Mr Willikar, my name is Elizabeth Hines. This is Louise Miller. We are detectives from Ossett Station.' They both showed their warrant cards.

'What is this about?'

Louise detected a hint of anger in his voice but also a wavering note of concern. It was the way his voice caught as he said *about*. A slight catch followed by an expelled breath as though he had to push the word out.

'Can we go inside, sir?' Hines asked pleasantly. 'It's a little parky out here.'

'I'd like to know what this is about?' he said again. 'Maureen!' he called, turning back into the house. 'Maureen, it's the police.'

'The police?'

Mrs Willikar, Maureen, appeared at the door. She'd left her cup and saucer but carried a worried look on her face that told both detectives that she knew there was something wrong. 'Is this about James?'

'He's at the youth club,' Mr Willikar said, his eyes darting between the two women standing in his doorway. 'He goes there most Sundays. Some weekday nights as well. But he's there right now.' He turned briefly back to his wife. 'Though he should have been with me doing some windows, like we agreed. What has he done? Was it that Hallum woman again? Has she put in another complaint about him and his friends?'

'Can we come inside?'

Hines was struggling to control the narrative.

Louise could see the parents' minds already starting to spiral through all the possible outcomes of a conversation with the police on their doorstep about their son, each one like a stone skipping across the lake of reality. Eventually the right, or in this horrible case, the wrong, stone would be found and it would sink to the bottom of that lake, along with all their hopes and dreams for their son.

'David?'

Maureen Willikar reached for her husband. Already tears were starting to roll down her face. David Willikar looked stunned, his mouth opening and closing but no sound coming out.

They know. They know what's coming but their minds won't allow them to accept it.

Louise looked at Hines. She too was frozen, her eyes caught on the sight of the two parents as they began to collapse into themselves.

Louise stepped forward and took both parents by their arms, steering them inside the house.

'Mr and Mrs Willikar. We need to speak to you about your son James, and this needs to be done inside. Please, let's all go inside where it's warm and we can talk.'

Silently they nodded and allowed themselves to be led into the house.

CHAPTER
TWELVE

A large fire burned in the fireplace, the warmth almost a physical wall that they hit upon entering the living room. Two comfy chairs and a long crème sofa were placed around it, a faded rug between them. A small coffee table was between one of the chairs and the sofa, the Sunday papers strewn across it. A piano stood against the far wall. Music sheets were open on the small stand, and the stool lid was open. Louise caught sight of more music books before Maureen Willikar closed it.

'Do you play?' Louise asked.

'James does,' Maureen replied, 'though he prefers his rock music. He'll be practising when he gets back.' With the stool closed, she took a seat on the sofa. Her husband sat beside her.

'Will you please tell us what this is about? Is James in trouble? Is he okay?'

Hines looked at Louise. Louise held her gaze, the silent question between them. *What should I do?*

David Willikar made everyone jump by slamming his hand down onto the coffee table so hard the glass surface cracked.

'What the hell is going on?'

Louise moved so she was in front of the two parents, facing them directly. 'Mr and Mrs Willikar. I want you to prepare yourselves for what I have to say. I want you to listen to me very carefully...'

'No.'

'... and I want you to know that everything we can do to support you will, and is, being done.'

'No.' This was Maureen, her voice shaking. She reached out to take her husband's hand. 'Please. Don't...'

Hines felt tears rise in her eyes; the room turned into a blurred mess as Louise reached out and took one hand of each parent in hers.

'I'm very sorry to have to inform you that we believe your son, James, was found dead this morning in the graveyard of...'

Everything else Louise said to the parents of James Willikar was drowned out by their screams of anguish.

CHAPTER
THIRTEEN

While Louise sat with the Willikars, Hines went into the kitchen and made them all a cup of tea. As the kettle boiled, she wiped at her face, angrily getting rid of the tears that had started to spill. Louise had seen, of course she had, and suggested Hines make everyone a drink; the unspoken message – *pull yourself together*.

Maureen Willikar had stood to help, but her legs wouldn't do what she wanted them to, and so Hines went into the kitchen alone.

She was glad for that. Glad that she didn't have to make small talk with a woman whose son had just died. Hines found mugs for them all and dropped a tea bag into the pot that sat on the countertop beneath the window. Looking out she saw the stretch of garden running in a single strip, and like the lawn at the front, it too had a covering of snow. A pair of ladders were laid down the length of the garden. Partially hidden beneath a beige tarpaulin, their black feet poked out, a stark contrast to the white snow beneath them.

The houses on Healey Road were what Hines would call posh, certainly a lot better than the mid-terrace that she lived in just off Church Street. Unlike her two-up, two-down, this had at least three bedrooms, an upstairs and a downstairs loo, large front and back gardens and what appeared to be a shed at the bottom of the back garden. Space at the front for two cars to sit comfortably and turn round without disturbing the other. The Willikars were certainly well off.

Which made James' decision to kill himself all the more bizarre. It certainly appeared that he had every opportunity a fourteen-year-old could want: loving parents, a good home, money. It was all here on the surface... She just didn't understand why someone with so much going for them would choose to end their life, and especially in such a violent manner.

She had seen the knife wound on his arm. That wasn't a simple cut in the bath, body already numbed by the heat and steam. He had been out in the cold, and that cut ran up his arm, not across.

Maybe Louise was right...

The kettle let out its pained whistle, reminding Hines of the horrendous cry David Willikar had let loose from the depths of his being. She shuddered again and was glad there was no one nearby who could see that her hands were shaking. If Louise saw she knew the over-protective nature of her friend would start to smother her, and she'd never learn anything with that sort of support.

It was why she hadn't said anything yet about her... situation. She knew how Louise would react, and for some reason that angered Hines. Angered her because she knew Louise would be right. Again. That was why she was biting her head off, arguing with her about the case. Hines wanted to be right for once.

Even when she was wrong. She could see there was something off about this, but she wasn't sure what it was. It looked pretty straightforward, but she couldn't be sure, could she?

Why was everything suddenly so complicated?

She gave the pot another swirl then poured the teas. Into the mugs for the Willikars she added several heaped spoons of sugar. She didn't know if that was how they took their tea, but the sugar would help. Hines took a big gulp from her own mug, then refilled it. It was certainly helping her.

As she went back into the living room, Louise was putting a photo of James down on the coffee table in front of the parents.

'I met his girlfriend earlier,' Louise said, her tone as light as she could make it under the circumstances. The Willikars had stopped crying but she could hear the tears still below the surface.

'Wendy,' Maureen said, her eyes never leaving the picture of her son. 'Her name is Wendy Jackson.'

'Lives on Broadowler estate.' From David's tone, Louise could tell he hadn't approved of the girl or her relationship with his son. 'Came around a few times. Always late at night, always with the music.'

'Oh my God,' Maureen said, her hand rising to her mouth. 'Is she—?'

'She's fine, Mrs Willikar,' Hines said, handing her a mug of tea from the tray. 'She obviously liked your son.'

'You spoke with her?'

Hines looked at Louise, who gave a nod. 'In fact, Mrs Willikar, it was Wendy who found him. From the looks of things, she tried to save him, but he was beyond her help. Beyond any help from anyone at that time, but that didn't stop her from running into the church to get help.'

David kept his eyes on the brown surface of his tea. 'She was there?'

'She tried to help, sir.'

He slammed his mug down on the table, slopping tea over the sides. 'If they hadn't met... if they hadn't...'

'You can't think like that, Mr Willikar,' Louise said. 'This looks like it was James' decision and his alone. You can't go blaming anyone else.'

She spoke softly but the words were firm. 'Did you notice any difference in your son before this morning?'

'No,' David said with a bit more force than Louise expected.

Maureen glanced up as he continued. He stood, eyes flicking around the room. 'We should go to the hospital. We should be with him.'

'Please sit, Mr Willikar. We'll arrange for all of that, don't worry. Please. Let's just talk for a few minutes. Were there any changes in behaviour, erratic mood swings, that sort of thing?'

For a moment Louise thought he was going to bolt from the room, but slowly he sat back down. 'He was fine. Typical teenager, you know. A new argument every day. You know what kids are like.'

'I don't have children,' Louise said. 'What do you mean? Were there any arguments between you?'

'What parents don't have arguments with their teenage kids? You show me a family that doesn't argue and I'll show you a family always in trouble with the police. Of course we argued... we argued all the time.'

'And what did you argue about?' Hines asked.

'The usual stuff. Music always too loud, not enough time studying. Not helping with the rounds.'

'The rounds?' Hines asked. 'Willikar's Windows, you mean? I saw the van out front and the ladders in the garden.'

David gave a shrug. 'It's just something I do to keep me busy. Retirement does not suit me,' he said.

Louise put her cup down. 'What did you do?'

'I was a structural architect for thirty years. Designed some of the new office buildings in Leeds. A couple in Bradford centre. Hit fifty and decided enough was enough, but after I retired I got bored and started a little window cleaning business. Something to keep me active outdoors.'

'Bit of a unique choice,' Louise said. 'Why window cleaning? Why not golf or walking?' She had seen a few groups of older people on their weekend rambles through town and Horbury. She had expected her aunt to join them, but luckily that hadn't happened yet. When it did, she was sure Aunt Fiona would rope her into it as well.

'I hate golf, and this was a way to get James into a working mood. If he'd helped like he was supposed to.'

Louise smiled at that. 'I take it he wasn't overly fond of it?'

'We only did it at the weekends, but he was always off with his friends. Or more often than not, that girl.'

That girl. There it was. *That girl*. Not Wendy; not his girlfriend. But *that girl*.

'And how was he this morning?'

Both parents looked at each other then turned to stare into their drinks. It was David who spoke first. 'We didn't see him this morning.'

'Not at breakfast?' David shook his head. 'Was that normal?'

There was a long silence before David finally answered.

'No. We'd usually have breakfast together, but... well, last night we had a big argument about his room. He ran up, slammed the door and wouldn't let us in. He wouldn't turn his damn music down either. I went up several times but all we got was the thump-thump-thump of his cassette player. It finally went off but not before driving me insane. I could have kill—' The sound of David's mouth snapping shut was like the lid of the stool when Maureen had shut it, a solid harsh clap.

'I didn't mean that,' he wailed, falling to his knees. His mug of tea hit the corner of the table and spilled its contents over the rug.

Maureen buried her face into her hands and roared hot tears.

CHAPTER
FOURTEEN

Hines stood outside, taking in deep breaths of the cold, crisp air. The snow had stopped, and a silence had settled that was deceptively soothing. She could feel the burn of her embarrassment in her face, her cheeks reddened by more than the cold. As soon as David Willikar fell to his knees Hines knew she couldn't take it and left the room, thankful that Louise had understood and given her the okay with a barely perceptible nod of her head.

The family liaison officer, a large woman called Shirley Hanson, had arrived while they broke the news to the Willikar family and was waiting in the porchway, her arms clamped about her waist, her feet stamping against the cold. She wore a police overcoat, stretched against her large frame. Beside her was an oversized bag, zipped at the top. Next to that was a carrier bag, a bottle of milk clearly sticking out the top.

'Sounds a bad one,' she said as Hines came to stand beside her. 'Young kid, I hear. Shirley Hanson,' she said, putting her hand out.

'Elizabeth Hines,' Hines said, giving it a shake. 'Fourteen. He was just fourteen. Jesus, I wasn't expecting it to be this bad.'

'First time on the knock?' Hines nodded. Shirley offered a smile full of regret. 'I'd like to say it gets better, love, but it don't.

Twenty-five years I've been doing this, and each one hurts in a totally different way. I'm lucky in that my kids are all grown and out the nest, otherwise they'd be getting squeezed to death when I get home tonight. It'll be a phone call instead. You got kids?'

Hines paused a fraction too long, then shook her head.

'Course you don't. Not a young 'en like you. Hear me when I say you'll be best not dropping any till you've got at least ten years of this shit behind you. Get yourself some insulation first.'

Hines smiled. There was no way she was having kids. Never. She pointed to the bags beside Shirley. 'What's with the bags?'

There was movement in the house, and Shirley bent to grab the bags. 'Large one's a change of clothes in case I end up staying the night with them. There's a lot for them in the next few hours and chances are they'll be needing some support to get through the night. Doctor's always on call in case meds are needed, but I find a triple-C is the best medicine they can get.'

'Triple-C?' Hines asked.

'Cry, cuppa and a chat,' Shirley replied. 'Usually in that order.' She hefted the bag over her shoulder and picked up the carrier bag. There was the clink of glass and the ruffle of plastic from within. 'Granted, not all cuppas need to be tea,' she said with a smile, 'and there's a good chance they'll need some staples like milk and coffee, and shit snack food like crisps and chocolate. Always helps.'

Louise appeared at the doorway. 'Hi Shirley. I'd say it's good to see you again, but it really isn't. No offence.'

'None taken at all love. If I had my way, I'd never have to do this again, but we all know that's never going to happen. Besides, how else would I pay the bills? How's your aunt?'

'She's fine, thanks. In fact, I'll be seeing her a bit later on for lunch so I'll say hi for you.'

'You do that, love. Right... lead me on.'

'They're in the living room. Third door on the left. Maureen and David. James was their son. There'll need to be the formal identification a bit later. Will you go with them?'

'Of course, love. Leave them with me. You and me'll have a catch up tomorrow.'

Louise nodded. 'We need to take a look at his room before we go, but we won't be long.'

Shirley was already disappearing down the hallway. 'No problem. Give us a knock before you come in.' She saw Hines visibly shiver. 'It'll get easier,' she said giving Hines' arm a reassuring squeeze. With that she was gone, leaving Louise on the doorstep with an obviously shaken Hines.

'How're you doing?' Louise asked after a moment's pause.

'I'll never get that sound out of my head,' the younger detective replied. She didn't turn to look at Louise. Instead, she scuffed her shoe along the gravel, dragging a groove into the pathway. 'It was like an animal. A wounded animal.' She shivered, and Louise knew it had nothing to do with the cold.

'You did okay,' she started, but Hines cut her off.

'Don't. Don't do that. I was terrible. I made a bad situation a hundred times worse, and you know it.'

'First ones are always difficult. Training is one thing but it all goes out the window as soon as you're stood across from them. What do you say?'

'You knew exactly what to say. And I didn't listen to you. Jesus, I feel like shit.'

'This isn't about you though, Beth. It's about them. The parents. The relatives, the friends who are all going to be going through their worst nightmare today. All of them. It's about them, and about trying to make this as painless as possible.'

Hines laughed, the sound hollow and without emotion. 'That's impossible,' she said. 'There's nothing but pain here.'

'And for a time to come. That's Shirley's job though, to manage that pain or at least help them find the tools to do so.' It was also the family liaison's job to check them for any signs of concealment or deception. Not that anyone suspected anything here, totally different case, but sometimes, especially in missing person's cases, the behaviour of the family gave clues to what had really happened. Whatever she found, Shirley would let Louise know.

'And what's our job other than to inflict some of that pain?'

Louise could hear the wounds in her friend's voice and knew that Hines was taking this particularly hard. There was something behind it, something her friend wasn't ready to reveal. That was okay; she was patient and Hines was smart; she'd talk when she was good and ready.

'What are you smiling at?' Hines asked.

'I didn't realise I was, but it's good to know this bothers you. It means you care, and to answer your question, we're here to try and work out why he did what he did and hopefully relieve some of their pain. Come on,' she added, turning back to the open doorway. 'Let's go take a look at his room and see if we can find some of those answers.'

CHAPTER
FIFTEEN

James Willikar's room was not what Louise had been expecting. Not that she'd had much experience of teenage boys and their bedrooms; the last time she'd been in a teenage boy's room, she'd been sixteen and was pretty sure she didn't like boys. That experience had proved it, cementing the fact that she preferred girls, although it would be several more years until she had her first proper relationship with another woman. What little she could remember of that time was a heavy scent of unwashed clothes, sport magazines and Page 3 models plastered over the football-inspired wallpaper.

There was none of that here.

For a start the walls were all painted the colour of an old bruise, the deep purple adding to the overall gloom of the room. The curtains were black, as were the bedsheets. On the walls were posters cut from the front pages of music magazines; *Heavy Metal*, *NME* and *Kerrang!* Most showed bands clutching spiked guitars, their hair as black as the curtains, their instruments adorned with red horns, gold multi-faceted stars and depictions of fantastical beasts the likes of which would be best found in some bizarre nightmare.

'Interesting,' Hines said, moving into the room.

David Willikar stood outside in the hallway, his face pale, his eyes running. He had appeared silently as they looked round the room and now twisted at the hem of his jumper with nervous fingers. From downstairs came the hushed whisper of Shirley talking with Maureen, broken by the distraught mother's sobs.

'We kept telling him to clean it up, but he never did.' He looked up. Louise was shocked to see how sunken his eyes had become in the short time they had been there.

'Now he never will.'

Gone was the anger, replaced with the numb reality of grief, loss and intense pain. Not acceptance; that wouldn't come for some time, if ever, Louise knew. What he was feeling now was a shocked free-fall, the mind spinning relentlessly over and over, turning round and round everything they had said to James, analysing everything he had said to them, seeking desperately for some clue as to why he had done what he had done. Were they to blame? Could they have stopped him? Should they had known how bad he was feeling? Did they cause that pain?

Were they to blame?

Louise knew that each and every one of these thoughts would be rushing around in their minds and that only time would be able to silence them. Silence perhaps, but never fully answer.

'Do you mind if we take a look around alone?' Louise asked. 'Perhaps you could go back down and have a chat with Shirley. Maybe make us all another cuppa?'

David nodded numbly and turned away without a word. Louise watched as he made his way silently downstairs, turning back only when he had disappeared from sight.

Hines gave her an exasperated look. 'If I have another cuppa I'm going to be pissing tea,' she said, flipping through a music magazine. 'Big fan of the hair metal by the looks of things. I've got this one as well.'

'You like Metal?' Louise asked.

'Metal, rock, pop. Anything you can dance to,' Hines replied.

'I just don't see you as the head-banging type.'

'Seen a lot of that, have you?' Hines asked as she threw the sheets back and had a quick look under the bed. There was nothing out of the ordinary there; a few battered boxes of old games, some tatty trainers that had seen better days, a bunched-up jumper and some other clothes. Nothing that wasn't under every teenage boy's bed across the country.

'I've been to a few concerts,' Louise replied.

'Name one.'

'Queen,' Louise said.

The look Hines gave her was pure filth. 'Queen? Are you fucking kidding me?'

'Oh, right. Sorry. I meant to say Fleetwood Mac. *Rumours* is pure metal.' She threw her hand up, raising the thumb and little finger out in the sign of the devil-horns. She finished off the look by sticking her tongue out.

'You're having me on,' Hines said, her head tilted to the side.

'What about Huey Lewis and the News?' Louise asked.

'You really haven't been to a concert, a proper metal concert, have you? You can't name a single one.'

Louise thought for a moment, then laughed when she realised she couldn't. 'Okay, I might not have been to a concert, but I've certainly heard a few metal bands in my time.'

'Name one,' Hines said again. 'I'll bet you a free night at the Carps if you can name one heavy metal band. A recent one, mind.'

Louise had walked over to the desk beneath the window. It was a cluttered, yet orderly, mess. You couldn't see the surface of the desk as every part was covered, but everything had its place. Some books were piled to the left, stacked together into a tower, their spines facing out, their pages facing the window. *The light will fade them*, Louise thought as she trailed her eyes down the titles. There was an eclectic mix for someone so young, not exactly what she'd been expecting to see for a teenager. *A Writer's Craft, The Joy of the Short Story, Writing Poetry for Beginners* were mixed with some comics as well as several poetry collections.

The usual staple: Batman, The Incredible Hulk. Conan the Barbarian.

'I'm waiting,' Hines said.

'You're annoying is what you are. Have you found anything?' She'd be buying the drinks tonight, and she was okay with that.

Hines, looking around the room, shook her head. 'There's nothing that sticks out. You?'

Louise looked at the desk again. Another stack of books, these ones all hardback by the looks of them, was piled up at the other end. She picked one off the top. The cover showed golden doors being held open by a mysterious, green-robed figure. Tendrils of smoke swirled around them, while behind them was a vista of oddly shaped beings, their clutching hands grasping forward under a golden light. Intricate carvings adorned the door; twin-headed snakes wrapped themselves around notched shields, with great rents in the doorway probably caused by sword strikes.

'*Dungeon Master's Guide,*' Louise read aloud. The cover was impressive, a mix of scratched art and sun-bleached colour. The title was bold, the letters thick and white. The next book on the stack had a similar cover but this one showed a red dragon being attacked by pristine white-winged horses.

'*Monster Manual.*'

She dropped it back on the desk. Beside them were an assortment of figures. Cast in a white metal they resembled some of the characters from the covers of the books. Some wore armour, some robes. Most were humans but there were a scattering of creatures as well, bizarre renditions of the artwork from the book Louise was flipping through.

She reached out to one of the figures and recoiled when a sharp sting bit her fingertip. 'Jesus!'

'I've done that one or two times. You have to be careful of his models. They're just toys but they can be really sharp, especially those with the swords.'

David Willikar was standing again in the doorway, leaning

against it with one hand. The other was rubbing through his hair, first at the front, then at the back; left to right. Three quick strokes then back to the start. 'No one wanted another drink,' he said and then noticed Louise watching and realised what he was doing. He jammed his hands into his pockets.

'What is this?' Louise asked.

'Some game he likes to play with his friends. I don't get it myself, but he spends all his spare time reading those books over and over again, or painting his models.'

'They're pretty impressive,' Hines said. She'd come over to the desk to take a look. There was a rack along the back of the desk on which James had arranged a display of all the models he had painted. 'Danes' nephew paints these... Not as good as this though.' She picked one up, a skeleton brandishing a bow. 'These are almost professional.'

She put the model back down. 'There's a shop in Leeds that sells them. I've been a few times myself with Janet, Peter's sister. She's a friend, by the way,' she added sharply. 'You've heard of that word right? Friend. You should try getting a few yourself.'

A cold silence filled the room, turning an already awkward situation into something much worse. David coughed nervously, drawing both detectives' attention.

'Is this really necessary right now?' he asked. 'I mean... what can you possibly get from this?'

'I know it's hard, Mr Willikar...'

'Call me David,' he said.

Louise smiled and continued. '...but it helps us get a picture of what James was thinking. He looks to be very talented.'

David smiled. 'Oh yes, he really loved it.' He walked over to the desk. There was a box of paints on the table, their lids splotched with each colour so they could be quickly identified. In the box next to them were a selection of paint brushes. 'He'd waste many a weekend sat here in his room, painting his toys and listening to his music. Or he'd be reading his books and magazines.'

She ran her hand along the spines of the books. 'And these games... I take it he played them as well at some point?'

David nodded. He was looking at the models arrayed along the rack. He reached out and brushed his fingertips against them, an almost caress. His eyes leaked tears down his face, which he ignored. Louise tried to ignore it too but couldn't. She could feel her heart tearing at the sight of the father's growing grief starting to take hold. *What must be going through his mind right now?* she thought, watching the man as he continued to stare at the desk at which his son had sat only a few hours ago. *What must he be feeling?*

'Mr Willikar?' she prompted. 'David?'

He gave a cough and wiped at his eyes with the back of his arm. 'I'm fine,' he said, clearly not. 'I'm sorry. What did you say?'

'The games, Mr Willikar. Who did he play them with?'

'His friends,' he said. 'Most times down at the shop in Horbury on a Saturday. It's why we argued about the round. I do most of it on a Saturday but he wanted to go to the shop to play his games.'

He sat on the bed, elbows rested on his knees as he rubbed at his forehead. 'Maybe if I hadn't pushed so hard...'

Louise put her hand on his shoulder. He turned to look up at her. 'I know this is hard, but would you be able to give us a list of his friends' names so that we can talk to them?'

He jumped to his feet so fast she stumbled back from him, startled by the look of pure anger and grief that had crumpled his face. 'What good will that do now? He's dead! Nothing's going to bring him back, so what the hell is talking to his friends going to do?'

David swirled back to the desk and thrust his arm across it, dragging everything over until things started to crash onto the floor. 'None of this fucking matters anymore!'

'Mr Willikar!'

Louise went to hold him but he shrugged her off as easily as if she wasn't there.

'If he hadn't been into this... this shit, then this wouldn't have happened!' he cried out, picking up one of the game books. 'This is all madness! Demons and goblins and devils. She said it would come to this, and she was right. We should have listened to her. This is what made him do it! This and those other bastards! All of them!'

He threw the book at the wall hard enough that it tore the poster and wallpaper behind it. The book landed on the floor, its spine snapping with a loud crack. A second later and he was angrily ripping at the posters, tearing them away and throwing the pieces to the floor.

Footsteps pounded up the stairs and a moment later Maureen Willikar appeared in the doorway. Behind her was Shirley, a startled look on her face. Louise knew that the family liaison officer had been doing her job for nearly three decades, but this might be the first time she'd seen anything so brutally feral.

'David!' Maureen started forward, but before she could continue, her husband let out a howl of anguish so loud that everyone jumped. He fell to his knees and started to cry, huge wracking sobs that were soul deep.

Louise and Hines stepped back, allowing Maureen space to get to her husband, but she stood unmoving, her hand to her face, shock numbing her. It was Shirley who moved in to kneel beside David, putting an arm around his shoulder. Louise started to warn her that he might throw her off, but she waved it aside.

'Let it out, love,' she said gently, pulling the man to her. He let her do it, putting his head onto her chest and tucking his legs beneath him. 'You just go and let it out.'

The last thing Louise saw before they left was David Willikar being rocked like a baby while his wife stood in the doorway and silently cried.

CHAPTER
SIXTEEN

The car took a few moments to start up, the engine ticking and not catching as Hines tried to start it. They had left the Willikars' shortly after David's collapse, leaving Shirley to look after them as best she could. Louise didn't envy her the task one bit.

'What happens now?' Hines asked as she waited for the engine to settle before trying it again.

'You drop me off at The Lodge and then head back to the station and get started on the paperwork, I guess.'

'I meant with the Willikars. It seems... it just seems so... Jesus, I don't know. Like we should be doing something more.'

Louise knew the frustration only too well. She shuddered at the memory brought up from her time in Hulme back in '83. Hearing David howl like that... just as eerie as the first time she had heard a human being make that sound. Not as gruesome the circumstances, but still...

'This is now little more than process and paperwork,' Louise said. 'Suicide is no longer a criminal act. We won't be prose-cuting the family; we'll be supporting them. Uniforms will talk to the congregation from church just to get an overview of what happened; we'll have to talk with Wendy Jackson in more detail as she found the body; the parents will make a formal identification of the body, probably later today. We'll fill out the paper-work – well, you'll do most of it as I'm going for lunch. But other than that...'

Her voice trailed away. Sad though it was, there wasn't much else to be done.

But still the questions tugged at her. *Where was the suicide note? Why did he choose to do it in a cold graveyard and not the warmth of his home? Did he not want his parents to find him? How did Wendy find him?*

Again, the questions outweighed the answers, and until that balance was addressed, Louise wouldn't be confident with the official line, even if everyone else was.

'The police surgeon has probably already arrived and announced the death officially, and the body will have been taken to the mortuary over at Dewsbury. There'll be an autopsy, a brief hearing and then the funeral. It's just a formality now.'

She paused a moment, then looked across as Hines gave the engine another try. It ticked, caught then died once again. 'I'm still not convinced this is a suicide, though,' she said.

Hines slammed her hand onto the steering wheel, her frustra-tion not only directed at the car. 'Is that why you've been a real pain to me today?'

Louise fish-mouthed for a few moments before finding her voice, but all she could utter was a single, shocked, 'What?'

Hines turned to her. 'All day you've been riding me. Snide comments; you near damn bit my head off when we went into the church.'

'I just didn't think we were ready to confidently state this was suicide, is all.'

'And you said so every chance you got, undermining me in front of the DI. I'm still on probation, or had you forgotten?'

'What's that got to do with anything?'

'I'm trying to show I'm up for the job, and yet there you were making out like I didn't know what I was talking about. Just because you're always looking for the worst, doesn't mean I have to. And what was that remark about Peter Danes?'

Louise stared dumbstruck for a moment, then quickly gathered herself. 'You're the one who told me about Peter.'

'In bloody confidence. It was a one-time, drunken stupid mistake that we both regret.'

'And yet you act all flirty-girty around him. People will notice. People will start to ask questions, and it doesn't help that you're so friendly with his bloody sister.'

Now it was Hines' turn to get angry. 'Who I see or don't see in my own time is nobody's business but my own. I can be friends with whoever I want.'

'Not if you're screwing their married brother. Jesus, Elizabeth, you have to realise the position you're putting yourself into. People will start talking, you'll get a reputation and then you're done. Just plain done. Doesn't matter how good you are, how many cases you close. None of the important work you do will matter because all people will be talking about is the skirt in CID who puts it out there for anyone who wants a taste.'

'What the fuck?'

Hines' face was so red Louise was worried she'd have a stroke. But this was something that needed to be said. People *were* starting to talk, Harolds for the most part, unsurprisingly. And she was pretty sure Danes had been bragging to the lads. Thankfully no one was listening. *Yet.* Louise wasn't going to stand by and do nothing about it.

'You know I know you're not like that,' Louise said, her voice softening, 'but evidence to the contrary, people only believe what they see.' She pointed to the mark on Hines' neck. 'Another passionate night with Joe, I take it,' she said, seeing the hurt in her friend's eyes, but there was nothing to be done about that. 'At least I hope it was Joe.'

'I told you what happened. Maybe if you concentrated less on what I was doing, maybe your own love life wouldn't be as non-existent as it currently is.'

'You know that's complicated.'

The car gave a wounded cough, jerked forward and started. Hines pushed the accelerator down with a couple of quick pulses, making the Rover growl and spit out an angry blue-grey cloud of smoke.

'It doesn't need to be,' Hines said, as the car rolled forward. She came to the end of the Willikars' driveway, waited for a car to pass, then pulled out onto Healey Road, turning right towards The Lodge. 'Karla's nice. She's good for you.'

She was right. Karla was good for her; the psychologist always knew how to make her laugh, especially on the bad days.

Today was a bad day.

'Can we change the subject?'

All conversation was silenced. The hedgerows of the houses on Healey Road rolled past as the car made its way back up the hill, their large frames set back from the road and hidden behind towering trees of oak or large expansive bushes that were undoubtedly trimmed by a professional service. The detached houses each had their own driveway, garage and in one or two cases, sheds that were more than likely filled with a separate bedroom and bathroom as opposed to gardening equipment, lawn chairs and discarded flowerpots. That the residents of Healey Road were in a totally different price band to the rest of Ossett was patently clear; it was the reason why The Lodge existed, after all. At first a private residence, it was where the not-quite-a-lord lived; this was back in the 1600s when the lands of England were divided amongst the elite, ruling over the local populace by granting them work on their lands in return for lodging, food and work.

Not a lot has changed then, Louise thought as she indulged herself in the daydream of one day owning such a house. Her flat and all its contents could fit in one room of these opulent homes, she was sure.

'There was another break in last night,' Hines said, tearing Louise away from grand dreams of lavish dinner parties,

Christmas gatherings and family get-togethers where everyone lounged in the garden drinking wine and laughing. 'Strangely enough, right back on Church Street,' Hines added when Louise didn't say anything straight away.

Louise pushed her annoyance down and took in a deep breath before answering. Nothing good would come of continuing their argument. Hines would either change her behaviour or she wouldn't.

'One of the houses?'

The car gave a judder as the Rover's engine coughed. A red warning light blinked on, then off, on the dashboard. If Hines was concerned, she didn't show it, but Louise made a mental note to speak to Manby about getting a couple of new cars.

'No, not a house this time. One of the old, abandoned warehouses. Right beside the church actually. Someone heard windows being smashed, and apparently the door had been given a pretty good beating. Not exactly a break-in as such, just some vandalism, but it got me thinking if this was connected with the kid in the graveyard in some way.'

Louise shook her head. 'Doesn't seem likely. There's a big difference between a suicide and a warehouse having its windows smashed, even an empty one. Sounds like kids messing around to me.'

'Do you think the Willikar boy was one of them?'

Louise thought for a moment, then shook her head. 'He doesn't seem the type. Not been in any trouble before; can't think why he would now.'

'You're probably right, but that's where I'm off this afternoon. Doesn't hurt to take a look I guess, and it's better than sitting round the Shop with Harolds bitching about his foot, and Tom Bailey letting one rip every five minutes. Here you go, your grace. Luncheon awaits.'

The car pulled up just outside The Lodge, its high stone wall broken only by the gateway into the hotel car park. A black door to the left opened as a young girl in a black skirt and white shirt stuck her head out. She looked up and down the road, saw Louise in the car, then ducked her head back inside.

Louise unbuckled her seatbelt and opened the door. 'Well, thanks for this morning. Not exactly how I'd planned to start my day off. Fancy a drink later on? I remember something about a heavy metal bet.'

Hines shook her head, staring directly ahead.

'Don't worry about it. I'm seeing Joe tonight for the pub quiz. Enjoy your lunch, and say hi to your aunt from me.'

Louise started to get out and turned back. She started to say something, paused, thought about it and then decided what the hell.

'What do you think David Willikar meant when he said, "She said something like this was going to happen"? Who do you think he was talking about?'

Hines shrugged. 'I don't know. His wife?'

Louise shook her head. 'No. It sounded like he was talking about someone else.'

'Who?'

It was Louise's turn to shrug. 'No idea.' Her voice trailed off.

Another question to be answered.

Another itch about this whole affair she couldn't scratch. And then there was Hines. Louise knew she should apologise for the way she'd been acting towards her this morning, but she couldn't explain it to herself, let alone her friend. This bizarre twisting in her stomach that had her all knotted up in her mind. Angry sadness was the best way she could describe it, but she didn't know where it was coming from or why.

It just was.

The car revved twice, and Louise got the message. She shut the door and watched as Hines drove away.

Whatever it was, she needed to get hold of it before it messed up her friendship with Hines any further.

CHAPTER
SEVENTEEN

The Lodge was a small hotel just on the corner of Healey Road and The Green. It was on the opposite side of the road to Louise's flat but close enough that she could see her cat in the window, waiting for her to return so he could be either fed or let out to go a-wandering.

Louise was sitting at a table in the room that held the bar, nursing a gin and tonic while she waited for her aunt and uncle to arrive. It was just after midday and the lunchtime crowd was starting to appear in small clusters; families out for birthday celebrations or semi-regular get togethers mixed with couples and the odd single.

Odd was correct; a man sat all alone at a table in the corner. He had a glass of water – too tall to be vodka, surely? – which he sipped from sporadically while he read a book. She couldn't make out the title but Louise was certain it was a Stephen King book. She had them all and she thought she recognised the cover. '*Salem's Lot*, possibly. Definitely not *The Shining*.'

The man had greasy hair; it fell around his face in long blonde strands. Dark at the roots, almost white at the tips, he had definitely coloured it. His gaunt cheeks were speckled with stubble and his eyes were set back from the prominence of his sloping nose. Late forties, early fifties at a push. She took a sip of her drink as she scrutinised his clothes. A faded tan overcoat was folded neatly on the chair opposite his and he wore a blue jumper that looked more than a little threadbare. Especially at the shoulders and elbows. The white collar of a shirt clutched his neck. The table between them obscured his trousers, but she was certain that's what they were: trousers, not jeans. One foot poked out – he must have had his legs crossed – to reveal a black shoe. Shoe, not trainer.

When she looked up she saw he was staring directly at her. He lifted his glass in a silent toast, his thin lips turning into an even thinner smile.

'Hi, love.'

Louise turned away from the man to find Aunt Fiona shrugging off her coat. Behind her, Uncle Bernard was trying to help but succeeding in doing little more than getting his wife's arm caught up.

'Bernard... please,' she said with a laugh. He leaned forward and gave her cheek a peck. 'What would you like?' he asked.

'G and T,' she replied. 'And make sure it's the proper Indian tonic this time.'

'Will do. Another one, Louise?'

She started to shake her head, realised she had nothing else planned for the day and changed her mind. 'Please.'

'Good choice, and not surprising after how your morning turned out.'

'Her morning,' Aunt Fiona said. 'What about mine? Bunch up, love. Let me scootch next to you.'

'There's a perfectly good chair right there,' Louise moaned but she did as she was asked, moving a little further up the bench so that her aunt could sit beside her. 'How was everyone at church after?' she asked. Uniforms would have taken statements, names and addresses, all of which would be followed up and channelled back to Hines, who in turn would brief the rest of the CID team.

Aunt Fiona was getting herself settled, fussing with her shawl and fidgeting until she was comfortable on the cushioned bench. 'You know these are never as comfortable as a chair, but they do look so much nicer, and it's so nice to sit next to you, love.' She patted Louise's leg and gave her a smile that warmed her heart. 'Is he a friend of yours?'

Louise looked confused. 'What? Who?'

'That man I saw you looking at when I got here,' Aunt Fiona said with a smile.

Louise shifted in her seat so she could glance back at the man. He was concentrating on his book, flipping the pages rapidly. She turned back to her aunt. 'Never seen him before. How are you?'

Aunt Fiona was looking around the nearby tables, offering wan smiles with each recognised nod. 'I'm fine, love. We said a prayer for that boy, and the girl. The Reverend said you had it all under control, so I should be really asking you how you are.'

'I'm okay. It's just work.'

'It's terrible work though,' Aunt Fiona said. 'A young life was lost and you say it's just work. That's cold, even for you.'

'Even for... What is that supposed to mean?'

Aunt Fiona turned away and tapped the woman at the nearest table on her shoulder. 'Good to see you, Eileen. How's your Trevor?'

And there it was, another unspoken argument waiting below the surface to snag them both, unwary swimmers on the sea of personal choice. Louise could feel her anger growing inside and knew if she didn't control it then words would be said that could never be taken back. The angry sadness was now just anger. Pressure built in her head, pushing behind her eyes with hot pulses.

Aunt Fiona patted Louise's leg once again. This time it didn't feel soothing. It felt patronising. 'I'm not saying anything, love. Nothing at all. I just thought it a bit cold, but I guess you have to put a little distance between the things you deal with and real life.'

Real life?

'It's my job, Aunt Fiona. It's what I do, and I'm pretty damn good at it.'

'There's no need to be like that. If you're happy, I'm happy.'

'Well, aren't I just pleased as punch to hear that?'

She closed her eyes and lowered her head, taking in several deep breaths before speaking again. When she did, the pressure didn't fully leave, but it did release a little of its grasp.

'I'm sorry,' she said. 'It's been a bit of a morning. I didn't mean to take it out on you.'

Aunt Fiona gave her another pat, this time on her arm, as well as a smile that said everything was all right. 'Of course, sweetheart. Terrible what happened this morning. Just terrible. That poor girl.'

'Wendy? She'll be okay in the long run. It's the family of the boy I'm more concerned about,' Louise said, snapping instantly back into work mode. She could still hear David Willikar's cries, see him being cradled like a baby while his wife stood mute and immobile, frozen in place by indecision and grief.

'Oh, of course. Those poor parents.' Aunt Fiona's voice fell to a hushed whisper as she leaned in. 'Did you have to go visit them?'

Louise nodded, her eyes closing momentarily again at the thought of David and the inhuman scream that left his body as the realisation of what had happened hit. *This isn't going away anytime soon*, she thought.

'I don't know how you do it,' Fiona said.

'Do what?' Uncle Bernard said as he put the drinks down on the table. He was wearing a tweed jacket that he shrugged from his shoulders, placing it around the back of the chair.

'I was just saying I don't know how Louise goes and says to parents that their child has died.'

'Made of strong stuff, our Louise,' he said. After sitting, Uncle Bernard raised his wine glass. Aunt Fiona and Louise both raised theirs. 'To absent friends,' he said. It was his usual toast, one that

Louise could always remember his using no matter the occasion. Birthday, wedding, a simple Sunday lunch, the salute was always the same. It was nice, familiar.

They all toasted and drank.

'Right,' Uncle Bernard said, passing each a menu he had brought back from the bar. 'What are we all having?'

CHAPTER
EIGHTEEN

Hines had parked the car on Church Street, the left wheels off the main road and part way onto the overgrown grass verge that led into the warehouse loading areas to allow other vehicles to get past without too much trouble. The road wasn't overly wide, just enough for a carriageway either side, the space between two vehicles in opposing directions scant to say the least.

The warehouses here were old and abandoned, part of the mills of the area back when the textile trade was the main source of business for the region. Now that time had moved on, trade had contracted to the point that only two mills still continued to this day; both at the bottom of Pildacre Hill. She supposed they would one day be used for something else; there was a sign that advertised the buildings, either for sale or let. A number for the local solicitors that handled them was below, along with the dimensions of the main building. And then she saw the white banner that had been stuck over the lower portion of the sign. It had blown back in the cold wind of the morning and now fluttered gently into place. SOLD PENDING CONTRACTS. Quite what it could be used for was beyond her; the buildings were all in such a story state, it would cost a fortune to get them safe to use.

Just who would want them? And for what?

Hines stepped through thick bushes, ignoring the scratching thorns that tore at her jacket, thankful that her legs were covered by her trousers and that her shoes had been replaced with boots that crushed a path for her to get through. Ahead, the abandoned warehouse loomed large, its brick walls adorned with a wide variety of sprayed comments in a rainbow assortment of colours. Rubbish was strewn all around the walls and across the broken gravel that surrounded the building. Empty beer cans lay like crushed cars, thrown aside as soon as they were used, while the smashed fragments of whisky and vodka bottles crunched under her feet.

The spire of Holy Trinty Church cast a shadow across the yard, a brief measure of shade as she walked towards the main door of the warehouse. The bells continued to ring despite everything that had happened, and she could see one or two official vehicles still in the churchyard.

The doors had been boarded up and it didn't take long to find the one that had been reportedly smashed with a brick. Sure enough, chunks of red brick lay nearby, while the wood of the boarded door had deep craters thumped into it. Luckily it had held, the brick breaking before the board did, and so whoever had done this had given up, choosing instead to throw the fragments of brick at the windows higher up the building. Three had been smashed, jagged holes looking like dark pupilless eyes.

Peering closer she could see that the door had been pulled forward to a point where someone could slip inside. She took hold and gave it a pull. There was a sound like a metal scream as the rusted hinges groaned and then the wooden board came loose.

Moving it aside, Hines slipped inside the building.

It was dark inside but not so that she couldn't see; a little light came through the gaps in the walls and the smashed windows.

The floor was littered with the dust and debris that several years of abandonment would bring, and she was careful not to tread on anything that could cause her to stumble.

Why anyone would want to come inside such a building was beyond her understanding. Why would kids come in here? It wasn't worth the risk. But then she thought about all the other reasons someone might want to come into an abandoned building. Hiding stolen goods was always a good one. Then there were drugs to consider. Wakefield was just down the road, good old Sin-City itself, and Leeds was just a short hop and a skip down the Mad Mile and onto the M1. Both cities were rife with drugs, which could come back here – they knew of two gangs in the area that dealt, but up till now they hadn't been able to do anything about it. A task force was being run out of Wakefield and the last update they had was that they were planning on putting an undercover officer into one of the gangs to gather more direct intelligence. So far nothing had happened, but that would change; DI Manby had a plan he was formulating, a combined strategy with the police forces of Wakefield, Dewsbury and Leeds. Operation Gypsy Rose or something; she hadn't been paying attention during the brief as it didn't apply to her. That had been weeks ago and so far they hadn't heard anything new.

Walking through the building, Hines was just about to give up and head back to the car when something caught her eye. She brushed through a couple of overgrown weeds to the small wooden overhang of a side building. Presumably used as a means to keep vehicles out of the weather when they came to pick up or drop off, this was now little more than a broken shack, open all around, the cracked timber roof barely held up by three solid beams.

She walked carefully down the corridor and stepped into a large room. She could see a dark circle burned onto the concrete floor. Several large stones had been placed in a crude effort to keep the make-shift campfire from spreading. Hines looked up; on the ceiling a dark patch of soot was burned into the roof, evidence that the fire had been quite large. How no one had spotted this and reported it along with the noise was baffling.

Next to the campfire were empty drinks cans and more than a dozen fag-ends, their stubbed bodies scattered in two small areas. *Two people then*, she thought. Two people sitting around, getting warm, getting drunk. Drunk enough that they started attacking the building.

She cuffed at the nearest stone, knocking it over with her boot. It rolled over a couple of times and thudded against the metallic double doors of the loading area, the clang echoing through the building. A splotch of colour caught the light and her attention.

Hines bent down and picked it up.

At first she thought it was paint, lazily thrown down by some graffiti artist's attempt at 'art'. Recently done, the red paint used to draw it was still tacky.

It was only when she rubbed at her hand to remove the paint that she realised this wasn't paint.

It was blood.

CHAPTER
NINETEEN

Their meal over, Louise, Aunt Fiona and Uncle Bernard sat outside in the hotel garden, waiting for coffee and mints to be brought to them. The whir of the outside heater gently mixed with the classical music being piped out from the bar.

Louise was looking up at her flat; Tom was still in the window, but he had curled up and gone to sleep now.

She could feel herself starting to get sleepy as well, the result of the full Sunday lunch complete with starter, main and pudding, plus the wave of heat that was lapping at her feet. It was the first full meal she could remember having in recent days.

The nature of her work meant that she grabbed snacks whenever she could; bacon butties or cold sandwiches from Jenny's Café and fish and chip suppers when she made her way home from the pub. She usually got home late, and after making sure Tom was fed and watered, she was usually too tired to cook anything for herself more complicated than heating up a can of beans and sausage.

These Sunday lunches with her aunt and uncle were welcome breaks from the intensity of work, mundane moments snatched wherever she could. At first she had tried to avoid them, uncomfortable in the posh environment, but now they were a strong foundation that kept her sane. It helped that her aunt and uncle were so grounded, so down to earth with their lot. They weren't Healey Road rich, but they were comfortably well off – Aunt Fiona was a retired teacher at Holy Trinity, while Uncle Bernard managed accounts for several high-profile council members – and had a prudent nature when it came to money. Thanks to them, Louise had been able to travel down to Manchester for the police training, and again when she was scheduled to move back to the area, it had been her aunt and uncle who had helped her. At first, they had offered to redecorate Uncle Bernard's office and turn it into a bedroom for her, swapping out the desk and chair for a new bed, wardrobe and anything else she might need, but Louise had refused; she would be working long and anti-social hours, coming and going at all times of the night, and while she could handle that sort of disruption to her life, there was no way she was going to inflict it on her adopted parents.

Seeking a compromise, they had agreed to instead help with payments on the flat, securing it so she had somewhere to move to that she could call her own.

That didn't mean she wouldn't accept the occasional Sunday lunch at The Lodge though. She loved the food, but it certainly came with a price-tag; there was no way she could afford it as regularly as they came. Maybe if she saved for a couple of months...

'Good afternoon, all.'

Louise turned from her flat to see the chef beaming down at them. Paul Bentely was renowned throughout Ossett and the three boroughs for a multitude of reasons. Most prominent were his cooking skills; as a Michelin-trained chef, he had worked in some of the highest profile restaurants around the country. A travelling chef, he would go where he was needed, bringing his signature dishes and hard drinking reputation with him. He had worked in London, Edinburgh and Cardiff, the biggest and the best hotels snatching him up for a season or two before he would move on to the next challenge. The latest was working at The

Lodge, bringing 5-star cuisine to what had initially been little more than a gastro pub-lunch in a small town. Now, the hotel attracted visitors the country over, with people who normally stayed at the large chain hotel on Queen's Drive choosing instead to stay at The Lodge.

'I trust all was to your liking,' the chef asked. Louise could see the heat-touched cheeks beneath his stubble, the result of work in a confined space packed with multiple ovens all at high-heat. He looked up over them and gave a little wave to the barman inside. It was a rare sight indeed to meet Paul the chef without a tipple in his hand or one on the way. He could be found most nights in the Carpenters, standing at the bar – never sitting – holding court with the other regulars. Either the Carps or the Taps, those were his haunts, though sometimes he could be found in the Lion on Church Street, and occasionally when he felt like a trip, up at the Boot in Gawthorpe, though that was usually reserved for May Day when the procession set out following the climax of the coal race.

'Everything was wonderful as always, Paul,' Uncle Bernard said. 'Can I get you one?' He raised his glass, empty though it was. Paul smiled and shook his head as a young girl, the waitress Louise had seen peeking out of the side entrance to the hotel when she arrived, slid up beside the chef and handed him a pint of beer.

'I'm good thanks, but if you want to put one behind the bar for me for later, I wouldn't say no. Tess, tell Jack the Millers have added a pint on for me, will you? There's a good lass.'

The waitress, Tess, smiled and headed back inside. 'Oh, and add a few more of those mints to the Millers' coffee, will you?' he added with a wink. The waitress waved and disappeared through the patio door. 'She's a good kid but a little quiet. Getting a word out of her is like getting blood from a stone.'

He looked down at Louise.

'I heard you were the one that saw the Willikar boy. Bad business that, in a graveyard as well.'

'You know I can't talk about it,' Louise said.

Paul waved her comment away. 'Oh, I know, I know. Not wanting to get you into it at all. Bad trouble that. Parents must be beside themselves. They come here now and then, you know, but then again, who doesn't?'

'With food as good as this, why wouldn't they indeed?' Aunt Fiona said, continuing to stroke the chef's ego. He took the compliment as he always did, with a toast of his glass and another long drink. Two more swallows and it was gone.

'I best get back to it, but before I do, can you answer me one thing? Is it true that the Willikar boy was into some sort of devil worship?'

It was like a slap to the face. Aunt Fiona's mouth dropped open and even Uncle Bernard, who was usually as cool in any situation as Louise, looked shocked. Louise's blood ran cold, and she could feel that anger turn hard as ice in her chest. 'What?'

'I heard that the boy was into some pretty nasty stuff?'

'And just where did you hear that?' Louise asked, her voice cold and hard.

'You'd be surprised how fast the rumours start to spread when Catherine Hallum's around,' Paul said, giving a nod back into the restaurant.

Louise turned to look through the window. Catherine Hallum was just starting to tuck into her pate and toast starter. Sitting opposite her was the man with the greasy hair and the Stephen King book. 'I'm not surprised in the slightest,' Louise said before turning her gaze onto Paul. 'The Willikars have enough to deal with, without these sorts of malicious lies being spread about by people who should know fucking better.'

'Louise!'

As Aunt Fiona looked on in astonished shock, Louise stood and gathered her things. 'I'm going home,' she said, pulling on her jacket. 'Tom's been waiting all morning to go out and I need a lie down.'

'What about the coffee?' Aunt Fiona asked.

'I'll make one when I get home,' Louise said. 'Paul.'

The chef gave a nod. 'Bad business,' he said. 'Well, those prof-iteroles won't cream themselves,' he said with a wink. 'Enjoy your afternoon.' He moved aside so Louise could slip past. She could feel their eyes on her back as she walked down the path to the entrance. She could hear them talking about her as well, but she didn't care.

CHAPTER
TWENTY

Tom was waiting at the door when Louise got home. As soon as she opened the door he shot out and disappeared over the wall into next door's garden.

'Good to see you too,' Louise said, pushing the door wider so she could get inside. 'Don't be too long; I got you tuna!' She'd made a stop at the Wadees' shop, getting a bottle of wine and some sweets as well as a special treat for Tom. She'd had her own treat with lunch, and so it was only fair he had something as well. All she wanted to do now was curl up on the sofa and spend the afternoon reading, doing her best to salvage her day off as well as she could. She felt a momentary pang of guilt, remembering that Hines was still working, called in on her day off to help out, whereas Louise had been actively on-scene when it happened.

There was still that dark cloud from speaking with the Willikars. If her afternoon was bad, how much worse was theirs? By now they would have visited the hospital and the body of their son would have been officially identified, presumably by David Willikar.

She searched in her kitchen for a clean glass. Several were stacked on the side waiting to be washed, along with a tower of dishes that rivalled James' pile of books. A dirty dishcloth hung from the tap with two tea towels draped across the draining board.

On the floor, Tom's bowl was empty save for some dried husks of food that her cat's pride would not let him touch, no matter how hungry he might be. She picked it up and dropped it into the sink. Turning on the tap she started to fill the bowl with hot water. By the time he came back from his wander – he used next door as his poo-garden, a fact she was extremely grateful for after his first large deposit in the litter tray she had bought him; it had forced her to crank open every window that she could in the flat – he would be hungry again, and she wanted to be able to relax on the sofa without the worry of having to keep getting up to minister to her cat's needs. That was where the tuna came in.

Even as she thought this, her face broke into a welcomed grin. She knew only too well that if he wanted anything, he had her trained well enough now that she would get it for him. More food, a fresh water bowl, his favourite blanket to sleep on. Yes, he had a favourite blanket; that it had once been her favourite jumper, well, that didn't really matter now, did it? It belonged to Tom, as did the rest of the flat.

Louise cleaned his bowl, opened the can of tuna and filled the bowl. After that she gave his water bowl a refresh. She then checked his litter tray and was pleased to see it hadn't been used while she was out. That meant he'd be making use of next door's garden for sure.

The cat was sorted; it was now time to sort herself out.

She poured a glass of wine and took a sip. It tasted wonderful, and by the time she had changed and was ready for her afternoon's reading session, Tom had come back and was eating in the kitchen. She went down the steep stairs to shut the door and was just about to close it when someone appeared, their shadow thrown on the wall beside her.

'Knock, knock!'

Louise opened the door wider to see Karla Hayes standing

there, her face beaming, her hair shining in the afternoon sun, and a carrier bag in her hand.

'What are you doing here?' Louise asked. 'I thought you were working?'

'I was. Now I'm not. Now I'm here, and I brought provisions.'

She lifted the bag and Louise laughed when she heard the clink of wine bottles.

Karla was curled into Louise's arm, her head resting on her shoulder. Evening had fallen, the afternoon passing all too swiftly. They had finished the bottle of wine Louise had bought at the shop and then immediately started on the next, a nice Merlot. Louise's favourite. Another favourite of hers was the bag of Liquorice Allsorts that Karla had plucked from the bag and thrown at her with a laugh.

'What is this?' Louise had asked, laughing. 'It's not my birthday.'

'I heard what happened this morning and figured you'd need a little pick me up,' Karla said, refilling their glasses. 'I made some changes to my schedule, grabbed a few things, and here I am.'

She came back with the glasses, and they settled on the sofa. Tom was curled beside Louise, his deep purr vibrating against her thigh. A film was playing on the TV, the sound turned down but not muted. Occasional gunshots sounded, making Tom's ears perk up, but otherwise he slept on, his broken snores making Karla laugh, earning her a playful poke from Louise.

'It's not his fault,' she said. 'And I bet you snore just as bad.'

'How would you know?' Karla said. There was a playful sparkle to her eyes and Louise's heart leapt. But instead of taking things further, she pulled Karla into the crook of her arm, and they snuggled down to watch the movie.

'I'm glad you came,' she said.

'Me too,' Karla replied. 'I was at work when the Willikars were brought in to identify their son.'

Louise sat up. 'Did you see them?'

Karla nodded. 'Part of my job, unfortunately. I work with the family liaison unit on cases of suicide. Especially teen suicides. Shirley Hanson came with them.'

'I know Shirley,' Louise said. Karla smiled.

'Lovely lady, Shirley. Really knows her stuff. We've worked together on several cases before. Long before you came back,' she added, seeing the puzzled look Louise gave her. 'Maybe one day I'll tell you a couple of stories about Shirley. They'll raise your blood pressure and turn your hair white! So... the Willikars. They were in pieces when they came in. How bad was it?'

'It was awful,' Louise said, shuddering slightly as she recalled seeing James sprawled across the gravestone, his eyes sightlessly staring into an unseen void. 'And so unnecessary. They talk about needless deaths; well, this was a prime example of one.'

'James had felt it was necessary,' Karla said softly.

Louise decided not to tell Karla that she didn't think it was a suicide just yet. Do a little more digging first.

Karla pulled herself from Louise's embrace, settling herself back against the arm of the sofa, her feet tucked beneath her. She was wearing a skirt and brushed cat hair from it. Louise grimaced an apology.

'For some, like James, suicide seems to be the only option they're left with,' Karla continued.

'But I've been to his house, looked at his room. Talked to his parents. From what I can see he had no reason to do this.'

'From what you can see,' Karla said.

'He had no reason to kill himself. He had good, loving parents who provided well for him, gave him all the love and support he needed. There was nothing to suggest anything foul happening beneath the surface, nothing that I could pick up on.'

'And how long did you spend with them... twenty minutes? Half an hour? You're a good detective, there's no doubting that, but you weren't looking for a crime here. You would be looking for a cry for help.'

'I saw no sign of anything out of the ordinary,' Louise said.

'There's no sign when a shark comes along and grabs a swimmer, either. One moment they are happily swimming along, the next they're nothing but a red stain in the water. Think of the decision to commit suicide like the shark; it drifts silently unseen beneath the surface, a constant threat just waiting for the right moment, the most opportune moment, to strike. James might have been swimming for years with the threat drifting silently behind or beneath him. This morning it decided now was the time to feast.'

Karla took another sip of wine then stared into its red surface. 'No one knows exactly what anyone else is experiencing. He could have been having trouble at school – bullies, stress about his subjects. He would have been one of the first to take these new GCSEs, wouldn't he? Maybe he was worried about that?'

'We haven't spoken to his school yet.' In fact, Louise hadn't even considered it till now. She made a mental note to mention it to Hines tomorrow. It would give them a chance to speak again with Wendy as well.

'There's so many things that people worry about these days. I see it all the time, small things that normally wouldn't raise a single concern become overwhelming obstacles that force people to make decisions they wouldn't usually do. Stupid decisions that affect their lives in ways they couldn't possibly imagine or consider under normal circumstances. Knock on effects being divorce and separation; job loss; substance and alcohol abuse. Even physical abuse. I've seen it happen way too many times to too many good people.'

'Even kids?' Louise asked. She'd sat up now and was stroking the ruff of Tom's neck. He purred louder and pushed back against her fingers.

'Especially kids. They feel the weight of the world as they struggle to understand it and can't understand where the pressure is coming from or what it means. They act out, which gets their parents mad at them, adding even more pressure. It builds and builds and eventually has to find a release. For some it's as simple as acting out in school or at home, staying out late, swearing at their parents. Silly stuff. Dumb stuff...'

'We've all done it,' Louise said with a grin.

'We have,' Karla agreed, 'but we may have had better coping mechanisms in place. If we didn't, we wouldn't have chosen such high-pressure jobs. Not everyone has them. For those who don't, they act out in deepening ways of severity. Drugs, risky and dangerous sex, self-destructive behaviour that starts to infect those closest to them. What?' she added, seeing that Louise was staring off into the distance. 'What did I say?'

Louise gave her head a shake, as though brushing off a cobweb that had fallen over her. 'I was just wondering what other ways people might act out. James came from a middle-to-upper class family; they listened to classical music, obviously had money—'

'They live on Healey, right?'

Louise nodded. '—and they did all the usual things like yearly holidays, family gatherings, from what I could tell from the photos. Father was retired, was even trying to get his son into a work ethic with a small window cleaning service. Good clothes, two cars – well, one and a van – all that stuff. But James listened to heavy metal music, read metal magazines. He was found wearing torn jeans, a dirty t-shirt. Battered trainers.'

'Clear signs of acting out would be my guess, but that's all it is. Just a guess based on what you've said. Without knowing more, I can't really comment with any certainty.'

'I wish a few more people had your common sense,' Louise said. 'He didn't leave a note though, and that has me curious. A few other things as well, things I can't talk about.'

'Can't talk about with me, you mean.'

Louise sighed. 'You know how it is; I can't.'

'It's okay,' Karla said. 'I understand.'

Louise put her glass down and stood up. She thought better when on the move, and everything she had rolling round in her head needed the momentum. 'Already the rumour mill has started, saying he was a troubled kid, into some bad stuff. Devil worship, if you can imagine it? As if the family hasn't got enough to deal with.'

Karla leaned forward, intrigued. 'Devil worship? Where did that nugget come from?'

Louise was pacing now, walking the problem. Karla took another sip of her wine and waited for Louise to continue.

'That bitch, Catherine Hallum, apparently. She's been telling people over at The Lodge that James was into devil worship and that was why he went mad and killed himself. She also called them troubled kids without even knowing them. Called them Broadowler kids.'

'James lived on Healey,' Karla said softly. She ignored the casual slur Louise had thrown at this Hallum woman. It was something she had noticed Louise do more regularly over the months they had been seeing each other. Little signs that she wasn't being as cautious about how she referred to certain people who rubbed her the wrong way. When they had first met, people under her scrutiny were suspects; now they were perps, shorthand for perpetrators, with a high level of guilt already implied by the word. It was a shift in attitude that Karla found a little worrying, if not outright disturbing yet.

'Course he bloody did, and I bet that burned Hallum's tits. I bet she was jealous because the Willikars had more than she did and she was revelling in the drama. Wendy lives on Broadowler, not James, but she lumped them all in, like they were something to be classified, like some test subject.'

'Sickening.'

'It fucking is!'

The pacing was faster now, enough that it had woken Tom, who looked lazily from Louise to Karla and back. He gave a stretch and stood, jumped down from the sofa and plodded out of the room. They could hear his thick pads on the wooden floor of the hallway as he made his way to the kitchen.

Karla stood and walked over to where Louise stared out into the night. The lights of the funeral parlour opposite were on, and the gate was open. For several minutes no one said anything.

'Do you think he's going to be taken there?' Louise asked.

Gently, Karla took Louise by the shoulders and turned her away from the window. She wasn't surprised to see tears rolling down Louise's face and reached out to brush them aside with one hand, while the other snaked into her hair.

Slowly, Karla pulled Louise to her. The kiss started softly at first, Louise's sobs making her body shake as Karla held her tight. Louise kissed her back, pressing her lips harder, her hands roaming across Karla's back and down her sides.

Still kissing they made their way back to the sofa and fell on it, laughing when Tom leapt up with a startled howl. Breathless, Karla raised herself up on one elbow. Louise reached up and started to kiss her neck.

'You know, I don't have work until tomorrow afternoon,' Karla said, eyes closed to better savour the feel of Louise's kisses on her skin. Louise stopped kissing her and looked deep into Karla's eyes.

'What are you saying?' she asked.

Karla bit at her lip. Louise's heart felt like it had stopped in her chest, her breath caught in her throat.

'I can stay the night, if you'd like...'

Louise smiled.

As they started to kiss again, Tom glared at them, turned around twice and settled down to sleep.

CHAPTER
TWENTY-ONE

The song on the radio was distorted, the voices mixing with the music to create a wave of noise that hurt her ears. It dipped in and out, at first loud then instant silence, creating a disconcerting wave that made her feel sick.

She wished she could turn it off, but she couldn't reach forward past her parents' seats to get at the radio. In fact, she couldn't move at all. She tried, again and again, straining to move even a fraction, but every time she tried an immense pain shot through her arm and into her chest.

She also couldn't see anything. Everything was shrouded in a veil of darkness tinged with red.

And she could hear rain falling. Falling all around her in a scattered pattern that was slowly coming to a halt.

And then she could move. Whatever had been holding her back was suddenly gone and she fell forward and down. Or was it up and back, because she found herself on the roof of the car, the ceiling, to be more accurate. The car was upside down and so was she. Carefully she moved, turning herself over, finally free from the seatbelt that had saved her life.

The rain she had heard was glass pattering to the ground from the shattered windows.

There was a painful roar slowly working its way into her head. It sounded muted, as though coming from deep under water. Hollow. It pushed at her, forced its way inside her head where it let loose with a fury that shook her with shocked revelation.

The scream of (David Willikar, on the ground, hands in his hair, eyes wide) her father; primal rage unchecked.

And that was when she saw.

That was when, dear God and Jesus Christ in heaven, that was when she saw —

Louise gasped upright in her bed, clawing at her chest.

At her feet Tom lifted his head, gave a *pufft!* of annoyance then settled back down.

Louise took in several ragged gasps of air, the mixed screams that had woken her fading away as rapidly as they had come. Fading away, but never truly disappearing. The image of David Willikar hung before her like a wraith in the night, an ethereal terror that was only too real.

Louise fell back against the pillow. She was alone, save for Tom, who had begun snoring again. Karla had left, Louise not ready to take their relationship to that next stage. Not yet. She wasn't ready despite what she had said to her aunt. She wasn't ready and those around her weren't ready. Except perhaps Hines.

Closing her eyes, Louise listened to the happy snores of her cat and waited for sleep to reclaim her.

She was waiting a long time.

CHAPTER
TWENTY-TWO

MONDAY, 12TH

Elizabeth Hines was at her desk by 7.45, a bacon and egg roll from Jenny's Café in its bag, its smell making her stomach rumble all the harder as she made coffee. She'd stayed in the Carps until half-nine last night, nursing a lager and black and enjoying small talk with Joe in between him serving customers. For a Sunday night it had been busy, the talk being mostly about how well Ossett Town were doing in the League. Apparently league promotion was on the cards. They'd been riding the wave since the pre-season friendly with Manchester United and the lads were all keyed up.

Hines had listened with one ear, surprised that there wasn't much being said about the suicide in the graveyard, but thankful none the less. She couldn't get the horrendous sound David Willikar had made out of her mind, nor the way his wife had looked when they left, at once lost and anxious all at the same time. She still felt cold shivers ripple her spine when she thought about standing before the parents, desperately trying to think how to tell them their son was dead. She had looked over at Joe, lost in his own little world pouring drinks, and wondered just why she was with him. There was no way she could make him understand what she had gone through, tame in comparison to the poor parents, but traumatic, nonetheless.

And if she couldn't tell him about that, then how the hell was she supposed to talk to him about...

The whistle of the kettle stopped her from completing that thought, and she let out a silent prayer of thanks. She poured hot water and deposited three large spoons of coffee into her mug, and was stirring vigorously when a gruff voice called out from the other side of the pen, the area where the detectives all had their desks. There were nine desks, each with a couple of chairs and all stacked high with paperwork. Files of research, interview notes, crime scene photos; every desk was crammed. 'Organised chaos', Louise called it.

'Any water left, love? If so, make us a cuppa. I'm parched already.'

She turned to see Detective Sergeant Harolds shrugging off his jacket. She'd hoped to have the Shop to herself for a little longer this morning. There was a stack of paperwork to finish off, plus she had the briefing to give later this morning about what she had found in the warehouse and she hadn't prepared for it as well as she knew she could have. The others all seemed so much better than she did when it came to the morning briefs, jumping through their reports pretty sharpish, while she struggled and had to keep referring back to her notes. When she'd briefed everyone about the car thefts it had taken her nearly ten minutes, through which Harolds huffed and puffed and several others coughed loudly, thinking they were being clever and she hadn't heard 'boring!' or 'dishwater dull!' hidden beneath their coughs and laughs. She had. And she remembered.

Give her a subject that needed taking down and she had no problem, but ask her to stand in front of a group and talk for five minutes and she became a nervous wreck.

'Do I look like a bloody teas-maid?' she said, throwing her spoon into the sink. 'Don't answer that,' she added, seeing the grin already starting to form on the Sergeant's face. 'Water's still hot though and I brought in fresh milk.'

'And a bacon butty too, by the smell of it. Brought enough to share?'

Hines shook her head. 'Seriously... you want to steal my breakfast as well? Didn't your missus fix you something before you came in?'

It was well known throughout the Shop that Harolds and his wife were having difficulties. It seemed to be contagious; DI Manby and his wife had had issues last year, now Harolds. And then there was Joe.

And Peter...

Best not to think about it.

His wife thought it was time Harolds retired; he thought she was a daft cow and had clearly said so, judging by the fact that his clothes were creased, and he was always on the scrounge for a meal and sometimes a bed.

'What do you know about it?' Harolds said, throwing his coat to the floor. 'I'll make it me'sen.'

Instantly Hines felt guilty. She shushed him away, grabbing a mug from the side and dropping a teabag in. He grinned and relaxed into his chair with a heavy sigh. 'Three sugars, if you please,' he said.

Hines took in a deep breath, promised herself she wouldn't kill him, and made Harolds his tea.

When Louise arrived at eight everyone was in, the night shift having signed over and gone home. Footsteps echoed above the pen from the newly installed lab, a fact that Harolds had been grumbling about for the last ten minutes. Tea or no tea, he was in a foul mood.

'Are they using elephants up there?' he said, giving DC Tom Bailey, who was sitting beside him, a heavy nudge, and pointed to the ceiling. 'Pretty soon one of 'em's going to be coming through that; you mark my words. Someone needs to have a word with Peter about it.'

Bailey said nothing and continued flipping through his notebook. Hines was sitting at the front of the group, with Louise next to her resting casually against a desk.

'Morning,' Hines said. Louise looked up and smiled.

'Did you have a good time at the pub?'

'I had to listen to Joe going on and on about bloody football all night. How was your night?'

'Kar... a friend came round last night, and I totally forgot.'

Hines' smile grew wide. 'I know. I came round to talk to you but saw you had company. Didn't want to intrude. How is she?'

Louise leaned forward. 'Keep it down, will you? I don't want everyone knowing.'

'Knowing what, besides, it's none of their business who you—'

'Will you *shut up*?' Louise hissed.

'What are you two blathering about?' Harolds shouted over. 'Like a pair of gossiping gooses.'

Before either of them could reply, Detective Inspector Bill Manby strode out of his office and over to the huddle of police officers and detectives. 'Let's make this sharpish. I've to head over to Wakefield to see the Chief Superintendent at eleven so no trammel this morning, folks. Who's up first?'

Tom Bailey took the bullet, delivering a dry rendition of the three scuffles he'd broken up in the town centre after the pubs had kicked everyone out. 'Just the usuals,' he said, finishing up by closing his notebook with a snap. 'And I expect we'll be seeing them again next weekend.'

'Albion's playing at home,' Harolds said. That got a chorus of grumbles rumbling around the room. 'Still got the book open if anyone wants to drop a few quid on the game, all in the interests of fun,' he added, seeing Manby turn a stony gaze his way.

'I don't want any of that getting back to the CS. We're under close enough scrutiny as it is; last thing we need is word getting back about illicit gambling, so cork that for now, Dave, all right?'

Harolds said nothing but nodded along, slyly sliding the paper he kept everyone's bets on back into his pocket.

'Beth, you go next.'

Louise felt a pang of guilt run through her. No one was mentioning the obvious: James Willikar's death. She still couldn't call it a suicide. Not yet. But no one was saying anything about it, just another 'suey'. No biggie.

It wasn't a question. Not really.

Hines sighed but stood up, fishing for her notebook. 'We've had a report of another break-in over the weekend. Dimple Well Junior and Infants' school. A stolen bike and a few smashed windows. I'm going over this morning to take a look.'

'How many break-ins is that now?' Manby asked. He sounded tired and looked even worse. It seemed he was giving Harolds a run for his money on who could look the scruffiest this morning, with a weekend's growth of stubble stuck to his face and a shirt that had more lines than Leeds train station.

'Six, over the course of three weeks, although other than the bike being taken from the school, there's nothing else gone missing. At least nothing reported.'

'Kids doing it?' he asked.

'Sounds like it,' Louise said. She'd taken a look at Hines' notes and so far everything pointed towards nuisance, rather than criminal, intent.

'And the warehouse?'

Louise gave Hines a puzzled look. 'What warehouse?'

'The one I went to after dropping you off at The Lodge. Seems there's more to it than a simple break-in. It's what I came to talk to you about. Someone phoned in a report of noises early Saturday night coming from the old warehouse next to Holy Trinity Church. A uniform had checked it out but found nothing and I had it down to check this morning but then Sunday happened. I figured now was as good a time as any to check, so after speaking with the parents of James Willikar I headed back to Church Street. When I got there, there was evidence that the main door had been pried open. I went inside for a look and found evidence of people being there. Empty beer cans, dead fags and a makeshift campfire. There were also tyre marks in the dust, as well as evidence that the building had been used as a knocking site. Several used condoms and wrappers in the empty offices.'

'Sounds like you've been busy, Bailey!' Harolds called out.

'Fuck off, Harolds,' Tom Bailey snapped back amidst a chorus of jeers and laughter from the others. 'If it's anyone putting it out there, it's Danes.'

'What else, Beth?' Louise asked, ignoring the laughter.

'I found traces of blood, not a huge amount but enough to make me curious, and so I went over to the churchyard where Danes and the SOCO team were closing up after the Willikar suicide to get them to come take a look.'

Manby turned to Peter Danes, sitting at a desk nearby. 'And?'

Danes shrugged. 'A little blood, like she says. Not enough to warrant a crime scene though. Could be from anything; kids messing about, a transient falling over drunk or in the dark. Sorry,' he said, turning to Hines.

'Not a problem. That's why I got you to come take a look. I did find something else though.' She held out a clear evidence bag. Inside was a wallet. 'Belongs to a Daniel McKensie. No cash inside but there was a library ticket for Ossett Library and a driving licence. Both match names and have the same address. Strangely enough just across the road.'

'What're you thinking?' Manby asked.

Louise watched all this with a growing sense of pride. Okay, she was only a few years older than Hines, but she was vastly more experienced than her, and yet here was Hines sounding like she'd been doing this for years.

'Best guess is he got it lifted while getting gobbled,' Hines continued. 'We've a few locals who work usually in Leeds or

Wakefield, but sometimes shop around in the town centre of a weekend. I'll take a couple of pictures of the most likely ones and have a chat with him. At the least, he got robbed on a night out in town. Either way, he gets his wallet back.'

'Sounds like you've got it covered, Beth. Good work.'

Hines smiled, blushed, and sat down. Manby turned to Louise.

'What about your not-a-suicide?' he asked. 'How did the family take it?'

'As well as could be expected,' she replied carefully, not liking the sarcastic tone he was taking.

'When does the autopsy get finished?' Manby asked, eager to move on.

Louise's cheeks had reddened but she recovered quickly. 'Either later today or tomorrow.'

'Well, no matter what I, or anyone else may think, it'll be the coroner who decides if there's an inquest needed. We follow where the evidence goes, not the other way round. Right, Louise?'

Louise paused before answering. Yes, all signs showed an apparent suicide loathe though she was to admit it; the sullen nature over the last few weeks; the arguments at home. Classic signs all, and they'd need to be explored a little further, but there was something about this; she had that feeling, that copper's gut, the warning bell clanging loudly enough that she paused in her rush to close the case and move on.

James Willikar's parents wouldn't be moving on anytime soon, and neither was she.

Wendy knew something she hadn't told them yet. So did James' body, and the autopsy would, hopefully, reveal those secrets.

'We're close to sticking a pin in this one,' she said as diplomatically as she could. 'Maybe one or two lines of questioning to explore and then we're finished. We should have it wrapped by the funeral, I'd expect.'

Manby was nodding. 'Good. Good. Okay, Charlie. What you got?'

Louise tuned out the rest of the briefing. She tried to catch Hines' gaze, but the younger woman had her eyes bored into the back of her notebook.

Great.

CHAPTER
TWENTY-THREE

'Why didn't you come get me when you found the blood?' Louise asked Hines as the pair got themselves ready to set off.

They were going to head to the school first to check on the stolen bike, before returning the wallet to Mr McKensie. As Louise grabbed a fresh notebook, Hines checked through the messages left on her desk by the night shift. There were always at least five officers stationed at Prospect Road overnight: two detectives and three uniforms. Last night it had been DCs Jon Williams and Gary Richards. Both were new to the area, having been posted to Ossett a few months ago. Coming from Leeds, the two were experienced, eager and, like Hines and Louise, relatively young. Harolds had complained that they were trying to push out the old-guard, and that these two whippersnappers were only giving his wife more reason to ask for his retirement.

Richards had left a message for Louise, which Hines passed over.

'I told you: I saw Doctor Hayes' car parked up the side street by your flat and didn't want to disturb you.'

'Why was Doctor Hayes visiting you?'

Louise turned to see DI Manby, coffee cup in hand, slowly

heading to the door for an early morning crafty cigarette. He had promised his wife he'd quit; he just hadn't said when.

'I asked her to come round to give me some advice regarding suicide. The psychology of it,' she added when she saw Manby's brow begin to wrinkle. Hearing the 'P' word, it loosened immediately, his brain already starting to tune out. It was a giveaway that Louise was sure he didn't know he had, and probably one of the contributing factors to his degenerating marriage, no less. He was not a fan of the science of the mind, even though he knew how important a role it played in their jobs. He didn't understand it, didn't want to understand it any more than he wanted to understand how an autopsy was carried out. All he wanted was the final details. The facts of the matter that he could use in court.

'What did she have to say?' he asked as the three headed towards the door together. Hines passed Louise her handbag after making sure she had everything they needed. She grabbed the keys to the Rover from Harolds before he could object, having already signed it out.

'She answered a few of my worries regarding the fact there was no note, and about the placement of the knife. I'm still not a hundred percent convinced—'

'No shit.'

'—but I'm working through everything and checking them off my list.'

'You and your lists,' Manby said. 'Bugger me; it's chill this morning.'

They were outside now, having stepped from the warmth of the Prospect Road CID building into the cold bitter wind of Monday. It was quiet, save for the heavy drone of the 126 bus as it left the bus station, trundling past on its way to Wakefield.

'Well, we talked, and she suggested we go speak to the kids at the school James went to.'

'North Ossett?'

Louise nodded. 'She thinks having an honest chat with them

about what happened would be a good idea. Might help a few of them, and we might get some background to his situation.'

'You're just not letting this go, are you?'

'Not until I'm convinced,' she said. 'Isn't that what I'm supposed to do?'

'As long as it's not at the expense of other cases that need your attention,' he replied. 'Sounds like a good idea though. Sueys sometimes bring out copycats, so having a professional head shrink talk to them might put a few off. Last thing we need at Christmas is a bunch of kids trying to top themselves. Okay, let her know I say it's fine. Sooner rather than later, though. Maybe go to South Ossett as well. Word will have spread. I'm pretty sure Ms Hayes has statistics about the spread of copycats amongst teenagers.'

Louise nodded. 'Will talk to her tonight.'

As Hines unlocked the car, Louise watched the bus make its way down Prospect Road. As it began its signal to turn left onto Station Road, Hines finally unlocked the car door with a cry of triumph.

'Bloody thing was frozen shut,' she said. She got inside and settled behind the steering wheel. A moment later and the car coughed to life, a thick plume of blue smoke billowing behind them. Hines wound the down the window and looked at Manby, who was still standing outside the front doors to the police station, enjoying the cold air and the last dregs of coffee. 'When are we getting new cars? This one is just about ready for the knacker's yard.'

Manby took a final sip of coffee then threw the rest to the bushes. 'Sanderson's do us a good deal on all the motors,' he said. 'There's still life in them yet.'

Hines reached across and popped the lock on the passenger door for Louise. She pulled it open and paused.

'Sanderson's are a bunch of crooks who do Sanderson's a good deal,' Louise said over the roof of the car. The Sanderson garages were on the corner of Ventnor Way just before it became

Queen Street and had been there for the last twenty years. A sudden cash injection a few years ago had seen them expand their business from a single bay to four, with car sales from a lot on Dewsbury Road. It was where the Ossett police had got the last two cars and they had a contract with them for maintenance. It was no secret that Sanderson's had ties to the Chief Superintendent; Colin Sanderson, who owned and ran the business, was the Chief's brother-in-law, and as long as Ruth Freeman was married to Colin Sanderson, that was where Ossett police got their cars serviced.

'I'm off back inside before I catch my death. Have a good morning, girls.'

His cigarette, now nothing but a filtered nub, went the same way as the coffee. A moment later the doors to the police station swung shut.

'Come on,' Louise said, yanking her door shut. 'Let's get the day started.'

CHAPTER
TWENTY-FOUR

Following an early-morning phone call with the head, assembly had been postponed until ten that morning, giving Louise and Hines time to get to Dimple Well Junior and Infants' school and take a look at the smashed window and where the bike had been stolen from. There was a long shed just to the side of the school against which several bikes were now chained. All were BMX bikes of various colours and states of repair. Most had bald tyres and one had Star Wars bubble-gum cards stuck into the spokes of the front wheel.

Louise knelt to look at them; a big Star Wars fan, she collected everything from the action figures to cereal transfers and even bubble-gum cards like these. She had a pretty large collection, with every action figure that had been released still on their cards and kept in bubble-wrap in boxes. These hadn't been unpacked and were crammed into the small cupboard-come-wardrobe in her bedroom. There was a loft in the flat but one she hadn't been able to access yet; she kept meaning to ask her uncle to lend her some ladders so she could use the loft to store some of her stuff and get it out of the way, but she kept forgetting.

Work got in the way, or the Dude.

Or Karla...

Yes. One or two times she had meant to grab the ladders and get the boxes sorted but Karla had turned up and the two of them had ended up either going to the pub for drinks or into Leeds for a meal and a dance.

And sometimes a hotel room.

Neither had stayed over at the other's home. This was a line they hadn't crossed yet, something they hadn't even discussed, although Karla had tried to push the point a few times. Why was that? What was stopping them from taking this to the next stage?

What was stopping her?

'That was where my bike was chained up. When I came back Saturday morning for it, it was gone.'

Louise craned her neck to look up at Deborah Jones. Young, perhaps a year or two younger than Louise, Deborah taught an infant class. Her long blonde hair fell across her shoulders and down her chest. She lifted a strand and tucked it behind her ear. 'It was stupid of me to leave it, but we were going out for drinks after work, and I didn't want to take it with me.'

'Where did you go?' Louise asked.

'Just up the road. The Taps. You know it?'

Louise nodded. 'And the chain?'

Deborah shrugged. 'That was gone as well.'

Hines stood a little further down the wall, beside the window. It had been boarded up by the caretaker and any broken glass removed before little feet could be cut. 'Was that when you saw the broken window?'

'Yes. I had a look inside, but nothing seems to have been taken. It didn't look like anyone had actually been inside, to be honest. Perhaps they fell against it when they were taking my bike.'

There was a compost bin opposite, placed against the large, fenced wall that ran all around the school grounds. On the other side was an allotment, several sectioned gardens that people tended from the surrounding houses. Some ran onto Healey

Road while others stretched behind the school and onto the back of The Lodge hotel.

'Someone could have climbed over the fence, snatched the bike and, when they were climbing back, slipped. Perhaps they dropped the bike, which smashed the window.'

'I'm not going to get it back, am I?' Deborah asked.

'I doubt it. It does happen, but I doubt it. Especially at this time of year; it's probably under someone's Christmas tree. We'll keep an eye out, but it's probably already been sold on.'

Deborah sighed then kicked out at a stray pebble. 'Bloody kids!' She looked up suddenly, realising that young ears might have heard her. Seeing no one nearby, she let out an audible sigh of relief.

'Sorry. I just really liked that bike.'

They told Deborah they would be in touch if they heard anything but not to hold any hope out. The young teacher said she wouldn't, but she would hope to see Louise in the Taps one night for a drink, perhaps. Louise had smiled and they had left.

'Well, you're a sly one,' Hines said as they got back in the car.

'What? I didn't do anything.'

'You obviously didn't have to,' Hines laughed. 'Hey, it's good to know you have options.'

'Shut up. McKensie's next?'

Hines shook her head.

'I think I should show you something first.'

Louise stepped carefully through the broken wooden door, being extra careful not to snag her trousers like Hines had just done. The younger officer cursed silently as she plucked at her trousers, trying to get the splinter of wood off her without cutting her—

'Jesus fucking Christ!' she yelled, snatching her hand back.

She sucked at her finger, which wept blood, and tried to ignore Louise's laugh. 'It's not fucking funny. It hurts.' Hines took a tissue from her pocket and wrapped it around her finger. The stain quickly spread from a single dot of blood into a widening crushed circle.

'That looks like a deep one,' Louise said, reaching for her purse. 'You want a plaster?'

Hines shook her head as she pulled the thorn free. Louise could hear the cloth rip. Hines' head drooped.

'Today is not a good day,' she said.

'Seems you've been having a few of those lately,' Louise said to Hines' back. They were walking down the ruined corridor of the abandoned warehouse. It was as deserted today as it had been when Hines came to look on Sunday. Puffs of dust and dirt were scuffed up as the pair moved further inside.

'Well?' Louise asked. 'What should I be seeing?' She looked around the stone circle at the scattering of dead cans and fag ends. One stone was out of place, and it was next to this that Hines knelt.

'Over here.' There was a red pentagram crudely drawn inside a circle. 'I saw the same symbol in one of the books on James Willikar's desk. And this,' she pointed to the scuffed tyre marks in the dust, 'leads me to believe that James was here.'

'You think he might have been the one to steal the bike?'

Hines nodded. 'It's a possibility, and then he came here.'

'And he wasn't alone,' Louise replied. 'All these cans and fags... Looks like at least two people. And what's this?'

She pointed to a small black puddle. Three conical towers melted into slag poked out from its jet-black surface. An acrid scent filled the air, its tang snapping on their tongues. A faint scent of memory that filled her mind. Going down the steps into the church, she had thought she smelled old cigarettes. Now it seemed it was this.

'Candles, by the looks of it.' Hines moved over and stared

down at the black puddle. 'Those weren't there before. Some-one's been back overnight.'

'Well, we know it's not James this time,' Louise said. 'Where did you find the wallet?'

Hines pointed to the darkened recess of a small room. It branched off to the right, a discarded storage room of sorts, Louise supposed. Now it was used for nasty meetups; a pile of old discarded used condoms lay next to the abandoned door, their grey, twisted forms looking like dead worms in the scattered debris at its entrance. A low moan sounded as the breeze found its way through cracks in the surrounding walls, a distant echo perhaps of dark, illicit connections made after too many beers and not enough good judgement.

'Not the most romantic of spots for a hook-up, eh, Beth? So, what are you thinking?'

Hines dropped the rock and scuffed it back into place with the heel of her shoe. 'I don't know. I was thinking maybe James had been here with some friends Saturday night. Maybe one of them stole the bike as well on Friday.'

'And what... while they were here, some prossie brought their work here?'

'Well, it certainly looks like that. We'll know more when we speak with Mr McKensie. I just think it's a huge coincidence that there's all this stuff here, right beside the churchyard where James committed suicide.'

'So... you're now thinking maybe it wasn't suicide?' Louise asked. 'I could have done with that backup back in the pen this morning.'

'I don't know!' Hines shouted. 'I don't know a damn thing!'

Her voice echoed off the walls, hanging in the air as it hollowed out and finally disappeared. She breathed heavily, her hands opening and closing, the nails biting into her palms.

'Are you okay?' Louise asked. She watched as Hines stalked up and down the corridor, her footsteps echoing throughout the building. There was a stale scent in the air, a lingering hint from the candles. It wasn't entirely unpleasant.

Hines was shaking her head as tears began to fill her eyes. She stopped pacing and turned to look at Louise.

'No,' she said, the words now empty and hollow. 'I think I'm pregnant.'

CHAPTER
TWENTY-FIVE

The drive back up to town was nearly silent, Hines' declaration hanging heavy between them, broken only by the sporadic sniffles as she wiped at her nose. She kept her eyes on the road as they made their way along Wesley Street towards the town centre. Their destination was the Co-operative, the only shop in town Louise could think of that might sell black candles. She wanted to follow this new lead before moving on to McKensie. Returning a lost wallet to a prostitute's 'client' was now low down on her priority list. She could remember seeing some red candles when she went into the homewares department looking for a basket she could put clothes in. There wasn't a lot of storage in the bedroom cupboard; baskets seemed the best option.

It had actually been Karla's suggestion, something she did with her own clothes, made when she had popped into the bedroom looking for her jacket. She had seen the puddle of jumpers and shirts in the corner and immediately started planning a trip to the Co-op. 'How can you live like this?' she had asked, gathering them all together. As she folded them neatly, Louise watched with detached fascination. The Dude had poked his head in, found there was no food, and wandered off in search of treats.

They parked on Kingsway, making sure the 'ON DUTY' sign was displayed prominently in the car window, and walked to the shop. Louise tried to start a conversation several times during the short walk, but Hines wasn't having it.

'Can we not do this right now?' she asked, her tone making it clear she didn't want to talk about her maybe-baby anytime soon. She held the door open for Louise, who slipped by her with a muted acknowledgement. If Beth didn't want to talk about it, who was she to argue? Who was she to give any advice anyway? Having children was not on any to-do list of Louise's by a long shot. And she was okay with that, although her aunt had had a few choice words on the matter when it was once broached.

That had been when Aunt Fiona had asked about Karla. Was it serious? Were they going to make it all official and let everyone know or was it always going to be a secret hidden from everyone, except her closest family?

Lots of questions, Louise thought. *I wish I had the answers.* Right now, being with Karla was fun, and that was all she wanted. Some fun. She needed it, she deserved it. She wasn't ready for anything long-term, and marriage wasn't on either of their radars. Like Louise, Karla had her own career that she was trying to steer the choppy waters of. Perhaps not as aggressive as the one Louise had chosen, there were still those in the health service who looked down on female professionals, even such acclaimed ones as Karla Hayes. Add into that the knowledge that she was gay, and doors wouldn't just slam shut against her, sealing off potential career paths, but they would be locked and double-barred.

And maybe the entire building would be burned down around her as well.

Luckily not everyone was as closed minded as some, but still the struggle was there, the juggling of career, relationship and family life. Apparently, there was some ideal, perfect woman who could balance all three in perfect unison. .

Louise knew that to be the bullshit that it was. Something had to give, it always did, and usually it was the career. A woman's ambition was second to that of a man's, pushed aside for the sake of family, or more accurately, *having* a family. Pushing kids out into the world and caring for the family unit with three squares a day and a clean home; that was the norm, the expectation. The dream.

To Louise, that was the nightmare.

'Over here.'

Hines stood at a display of candles. Their cream stalks were stacked like logs, fallen trees ready to be chipped or chopped. Multi-coloured wicks poked from their tapered ends. Alongside the dinner candles were cathedral-style ones, thick round towers that would look ideal on any kitchen table or dining board. Aunt Fiona had a few of these, she remembered. Louise looked around the display.

'No black ones?'

Hines scratched her forehead and looked for an assistant. Seeing one by the pots and pans she wandered over, Louise following. She recognised a large skillet that Karla had brought to her flat as a housewarming gift. True, it was nearly a year after Louise had moved in, but it was the thought that counted. She had used it to fry them both a steak that night. The Dude had approved.

'We don't sell black candles,' the assistant said, her clipped response accompanied by a haughty scowl. 'Who on earth would want such a thing?'

'They're quite popular, actually,' Hines replied. Before the assistant could respond, Louise jumped in, hoping to stave off the impending argument.

'Do you know who might sell them? Anyone in Ossett? Allwares, perhaps?'

'I work for the Co-op. I can't speak for anyone else, but I highly doubt anyone of good standing would sell such a thing.' Her voice dropped as she leaned in. 'Devil's fire,' she said in a low whisper. 'Black candles bring the devil's fire, his evil gaze, on those that light such. No one in Ossett would sell such a thing, though I hear the Dragon in Horbury might have that level of taste.'

'The Dragon,' Hines replied, turning to Louise. 'I've heard of that shop. Sells comics and books. Videos and games as well.' She turned back to the assistant, whose sneer was in danger of splitting her head back. 'I've never heard of devil's fire.'

'Have you not read your bible?' the woman asked. If she was shocked before by the request, she was now completely horrified. 'From the scriptures comes the immortal truth. You should read them, child.'

'Child? I'm about three years younger than you, you condescending bi—'

'Thank you for your time,' Louise said, hurriedly taking Hines by her shoulder and steering her away from the assistant.

Hines shook her hand away.

'What the hell was that? Child? Who the... oof, that's got my back right the fuck up. Child? Did you hear that?'

'Yes, and everyone in the Carps can hear you as well. Bring it down a notch, will you?'

Hines took in a few deep breaths, calming herself with each one.

'Maybe you are pregnant after all,' Louise said laughing, then ducked as Hines threw a tartan slipper at her.

CHAPTER
TWENTY-SIX

They were walking out of the Co-op and headed back to the car when Hines grabbed Louise's arm, yanking her to a stop. She pointed across the road to the side of Johnson's Butchers. The phone box was as dirty as the one on Pildacre Hill, its red paint all scratched and mucky, but she could see movement inside.

'Isn't that Scruffy Pete?'

'You've better eyes than I have if you can make that out,' Louise said. 'Definitely someone in there, but I can't tell you if it's a bloke or a woman.'

'It's Scruffy Pete!' Hines said. She let go of Louise and was already dashing across the road when the door to the phone box creaked open. A head popped out, the hair long and greasy. It sat atop thin shoulders covered by an equally greasy-looking green coat, yellow streaks down the arm where the fabric had ripped and padded stuffing had leaked out.

'Pete!' Hines called. 'Wait up!'

He looked up, saw Hines coming towards him and started to scurry away.

Scruffy Pete was well named. His coat, perhaps two sizes too big for him, caught on the door as it swung shut so that he was still struggling with it by the time Hines got to him. As well as rips in the coat, his trousers were torn and a sock peeked out from the ruined lip of his shoe. An unkempt beard wore his face like an afterthought, growing in patches of grey and brown hair that poked out at odd angles.

To Louise it looked like the matted fur she'd been meaning to brush out on Tom's back. Out of the two of them, she suspected Scruffy Pete was more likely to be the one with fleas.

'What you up to, Pete?' Hines asked. Unlike most people in Ossett, Hines and Louise treated the homeless man as the human being he was. Most people ignored him, choosing to look through him when he approached begging for coins for a sneaky pint, rather than engage. Louise couldn't blame them though; he stank like last week's chip supper.

'I didn't do nuthin',' he said, his eyes never leaving his shoes. 'What you wanting?'

'A chat,' Louise said. 'You up for a chat?'

His eyes lit up.

'I'm up for a pint.'

The Carps was the best place to go. It was just after twelve, the doors were open, and the bar already packed with Christmas punters. Louise found their group a table while Hines went to the bar.

Standing behind it, naturally, was Joe. He smiled when Hines came up and, ignoring several other customers waving money at him, grabbed a glass.

'Pint of 'top?'

'Make it a half; I'm working,' she said. He swapped glasses and started to pour. 'Same for Louise and whatever Scruffy has.'

Joe peered round her to look at where Louise had stashed Scruffy Pete into a chair. 'What's he done now?' he asked. Joe flicked the beer tap shut and added a generous splash of black-currant cordial to the drink. He placed it in front of her.

Hines looked at the drink then up at Joe. 'Sorry – better make it two lemonades for us seeing as we're working.'

Joe gave her a strange look.

'Really? It's not bothered you before, working or not.'

'New rules,' she said. 'You have it. My treat.'

Joe laughed and took the glass back. He poured it down the sink. 'I've got rules to follow as well,' he said. 'I'll bring them over. You all right?'

Hines nodded.

'You look a bit peaky, is all.'

'Just bring the drinks over, all right,' she bit back.

Scruffy Pete sat hunched into his chair, picking at a rough scab on his finger. His fingers were nothing but dirt-covered husks, the crap beneath what remained of his nails the detritus of alcohol-fuelled nerves, drug-riddled anxiety and a constant urge to pick.

He was doing it now, scrabbling at the scabs, not bothered by the flakes of skin and dried blood that dropped onto the table. Louise ignored it, but when Hines saw she swatted his hand away.

'Stop that!' she said. 'That's fucking disgusting.'

'Wha'?' Pete said. The stink of his breath reached Hines and she couldn't stop herself from covering her nose.

'Jesus, Pete. When was the last time you had a bath? You smell like you shit yourself and then threw up on it.'

'Beth...'

Louise gave her a look that said *shut the fuck up*! Hines shrugged. 'Sorry, Pete, but you've got to admit; you stink, fella. That's not usually like you. What's going on?'

Pete kept his eyes on his hands, still idly picking at them. He caught himself doing it and closed his fists. Tight.

'It's been a bit tough lately,' he said. His voice was hoarse, as though he'd been shouting recently. Or crying, Louise thought, noticing the redness of his eyes. That could also have been from whatever drug he was using these days; when she first got back to Ossett 'Scruffy' Pete Williams had been a serious heroin user, along with his prostitute sister Helen. The Williams were known throughout the local police forces right across West Yorkshire, having been arrested for one petty crime or another in Leeds, Dewsbury, Wakefield and, of course, the three boroughs of Gawthorpe, Horbury and Ossett. It was in the latter where they had found a small measure of respite; Detective Inspector Bill Manby had befriended the siblings, taking them under his wing and offering them a little protection in exchange for timely bits of information they could give him, insights gleaned from the criminal underworld that naturally attracted those as down on their luck as Helen and Pete Williams.

Louise knew all this, as did Hines. What they didn't know was where Helen Williams was. And apparently, neither did her brother.

'I've not seen her since Saturday,' he said again, this time with a moustache of beer foam clinging to the dirty strands of his beard. He wiped his mouth on the sleeve of his coat. Louise was pretty sure all he did was leave a cleaner smear on the coat arm.

'It's Monday, Pete,' she said. 'She didn't come home?'

Pete shrugged. A small cloud of what they hoped was dust rose from his shoulders. 'It happens. Sometimes she goes off and does her thing in the cities. Leeds more than likely. There's more about of a weekend. You eating those?' he asked, pointing to the bowl of chips Louise had ordered. She shook her head and slid the bowl across the table. Pete tucked in.

'How would she get there?'

'She'd get one of her punters to drive her in for a discount,' he said around a mouthful of chips. He dotted a splotch of ketchup on them, not bothered that most of it got on his fingers rather than the crispy chips. 'I've seen her do it tons of times. She did it on Saturday.'

Louise leaned forward. She reached out and pulled the bowl of chips back towards her.

'Helen got in a car Saturday? Do you think she'd have gone up to the warehouse on Church Street with him?' she asked. Pete's eyes were glued to the bowl of chips, which seemed to be disappearing. Louise pushed them back and he snatched at them.

It could have been days since he'd last eaten, getting by on stolen pints and whatever scraps could be found in the bins around town.

'The abandoned shoe factory? Hell, that's one of her favourite places to take 'em. Seems a bit daft doing that with a car though. People live nearby; they'd hear it.'

People like Daniel McKensie, Louise thought. She made a note to check what car he drove.

Scruffy Pete pushed the bowl aside and looked up at Louise. 'Is my sister all right?'

'I hope so,' Louise said. 'Like you said, Pete, she does this all the time. Louise reached over to place her hand on his. She could feel a week's worth of dirt layered on his rough skin, but she pressed her hand down, nonetheless. 'I'm sure she's fine, but if you hear anything from her, can you let either of us know?'

He nodded. 'I have the number,' he replied. They would usually get one or two calls from him each week, little slivers of information he thought they needed. Most of them went nowhere; sometimes he gave them the golden goose. It had been a timely tip from Pete Williams that had led to the capture of the gang who had been clocking cars on the Farsham Industrial Estate just off Dewsbury Road.

'Is there anything else, Pete? Anything at all?'

He didn't waste a second in thinking. 'Can you put a fiver behind the bar for me?' he said, dropping the last of the chips into his mouth.

.   .   .

Hines stood outside, eyes closed, thankful for the cold, crisp, yet fresh air that closed around her. Louise was making a quick visit to the loo. Scruffy Pete had gone for a wander around town after making sure Joe knew he had a few halves waiting to be claimed. She heard the door to the pub open and turned. Joe stepped out, a lit fag in his hand.

'It's all quiet so I figured I'd grab a cheeky one,' he said with a grin.

'I thought you said you were going to stop?' she said.

'I thought you said you didn't care?'

'Well, I do.' She stared at him. 'So?'

Joe let out a sound of mixed annoyance and amusement as he stubbed the cigarette out on the nearby bench. He made a show of it, really grinding it into the wood, then held out the ruined nub for her to see.

'Happy now?' he said, flicking it away into the brush. 'What's going on with you anyway? You've been all moody the last few days. What's up?'

'Oh, I don't know. Maybe looking into the death of a child is playing havoc with my good nature.'

'I thought he topped himself in a bit of devil worship gone wrong?' Joe asked.

'Don't let Louise hear you say that,' Hines said. 'In fact, don't let anyone hear you say that. You couldn't be further from the truth if you fucking tried.'

'Okay,' Joe said. 'Sorry. Am I going to see you tonight?'

Hines started to walk off. 'Not tonight. Tell Louise I'm going to Smith's, will you?'

And with that she was gone.

'Everything okay?'

Louise had seen the two talking through the pub window and had chosen to wait before coming out. It had looked heated, and she didn't want to get into the middle of it while they were sorting things out.

'I don't know,' Joe said. His face was sullen, his eyes drooping. The next moment he swept a hand through his hair and tried to put on a smile. 'Probably her time of the month,' he joked. 'She's gone to Smith's newsagent.'

'Cheers, Joe. Don't forget those drinks for Pete. And I don't suppose you've seen Helen, have you? Perhaps Sunday? Maybe even today?'

'Yeah, I saw her Saturday, but it was busy. Not sure what time she left, but it was late on and she was with some greasy-looking guy. Everything okay there? She's not in any trouble, is she?'

Louise offered him a smile that she hoped was more convincing than it felt. 'Everything's fine, Joe. Just let me know if you see her.'

He said he would and then headed back inside as a queue had formed at the bar. Joe was good people, a bit young and immature perhaps, but Louise thought he genuinely loved Hines. Or at the very least, cared a lot about her. Perhaps theirs was not the best relationship, but then who was she to give advice?

Pulling her coat tight, Louise went to find Hines.

CHAPTER
TWENTY-SEVEN

Daniel McKensie lived on Ryecroft Street, barely a stone's throw from the warehouse and graveyard on Church Street. The street was lined either side with two-up, two-down houses, their quarry-hewn rock clutched together with sandstone. It was a mirror image all along the street, the only differences being the colours of the doors and window mounts.

Number 73 belonged to Daniel McKensie, and Hines was able to park the car directly outside. A low stone wall fronted the property, broken by a black iron gate with a circular number plate fixed to a metal post box. The flap was up and several letters poked out.

Getting out of the car, Louise looked up at the house.

'Curtains are drawn,' she said pointing up. There were two windows facing onto the street. One was frosted glass, the bathroom no doubt. The other was a bedroom, green curtains blocking the day's light.

'Bit late for a nap, don't you think?' Hines asked, coming round the car. She had her notebook out and was jotting down the time they had arrived. 'Two-thirty on a Monday. Surely he'd be at work?'

'Let's find out,' Louise said.

She opened the gate, grabbing the letters from the post box as she went past. She went up the three short steps and rapped her knuckles on the door. When there was no answer she used the red door knocker, giving it several hard knocks.

The door to number 71 opened and an elderly woman's face poked out.

'He's not in, and if I have to tell another soul the same thing, I swear to you and the great God above us, I'm going to go insane.'

Her voice was like crushed gravel, throaty and the obvious result of decades of smoking. In fact, as she stepped out of her own doorway, Louise could see the cigarette held between nicotine-stained fingers. She wore a housedress, white with blue and white flowers across it and tied at the waist by a red sash; she clutched it tighter to her chest as she stepped out onto her front step.

'You want to leave a message like the others?' she asked.

Louise got her warrant card out and showed it. 'We're from the station,' she said. 'We've got some lost property to return to Mr McKensie. Do you know when he'll be back?'

'You're police? About bloody time.' She waved her hands all about, the fag ash drifting around her in grey sprinkles. The robe came loose to reveal that she was naked beneath. Hines turned her head away so fast, Louise thought she might have whiplash.

'Diedre Aldwin, I live at number 71,' she said, holding her hand out. Louise took it and they shook over the garden wall. Diedre must have sensed the cold on her skin because she looked down, tutted and snatched her robe shut. If she cared, she didn't say anything about it. 'Comings and goings at all hours. It's enough to drive you insane. I don't know what he does for a living but whatever it is, he needs to sort his bloody car out. Engine growls like a wounded lion and farts out smoke like a chimney. It's not what we're used to round this street, I'll tell you for nothing.'

'I'm going to check round the back,' Hines said, doing her

best to hide her laugh. The old woman at number 71 might not have noticed but Louise had.

'Did you hear his car Saturday night?' Louise asked.

'What day is it today?' Diedre asked. Louise told her it was Monday. 'Last I heard him knocking about was yesterday. Sunday. He's one of the God-botherers down at the wacky church.'

'Wacky church?'

'The church that isn't really a church. Behind the pub.'

'The Church of Divine Light? Do you mean that one?'

'I don't know what they're calling themselves these days. They've had many different names, been called many-a-different thing as well, 'specially by those they piss off, which is many.' She gave a chesty cough and clutched at her robe, making sure it didn't spill open again. Louise stood silently and watched as the woman spat a great big ball of phlegm out onto the garden path. She stubbed out the cigarette, reached into her pocket and pulled out a pack of Regal Blues. A second or two later she had another one lit and was pulling deeply on it. The smoke that drifted from her mouth and nose was smoky-grey and stank like an old sock.

'Damn things will kill me,' she said and laughed. 'Least I won't have to listen to his damn car any more. You going to do something about it?'

Hines was coming back down the side path. She shook her head. 'Back gates locked and I can't see in.'

'You won't get in that way,' Diedre said. 'He keeps it locked all the time. Keeps his curtains drawn all day as well.'

Louise turned to Hines. 'We're not going to get anywhere with this today.'

'I agree. Waste of time when we have lovely paperwork to get done.'

Louise turned back to Diedre, who was watching the two of them closely. 'If he comes back could you ask Mr McKensie to either call in to the station or give me a call. Here's the number.'

She handed over a scrap of paper with the phone number to the main desk. 'Ask for either Detectives Miller or Hines.'

Diedre looked at the note then at the two police officers. 'You're detectives? Well, I never.'

Hines smiled but said nothing.

'Thanks a lot, Mrs Aldwin. You enjoy the rest of your day.'

They walked back to the car under the gaze of Diedre. She inhaled another cigarette as she watched them.

Unseen by either the neighbour or the two police officers, the curtain in the upper window gave a twitch as though someone had pulled it aside for the briefest of moments before letting it fall back into place.

CHAPTER
TWENTY-EIGHT

Wendy Jackson hadn't stopped crying once since Sunday. The tears didn't fall as hot or as heavy as when she first discovered James Willikar in the graveyard of Holy Trinity Church, but they still lingered, snaking down her face, leaving their faint imprint on her skin and on her soul.

She was in her room, the door closed, the curtains drawn; a dark cocoon into which she had dived headlong, intent on keeping the world out and her pain enshrined. It was a dull ache, hiding just behind her eyes, pushing with each rhythmic beat of her heart, pulsing with each agonising memory of James.

His laugh still lingered in her mind, its high notes catching in her throat as though she was the one laughing, laughing along with his jokes and his pranks. With James. Instead of laughing, she was crying, crying with as much passion as he had laughed. That was how she would always remember James, her friend and so much more.

Wendy leaned back against the bed, her head pushed back as far as she could so that she stared at the blank canvas of her ceiling. It hurt; the wooden slat of the bed was pressing into her neck, just below the curve of her head. She liked it. She welcomed the fat heat of pain; it cut through the thin chill of her broken heart, slicing deep, opening slivered wounds as deep as the ones James had cut into his wrist.

In her hand she held the model James had painted for her, for their game. She turned it over and over again, staring at it but seeing only the love James had put into each brushstroke, each colour choice. The figure was that of an Elf ranger; Tomaris was her name. Wendy had created her, rolling the dice that James told her to, marking down the numbers on the paper he had given her. She didn't know what any of it meant but James did, and that was all that mattered. He had included her when so many others wouldn't. He had welcomed her and, over time, come to love her as much as she loved him.

A sob broke between her lips, stifled as best she could by pressing the palm of one hand tight against her mouth, pushing the cry back inside. In the other she continued to hold the model, the last thing she had that James had touched. She didn't want her parents to hear. They were downstairs talking to the woman from the police. Talking about her. Not with her; about her. Just like always. They didn't know. They didn't understand. She didn't want them coming back up here into the one place she felt safe, talking at her. Talking down to her. Pretending they understood. Pretending they could help. She didn't want that.

She wanted James.

She had been his first; he hers. No one knew, though she thought her mother suspected. It had been during the summer holidays when they got together, spent time together in Ossett park on the Green. In Holy Trinity park. In the graveyard. Talking, listening to music, making music of their own. Playing games. Eating crisps and drinking Panda cola. Ice pops in long plastic tubes, which they used as lightsabres, swinging them at each other until they fell to the ground in sticky patches of pop, rolling over and over, tumbling. Wrestling.

Kissing.

Touching.

And then...

A smile snuck onto her face, sad and happy at the same time. It tugged hard on her heart. Stabbed into her memories with hot tips of anguish. She could see him still, not as she had found him sprawled across the grave, cold as distant time with his blood all around him, but as she had known him. A beaming smile that melted away the frozen cage of her heart.

Wendy put the model down beside her and wiped at her eyes with the back of her arm. She felt the cold sting of her tears on her skin. She heard the murmur of voices from downstairs. Reaching beneath the bed, she brought out a notebook, its corners frayed and scrappy. A black rubber band kept the pages together and a pencil trapped inside. She snapped it open and took the pencil. Hidden in the stem was a nail she had stolen from her dad's toolbox. She pulled it free and tested the tip; still sharp.

She pressed it against her arm, teeth biting down on her lip as the pressure shifted from uncomfortable to painful.

Keep going.

She closed her eyes and pressed harder.

Harder... there.

The sting and pop as her flesh tore open drew a sigh from her. Just a small puncture dragged open by the nail tip. Nothing anyone would notice. *They hadn't noticed the others, had they?*

She pushed harder and winced as the sting became heat, almost molten along her nerves. She opened her eyes and looked as around the tip of the nail a pool of red began to form, her blood become ink. It gathered at the wound then slowly began to roll down the side of her arm.

Wendy smiled at the sensation. It rolled inside her mind, turned itself over and over again, making the room start to spin. Slowly she pulled the nail towards her, up her arm, creating a snaked line along her skin from which bloody tears rolled.

Not too far, not too much, she thought.

She paused and admired her work.

Another.

Five minutes later, a second line ran perpendicular to the first.

Another.

Slowly, Wendy placed the nail's tip against her skin a third time and began to press down.

CHAPTER
TWENTY-NINE

THURSDAY, 15TH

Tuesday and Wednesday had been a complete waste of time. Twice they had gone back to the McKensie home, and twice they had left disappointed. It was as though he had vanished into thin air; even Diedre Aldwin still hadn't seen him, although she was sure she had heard his car farting its way down the street in the early hours of Wednesday morning. By the time she had struggled to her bedroom window, Ryecroft Street was empty once again.

With no other choice, Louise asked a couple of uniforms to keep checking the address on their patrol. If he was there, they were to let him know they had his wallet and he could collect it from the station, pretty much the same message they had left with his neighbour. Until they talked with him, they couldn't prove he had done anything wrong; they couldn't place him with Helen Williams and had no just cause to pursue any formal investigation into Daniel McKensie. For all they knew, Helen had stolen his wallet in the pub. With little else to do, they just put it down to a simple case of returning lost property; not exactly high priority.

The only good news they had was that the inquest on James Willikar had been granted a speedy hearing. Doctor Robert Wilkinson would be conducting it, and interviews with the family, Danes and the SOCO team and even family liaison officer Shirley Hanson had been arranged to get a full and detailed understanding of the events that had led to James' tragic death. He had also requested an interview with Louise to discuss her concerns. The family had requested their son's body be released so they could hold a funeral as soon as possible, wanting to have it done before Christmas. Seeing no major issues before his investigation, Doctor Wilkinson had agreed, and plans were put into place.

It was just after nine in the morning and Louise was still at home, getting ready for the funeral of James Willikar, and seriously considering calling in sick. She hated funerals, had been to too many already, and she was only twenty-eight. It wasn't even as if the Willikar boy was someone she knew; DI Manby had requested that Hines go along to show support to the family, and that meant Louise was going as well. The investigation into the boy's death was all but closed and this would be just another step closer to putting it to bed. Hines had said something about the girl who had found him, something that scratched at the back of her mind and wouldn't go away. She wanted to talk to her again if possible, and Manby thought that the funeral was a good excuse, if not the best of locations.

Louise wasn't too sure. Funerals were funny places, the atmosphere thick with emotion, people on guard, keeping back their true feelings lest they be judged. That was how she saw them, anyway. That was how she felt about church and religion in general, ever since her life had changed back in '74. As she had stood in the same aisle that Wendy Jackson had collapsed in, staring at the coffins of her parents, the teenage Louise Miller, eyes blurred with tears, vowed never again to trust a god who could inflict such pain, and other than the occasions when she accompanied her aunt, she had barely set foot in another church since.

She pulled off the black cardigan she had been trying on and threw it onto the bed. Her cat gave it a cursory sniff then settled back to watch what she would try next. Louise smiled. *Her cat*. That sounded nice. That sounded like home.

'What do you think?' she said, pulling a dark maroon cardigan from the walk-in wardrobe. She dragged it over her arms and turned round to get the reaction from Tom.

He was washing his arse, one leg pushed up high like a ballet dancer.

She looked down at the outfit and sighed. 'My thoughts exactly,' she said as she began undressing for the third time.

When Hines arrived at the flat, Louise had finally settled on a black two-piece dress with dark green scarf. It was cold out; a shine of ice was steadily growing on her bedroom window, and she could see that snow was again a very distinct possibility by the sky's grey, cloudless colour. That gave her a small thrill. She loved snow, the more the merrier. She could remember the bad snowfall of '73 when it was thick and deep enough that she lost a wellington boot on Pildacre Hill, out on one of her parents' afternoon wanderings.

'73 was a year before they had died. She'd been thirteen and it was one of the last happy memories of her parents she had. Walking down the hill towards Chickenley Fields, a long swathe of farmland on which grew the tangiest gooseberries Louise had ever tasted. The farm, like so much of Louise's past, was no longer there, but the memory remained. She smiled as she remembered the sudden cold as she had plunged her bootless foot into the snow drift ahead. Her other foot was stuck, held fast in the thickly packed snow. She'd screamed in laughter for her father to help, but all he had done was collapse into laughter of his own. Her mother had been the one to pluck her from the snow, and together they had searched for her wellington.

Before she could fall too much into the past, Louise tore her mind back to the present; the abandoned warehouse that she had looked at with Hines. The melted black candles. The discarded beer and vodka bottles. The fag ends. The used johnnies.

Perhaps Hines was right. Perhaps James had been there. The johnnies would belong to whoever Helen Williams had taken there, most likely Daniel McKensie, due to the wallet, but James was a teenager – had been a teenager, she corrected herself – and what were teenagers, if not horny? The black candles, the firepit, the beer... a romantic getaway that only kids would appreciate, perhaps?

After more phone calls than she cared to remember on Tuesday and Wednesday, they had tracked the candles to the Green Dragon in Horbury, but the owner said there was no way of checking who had bought them. It was a fascinating shop packed to the rafters with books, comics and games, everything from Cluedo to Chess. They also sold Dungeons & Dragons and confirmed that James had been a customer, a very good one in fact.

Hines came in from the kitchen carrying two mugs of tea. She put one before Louise and sat down opposite her. Her face was pale, made more so by the black dress and jacket she was wearing.

'I hate funerals,' Hines said, blowing on her tea. 'And for kids? I am not looking forward to this at all.'

'Same here, but Manby wants us to go.'

Hines shook her head. 'I don't see why. I mean, what are we supposed to do? I am not happy about pestering a grieving girl on the day her boyfriend is being buried.'

'We're not pestering,' Louise said, not believing a word of it. She agreed in part with what Hines was saying. 'We're not pestering,' she said again, 'we're showing support to the family and friends at a really shit time for them.'

'But we're going to ask Wendy Jackson some questions, right? And that's not pestering how, exactly?'

This was another argument waiting to happen and one Louise knew she wasn't going to win, so she changed the subject. 'So... are you pregnant then, or what?'

For a moment Hines was stunned into silence by Louise's uncharacteristic bluntness. She blinked a couple of times and Louise drank some of her tea with a devious smile on her face.

'It's complicated,' Hines finally said.

'How exactly? You either are or you aren't. Did you take the test?'

Hines took in a deep breath but stayed silent. Louise could see this was bothering her, but she pressed on. 'Did you tell Joe?' Hines shook her head. 'Don't you think Joe has a right to know he might be a father?'

There was a long pause before Hines replied. 'It might not be his.'

Her voice was a child's confession, almost silent, not really wanting to be heard but needing to say something. Now it was Louise's turn to be stunned to silence. It lasted all of four seconds.

'What... the... fuck? Are you serious? Joe's not the father? Who is it?'

And then cold realisation hit her; there was only one person it could be. Hines saw the dawning understanding on Louise's face and tried to put a halt to it. This was a conversation she clearly did not want.

'Don't. Just don't!'

'Please tell me it's not Danes. You can't have been that stupid or careless. Can you?' Louise pressed her hand across her mouth. 'You have to be kidding?'

Hines stared at her but some of the anger in her eyes faded. Louise drank more tea, grimacing at the taste, but still draining the cup. At her side Tom rubbed against her leg, depositing strands of fur on her dress. His purr was a loud engine roll that hummed against her, the vibration a pleasant distraction from the conversation Hines did not want to be having right now.

'It's complicated,' Hines said again, standing up. 'And we need to go.'

Neither of them said anything more about it as they drove to Holy Trinity Church. Instead, Louise fiddled with the radio while Hines drove. She found Queen on Radio One: 'Crazy Little Thing Called Love'.

'Not a fucking word,' Hines said, her eyes intent on the road. A little of the anger still bled through her jokey manner, but not as much as Louise had feared.

Louise smiled, thankful that they had somehow managed to dodge a breaking of their friendship, but said nothing.

CHAPTER
THIRTY

When they arrived, they could see that there was quite a crowd gathered outside the church. Several cars were parked either side of Church Street, not enough to cause a blockage but enough that Hines snail-crawled between them, careful not to scratch either the parked cars or the unmarked police car. It was only the second unmarked vehicle the Prospect Road CID branch had been given, bought from Sanderson's on Ventnor Way, and there was no way it was getting damaged under her care.

'Bit of a turn-out,' Louise said, looking at the crowd. Something felt off and she could see that Hines felt the same. James Willikar might have been popular, but he was just a teenager, and from what they did know about the family, it was quite small. Perhaps one or two aunts and uncles, nothing overly massive.

Nothing that would suggest a gathering such as this.

'I don't like the look of this,' Hines said as she pulled the car into the side of the pavement. She'd had to park a little up the road away from the church itself, but it gave them time to scrutinise the crowd as they walked back down the street.

There was a throng of about ten people clustered together just inside the entrance to the churchyard. They huddled close, almost shoulder to shoulder. Each wore their Sunday best; a couple of the women were wearing colourful hats. Each of them also held in their hands a book, dark blue in colour with gold letters. Louise couldn't make out what they said, not at this distance, but she had a good guess. Her heart sank at what she thought this might be and was really hoping she was wrong.

When she saw Catherine Hallum standing in the centre of the throng, a smug expression on her painted face, a deep sick feeling came over her.

As the two women approached the church, Catherine saw them and smiled. She turned to one of the men nearby and gave a nod. From within a bag kept to the side, he took out a stack of papers and what appeared to be a folded blue sheet. This was stretched out in front of the group, the sides taken up by three other people so they could pull it tight. Written in bright, bold letters of gold in the same font as the bibles they clutched to their chests were the words: THE DOORS OF THE LORD REMAIN SHUT TO THOSE WHO COMMIT THE SIN OF SUICIDE.

'Oh, shit.'

Another banner was unfurled, similar to the first. A group of four moved to the other side of the entrance and held it tight so that it could be read. FOR THE SINS OF THE CHILD SHALL THE PARENTS' FAILINGS BE JUDGED.

'Do you think the Willikars have seen this?' Hines asked

Louise shook her head. There was no funeral car outside the church, no hearse either. They hadn't arrived yet.

Louise walked directly to Catherine, who gave her a wry smile.

'Good morning, Louise,' she said. 'I'm surprised to see you here.'

'Not as surprised as I am to see you,' Louise replied. 'And it's Detective Constable Miller, Mrs Hallum.' Her tone was sharp and as cold as the wind that had risen.

Catherine's gaze turned stony, her smile locked in place. 'Is that how it's going to be?' she asked. She looked to the group beside her. 'Did you hear that, brothers and sisters? Did you hear the venom in her voice?'

There was a rumble of acknowledgement from the crowd. Heads nodded. Louise ignored them all, keeping her attention solely focused on Catherine.

'What do you think you're going to achieve, doing this?' she asked. Subtlety was not a trait associated with the woman, and this, this callous stunt, was far from divine.

It was shit, pure and simple.

'Don't you care what this will do to the family, for Christ's sake?' Louise continued. She could see Hines had moved towards the church. At the entrance stood Reverend Dawson, a worried expression paining his face. His hands wrung at his cassock, twisting the fabric round and round as he bit at his bottom lip. She turned back to Catherine, who gave her a smug grin in response.

'Oh, but I care. I care a lot. I care for those who don't commit the sin of blasphemy against our great Lord by taking their lives. Only He has the divine right to call us back into His grace. I care for those who don't take His Name in vain. I care—'

'You care about yourself and fuck everyone else.'

Catherine's face fell, white as the snow about them. Her hand rushed to her mouth and a strangled gasp of shock erupted from those gathered beside her.

'No. I'm not having it,' Louise continued. 'Mrs Hallum, I am asking you... No. I'm telling you. Pack this up. All of it. I want you out of here. Now.'

She reached for the banner and gave it a tug, hard enough that it was ripped from the hands of the nearest member of the so-called church. They started to speak but Louise glared at them, her anger an oppressive presence that crushed their spirit, forcing them into silence.

'You can't do that,' Catherine said, her voice as haughty as her stance. She straightened her shoulders, thrusting them back, and lifting her head so her voice would carry across the church-yard. 'Do you see this, Reverend?'

Reverend Dawson didn't reply. Hines stood beside him, her hand laid reassuringly on his arm. He looked beyond shocked. He looked sick.

'Do you see the fist raised against the Lord?' Catherine continued, playing up to the crowd. 'This is the first, desperate act of a coward, though it shall not be the last!'

Louise turned to the small crowd. 'All of you. Out. Out of here right now. If you haven't left the premises in the next two minutes, I will be arresting each and every one of you on grounds of trespass, harassment and six other violations of public misconduct that I can think of just off the top of my head. Imagine what I could do with ten minutes of thought.'

There wasn't any real legal cause for her to arrest these people, but she didn't think they knew that. Maybe she could get them for not having a permit for an organised protest, but she doubted it. No, Louise was relying on their arrogance and their ignorance of the law in order to prevent something even worse happening.

The Willikars would be here soon, and they didn't need to see this. Who cared if she was bending the law a little?

'Come on,' she snapped, grabbing the banner from the other side and balling it up with the first. 'Get a move on. Out and away or you're spending the rest of the day in Prospect Road's cells before going on to Wakey for a lengthier stay.'

'There will be consequences for this,' Catherine hissed. Her face had gone tight, her lips disappearing into a line so thin it almost looked like she had no mouth at all. Her eyes glistened and Louise could see tears of anger beading at the sides. It gave her a not-unwelcome tingle of pleasure that she quickly pushed back down.

'You're damn right there will be,' Louise said quietly. She pushed the balled-up banners hard into Catherine's chest until the woman grabbed at them, taking them from her. As she did so, Louise pulled her forward, nearly jerking Catherine off her feet, until their faces were inches apart.

Her voice fell to a bitter whisper, colder than the wind and twice as sharp. 'Now take this shit and fuck off.'

Without another word, Louise turned her back on the woman and walked away.

'Has she gone?' Louise asked as she reached the top of the steps of the church entrance. Hines nodded, smiling. 'And the rest of them?' Another nod. Louise let out a breath she hadn't realised she'd been holding in. A wave of tension rolled off her. 'Good. You okay, Rev? You're looking a bit peaky.'

'I can't believe what I just saw,' he said, shaking his head.

'Yeah. Sorry about that language, but you know. Needs must.'

Some of the colour returned to his face as a smile broke out. 'No. Not that. Not you, although I think you could have perhaps chosen your words a little more carefully. No. I meant those people. What they were here to do. Ghastly.'

'Some very strong opinions, for sure,' Hines said. 'Arseholes.'

The vicar and Louise turned as one to stare at Hines. To her credit she didn't blush, just looked back at them. 'What... I'm right though, aren't I? Look, some folks you can talk to, some you can even reason with, but those... those were the arseholes.'

'But Catherine Hallum... She's a member of this church as well as her own.'

'Her own?' Hines asked.

'Didn't you see their sign?' Louise asked. When Hines shook her head Louise shrugged. 'Our Mrs Hallum – who's probably writing a letter of complaint to DI Manby at this very minute – runs the Church of Divine Light, a member of the Puritanical Society.'

'What, are they like Methodists?'

It was Reverend Dawson who laughed. 'Not at all. They're not a real church, not a recognised religion in any shape or form. More a social club that meet every week. Organised and run by Mrs Hallum; named by as well.'

'They have their meeting hall beside the Carps,' Louise said. 'Surely you've seen it. It's right against the car park.'

'That building? It's nothing more than a long hut. I honestly thought it was part of the Carps, used to store old benches and tables or other shit.'

'It's certainly got some shit in it,' Louise said.

'Ladies, please. If we could hold back some of the language. God's children come in many shapes and forms, and we should learn to tolerate all.' He gave Hines a mischievous wink. 'Even the arseholes.'

For a moment no one said anything, and then all three of them broke into laughter, the vicar laughing so hard he began to hiccup. This went on for a few moments, which only made them all laugh harder. Eventually he had it back under control.

'I do apologise,' he said, wiping at his face, 'but I just couldn't resist. No one heard, did they?'

Hines shrugged. 'I don't think so, and no apologies needed, Rev. These lot probably come in socks and throw them at the wall to see if it sticks. Sorry,' she added, seeing the new look of horror on the vicar's face. 'So this Church of Divine Light is just a glorified knitting circle?'

'A knitting circle that likes to protest anything their great leader thinks unsavoury. Did you know they initially protested when we started running the Sunday club here in our basement for those kids who were a little, unruly, shall we say?'

'Kids like James?' Louise asked.

The vicar nodded.

'Such a shame,' he said. 'Such a sad, sad loss.'

Before anyone could reply, the sound of approaching vehicles grew louder. A moment later and the first of the funeral procession turned into the churchyard. The black Ford drew up to the steps and came to a stop. Reverend Dawson straightened, his face tightening and his demeanour totally changing.

'And so it begins,' Reverend Dawson said, his voice low.

He stepped forward to open the car door.

. . .

With the protesters thankfully moved on without further incident, the funeral proceeded. For the parents of James Willikar, the day was a short crawl through a long nightmare, an endless slog through the treacle of their new pained existence that seemed without end. Numb to all around them, they went through the motions, sleep-walking through their grief. Their smiles were painted on the hollow shell of their faces, their hand-shakes little more than the cold touch of a mannequin's grasp.

With their son's coffin arranged at the front of the nave, Mrs Willikar sat on the edge of the pew, head down throughout, a black veil drawn down over her face. Her husband slowly walked back, his strides short and stilted as though he was struggling to remember how to walk. Once at the pew, he placed his hand on the back and waited for his wife to move up. When she didn't immediately respond, he leaned forward to whisper in her ear.

His hand slipped, sliding along the back of the pew, and he fell to the ground, his legs giving way beneath him. A loud gasp rolled around the church, its echo like that of an approaching thundercloud, here yet distant all at the same time.

He got to his feet, hand raised to the onlookers, a gesture that was meant to be reassuring but was all the more heart-breaking as tears rolled down his face.

Hines looked to Louise, but she had her eyes set firmly ahead, jaw clenched. She sat rigid in the pew, hands clenched in her lap as tight as her jaw. Hines knew how she felt.

She fucking hated funerals.

CHAPTER
THIRTY-ONE

It was nearly Christmas, 1974.

Same cold chill air that bit into her skin, turning the tears on her face into ice slivers that cut as deep as her grief. Deeper. Fourteen years old and orphaned. Fourteen years old and alone. Sitting alone on the cold wooden seat, the thin cushion little more than a blue divider to the hard uncomfortable pain that sitting on it for the last thirty minutes had provided.

Fourteen years old and wondering what would happen next. Not here. Not now. The two coffins placed side by side in the centre of the nave of the church, just before the steps up onto the area where the choir now sat, singing soft hymns while people walked up to say their last goodbyes.

Goodbye. A word she would never be able to say to her parents. They had been dead before the car had come crashing to a stop. Necks broken, flesh torn, the harsh rubber of the other car shredding into her father's face even as she screamed.

And now she sat alone in the church as strangers walked up to her

*parents' coffins and said words she would never hear again, never say
again to the two people she had loved most in the world.*
*From somewhere came a keening wail. It grew slowly, rising out of the
silence of the church like a wraith, getting louder, getting shriller.*

People turned to stare. At her.

At Louise.

*Only then did she realise that it was her crying out, roaring out her
pain and her grief and her anger at being left alone. The pit of her
sorrow was swallowing her, sucking her in with each new tear of her
throat as her voice gave way beneath the onslaught of heartache.*

*And then arms were sweeping her up, crushing her to a warm chest and
rocking her back and forth. Back and forth.*

'It's going to be okay, Louise... it's going to be okay. Louise...'

She recognised the voice.

'Louise... Louise...

'It's okay, Louise. Louise...'

CHAPTER
THIRTY-TWO

'Louise. It's okay.'

Louise woke with a start.

She was on her sofa in her flat, no longer in the cold of the church. No longer at her parents' funeral all those years ago.

Karla Hayes was sitting beside her, holding her and stroking her hair as Tom sat on the sofa arm, head cocked to the side as he looked down on Louise.

She sat up. The clock on the windowsill ticked loudly, the green dials glowing in the half light. Nine-thirty. *Just where had the day gone?*

The room was dark, lit only by the small lamp in the corner and the puttering flicker of a candle close to death. Wine glasses near empty had been placed on the side table, along with small plates that had once held cheese and biscuits: the perfect end to a shitty day.

Gradually the fog of the (*nightmare*) dream began to part. Louise brushed at her face and was surprised to find the tracks of tears drying on her cheek. 'How long was I asleep?'

Karla smiled and pointed to the wine bottle. 'Long enough for me to finish that, and this,' she added, lifting the book that had been in her lap. It was a Stephen King, taken from Louise's collection. Well-read, as evidenced by the battered slip of a cover and the loose flap of its spine. To Louise, a book was meant to be read, and if that meant cracking its spine to make it easier to rest on her lap while she fussed Tom, then so be it.

'I'm so sorry,' Louise began, but Karla brushed her concern aside by running her fingers through Louise's hair. It had come loose while she was asleep, falling down across her shoulder, partially obscuring her face. Karla smiled.

'It's not a problem.' To emphasise the point, Karla placed a kiss on Louise's forehead, one finger lightly tracing down her cheek.

'But it is,' Louise said, sitting up. She stretched her back, the crack of her spine as loud as the books had been. 'We barely get to see each other as it is, and when we do, the last thing you want is me falling asleep on you.'

Karla smiled mischievously. 'You know I wouldn't mind that, but I appreciate you saying that, love,' she added, seeing Louise about to argue her point. 'You've had a long day, and a tough one by the sound of it. And what's a ten-minute cat-nap between friends?'

Louise reached for her wine glass. There was a little left, not much. Enough.

'Is that what we are?' she asked. 'Friends?'

Now it was Karla's turn to sit up. She scooted to the side of the sofa, away from Louise, to get her own glass. Louise stared intently at her when she turned round again.

'That's not fair,' Karla said. 'You know it's complicated. I like being here. I like being with you. Even you, fluffer-nutter.'

She reached across Louise and gave Tom a scrunch behind his ear. His eyes closed and his purrs began to rev. Pretty soon his pigeon-coo-purr began, and Louise couldn't help but laugh.

'Traitor,' she said but she joined in and gave his back a rub. This lasted all of three minutes, time enough for Tom to realise there was still food in the kitchen that required his attention. He jumped down from the sofa and sauntered off without a backward glance. They could hear his claws skittering on the wooden floor of the corridor, making both women smile.

A silence settled between them, becoming uncomfortable as neither one ventured to say anything that might ignite the kindling of their conversation. Louise tipped her head back and tried to drain the very last drop of wine from her glass. Karla handed her the bottle, but nothing came out.

'I think I saw another one in the kitchen,' Karla said, standing up. Louise caught her arm and shook her head.

'That's all right. I've an early start anyway tomorrow. Probably best not to talk to a bunch of schoolkids nursing a hangover.'

Karla sat back down. 'You're really going to the school?'

'Yes. It was your idea.'

Karla raised her eyebrows. 'I'm shocked you took it. Pleased, though – I think it will do a world of good. Which school?'

'Both.' She let out a sigh. She was dreading it. Really dreading it. 'Manby agreed we need to talk to the kids about suicide. About talking to someone if they're feeling depressed rather than slitting open their wrists.'

'Jesus,' Karla whispered.

'I know. I am not looking forward to it, at all.'

'I'm not surprised. Talking to kids is tough enough at the best of times, but talking to them about the death of one of their friends, plus suicide, plus the need to open up to others... all that, all at once—'

'In twenty minutes. Tops.'

'—Jesus. That's going to hurt. Have you thought what you're going to say?'

'There's so much, I honestly don't know where to begin.' Louise sat back into the sofa, already exhausted at what was to come in the morning. Karla did the same, nestling into the crook of the sofa arm and the back so that she could take Louise's hand in hers. Louise smiled. Neither said anything; they just sat there, holding hands.

. . .

'I once thought about suicide.'

Karla's voice broke the silence that had fallen around them, shattering the comfortable cocoon into which Louise had settled herself. If she didn't think about it, maybe it wouldn't happen. And if her granny had wheels, she'd be a bike.

Louise turned to her. She could feel Karla's hand get warm in hers, see the flush of blood in her cheeks. 'Really? When? I'm sorry, it's none of my business, but... wow. Really?'

Karla nodded so gently it was hardly there. But Louise noticed. She also noticed the way her eyes had started to glisten with tears. She gave her hand a squeeze. 'You don't have to talk about it,' she said.

'But that's the thing... I do.'

Something passed across her face, a decision made. Karla let go of Louise's hand and stood up. She cleared her throat. 'And so do those kids. Not all of them, hell, hardly any of them, if I remember my time at school. There's only going to be a small crowd who are directly affected by the kid's suicide, but they are going to need to talk. They are going to want to talk, more importantly. That's one thing I still remember to today; the powerful urge to talk to someone about how I was feeling.'

'But you couldn't.'

Karla shook her head.

'What was the problem... the initial problem that made you consider suicide?'

Karla gave her a look. Long. Hard. Eyes raised. *What do you think?*

Louise blushed. 'Oh. Of course. Wow, it was really that bad?'

'I was raised by parents who followed the bible *very* closely. I mean, close. Dedicated Christians is putting it mildly. Church every Sunday, no drinking, no swearing. Marriage between a man and woman only; everything else is a sin to be condemned. Not to the same level as Catherine Hallum and her Divine Light nutters, though. Let me make that clear. They were strict... not crazy.'

Louise couldn't help but laugh. 'Seriously. What's wrong with those people? Protesting at a funeral of all places.'

'If anyone deserves to burn in a non-existent hell, it's them.'

'Not a believer then?'

'I had it purged from me, thankfully,' Karla said. She lifted the empty bottle. 'See?'

Louise laughed again then stopped. A sudden thought hit hard. *Of course!*

'You should do it,' she said.

'Another bottle?'

'No, silly. Tomorrow. Talk to the kids.'

'Wait a minute—' Karla began, but Louise wasn't hearing her.

'This is directly in your area of expertise. Psychological stuff. You know what to say, what they need to hear. And you have the experience as well. Beth and I will be there too, of course; we could do with speaking with Wendy again. This is perfect. I'll talk to Bill and have it changed to Monday so you have time to prepare. Perfect,' she said again with a huge smile on her face, the relief evident in her voice.

'For you maybe.'

'Come on. You'll be a great help. You know all the right things to say. I'll fuck it up, you can guarantee that. Come on. Please? Pretty please?'

Karla pursed her lips and glared at Louise. Her eyes slowly softened, and she reached behind the sofa. A moment later she straightened up, a fresh bottle of wine in her hand and a wicked smile on her face.

'Well in that case, if you're not going to school tomorrow...'

Her voice trailed away as she saw Louise's face.

She put the bottle down.

'I'm not staying again, am I?'

'I'm sorry,' Louise said. She sat up and pushed into the sofa's arm, tucking her legs beneath her as much as she could. It was a protective measure, she knew this, trying to get as much between her and the perceived threat, and she knew Karla knew. She could see it in her lover's face, all the same disappointment and frustration that she felt, but more. Anger. Anger lay beneath the surface, checked for now but always ready to be unleashed at a moment's gasp.

'I'm sorry,' Louise said again, reaching towards Karla, hoping to draw her near to lessen the disappointment. They had been dating seriously now for over six months, but Karla had yet to stay the night.

Was it serious, though? No one other than Hines knew they were seeing each other, although Aunt Fiona had a strong suspicion that they were more than friends. And what did 'serious' mean anyway? They certainly weren't exclusive; neither of them had prompted that conversation, and in truth, Louise didn't know how she would respond if asked. Was this what she wanted, was Karla who she wanted to be with? Permanently?

'I won't ask what you just thought,' Karla said, standing up. 'I can tell it wasn't pleasant.'

Louise struggled to her feet, the aged sofa refusing to give her up from its saggy clutches. The cushion was an inverted trap, comfy, but a trap nonetheless. 'Don't be like that,' she said as she finally got up.

'Like what?'

Karla's back was to her, the psychologist pulling on her jacket and stabbing her arms into the sleeves. She threw her hair over and down the back of the jacket.

'It's late, and like you said, it's been a long, rough day. Best you get a recharging sleep in.' She picked up her handbag and walked out of the room. Her shoes were at the bottom of the steep stairs; safer to keep them there than struggle up the stone staircase and risk breaking an ankle, or a neck.

Tom was also at the bottom of the stairs, staring back up as Karla made her way down.

'You wanting to get out too?'

His answer was a throaty yowl.

At the top of the stairs, Louise looked down, totally thrown by how the night had gone. 'Karla... love. Don't leave it like this. Let's talk.'

Karla paused for a second and then pulled the door open. Tom shot out into the night. A moment later, and without another word, Karla was gone as well. The door shut with a solid thump that echoed throughout the flat.

Louise let out the breath she had been holding.

'Fuck!'

CHAPTER
THIRTY-THREE

The pain was like nothing Wendy had ever felt before. Not the dull throb that ran along her arm, hidden beneath the long-sleeved shirt she wore pulled down as far as she could, but the aching pain of loss that threatened to consume her.

Her shirt was black, an early gift from James for Christmas. Her favourite band, AC/DC, the design on the front taken from their *Blow Up Your Video* album, tour dates on the back. It had been the best concert ever. Their dads had taken them, driving to the Birmingham National Exhibition Centre in the Willikars' Saab. How James had managed to get her this without her seeing, he had never said, keeping it a secret all those months, but it had been the best present ever.

And now he was gone, never to come back, and she was alone once again.

The ache from where he should be filled every part of her. Every heartbeat pounded the fact he was gone, to the point she could almost hear the words with each beat. *He's gone... he's gone... he's gone.*

Her throat was raw from the crying, but she still cried.

Her head hurt from the pressure her thoughts applied, but she still thought them.

Still toyed with the ideas that rolled over her in black waves, leaving behind nothing but her raw self.

A knock sounded at her door.

'Wendy?'

Her mother's voice. She could hear the concern in her voice, but Wendy knew it was fake. Not directed at her, not sent with love but embarrassment. The concern that was there was directed at herself, at a mother more concerned with how she was perceived than her daughter's pain. She had known that the moment she had come home, her mother saying over and over again that she hoped no one had known how close the two had actually been. That she and James had...

'We love each other,' Wendy said to the room.

Loved.

The single word cut deeper than any blade or pencil ever could.

Another knock at the door. Harder this time. More insistent.

'Wendy, love. Are you coming down for tea? I've made your favourite.'

Spaghetti bolognaise.

"I've made your favourite," was a bit of a stretch, even for her mum. What she meant was she'd boiled the bags in a pan for the fifteen minutes the back of the box said, snipped the corners and poured the slop onto the plate. The garlic bread slices were just Co-op extra thick white with garlic mayo spread across in a sickly wave.

You like it.

That was James. In her head once more. Always in her head.

Only in her head forever now.

Wendy pulled her sleeve up. Red tracks ran along her skin, three long cuts that had healed into raised welts. How could he have done this? The pain was too great, the blood too much, always turning her stomach the moment she saw it begin to flow. The pressure always released, though, as soon as the first cut was made; the valve turned, and all the dark shadows were released into the light.

For her that was enough. For her. Not James. James had needed more, had hurt more; that was obvious now, but now was too late.

Now didn't matter any more.

They had shared the pain together but now she was alone with it.

She reached over to her cassette player. Flipped the tape round and pressed play. Turned the sound up. Way up.

The heavy staccato opening to 'Heatseeker' filled the room. The memories of that concert, holding James' hand, dancing with James, and sneaking quick kisses when their dads weren't watching, flooded back.

There had to be a way to release this pain, to get it out of her before it ate her up completely. There had to be something she could do.

Perhaps James had been right. Perhaps James had known.

Wendy put her head back, turned the music up and let the darkness fold in around her once again.

Downstairs in the kitchen Wendy's mum sat at the table and listened to the heavy thump of the music coming from her daughter's bedroom. She hoped it wouldn't wake Karly.

A darker hope that it wouldn't anger her husband into taking action pushed any other thoughts aside.

CHAPTER
THIRTY-FOUR

FRIDAY, 16TH

The day began just like any ordinary Friday. With Tom fed and watered, Louise was out of the door and at the police station by seven-thirty. Following the morning brief, Louise and Hines were called into DI Manby's office.

He slowly shut the door behind them, before directing them into two new chairs in front of his desk. They were thick, white and gleaming.

'Been to Woolworths, I see,' Louise said, taking one of the two seats. 'I've always fancied something like this, but never had the patio to put it on.'

'Sturdier than it looks,' Hines added, giving her chair a good rocking. Louise smiled. Manby didn't.

'I think putting you up for Detective did something to that ego of yours,' he said to Hines.

'Invigorated it, you mean?'

Manby didn't respond. Instead, he pulled out a pack of cigarettes, tapped one into his hand and lit it, settling back into his own seat so he could stare at the two officers.

'Tell me about Catherine Hallum,' he said, after the silence had grown stifling. Smoke hung between them, drifting slowly across the desk.

'What's there to tell?' Louise said. She had known this was coming, she just hadn't expected it to be so fast. 'She was holding an unlicensed protest on church grounds, which are considered private property. I asked her to move on. She did. End of.'

Manby blew out another haze of smoke, which drifted to the ceiling to hang with the rest. 'That's not exactly how Mrs Hallum puts it.'

'And?' Louise's tone gave no doubt that she didn't care one jot what Catherine Hallum thought.

'And she's making quite a stink about it. I had the Chief Superintendent on the phone last night when I was trying to have a quiet evening with the missus. You know how that went down?'

Louise could guess. That Bill and his wife were still having issues was no secret throughout the station. It wasn't gossip; they didn't do that here. No hidden whispers when they thought the boss wasn't looking, no huddled chats around pints or fags down the pub. They just came out and said what they needed to say. They'd said one or two things about Louise; she'd said one or two things back.

'Sorry about that – Bill,' Hines said, letting his first name roll uncomfortably off her tongue, 'but come on. I mean... it was a funeral. A kid's one at that. Hallum and her cronies even had banners, calling the Willikar boy a sinner. Calling his parents even worse. And legally, they didn't have any right to be there.'

'Forget legally,' Louise cut in. 'What about morally? Who the hell does she think she is? It's not even a proper church she runs, is it? Does she collect dues like a club or pass round a collection plate? Maybe the tax folk might want to give her a nosey. Catherine Hallum runs the Church of Divine Light like her own personal religion, from what I gather.' Louise looked thoughtful. 'Maybe someone should start to take a closer look at what goes on there.'

Her face had reddened, not through embarrassment or shame at being drawn across the coals by her boss, but by the sheer audacity of the situation. 'Speaks out on many a subject that she finds "taints the soul". What a load of shit. Maybe I will take a lookey-look.'

Hines was nodding along. 'Then count me in,' she said before turning to point a finger at Manby. 'Do you remember the cricket match a couple of years ago? Down on the Green when it still had the cricket ground marked out?' Hines turned now to Louise. 'Stupid bitch organised an event called Rally Against Gay Extremes.'

It took barely a second for Louise to figure that out. 'R.A.G.E.? Really?'

'Just goes to show you where her mind's at, doesn't it? They all had banners, just like the ones they had at the church yesterday. Deplorable statements, intimidating tactics. Just disgusting, and all because the visiting cricket team had three openly gay players.'

'What did you do?' Louise asked Manby.

Manby sat back in his chair, reaching forward to stub out the cigarette. 'We had a chat with her, got her to put the banners down and finally moved her little group on.'

'So, exactly what I did?'

He brushed the remaining smoke aside and opened a drawer. From within he pulled out a pack of Polo mints, threw a couple in his mouth and dropped the packet on the desk. Hines grabbed the pack and stole a couple.

'Pretty much.' His voice had dropped.

'And how is it any different?' Hines asked.

'Well for a start, Hallum didn't get in touch with the fucking Chief Superintendent to complain. Look, I don't agree at all with the woman or her beliefs. I also don't agree with the Chief that there is cause for an investigation. But let's just not do one and say we did, all right? I'll give it a day, then call him and say I found no evidence of you overstepping the mark. Good enough?'

'I honestly don't care,' Louise said. She turned to Hines. 'What about you?'

Hines gave a half-hearted shrug. 'Hallum who?'

'Right,' said Manby. 'That's all settled then. Other than that, how did the funeral go? Anything new from the girl?'

'Wendy?' said Louise. 'She was there with her family, but we couldn't talk to her. She was obviously distraught. In fact, there's not a strong enough word to describe what she's going through right now, but it was obvious she was in pain. Every time her father or mother hugged her she winced and pulled away. I felt it best not to try and talk to her then.'

'Maybe when you go to the school? In fact,' he said looking up at the clock above the door to his office, 'shouldn't you be heading there now?'

'I've moved it to Monday,' Louise said, ploughing on when she saw Manby's face darken. 'It's the last day of school before the holiday. We talked earlier about Karla Hayes coming with us both as she has a unique perspective she can bring to this, and I'd feel a lot more comfortable having her expertise on hand to answer the inevitable questions that will come up. Monday works best for everyone, even the schools. It's a bit short notice, but they understand the urgency of the situation.'

Manby stubbed his cigarette out. 'Hayes... She was the psychologist from the Jacobs case?' Louise nodded. 'Makes sense,' he said, tapping another out of its pack. 'I guess, but she's doing it on her own time and cost. We can't afford to pay for outside support right now.'

'She's happy to do it and didn't once mention any sort of fee. She agreed last night.'

'You spoke with her last night? When?'

She saw the sparkle hit his eyes.

'When doesn't matter. So... is that a yes?'

He turned to look at Hines, who stared back, stony faced.

'Fine. Keep your secrets. And yes, she can go with you.' He went silent. Louise could see the cogs whirring but kept quiet...

best to let him get to the same conclusion she had last night on his own.

'You know,' he said, taking another Polo from its wrapper. 'It's probably a good thing to have a psychologist on the team. Maybe we should try and find a little money after all...'

CHAPTER
THIRTY-FIVE

Back at their desks, Louise and Hines planned out their day over a cup of tea. Louise had made it; the ones Hines made were the worst. Louise couldn't work out how Hines managed to make a cuppa taste like wet socks and cold sweat; it was a mystery she knew she would never solve, no matter how good a detective she was. It was easier to just make them herself rather than suffer through that slop.

She was just giving the brew a final stir when Sergeant David Harolds came over with a middle-aged woman at his side. His face was pale, the eyes sunken so that they looked like the coal pits of a snowman. It had started a few months ago, the lethargy. He had always been seen as being lazy, putting a comfortable seat in front of a hard investigation, but now that the diagnosis had come in, pancreatic cancer, it answered a lot of the perceptions about the man. He never spoke about it, would never speak about it when asked. Rumour was he was thinking of retiring soon.

The woman coughed delicately into a handkerchief, which she stashed away as fast as she could. She wore a long tan coat, tied at the waist. Her white skirt poked out beneath the coat's hem; its edging was laced with some decorative pattern Louise couldn't quite make out, but looked floral in nature. Floral; that was the best way to describe the woman who smiled softly at her as Harolds made the introductions.

'Mrs Hambly here says she thinks she's bought some hot gear from the indoor market. Thinks it might have been nicked from the school.' Without waiting for a response, Harolds walked away. Louise watched him for a few seconds, watched as he moved back to his desk, head down against the world, his right-hand clenching and unclenching. She didn't think he knew he was doing it.

Louise turned back to the woman and held her hand out.

'Hello, Mrs Hambly. I'm Detective Miller. Louise. I've just made a cup... Would you like one?'

'Please. Two sugars if you don't mind.'

'The perfect cup,' Louise said and handed her the mug she'd made for herself. 'Let me just drum up another mug and we'll go have a little chat. Please... take a seat over there next to Beth. I'll be over in a minute.'

'Thank you, and it's Miss Hambly. I'm not married. Very much single,' she added with a smile. 'Please call me Jeanette.'

Hines pulled another chair over and sat to the right of Louise. Jeanette Hambly sat in front of the desk, the mug of tea held between her hands. She had shrugged the long coat off, hanging it over her lap. Her white dress was buttoned down the front and was indeed as floral as Louise had suspected. Red flower heads were dotted in an intricate spiral pattern down the right side, twisting along the hem to disappear round the back.

Her hair was blonde and tied up behind her with white floral ribbon that matched the dress.

'What was it that you wanted to tell us, Miss Hambly? Sergeant Harolds said something about stolen property?' Hines asked.

'Jeanette, please,' she said with a smile directed towards

Louise. Hines noticed and gave Louise a nudge with her foot under the desk. Louise ignored her as Jeanette continued. She leaned forward to put the mug of tea down on the desk.

'I went to the market this morning looking to get my nephew something for Christmas. Like always, I left it to the last minute.'

'I do that,' Hines said. 'So much easier... less stressing about it when you have an immediate deadline.'

To Louise, who planned everything down to the minutest detail, doing last minute shopping was an anxiety attack waiting to happen. She'd already got most of her Christmas presents bought and wrapped, and there was still over a week to go. The only gift she hadn't bought yet, not even thought about yet, was what she was getting Karla.

'He's a very outdoor focused lad,' Jeanette was saying. 'Loves playing outside all the time, so I figured I'd get him something he could use outside.'

'Like a football or something?'

'I thought a bike would be good.'

Hines leaned back, obviously impressed. 'A bike? Wow... I wish my aunt liked me that much to get me a bike. Best thing she ever gave me was food poisoning from one of her fairy cakes. She can't bake for shit.'

Jeanette laughed. Louise didn't.

'Sorry,' Hines mumbled into her tea. Louise turned back to Jeanette.

'A bike is a pretty expensive gift.'

'I wasn't looking to spend a fortune. In fact, I don't have a fortune to spend. I work at the library, and while the job is fantastic, the pay isn't. I've seen you there once or twice. Stephen King fan, if I remember correctly?'

Louise could feel the heat rise in her cheeks, and she knew Hines had seen it too because her friend and colleague had given her foot another cheeky kick under the table.

At least she hoped that had been Hines.

'Anyway,' Jeanette continued, 'the indoor market has a few

second-hand stalls, so I thought I'd try my luck, and I was lucky. I found a bike for twenty pounds. It looked brand new, and those tend to be about fifty or even sixty pounds, so I snapped it up. I was going to give it to Jake tomorrow, Jake's my nephew, but then I remembered in the *Herald* that there'd been a break-in at the school and that a bike was missing.'

'It isn't missing... it was stolen,' Hines said.

It was Jeanette's turn to redden.

'That's why I came here straight away.'

'Is the bike outside?'

Jeanette nodded.

Louise got up. 'Okay. Let's take a look.'

It was the same bike that had been stolen from Deborah Jones at Dimple Well School. She had come into the station during the week with a photo and it matched perfectly. There was even the chain that had been taken, wrapped around the neck of the bike. Hines made sure by flipping the dials on the lock to the combination Deborah had supplied – it clicked open; definitely hers.

Jeanette Hambly was given a receipt for the bike with their apologies as it was now officially stolen property and evidence. Hines booked it in while Louise asked a few final questions. Jeanette answered them all and offered to take them to the stall where she had bought it. She was going to get a refund, and having two police officers with her would certainly be a help.

Louise agreed, and when Hines came back out, the three of them headed over to the town centre.

Fridays were market days, and it was naturally busy in the marketplace. A wide variety of stalls had been constructed Thursday night by the council workers, dragged out of storage beneath the Town Hall and erected in pretty short fashion. Come Friday morning, everything was in place for the traders to get to their stall and finish adorning them with their banners, goods and, in one or two cases, even chairs for people to sit on as they haggled over price or just had a general chit chat about the goings on in the world.

Louise had loved market days when she was growing up. She could remember spending the morning running through the marketplace with her friends, all of them hopped-up on pop and midget gems, running between stalls in a never-ending game of kiss-catch. Lisa Jennings had been her target; she had never caught her, always chasing after one of the lads instead. She had deliberately never caught them; Lisa had known, though.

That had been before the accident. Before everything changed.

They walked through the crowd, Hines stopping momentarily at a fresh fruit and veg stall called Jackson's. Standing behind the long row of fresh produce was Wendy Jackson. She was unboxing apples, giving each one a wipe over with a waxed cloth before stacking them in rows on the rough green mat.

'Morning, Wendy,' Hines said. 'Those apples look good.'

She picked one up. 'I can see myself in it.' Wendy smiled but said nothing. She looked nervously around for her parents. Instinctively her mother saw and came over.

'Can I help you?' she asked, putting herself between Hines and her daughter. 'Five pence, or six for a twenty.'

Hines handed over a note. 'I'll just take the one, thanks.'

Mrs Jackson rattled around in a biscuit tin for change, which she handed back without comment. Hines smiled.

'How's Wendy doing? Not at school today?'

'She's fine, but after everything what happened, I wanted her with me. The school said it was all right and she'll be back Monday. Sorry, I have customers.'

Mrs Jackson moved away to go talk to an elderly couple who were testing the firmness of pears. Wendy hovered at the back of the stall, seemingly looking for anything to do other than speak to Hines.

'You take care, love,' Hines said, giving the girl what she hoped was a friendly smile. There was no point trying to force the issue today. Monday would be better when she was at school, with her friends. They would also have Karla Hayes with them, an expert in getting people to open up and talk about things they would much prefer stayed secret or locked away.

Taking a bite out of the apple, Hines hurried on to catch up with Louise and Jeanette.

While the marketplace was full of a wide variety of stalls, inside the Town Hall were a motley collection of traders. They were gathered in the main hall, arrayed in a square with each trader given a fold up table on which to place their products.

As soon as they walked in Louise and Hines could see the marked difference; there were no banners advertising each business, unlike outside where it was almost as gaudy as a May Day celebration. Instead, each table was simply stacked with goods that looked like they had been taken from a cupboard and dumped. No price tags; some didn't have all the parts needed for the item to work. Louise could see a radio cassette player that was missing three buttons on top. Another table had a kettle whose handle was black while the rest of it was a deep red – obviously some home-made repair. One stall specialised in jewellery; three open multi-compartmentalised wooden boxes held a varied assortment of rings, brooches, bracelets and neck-laces. The owner of the stall didn't look like the typical jeweller, certainly not like anyone who worked in Deans on Bank Street, at the other end of town. Dirty denim jacket, hair that looked like it had been combed through with chip fat. He saw Louise looking and turned away.

'Who's that?' Hines asked.

'No one to worry about today,' Louise replied. The man was talking to a woman beside him. Her stall had books stacked in several towers. Battered covers, some missing them entirely;

Louise could tell that the majority of them were probably stolen from the library; she recognised the symbol that all library books had at the bottom of the spine.

There were about a dozen different traders packed around the square, maybe another half dozen on the outside of that. Some lined the stage edge and didn't have tables; these were the traders who sold larger goods like vacuum cleaners, furniture or bikes.

'That's the one,' Jeanette said, pointing to the far side of the stage.

Six bikes of different sizes were leaning against the stage, all showing signs of wear and tear. Paint was scuffed, chains were rusted. Three of them had flat tyres, one was missing its seat. A man sat on the edge of the stage reading a newspaper. He looked up when the three women approached, and went back to reading his paper, lifting it higher to hide his face.

'Tim Howard,' Louise began. 'I should have known it would be you selling on stolen property.'

'Don't know what you're talking about, sweetie,' he said from behind the paper.

Hines reached out and yanked the paper down and out of his hand. It tore in the middle and fluttered to the wooden floor of the hall.

'Oi!' he yelled out. 'I was reading that!'

'And now you're not,' Hines replied. She pulled the photo of the bike that Deborah had given them from her pocket and waved it beneath his face. 'You sold this bike this morning and we want to know where you got it from.'

He looked at Hines, not the photo. 'Ain't seen it before, and I didn't sell her—' he pointed at Jeanette, '—anything.'

Louise looked over from where she was checking out the other bikes.

'Well, that's interesting, because DC Hines never said who bought the bike.' She came right up to Tim. 'Turn around,' she said, pulling her handcuffs out. 'You and I are going to have a little chat over at the Shop. All of this will be seized, and I'll get a warrant for your shed down on the allotments just off Church Street.' She turned to Hines. 'I'll bet that's like Aladdin's cave – who knows what we'll find? Bet it's worth a fortune, as well.'

'At least eighteen months to five years,' Hines replied. If he got more than a slap on the wrists, they'd be lucky. But he didn't know that.

'All right, all right,' Tim said. 'Yes, I sold her a bike; what of it?'

Louise paused and turned Tim back round so he was facing them. He waved past her at some of the nearby stall holders. 'Just a joke,' he said. 'Little Christmas prank from my friend here.'

She kept the handcuffs out, letting them hang between them, a silent threat.

'It was stolen, Tim, and you knew it. I'm not arguing the point with you,' she added, seeing him starting to wind up to another ridiculous excuse-laden lie. 'We both know it happened. What I want to know is, who sold you it?'

'No one sold me it; it was mine to sell. I don't handle dodgy junk any more.'

'Right,' Hines said. 'So... you're one hundred percent certain the bike was yours to sell and not stolen property? Have I got that right?'

Tim nodded vigorously. 'Yeah... one hundred percent. A thousand percent.'

Louise shook her head, with a deep sigh. 'You logically can't have anything over a hundred percent. It literally means "out of a hundred". It really pisses me off when people say things like that.'

'Well, it depends on what the second value is,' Hines countered. 'That becomes the base and is represented by a hundred percent. That's how it works.'

Tim looked bemused. They had already lost him. Jeanette looked between the two as they continued their discussion.

'But it's logically, and literally, incorrect.'

It was Hines' turn to shake her head. 'I knew you were a little pedantic about things, but this...?'

'It's not pedantic to want to be accurate. You can't have more than a hundred percent of anything. You can't have a hundred percent more cake, can you?'

'You can if you buy two cakes,' Hines said.

'All right, a hundred percent,' Tim said. 'I'm a hundred percent sure the bike was mine to sell. Simple logic, right? Jesus, can we get this over? You two are bad for business.'

Hines and Louise now turned as one to stare at Tim. Louise brought the handcuffs out again.

'Woah... wait a minute? I said it was my bike,' Tim began.

'That bike was stolen from Dimple Well School a few nights ago. You said the bike was yours to sell, therefore you must be the one who stole it. Simple logic, right?' she parroted back. 'Tim Howard, I am arresting you on suspicion of—'

'No! No... I remember now. I thought you meant another bike. One I sold earlier. This bloke... it was a kid. A kid sold me the bike. Sold it to me for a fiver.'

'A fiver?' Jeanette said, throwing her arms in the air. 'You sold it me for twenty quid!'

Tim gave a lopsided grin and a shrug. 'A man's gotta earn a living, right?'

'So you did sell the bike on? Here's what we're going to do, Tim,' Louise began. She put the handcuffs away, eliciting a sigh of relief from Tim. 'First, you're going to give this nice lady her money back. In full. Right now.'

Grumbling, Tim turned round and pulled a money tin from beneath a mucky looking coat. Long and green, it was a poacher's coat, waterproof and dirty. With a grunt he hefted the lid off the tin and pulled out two ten-pound notes.

'Here,' he said, thrusting them towards Jeanette. She took them and gently folded them into her purse.

'Thank you,' she said.

'And the other thing?' he asked.

'You're going to tell us the name of the person who sold you the bike.'

'I don't know his name, just he's a local kid. I've seen him round here before. Bought a few other things... he's showed me a few other things, but I didn't buy them, obviously.'

'Obviously,' Hines said. 'What does he look like? Do you remember that?'

'Bit of a tall streak of piss, not much to him,' Tim said. He scratched at the back of his neck for a moment. The rasping sound dragged across Louise's last nerve.

'That it? Why am I wasting my time with you?'

'Hold your horses, love, I'm thinking. Tryin' to remember for you.'

Louise sighed but waited. Hines looked over at Jeanette and gave a smile. Jeanette smiled back. Hines leaned over. 'You can go, you know?' she whispered.

'I know. I'd just like to speak with Detective Miller first.'

Hines nodded.

'I remember now,' Tim said. 'He had a weird cut to his hair. Almost military looking. A buzz-cut, I think it's called. He also had a scar on the side of his neck. Here,' he said, reaching out to run his finger down the side of Louise's neck, from just under her jawline down to the top of her shoulder. His skin felt clammy and rough on hers and she flinched away.

'Okay, fine,' she said. 'A scar.'

'Pretty fresh one too, by the looks of it.' Hines said. 'Is that it?'

Tim nodded.

'Fine. Pack this shit up. You're done for the day.'

Back outside, Jeanette briefly talked with Louise to one side as Hines looked out across the marketplace. She could see the Jacksons' stall, but Wendy wasn't there now. Instead, Mrs Jackson was alone, bagging a customer's shopping. She kept watching until, a moment later, Louise came over to her.

'All sorted?' Louise asked.

'What did Jeanette want?' Hines asked with a smile.

'Nothing that concerns you,' Louise said. She paused, then continued somewhat sheepishly, doing her best to ignore the grin that was rapidly spreading across her friend's face. 'She was very pleased we were able to get her a refund. Still mortified she bought stolen goods though. She just wanted to say thank you.'

'Really? And just how did she want to express those thanks? Did she give you her phone number?' The flush of Louise's cheeks was all the answer Hines needed. She waved off any response. 'I don't need to know. That way I don't have to lie to Karla on Monday if she asks where you've been.'

'I didn't give her my home number,' Louise replied. 'I gave her yours.'

Hines stared back, lost for words. Then with a shrug, she started down the steps.

'Never say never...'

CHAPTER
THIRTY-SIX

Louise sat at her desk, the paperwork on the stolen bike finished. As cases went, it wasn't the most exciting, but true detective work wasn't like the television; all serial killers or mad bombers. That was what everyone wanted to talk about, though, when they learned she was a detective. They wanted to hear the exciting tales of chasing bad guys down alleys or car chases that ended in violent explosions, things that rarely, if ever, happened. At one particular party someone had asked the inevitable question, begging she recount for the whole group something nasty. When she had finished describing a post-mortem she had been tasked to observe, three of the guests had turned white, while another had excused himself to go to the bathroom to be sick.

After that, she wasn't asked to tell another work-related story all night.

She closed the file and looked at the clock. Five-thirty had rolled round quickly. Hines had already left for the weekend and Louise was ready to start hers. Manby had given the rota a tweak so she could catch up on her previous missed weekend, swapping Sergeant Harolds over. Strangely enough he hadn't complained as much as Louise thought he would; the chance to get away from his wife and her insistent demands that he retire obviously playing a big role in his sudden humanitarianism.

Hopefully this time nothing would come up to spoil it.

The Dude had just been fed when there was a knock at the door downstairs.

Giving his neck a ruffle, she went down, careful of the steep stone stairs. She'd slipped on them just that morning when she'd come back from the shop with a bottle of milk for her cereal. The melting snow had made the stones slippery and she'd nearly skidded back to the bottom in a heap. Luckily, she had caught herself, and not sent the milk bottle crashing either.

When she could, she would get a carpet laid down the centre, but that would have to wait. Money was tight right now with the run up to Christmas and she wanted to do something special for Karla.

If Karla still wanted her to.

She hadn't heard anything from her since their argument the other day. No phone call, no message left at the station. She didn't even know if she was still going to go with her to the school on Monday.

She hoped so... Karla was supposed to be picking her up.

Louise opened the door and was surprised to see Aunt Fiona standing in the darkening evening. She was wearing her long coat, her going-out coat, and she looked upset.

'What's wrong?' Louise asked, instantly worried. 'Is it Uncle Bernard?'

'No,' Aunt Fiona said. 'He's fine. I'm just... Can I come in?'

'Of course, of course,' Louise said, moving aside so Aunt Fiona could get past her.

'You know, you really need a carpet on these blooming stairs,' Aunt Fiona said as she started to struggle up them. 'Someone could fall down these and do a real mischief.'

'That sounds like a crackin' idea,' Louise said, shutting the door as a faint smile played across her face.

A cup of tea in her, Aunt Fiona had calmed somewhat, the colour coming back to her cheeks. There was nothing a cup of tea couldn't fix as far as the Millers were concerned, and it seemed equally true in this case. Aunt Fiona poured another from the pot, offering it to Louise, who put her hand over her mug.

'I'm fine. Any more and I'll be pissing tea, as Hines likes to say.'

'Oh, gosh,' Aunt Fiona said. 'She really is quite colourful, isn't she?'

'She's a good 'un,' Louise said, letting a little of her Yorkshire show. Many people couldn't place her by her accent, or lack of one, a fact that had helped on several occasions when she had been tasked with some very basic undercover work in Manchester. Having a voice that didn't betray her true heritage meant she could blend in more easily, a task she had performed several times; the Higgins gang; the dog-fighting circle run from the Soldier's Arms pub. None had suspected that she was a copper, and they certainly didn't know she was a Yorkshire lass.

Right now, Hines was probably neck deep in the weeds with Joe, she thought, remembering that Hines had said she was going to talk with her boyfriend about the possibility he was going to be a dad. No... that wasn't what she'd said. Hines had been a bit cagier about it. She was going to tell him she might be having a baby. Not that he was the father.

But if not Joe, then who...?

'Oh, shit!'

'*Louise!*'

Louise looked up, startled. Aunt Fiona was staring at her, brow furrowed, and a stern look on her face. 'Whatever is the matter with you?' her aunt asked, putting her mug down.

'It's nothing. Just something work-related. More importantly, what's the matter with you? You looked positively ashen when I opened the door.'

For a moment Aunt Fiona didn't say anything. Instead, she stroked Tom's back, long strokes that swept ginger-grey fur up into the air. Tom was a big cat, a Maine Coon, and his fur was soft. He shed all the time, forcing Louise to constantly keep changing the covers on her sofa and the bedding... Well, the bedding was now a hundred percent Tom-hair.

'I was at the book club tonight, and this time it was held at the Church of Divine Light.'

'All I seem to be hearing about these days is that bloody lot. You should have just gone to the Carps.' Louise said.

'Of course, you'd suggest a pub,' Aunt Fiona said. She didn't like the fact Louise went out drinking. As far as she was concerned, she was still a teenager to be protected. 'Anyway, we didn't like it, especially not after what happened at the Willikar funeral, but we had no choice.'

'You always have a choice,' Louise said. 'I take it things didn't go well?'

'That woman is a bloody idiot!'

As bad language went, that was damning stuff for Aunt Fiona. Louise could see the anger smouldering beneath the surface; her aunt's eyes were darting around, and she clenched and unclenched her hand several times while Louise waited for her to continue.

'Before we'd even begun, she was going on about the poor Willikars, how they had raised a devil-worshiping son, and that it was God's will he be punished. It was like something out of the Old Testament,' Aunt Fiona went on, her words coming out like machine gun fire. 'I tell you, if I didn't know any better I'd have thought it had been Catherine Hallum herself who had cut the boy's arm, as punishment for his behaviour, the way she was going on.'

'His arm?' Louise asked. 'What did she say about his arm?'

No one outside of the immediate family, police and medical

examiners knew the extent of his injury and exactly how he had died. No one knew that the cut had been made up his arm, and not the typical sideways slash that everyone expected.

'She said how it was the only way to make sure. That anything less was just practice. It was terrible, so I feigned a headache and left. I couldn't go home straight away, I was so mad, so I thought I'd come and see you.'

'I'm glad you did,' Louise said, putting her hand over her aunt's. 'I'm very glad you did.'

Because I think you've just given me a murder suspect and *a motive.*

'Another cuppa?'

CHAPTER
THIRTY-SEVEN

It had been a good day for Wendy Jackson, right up until the moment she had seen the two lady police officers.

She had been stacking apples, boxing pears and bagging people's shopping, and then they had walked past and instantly her head was filled with pressure. Luckily they hadn't tried speaking to her, but the damage was done. She couldn't concentrate, couldn't work out what change to give and knew she'd undercharged several people already. Her mum knew it too and sent her home with instructions to go straight there and have a nap.

That would be a neat trick if she could pull it off; she hadn't slept properly for a week. Every time she closed her eyes, she saw James lying there across the gravestone, his blood all around him. She couldn't even call it a nightmare, because she was sure she hadn't fallen asleep. Not properly. Quick naps from which she was jolted when James reached up from the gravestone, blood pouring from his arm, fingers outstretched to her.

'Please...' he would gasp, the word drawn out until it became a sigh. 'Pleeaase...'

The cold of that December morning couldn't match the chill

that filled her veins as she sat up in bed, the dark of the room pressing in all around her.

And now here she was again, back in the dark. Back in the lonely heart of her existence. Her mum and dad tried, they really did, to understand what she was going through, but they just couldn't. They just didn't.

They talked but said nothing; listened but didn't hear.

They loved but weren't loving; knew but didn't understand.

James was all those things her parents weren't, and now he was gone.

Wendy got out of bed, making sure the curtains were pulled fully across. She didn't want any light in her room save for the flickering light of the candle she had lit earlier. Tall and black, it sat in a saucer she had stolen from the kitchen. Her mum hadn't noticed yet, which Wendy was surprised about; the crockery in the kitchen was a collection of long-held family tradition, each piece passed down to the next generation. Blue and white patterned, folksy art that Wendy thought was dumb looking.

The candle flickered again. James had given her it as an early Christmas present when they were in the warehouse with the others.

She thought about the last time they had been together, sitting in their group around the fire as it burned, drinking cider from cans and talking. It had been fun, the three of them laughing and joking, telling stories around the makeshift campfire, telling tales out of class.

Ian had been there, smoking his cigarettes like a big lad. He was funny. Not in the ha-ha way, but on a more surreal level. He had an air about him, like he was the only one who knew the punchline.

But what was the joke?

Ian had talked that night and they had listened. Perhaps James had listened too much. Perhaps she hadn't listened enough.

When she said she wanted to go home they let her, James

staying for just one more.

Maybe she should have stayed?

Would things have changed if she had?

Wendy stared into the flickering candlelight, mesmerised by its incandescent dance. The house was silent; Mum was still out at the market. Dad was at work. She had the house to herself.

She took out her notebook and found a pen. Flipped through to a clean page.

Write it down, James had once said. *Write it out of you, get the dark on the page.*

Ian had laughed at that. 'There's only one way to release the dark inside you, and that's this...'

He'd taken a knife from his pocket and raised it over the fire.

'Watch,' he had said.

They had watched. Listened as he had talked.

And they had learned.

Wendy lifted her arm and looked at the scabbed-over scars of deeper wounds hidden.

Once again the darkness pressed in on her until all she could hear was the memory of Ian Peterson's voice, soft in the night, telling them all what they should do.

Showing them the way.

She knew what she had to do.

James, and Ian, had shown her the way.

It was several hours later when Mrs Jackson came home. Immediately she went straight upstairs to check on her daughter. She had been worrying about her all day, but work had to come first, even under such terrible circumstances.

She opened the door to her daughter's bedroom. She needn't have worried. Wendy was fast asleep in bed, the pillow clutched tight to her chest, a smile on her face for the first time in a week.

Being careful not to wake her, Mrs Jackson closed the door, thankful everything was back to normal.

CHAPTER
THIRTY-EIGHT

She sat in a dark room that wasn't hers, the curtains forever closed against whatever day it was. She sat on a bed that wasn't hers but fitted the small office-turned-bedroom perfectly. There was a bookcase directly at the end of the bed. The room was so small the bed blocked the lower doors, leaving them trapped shut. She didn't know what was inside, but she suspected it was her uncle's horse racing papers. His old ones, not the ones he needed for this week's races. There was another bookcase to her left, this one built into the wall. White paint that matched the white of the walls so it looked almost hidden. But she knew it was there; her uncle had told her not to look inside; there were private papers and documents that belonged to his clients, and not for the prying eyes of teenagers.

In the six weeks she'd been here she'd never once looked inside.
But she wanted to.

But she didn't, and never would.

They had been kind to take her in, to give her a home, though one that would never feel like it. That wasn't their fault; they did everything right. They always did. They loved her, she knew that, she knew that!

They had cried with her, hugged her tight whenever she needed it, most times without asking. They were going through what she was, but they had the benefit of experience to fall back on while she just had them.

Her cousins helped as well, but a step removed. She felt as if they looked at her like a social experiment, like a project that needed work.

Louise supposed she was. She supposed she did need work. She was broken. She needed fixing, but didn't know how to get it done.

She didn't think anyone did.

As she dreamed, Louise turned over suddenly, violently throwing the sheet aside as she punched the bed.

Startled, Tom jumped to his feet at the end of the bed and glared at her. His eyes caught the lamplight from outside and sparkled neon green for a moment. When she didn't move again, the cat turned round three times, patted the surface of the bed to be sure it was safe and then settled down.

A moment later his snores filled the room, accompanied by the occasional soft whimpers from Louise. Slowly, as night marched on, the time between them grew longer and her twists and turns in bed slowly ceased, until finally, eventually, Louise truly slept.

But the dreams continued.

The rage inside burned constantly, filling her with a heat that could never be quenched and one that she carried everywhere. All it took was a wrong word, a strange look, a perceived slight that wasn't there and she let loose.

Her shame burned even stronger, brighter even, than the white hot fury that had caused the argument with Aunt Fiona. She was wrong, she knew she was wrong but she wouldn't back down. She would never back down. How could she? Why should she? It was her room; they could keep the fuck out of it if they didn't want to find anything they didn't like.

It wasn't her fault they found her cigarettes, the blue Regals she kept hidden under the bed. It wasn't her fault they wanted to know where she got them and didn't like her answer. It wasn't any of their business; she wasn't their daughter. They couldn't tell her what to do.

Aunt Fiona's slap was as much a shock to her as it was to Louise. In her late forties, Fiona had never slapped anyone before, not one of her own children, and certainly not one of the many hundreds she taught at Holy Trinity. As the sound still echoed in the small kitchen, Aunt Fiona's own cheek burned as hotly as Louise's.

Now seventeen years old, she had never been slapped before and so she did the only thing that came to mind.

She slapped Aunt Fiona back.

And instantly burst into tears. So did Aunt Fiona, pulling Louise to her, crushing her against her chest, pressing her face into her hair and saying 'I'm sorry' over and over again. They both did.

That was how Uncle Bernard had found them, coming in with the Saturday shopping, the pair standing in the kitchen, crying together and hugging tight.

But still the rage burned, breaking out in similar instances throughout her life. But while the rage burned, the darkness was pushed momentarily aside.

And yet, there were times when the rage dimmed, and the darkness descended...

...and showed her other possibilities to release her pain.

The cutting began shortly after that incident. Nothing serious, she would think. Nothing that would show. Nothing that anyone would care about. Tiny nicks of her flesh, each weeping wound a scarlet tear she didn't have to shed.

But soon that wasn't enough.

The bathroom had filled with steam from the sink, only hot water running for fifteen minutes against a shut door. Everyone out. Her uncle's shaving blade, removed from the plastic casing. Louise looked in the mirror; she didn't recognise the creature that stared back.

She looked back down at her wrist, the skin so white against the green porcelain of the sink. When the blade met her skin, the area dimpled under the pressure. Not a lot. Not yet. She was building her courage. All it would take would be a simple twist, a sudden swipe, left to right. The porcelain would turn purple as her blood spilled into it, then, diluted by the water, it would wash away, all sins forgiven.

Everything would be fixed with a moment's action.

She was starting to push the blade tighter when there was a pounding knock at the bathroom door.

'Louise...!'

Her heart pounding as loud as her aunt's knock at the door, Louise sat bolt upright in bed. Her body was covered not in the slick embrace of a steam-filled bathroom, but in the flop-sweat of another nightmare endured.

Her face was wet as well, and when she touched trembling fingers to her cheek, Louise was unsurprised to find she was crying.

CHAPTER
THIRTY-NINE

MONDAY, 19TH

It wasn't a long walk from her flat to South Ossett High School, and frankly, Louise was glad of the exercise. The weekend had been lost to cleaning the flat, washing laundry and reading; all things she had sorely neglected in the last week. It had been some time since she'd last gone out on her usual early morning run, swapping the half-hour circuit along Ossett's streets for an extra hour in bed. She could blame Tom for that; his impatient yowls brought her awake at the same time as her alarm clock used to, but rather than jumping out for her run, she would drag her sleep-deprived body into the kitchen to feed her cat.

She found time to do a little exercise routine in the flat every other night, but that too had started to slip. Either Tom needed her attention or Karla did; the two of them seemed to be conspiring together to change her routines.

That had been part of the argument Karla and Louise found themselves in right now. It had been days since they had last spoken. That had been a particularly tense phone call when Louise had phoned Sunday night to double-check Karla was still going to go to the schools with her. It was important enough that the psychologist had said of course she was still going, but when Louise asked what time she'd pick her up, Karla had coldly said she would meet her at South Ossett at nine. She had then hung up before Louise could say anything else.

And what would she have said? 'I'm sorry. I'm not ready to commit yet?' Why should she have to apologise for how she was feeling? Why couldn't Karla just accept that the time wasn't right yet for them to be coming out to everyone? It was too early, both in terms of their relationship and her new role. What would happen if they came out and then their relationship crashed and burned? All the hassle, all the looks and the stares and the comments behind her back would have been for nothing.

That was hardship she wasn't prepared to suffer. Not now. Not yet.

Karla obviously felt differently, but she had already come out to her colleagues, and in all honesty, they were a totally different bunch to the ones that Louise worked with. She was suffering enough from the taunts of the lads in the Shop, sly side comments like 'on the rag again' when she said anything remotely against the group-think. It wasn't as bad as her time in Manchester; she supposed it helped that she was a local lass here in Ossett, born and raised in the town. Hines had her own share of crap to shoulder, and that would be so much worse if what she suspected had happened, had, in fact, happened.

But that was a worry for another day.

After stopping briefly at the shop to buy a couple of chocolate bars for later, peace offerings she hoped would smooth over the cracks with Karla, Louise continued along the Green, walking past the entrance to the park just as the groundskeeper, a wiry old man called Jack, opened the gates. He was as cliché as they came, complete with a flat cap and a pipe, but he also had a cheery wave that he threw her way as she passed by. He grabbed the gates and pulled. They creaked on rusted hinges as he swung them in, tipping another morning nod in her direction as she waved back. That was as far as his conversational skills went, though. Sometimes he'd offer a gruff greeting; most times it was a wave or a nod.

Today she got both and that made her smile.

She could hear kids already in the park, their laughter mixed with screams of feigned indignation at some slight. Hearing them gave her hope; perhaps things weren't as dark as she had feared. Hopefully, James had been the exception, a terrible, tragic exception, but an exception nonetheless. It hurt to think that there were more kids out there, suffering silently every day under fake smiles, fear tainting the joy that should be in every child's eyes.

Louise bit at her lip. She knew Wendy was having it rough right now, and they had planned time for them to sit with her when they went up to North Ossett later in the morning. If anything, this was all for her; Louise saw so much of herself in Wendy Jackson. Quiet, slightly nerdish in her pursuits, liked by others. But also fearful. Afraid. She had seen it in the girl's eyes when they had tried talking to her on that horrible Sunday morning. Saw the way she flinched at every touch. Louise had a horrible feeling she knew what that was. Karla had agreed with her when she had mentioned it, and they would try to get an answer that morning.

If she was right – and she really hoped she was wrong this one time – then Wendy needed a lot more help than anyone knew, especially her parents.

A blare of a car horn brought her up just at the corner where Manor Road began, its mechanical scream jolting her aware of the car that was turning from the Green. A two-fingered gesture from the driver as he drove past startled Louise. She blinked twice, watching the car disappear up the road. From behind came muffled laughter.

She turned around. Six schoolgirls looked back at her, each

one laughing at the crazy woman who had nearly walked out into the path of a car.

'Look both ways,' one of the girls said.

'Didn't you learn your Green Cross Code?' another one said. The others burst out laughing. Louise said nothing and crossed the road.

Karla was waiting for her outside the school when she got there a few minutes later. She had arrived in her Saab, parking it in the car park of the Weavers Arms across the road.

Louise had walked briskly, followed closely by the gaggle of schoolgirls, who took great delight in throwing barbed taunts as she headed to the school.

'Careful of the parked car,' one of them shouted. 'It might jump out and get you!'

'What's that all about?' Karla asked as Louise came to a stop beside her. The girls continued on, swinging their school bags and laughing.

'Nothing,' Louise said. 'Girls being girls, I guess. How are you?' she asked. The urge to kiss her nearly overpowered her, but she resisted, choosing instead to reach out to touch her hand. At first Louise feared Karla would remove her hand, but instead she let their fingers entwine.

'People might see,' Karla said quietly, leaning in a little closer. Despite everything she had been running over and over in her mind, Louise didn't care. She took a deep breath.

'I don't care.'

Karla smiled, and some of the fear Louise had been carrying disappeared.

The headmaster introduced Louise to the gathered assembly.

It took a few moments to get everyone to silence their shuf-fling, and even as she spoke, Louise could hear some hushed whispering taking place. *Nothing changes*, she thought, recalling the many times she had sat in similar assemblies ignoring whatever it was the teachers felt compelled to tell them before first class.

She couldn't remember anything discussed being this serious, though.

'You may have heard about the death of James Willikar last week,' she began. 'Some of you may have known him, even though he went to North Ossett.'

A chorus of boos rang out at the mention of their rivals. Louise let it go for a moment or two, then continued, raising her voice slightly and injecting a little of her 'police tone' into it.

'Don't you think it sad when someone feels they have no one to talk to, especially when they are suffering? I bet you've felt that way once or twice. I know I have.'

'Me too,' Karla said beside her. 'I can remember being at school and thinking that no one understood what I was feeling, that no one ever had gone through what I was going through. I mean, how could they? They couldn't... because I didn't tell them. I kept it all to myself, all the worries and the things I was scared about. And I was scared about a lot of things.'

Louise took a step back, letting Karla take the spotlight.

'I was scared about my classes, that I wasn't as clever as some of the other girls. I knew I was better than the boys, because, well... boys.'

That got a laugh. 'But I was also scared at how my body was changing. I know, I know... embarrassing stuff, right? I can hear you giggling out there, but I know it's a nervous "she's right" sort of giggle. Right? And that's okay. It's okay to be nervous. It's okay to be embarrassed. Growing up is embarrassing at times. Changes in our bodies, in the very chemicals that make our bodies unique. Make you unique.'

'And that's okay,' Louise said. 'But sometimes it gets a little too much, right? And you don't want to talk to anyone, prefer-

ring to hide away in your bedroom. Shut the door and the problems go away.'

'But that's not healthy,' Karla said, taking over again. 'It's not
the best way to deal with an issue, no matter how serious you
might think it is. You might be scared about getting in trouble
with your parents if you told them, or that they might be embarrassed as well, but I promise you... I *promise* you... they would
want to be embarrassed, they would prefer to be a little angry
with you if you had done something wrong, than not be able to
talk to you about it. Talking gets everything in the open. There's
a saying, one of those grown-up sayings you might have heard.
Can anybody finish it for me? A problem shared is a problem...?'

At first no one said or did anything. And then a moment later,
a couple of hands went up. Louise pointed at one, a boy with
sharp red hair and freckles. A prime candidate for bullying.
'Yes?'

'I think my mum said this,' he started, his voice cracking with
nerves. 'A problem shared is a problem aired.'

'That's good. I like that. Not what I was thinking, but it
works.' Louise said.

'What do you think it means?' Karla asked.

The boy's cheeks went as red as his hair. He thought for a few
moments and then put his hand back up again. 'Go on,' Karla
encouraged.

'Erm... well, I think it might mean that if you tell someone
about your problem, it is no longer all stuffed up inside any
more. I think that's what aired means. My mum says she always
has to air my dad's underpants outside on the line because they
stink the airing cupboard out.'

Everyone laughed. The boy looked around then joined in.
One of his friends gave him a couple of good-natured thumps to
his back, something he wasn't quite used to, judging by his
nervous reaction.

'That's good,' Karla said, waving her hands up and down to
encourage everyone to be quiet. 'I like that as well. Another way

of saying it is "A problem shared is a problem halved". Now, who thinks they know what that means?'

This time a dozen hands shot up.

Louise was impressed by how Karla was handling the kids. A few teachers were, too. She watched as Karla made a show of walking up and down the front row of the assembly, looking over the eagerly waved hands. She was captivated by how confident Karla was. One girl, a few rows in, was holding her left arm up with her right, stretching it as high as she could and fluttering the hand side to side like a peacock attracting its mate.

Louise smiled at the memory of her own time at school, up at North Ossett, their next destination.

'Okay, you.' Karla pointed at the peacock-girl, who seemed to nearly explode with enthusiasm. 'What do you think?'

'It's easy,' the girl said, throwing a look to her friends on either side. She held her hands together as though in prayer, holding them up so everyone could see. 'If you tell someone you need help with something, then they'll probably help. One person becomes two.' As she said this, she pulled her hands apart.

'Spot on,' Karla said and started clapping. Everyone else joined in, even Louise.

'If you tell someone that you're having a problem, they can help you. If they can't sort it directly themselves, then chances are they can help you find the solution, so you're not alone any more.'

'That's really important to not only understand, but to *hear*,' Louise said, moving forward once again. 'You are not alone at all, and you can always, *always*, talk to someone. Your parents are the best choice—'

'You've not met my dad,' a boy's voice called out. Laughter rippled around them, but Louise ignored them and carried on.

'—followed by your teachers. They're not all scary, certainly a lot better than when I was at school, and then there are your friends. Talk to them. Tell them how you feel. Just doing that, sharing your problems, will help. It will also make you feel a little better.'

'It may not solve the problem,' Karla jumped in, 'but it will be a step in the right direction. And it is so much better than taking a drastic, permanent solution to what is more than likely a temporary problem.'

'You mean suicide, don't you?' Peacock girl asked. 'Like James Willikar.'

Karla nodded. 'Yes, sweetie. What he did was terrible and tragic because he thought there was nothing else he could do. No one wants that to happen to anyone else, and that's why we're here.'

'Now,' Louise asked, 'are there any questions you'd like to ask?'

A forest of arms shot into the air.

Karla and Louise did their best to answer as many questions as they could, but when they saw the time starting to creep towards ten they called a halt, asking everyone in the hall to promise that they would speak out if they were ever feeling sad, stressed or just plain angry. There was the expected rumble of agreement, and then the teachers were herding them all out and back to their classrooms.

After a few minutes with a group of teachers who had some more questions, Louise and Karla found themselves walking across Storrs Hill towards the car park of the Weavers Arms, keen to get up to Gawthorpe and North Ossett High School for the next assembly chat.

'I think that went well,' Louise said as she walked round the front of Karla's Saab to the passenger door.

Karla unlocked the doors and they got in.

'They asked some good questions, more than I was expecting,' she said as she got the car started. They pulled out of the car park, turned right and headed back up Storrs Hill. 'You need to get anything from the flat before we go to the next one?'

Louise shook her head. 'Tom stayed in today. I think he's a little under the weather. Missing his buddy,' she added, stealing a sideways look at Karla as she drove.

'His buddy... oh.'

Karla and Tom had struck up a pretty good friendship over the last year. He usually didn't like it when people came round; he would hide in the bedroom, or shed on their legs until they left, but with Karla it was different. He purred for her. He actually purred for her, rubbing against her until she gave him the attention he craved. And the pigeon-purrs would begin. At first Louise had been a little jealous; he normally only purred like that for her, but then she realised that he had accepted Karla into his family, just as he had accepted Louise.

Karla turned away from the road briefly and smiled at Louise. 'Perhaps I should pop round tonight? You know, make sure the Dude is okay. What do you think?'

Louise smiled.

'I think that sounds perfect.'

CHAPTER
FORTY

Unlike South Ossett School, North Ossett School had its own car park for teachers directly on the grounds. There were more than enough spaces and Karla was able to park close to the entrance. They could see children running around the large circular plant pots, shouting at each other and generally having a good time. Some stood around in small groups, or sat on the benches sharing sneaky snacks of crisps and chocolate bars.

Seeing that reminded Louise she had a couple of bars still. She reached into her purse and brought them out. 'Marathon?' she asked, handing one of them to Karla. The psychologist looked at it, looked at Louise and shook her head. 'Oh... too good for a choccy-bar?'

Karla laughed. 'No, you idiot; I'm allergic to peanuts, and besides,' she reached into her pocket and pulled out a pack of sweets, 'I've got Opal Fruits.' She unwrapped them and held the pack out to Louise. 'Want one?'

Eagerly Louise took one, laughing as she held it up. 'Green ones are the best!'

'Lime? You've got to be kidding. Orange all the way!'

Laughing together, the pair walked down the path to the school's main entrance.

. . .

They made their presence known at the reception and took a seat beside the doors that led to the hall where the assembly was to take place. As they waited for the headmaster to come and meet them, a loud bell rang throughout the school grounds, making both Karla and Louise jump. It rang three times, then one long drone before falling silent, its metallic echo reverberating from the open staircase they sat beneath.

'Jesus, I'm deaf,' Karla whispered. Louise giggled.

There was the scuffling of feet as children, teenagers all, came in from outside, their combined chattering broken by the sporadic bark of laughter, or the squeal of a secret pinch. Most gave the two women a stare as they trooped passed, heading inside the hall.

Eventually the traffic died down, the door swinging shut behind the last of the kids. At that moment the door to the reception area opened and the headmaster came out. He was accompanied by David Willikar, his face drawn, his eyes red and watery as though he had been crying.

'Do you require anything else, Mr Willikar?' the headmaster asked, his tone sombre but pleasant. It was hard to watch the obvious grief of a parent, but Louise found herself looking at Mr Willikar as he shook his head silently. 'James' locker is down the hall and on the left. Lucy, the head girl, will show you. If there's anything more I, or my staff, can do to help you or your family, please do not hesitate to ask. James was a wonderful student, and he is sorely missed by staff and pupils.'

David gave another nod and took the headmaster's hand, giving it two quick shakes. He turned and walked down the corridor to where a girl – Lucy, Louise supposed – stood waiting by the door into the student rec room.

The headmaster was a tall middle-aged man with thinning black hair that had silver streaks either side just above the ears. He came over to the two women and gave a sad smile.

'Such a terrible, terrible thing,' he said. 'Gerald Pitchford. Headmaster. I believe we spoke on the phone?' Louise took his hand and shook. 'They're all waiting for you through there,' he said, indicating the double doors into the hall.

'Afterwards we'd like a few minutes with Wendy Jackson, if that is all right? Just a classroom that isn't being used.'

'We can do that,' he said, 'but I'll have to get her mother's permission. I can go ring her while you talk to them, if that's all right?'

'That's perfect, thank you.'

'We won't be long either. Ten to fifteen minutes, tops. I'd just like to have a quick chat, make sure she's okay. See if there's anything she needs. Poor love had such a big shock.'

'I'm sorry, you are?' Mr Pitchford asked, turning to Karla.

She introduced herself but didn't offer her hand. 'It's my role to evaluate Wendy's psychological state. A few questions will do that. We've spoken to Mrs Jackson before; I'm sure she'll be fine with it.'

'Best to make sure, though.'

'Of course. We'll get started then.'

By the time they had finished talking to the children, Louise was glad she didn't have to do this again today. The teachers for the older kids had now been briefed and her phone number and that of Karla's office had been given out if there were any follow-ups required.

Mr Pitchford was waiting by the door as everyone filed out.

'That seemed to go well,' he said. 'I don't know how many took anything from it other than having another twenty minutes out of class, but I'm sure it helped one or two.'

'I hope so,' Karla said. 'I wouldn't be surprised if a few teachers get some awkward questions over the next few days. Let me know if they need anything, anything at all.'

'I will. Thank you. The kids might not appreciate what you're doing but I do, so again... thank you. I've also spoken to Mrs Jackson and she's perfectly happy for you to talk to her daughter.'

'Good. Now we just have to find her. Did you see her?' Louise looked at Karla, who shook her head.

'I was looking through the kids but couldn't see her.'

'She's definitely here because I saw her this morning talking with her friend Jenny,' said Mr Pitchford. 'In fact, there's Jenny now. Jenny? Jenny Cavandish... Wait there, will you?'

The three of them went over to the far side of the hall where a couple of girls sat on the floor. Between them was an open bag of crisps, ripped down the middle and spread so they could both get to the snack more easily. When they saw Mr Pitchford walking over they started to scoop up the crisps. The headmaster waved at them.

'Don't worry about that,' he said, 'though don't let Mrs Kent see you with them. Jenny, do you know where Wendy Jackson is? We can't seem to find her right now.'

Jenny looked from Mr Pitchford to Louise and Karla, who both smiled. 'It's okay,' Karla said, kneeling down so that she was at the same level as the two girls. 'She's not in any trouble. We'd just like to see how she's doing. We know she was close to James.'

'They were boyfriend and girlfriend,' Jenny said.

'Yes. So I'm guessing she must be really sad. Remember what we said about how some people can be sad and it can get really bad for them, especially if they don't talk about it?'

Jenny nodded. So did her friend.

'Well, we just want to make sure she has all the help she needs. Do you know where she is?'

'I've not seen her today,' Jenny said, scooping up a couple of crisps. 'I think she's taking a day off. You know, because of everything that happened.'

'I know she's been here, because I saw her this morning talking with you. It's all right, she's not in trouble. Where is she?'

Mr Pitchford asked. Louise could hear a note of concern edge into his voice.

Louise looked both girls in their eyes, turning from one to the other. She could feel a tremble of worry start to build. Karla leaned forward, Louise's concern mirrored in her own.

'This is very important, girls. Do you know where Wendy is?'

They shook their heads.

'We haven't seen her since this morning.'

CHAPTER
FORTY-ONE

'And you are certain she's not at home? Hiding upstairs in her bedroom perhaps?'

Louise knew the answer as soon as Mrs Jackson started speaking. Wendy was not at home. The worry in her voice was like a cold knife in her chest; every parent's nightmare come true.

'She left for school this morning as normal,' Mrs Jackson continued, her voice trembling further with each word. 'I asked her how she was, and she said she was fine. She'd had an episode over the weekend, a nightmare about that Hallum woman. She said she was fine.'

Louise could hear the tears now, hoarse and genuine, as the guilt deepened behind the words. Token gestures spoken over breakfast, casual conversation that skirted the issues and didn't address them directly. The root of many deep problems.

Listening but not hearing. Talking but not saying anything of value... of worth.

But the parents of Wendy Jackson were not alone in their failure to come together as a family. Wendy also chose to take the solo route, to bottle everything away. To try and tackle the over-whelming force that was her grief.

Failure was too harsh a word, too guttural. Too emotional a

word for what had truly happened here, for what had happened for centuries in families the world over. Teenagers and parents; a volatile mix.

'And you are absolutely sure she isn't in the house?'

She could hear Mr Jackson in the background, stomping down the stairs, slamming doors, calling out for Wendy over and over. The anger in his voice was white-hot; Louise feared that if Wendy was at home she wouldn't want to come out and face that anger head-on.

'Okay, Mrs Jackson, what I'm going to do is this. I'm going to hang up and call my station immediately. They will send officers out to your house to start looking in your immediate area. I will also arrange to have officers come to the school and we will start a search around the streets here. It could just be that Wendy wanted some time alone; God knows she's been through a lot this last week. She may have simply gone for a walk to clear her head; I've done that myself a few times when I was her age.'

The death of her boyfriend, local protests at his funeral. The funeral itself. So much pain and grief for anyone to handle, let alone a fourteen-year-old. She hadn't gone for a head-clearing walk. Louise knew that.

'By the time the officers get to you, I'd like you to have put together a list of all her friends that you can remember, along with addresses and phone numbers. That will give us a good place to start. Can you do that for me?'

Mrs Jackson said that she could, and Louise hung up.

'No luck?' Karla asked. Louise shook her head as she pulled her radio from her bag. Over the last year there had been some improvements to the Prospect Road CID branch, one of them being better radios. Handheld, multi-channel beasts, these bricks of plastic enabled detectives to speak directly to the Shop without the need to find public phones or rely on the crackly inconvenience that were the shoulder radios most uniformed police used.

They also made a great bludgeon for when a suspect was being too unruly. Their head would crack before the radio did.

'I'll radio Sergeant Harolds and get the ball rolling. Can you call Beth directly? She'll still be at her desk.'

Karla was already reaching for the phone. 'What do you want me to say to her?'

Louise told her.

Karla smiled.

'That's a bold move,' she said.

Louise nodded in agreement, the radio in her hand. 'I'm either wrong, and we have another able body helping with the search,' she said, flipping the dial to the correct channel, 'or I'm right, and we have a potential murderer right where we want them.'

CHAPTER
FORTY-TWO

In less than ten minutes, police officers were at the home of Wendy Jackson. Sergeant David Harolds took the radio call from Louise, started to make a snide comment about her need to go back to school to learn a thing or two then shut up as soon as he heard the tone in her voice. The urgency as she gave her instructions brokered no time for his one-sided banter, neither did the cause of her call.

A missing child was serious, and every moment wasted was another moment closer to disaster. They had learned valuable lessons from the Jacobs case and had put in place specific local responses should another call come through. Lower priority cases were flagged, and, while not put aside, they were superseded by the immediate situation. Off-duty officers would be contacted, and if not called in immediately, they would be put on notice that they might be needed. Most of them came in anyway, eager to help.

He made frantic notes as she talked and was already making a checklist of what needed to happen in the next few minutes. As soon as she rang off, he dispatched two cars to the Jacksons with instructions to take statements from the parents and start knocking on doors nearby. Detective Tom Bailey would go with them and take a look at the girl's bedroom in the hopes they could find a clue as to where she had gone.

Secretly, Harolds hoped this was just another example of the foolishness of teenagers not thinking about the consequences of their actions, dashing off with friends to smoke a crafty tip or two, or just play sick from school. If it was his kid, she wouldn't be able to sit down for a week when she came home; it wasn't a popular belief amongst many parents, but for Harolds, a good hiding never hurt him in the long run.

He then sent three cars up to Gawthorpe to meet with Louise and start a search there. His next call was to DI Manby. For that, he went in personally.

DI Bill Manby was sitting at his desk on the phone. He looked up at the single rap on the door then beckoned Harolds inside.

'Yes, I'm sure it must be some misunderstanding... I don't think it's as... Well, that's a bit harsh, don't you think, but as I said, a misunderstanding that can be easily sorted, so if you could just... Again, I don't think that's really an issue here, but...'

'Sir... Bill?'

Manby put his hand over the phone. 'I've got Catherine Hallum having a right pop because someone's at her house wanting her to come to the station for a chat.'

'Bill... we have a missing kid.'

Manby sat forward, totally ignoring the tinny voice that escaped the phone. 'Tell me.'

'Wendy Jackson. Supposed to be up at school, same one Miller went to for that touchy-feely, kumbaya crap to the kids. Miller called it in about ten minutes ago.'

'Co-ordination plan?'

'We've sent uniforms there and to the home to start searches. All hands on deck, but I can't find Hines anywhere. She's pretty good at door-to-door and I could use her up in Gawthorpe. It's bigger than people think.'

Manby nodded, sighed and gestured to the phone.

'Who do you think's with Catherine Hallum?'

Catherine Hallum was red with anger.

She listened to the phone, started to say something, stopped, then turned to WDC Elizabeth Hines. Hines was standing in the doorway, her feet scuffing the Welcome mat as she tried to get some days-old slush from her soles. The mat had a black and white cat on it, the whiskered face beaming widely beneath the legend: *clean your paws or no indoors.*

Hines looked up and smiled. Catherine held the phone out.

'He wants to talk to you.'

The smile faded but didn't leave Hines' face. Catherine gave a smirk that Hines ignored. She gave her feet another good scrape then stepped inside the hallway.

The inside of Catherine Hallum's home was decorated just as Hines had expected. Chintz was everywhere, from the fake chandelier that hung over the wide staircase, to the pastel-coloured rugs that were perfectly centred on the wooden floors. Pastel pink wallpaper ran from the floor to the dado rail running the length of the wall; above that the walls had been painted an off-white. The off being a shade of pink that even Hines thought was sexually vulgar.

Taking the phone, Hines expected a tirade from her DI.

She'd got the call from Karla, surprised that she would be calling her and not Louise, but when she heard what was going on, and what Louise wanted her to do, she was more than happy.

'Yes sir?'

'Having fun, are we?' Manby asked.

'I'd be lying if I said no, sir, but Detective Miller's pretty much spot on with this. When I got the word I was already nearby, so it wasn't a major inconvenience to get here.' She couldn't say any more, not without alerting Catherine as to what was going on, and Manby obviously understood.

'Okay. A long shot – all we have is a missing kid right now, one that probably just wanted to get away for a bit under the circumstances – but on the side of caution, I'll back it.'

'Yes sir. Thank you, sir,' Hines said.

'And enough with the sir shit. No need to butter me up like a bap. It's Bill. Got it? Bill.'

It wasn't for him, and he knew it. 'Of course, sir.' Hines handed the phone back to Catherine, who had been staring daggers at her the entire time. It was Hines' turn to smirk now as Manby no doubt was telling her what was about to happen.

One step out of line, Hines thought as she saw Catherine's face darken. *Just give me one reason.*

'Well, I... I don't think...' Catherine said, her voice rising at the end of each utterance. Hines could hear the arrogance in her voice being slowly sapped of its strength. Whatever Manby was saying to her, it was working.

'Fair enough. I shall see you shortly,' Catherine said and then hung up. She turned her back to Hines as she took a long white coat from the stand beside the staircase. She draped it over her shoulders and turned round.

'Shall we away?' she said, and it was all Hines could do to stop herself from laughing.

CHAPTER
FORTY-THREE

Detective Constable Tom Bailey stood in Wendy Jackson's bedroom and looked around, taking in the music posters on the dark purple walls, the black curtains and the dark maroon of the carpet.

'Not exactly a cheery place, is it?' he asked the uniformed officer standing just inside the door.

'It looks like my niece's room if I'm being honest, Tom,' the officer replied. He removed his helmet and gave the back of his neck a rub before putting it back on. 'What are you looking for, anyway? It's not as if she's going to have written down: "running off for the day. Back at six. Will bring chips".' He paused as Bailey stopped at the bedside table and reached down behind it.

Standing up, Bailey lifted a green and purple notebook, which he showed the officer.

'You never know,' he said, flipping it open. 'She very well might have.'

He started to read.

With three police cars full of officers now dispatched onto the streets around the school, Karla felt a little better. She knew from

Louise that time was vital in first stage searches for missing children, and the more bodies that could be thrown to the problem, the better. She also knew how unique this situation was, that there were special circumstances to take into consideration, and throwing everything they could at finding Wendy as fast as possible was worth bending a rule here or there. It wasn't standard procedure, far from it, but this wasn't a standard missing kid scenario either.

Headmaster Gerald Pitchford stood outside the school, a folder resting on one of the large stone planters. He flipped through it, checking each entry carefully.

'The daily register for all the classes,' he said when Karla asked him what he was doing. 'I thought I'd go back and see if she had checked in at all earlier. Also, I can find out if she missed any other days. Perhaps if she did, then this is just another example of her bunking off for the day. And who can blame her?' he added with a grimace.

Karla had to agree; the girl had been through the wringer, that was for sure, but right now, she was putting her parents through one as well.

'Anything?' Karla asked. She looked over his shoulder at where Louise was standing, co-ordinating the search with the police officers who had arrived. She knew what Louise did for a job, had even been on the receiving end of some pretty intense questioning by her in the past, but she had never really thought about what she actually did. How she actually acted when on the job. It was an eye-opener to be sure.

Karla knew how self-conscious Louise was in private, but here, with a dozen police officers to control, a missing girl to find and the horrendous reality of a possible child abduction and murder to contend with, it was a surreal experience for Karla to witness just how take-charge Louise was.

There was no hesitation in her voice, no stammered orders given. She knew what needed doing and who needed to be doing it.

And it was getting done.

'I'm sorry. Can you say that again?' Karla asked when she realised Mr Pitchford had stopped talking.

'I said, there's no mark against her name in the register today, and a few days last week she wasn't marked as down either. Monday and Friday.'

'What about Monday and Friday?'

Louise walked up behind them as they were talking. She held her radio in one hand, a clipboard in the other. Her purse was slung over her shoulder, its strap threatening to slip off. Karla reached out and adjusted it, giving Louise a soft smile as she did so.

Louise gave a curt nod in reply.

If he had noticed anything, Mr Pitchford gave no indication.

'Wendy Jackson wasn't marked down as attending either on Monday the twelfth, or Thursday the fifteenth.'

'The day after James died, and the day of his funeral. I'm not surprised. And she wasn't down for today either?'

Williams shook his head. 'I can check with her class teacher if you'd like?'

'We'll need to speak with them, yes. They might have noticed some behaviour out of the ordinary, or overheard something that could explain this absence.'

Pitchford gave a cough, nervous about what to say, but needing to say it anyway. 'Well, we all know what's going on here, right? Isn't it obvious? The poor girl has become over-whelmed and taken the day. I can't say I blame her.'

'In all honesty, Mr Pitchford,' Louise began, handing the clip-board off to a uniformed officer who came up, 'I agree with you. That is *probably* what has happened, and she'll be embarrassed by all the fuss she's caused when she comes home, be in the shit with her parents for some time, but thankfully she'll be home and safe. But...'

She let that hang between them.

It was always there for her, that extra point of concern, her mind going to the darker possibilities, ones that still needed checking, if only to cross them off. She couldn't rely on probable or hopeful outcomes. She had to follow the evidence no matter where it went, no matter what dark paths it led her down.

No matter the outcome, however monstrous or evil it became.

And right now, all they had was a missing girl, a girl who was troubled, a girl who had suffered the loss of someone close to her. She had also suffered at the hands of others, people who should know better.

Adults who should know better.

Adults like Catherine Hallum.

Hines had offered Catherine a cup of tea when they got to the station. Thanking her, she had taken a seat at Hines' desk while the young detective went to make the drinks. When she came back, DI Manby was now also sitting at the desk, talking with Catherine as though the two were old friends.

Hines took great delight in handing the thin beige plastic cup of weak tea to Catherine, relishing the wrinkling of the woman's nose and the quick bite of her lip when the heat roared through the plastic.

'Not the best cuppa,' Manby said, 'but it's good in a pinch.'

Catherine didn't take a sip but put the cup on the desk. On a report Hines had been working on for the best part of two days. She could see the ring form beneath the cup and knew she would have to type it all out again.

'Tell me again why I am here?' Catherine said, speaking directly to Manby.

'Well, Catherine,' he began, uncrossing his legs and smoothing his trousers down. They were worn at the knees and about an inch too short, showing off the threadbare brown socks he wore. 'It's like this. We've had a few complaints come in regarding statements you and members of your church have made recently. Statements that some find... distasteful.'

'I would very much like to know who has been saying such things,' Catherine said, each word pinched off and taut. 'I stand by everything and anything I, or members of my congregation, have said.' The way her lips pursed together into a line as thin as a spider's leg told Hines everything. It told her she was speaking with a true and honest believer. The most dangerous kind of suspect.

'Yeah, but it's not like you're a real church, are you?' Hines said. 'I mean... you're not even a real religion, right? Just a bunch of people who get together now and then to bitch about your perceived slights in the world. And occasionally you gather outside funerals and shout hateful remarks at grieving parents, family and friends.'

'I... am... shocked! Is this how you treat people? Drag them in to hound and harass them? Why am I here anyway? That all took place a week ago. This is harassment, William, and I will not be standing for it, and neither will my solicitor when I contact him as soon as I am able, and neither will the Chief Superintendent when I tell him, I expect.'

If that had any impact on her DI, Hines couldn't see it. Neither did the woman's fake tantrum as she jumped to her feet.

'Sit down, Catherine,' Manby said, quietly but firmly.

She didn't, but she also didn't continue towards the door. Hines would have stopped her leaving, and the detective thought she realised that.

'What is this all about?' she asked again. Hines took a breath; Catherine's constant repeated question about what this was about was really grating her last nerve.

'This is about a missing girl.'

'What missing girl?'

'Wendy Jackson,' Hines said. 'The girl you called "another suicide waiting to happen" and that it "couldn't happen to a more deserving person".'

The colour drained from Catherine Hallum's face.

Louise had gathered everyone around the larger of the planters. A wooden board had been placed across as a makeshift desk, and a map of the area had been sourced from the geography class. A more detailed one would be brought from the station later; for now this one was adequate enough to get the search started.

Around a dozen men and women had joined them, offering to help with the search for Wendy. An officer had taken everyone's names and addresses, noting them down on the clipboard Louise had given him. These would all be scrutinised later, their backgrounds checked and any further follow up interviews taken. It was a disturbing fact that out of all the searches undertaken for missing people, two percent of them included the abductor, the lure to inject themselves into the investigation too strong to resist.

'We've broken the area up into sections. I want an officer controlling each one.' Louise pointed to the clump of houses that made up part of Gawthorpe's winding network of roads, cul-de-sacs and alleys. About a thousand houses altogether, now divided by red pen into roughly equal sized squares, each one numbered and assigned to police officers. The closest batch was number one. The furthest section was number seventeen at the top of the town by the May Pole opposite the Shoulder of Mutton pub.

'How do we know she was even here?' someone asked.

'She was seen before school started by the headmaster and a couple of her friends. Has everyone got everything they need? Knock on doors, ask to look in any sheds and gardens. Garages can sometimes be a hiding place that kids use.'

Karla stepped forward. 'Remember, she is very vulnerable right now. If you find her, stay with her, and officers, you each have a radio so let Detective Miller know and we'll be right with you.'

The groups started to disperse, heading to their respective search areas, an officer checking them off as they went.

'And what about us?' Karla asked.

'We stay here and co-ordinate this,' Louise said. She looked down at the clipboard – there were seventeen police officers and fifteen members of the public now searching for Wendy Jackson, and that was just here at the school. There would be a similar number of officers now around the area of her home, and at the station, Hines and Manby would be talking with the person Louise suspected had contributed greatly to this entire mess.

'That is utterly preposterous,' Catherine Hallum said, her voice rising once again with shock. 'I am in no way responsible for a very troubled teenager going missing. And you can't prove that, either!'

'Strange that you would take such a stance,' Hines replied. She was thoroughly pissed off with the woman and didn't bother to hide it any more. If he objected to her combative tone, DI Manby didn't show it.

Instead, he sat back in his chair and smoked another cigarette. 'I mean, for such a woman, a *Christian* woman, I mean... that's pretty strong language. Not exactly love thy neighbour, is it?'

'The sins of temptation constantly threaten the weak.'

'And shouldn't you be protecting the weak... again, as a Christian woman?' Hines asked. 'Not harassing them, or calling them out?'

'I did no such thing. I—'

'Enough with the bullshit, Catherine,' Manby said, stubbing his cigarette out in the overflowing tray. 'You said some pretty heinous shit before the funeral, and by all accounts once you got back to your little hut you continued with your spiteful barking. That got back to the Willikars and no doubt the Jacksons, and here we are.'

'It's nothing to do with me that a girl runs away. Maybe her parents should be dragged in here and subjected to the same gestapo questioning? What's next? Rubber hoses and pulling nails?'

Manby looked like he was about to say something, but he stopped himself. Breathing in deeply, he took a moment to compose himself, taking another cigarette out. He offered the pack to Catherine, who sneered at him.

'Cigarettes are the sign of a weak soul,' she said.

'Guilty as charged,' he replied, lighting up. He took in several long pulls, blowing the smoke out so that it drifted towards Catherine, gently rising until it hovered above her. She coughed and waved at her face theatrically. Hines shook her head with a resigned sigh.

This wasn't getting them anywhere.

For a moment, no one said anything, and then Hines took a gamble.

'Do you have kids?' she asked, knowing the answer but asking anyway.

Catherine shook her head. 'I wasn't fortunate to be blessed by God in such a way,' she replied.

'That explains quite a lot,' Hines said. Manby raised his eyebrows, but she ignored him. 'Because I don't know of any mother who could react so callously to the knowledge of a missing child. A *child*! You speak a lot about the love you have for your fellow man, but it's only on your own terms, isn't it? Anything that falls outside that precious belief of yours is what... tainted? Evil? The work of Satan, I believe, is what you said outside the funeral. No mother would ever say that about a child, let alone one who had recently died.'

'James Willikar didn't die... he killed himself. There is a difference, a vast difference, and it is a sin in the eyes of the Lord.'

'You're not God, despite what you may believe. You're nothing but a human, with human vulnerabilities. Just like James, and yet you don't afford him the same respect you demand for yourself. And the things you said about Wendy. Devil's harlot, you called her. A troubled, grieving young girl.'

'A girl who no doubt fornicated with that boy, fired by the devil's music and lit by the devil's fire.'

Hines looked up. 'I've heard that before. Devil's fire.'

'The devil's accessories: black candles, and the loud, heavy music that calls out to the devil himself.'

'You mean heavy metal?' Manby asked. The phone on his desk began to ring. 'It's music, not my taste exactly, but it's just music.'

He lifted the receiver. 'DI Manby...'

'Through which the devil commands,' Catherine said, turning to Hines. 'And the tainted obey. Mark my words, this won't end well until all such evil is wiped from the face of the earth, and we will not stop in bringing the Lord's word to those who would not listen.'

'Are you even hearing yourself?' Hines said. '"Wiped from the face of the earth!" – what the hell are you on? You might not be smoking cigarettes, but you're surely smoking something.'

Manby looked up at Hines. His eyes had turned hard, and as soon as she saw them, she knew what was coming. A cold pit swallowed her anger, quelling it instantly.

'Okay,' he said, his voice dropping in tone. 'We'll get Danes and his team organised and on their way.' He listened a moment longer then hung up.

'Well, I guess you were right about how this would end.'

He stood up and stubbed out yet another cigarette.

'They found Wendy Jackson.'

CHAPTER
FORTY-FOUR

The two boys had also had the idea of bunking off school. Dropped off at North Ossett by their dad, they had waited for his car to leave the grounds before heading down to the playing fields behind the school.

From there they had snuck through the outer fence and onto Gawthorpe Lane, a single dirt road that ran all the way from the bottom of Gawthorpe to Outwood. Not much more than a car width wide, the lane was used by the local farmers in the area to get to the numerous fields that lay either side of the track. A couple of fields had horses, and the boys avoided these, not wanting to get a kick or worse.

Their destination was the thick woods known locally as Frampton's Folly about halfway down Gawthorpe Lane. A favourite haunt of the older children, it was used for playing games of gang war, sneaking illicit smokes or indulging in heavy petting sessions that resulted in ruined reputations for all concerned.

Running towards the woods before anyone could see them, they had felt the grass soak through their trousers and trainers, the grass still sodden from the morning's dew. They had ducked when they heard a car's engine start, worried one of the local farmers would catch them. The last time it had happened, the kids involved had been dragged in front of the entire school to be made an example of. Their parents had also been forced to pay a fine for trespassing.

Ignoring the PRIVATE LAND sign that had been nailed to a tree, the two boys ducked inside the woods.

They had got about ten feet inside the protective shadow of the trees when they found Wendy Jackson. At first they thought she was messing with them, swaying side to side like a ghost in an effort to scare them.

It was only when they moved closer that they realised that Wendy had, indeed, scared them after all.

Together, they ran screaming from the woods all the way back to the school.

CHAPTER
FORTY-FIVE

Within half an hour of the boys running back into the school grounds and alerting everyone to what they had found, Louise and Karla stood in Frampton's Folly, watching as uniformed police officers strung tape between the trees, creating a strong protective cordon around Wendy Jackson.

She was hanging from the twisted lower limb of a tree, her arms limp at her sides, the gentle sway of her body as the wind rocked her a ghoulish hypnotic motion that made Louise's stomach lurch. She looked across at Karla; her face was pale, a mirror of her own, she suspected. Her eyes were captivated by the girl, locked on the way she hung, head cocked to one side at an unnatural angle. Her tongue, swollen and purple, pushed between her lips, twisting her face into a tortured mask.

Karla turned away and took in several deep breaths.

Louise placed her hands on Karla's shoulders as her friend bent over and retched, dry heaves that echoed through the stillness of the wood. An officer looked over, saw what was happening and quickly turned away.

'Take it slow and easy,' Louise said, remembering the first time she had seen a dead body. Back in Manchester on the bank of the River Irwell in the city centre, the body of a young woman had been found. Stabbed over twenty times in the chest and head, it had taken Louise a moment to understand the geography of the face. Added to that was the complication that animals appeared to have got to her before she had been found, and several chunks of flesh were missing from her arms and legs. It was only later during the post-mortem that they had realised that the bites had been made by a human, not an animal.

Louise hadn't slept that night.

Karla stood up and let out one long breath. 'I'm okay,' she said, looking anything but. 'It's just that...'

She doubled over once again; this time unable to stop herself from being sick. Luckily, they stood well outside the cordon, so Louise knew there was no danger of contaminating the crime scene. She still made a note to mention it to Danes when he got there.

Immediately she hated herself for thinking in such a clinical fashion; her friend, her lover was struggling with the horrific reality of the situation and here she was thinking in cold, hard police logic.

Because that's my job.

She could see the police uniforms finishing with the tape and could hear the approaching car engines; Peter Danes and his SOCO team, no doubt. The turbulent chaos of a police investigation was about to begin again. A young girl had died in the most tragic of ways, alone and probably scared in the woods. Was this another suicide, like James, like her boyfriend, or was this something more? Something much more sinister?

Already she had her doubts; she would need to get closer before she could make any serious determinations, but first she had to deal with Karla.

'I'm sending you home,' Louise said. 'This is going to get treated like a crime scene until I know different and so I can't have you here.'

Karla was already nodding. Louise could see the relief flood her eyes and she felt a pang of jealousy; Karla could escape the horror while Louise would have to immerse herself in it once more. But this wasn't what Karla was trained for, and it wasn't something that Louise wanted her to experience. She didn't want her to see how close Louise had to get to the girl in order to examine her; she didn't want Karla flinching under her touch, knowing those same hands had lifted the girl's head, or touched her dead skin.

It was one thing to know that the person you loved dealt with such terrible things; it was another thing entirely to watch them do it. Louise had scrubbed her skin almost raw following the discovery of the woman on the Irwell, not wanting to feel the cold, wet slickness of dead flesh on her. Her mind had tricked her into that awful sensation at least once a day for the next six months. Eventually she'd hardened to it; working the streets of Manchester in the early eighties there were a lot of bodies to be found.

'Take one of the cars back up to the school and then go home.'

'I'll walk,' Karla said. 'The air will be good for me. Are you going to be okay?'

'I'll be fine,' Louise said, watching as Peter Danes and Elizabeth Hines walked towards them. She leaned forward and gave Karla a quick peck on the cheek. Some of the colour came back into Karla's cheeks and a brief smile warmed her lips.

'What was that for?' Karla asked.

Louise smiled. 'You know why.'

'Afternoon all,' Danes said. He was wearing a protective plastic suit, the hood hanging down his back. In one hand he carried a metal suitcase, in the other a bundle of evidence bags. 'Not the result you wanted, I'm guessing.'

'Far from it,' Louise said. 'You got a spare suit in that case?'

Hines handed over the folded suit she had been carrying. 'Got it right here for you. Hi, Ms Hayes. There's a car waiting to take you back up to the school. DI Manby will meet you there and a uniform will take a statement from you.'

Karla looked worried. 'Why do I need to make a statement?'

Louise touched Karla's shoulder, a tentative touch to reassure. Karla leaned into it. 'We were both close by, Karla, then the first down here. They'll want to know what we each saw and if we touched anything. It's standard practice. Nothing to worry about.'

'Oh. Okay.'

Louise was worried that Karla was starting to suffer from shock, but Hines seemed to have that covered as well. 'Make sure you grab a tea when you get there. Plenty of sugar. For the shock, okay?'

Karla mumbled something in reply. Louise looked beyond her and waved a uniform forward. 'I need you to drive Karla back to the school.'

'I'll walk,' Karla said again, but if she could walk all the way back to the school without collapsing, then Louise was the Queen of Egypt.

'You'll get driven and be thankful,' Louise said. She gave her another kiss on the cheek. 'We'll talk later.'

Karla nodded and allowed herself to be led away. Louise watched until she had got in the car and it had left.

Slowly she started to unfold the plastic suit. Hines had already put hers on. Danes readied his camera. If he had seen her kiss Karla he didn't say anything.

'Let's take a look, shall we?' he said.

The first thing Louise noticed was that Wendy wasn't hanging by a rope. She had one arm of her jacket looped around the tree branch, tied off in three thick knots. The other coat arm was wrapped around her neck.

'It looks like she then raised her legs, putting all her weight on her neck,' Danes said as he snapped off three quick pictures. 'It would have been slow.'

'And extremely painful,' Hines said. She was standing behind Wendy, slowly walking around the dead girl to look at her from as many different angles as she could. 'How could she do that?' she asked.

'She just couldn't take it any more, I guess,' Danes replied.

'No. That's not what I meant. How could she just raise her legs and keep them raised long enough to... you know.'

Louise was nodding. 'I was thinking the same thing. After a time, the fight and flight response would kick in. Her brain would be telling her to do whatever she could to stay alive.'

'And all she had to do was put her feet down. Okay, she might not have been standing with her feet fully level on the ground, but her toes would be able to take some of the weight,' Danes said. 'Would that have been enough so that she'd be able to breathe, though?'

Louise was staring at the branch to which the coat arm was tied. 'There's something definitely not right about this. How did she tie that off?'

Hines moved closer to the tree. 'Knot looks like a basic one. Not a slipknot. There's no marks I can see on the tree that indicate she used it to climb up, either.'

'So how did she get up there?' Louise asked, the frustration in her voice. 'Peter, can you get pictures of all around here?' she said, indicating the ground directly beneath the tree and its surroundings with a sweep of her arm.

'Not a problem,' he replied, moving to one side as three suited SOCO members came up. They held a body stretcher between them. Danes gave a nod of recognition, then indicated the body. 'All photos of the body have been taken, Stuart, so she's ready to be taken down. I just need to photograph the ground.'

'There,' Louise said suddenly, pointing at an area just in front of and to the side of the tree limb Wendy had been hanging from. 'Right there.'

. . .

Hines, Louise and Danes all hunched together in a crude circle, backs bent, knees bent so they could look at the four indentations in the ground. Spaced equally apart, the grass had been crushed into four shallow wells, each one four inches long, three inches wide and with a depth between one and two inches depending on the thickness of the grass.

'What are you thinking?' Hines asked.

'Ladder. Has to be,' Danes said. He had measured the spacing between the marks left to right, front to back and even diagonally. 'Big one as well, I'd say, judging by the measurements.'

'Could it be anything else?' Louise asked.

'Don't think so,' Danes replied. 'Looks like ladders to me, but I can get into more detail when I examine the photos we've taken close up. I could take plaster moulds, if you want? I doubt I can get anything much from them though – no idea of when they were initially made, that sort of thing.'

Louise stood up and cracked her back. 'Please. Best to cover everything, don't you think?'

Danes shrugged. 'No problem, but I'm positive it's just ladders. Hard rubber feet, no major markings usually unless they've been damaged. It's not like you'll get an impression like that of a car tyre or shoe sole. Worth a shot though.'

Hines let out a laugh. 'Know a lot about ladders do you? Use them for quick escapes from married women's bedrooms, do you?'

'Once or twice,' he replied.

Louise saw the look that passed between them. The last thing they needed right now were those sorts of complications. Or rumours.

'If she used a ladder though,' Hines asked, 'then where the hell is it?'

'More importantly,' Louise said grimly, 'who the fuck took it?'

. . .

Solemnly, the three forensic officers began the process of removing the makeshift noose from around Wendy's neck so they could lower her to the ground and put her on the stretcher to be transported to the mortuary for autopsy.

As they began to work, Louise turned away, ducking beneath the tape, and headed towards the nearest car. Hines was quickly behind her, shrugging out of the plastic suit as she went.

'What next?' Hines asked as she kicked herself free from the suit. Louise sighed, her expression cold and resigned.

'No,' Hines said.

''Fraid so,' Louise replied, opening the car door.

'I fucking hate door-knocks,' Hines said, starting the car.

CHAPTER
FORTY-SIX

The Jackson house was in a better part of Broadowler estate, if that description could ever be possible or accurate. The garden wasn't as unkempt as some of the others they had driven past, the gates still intact and not just broken boards of wood or rusted metal. Proper curtains hung in the window, something beige with a subtle pattern hidden in the fabric, and not a Union Jack beach towel. As always whenever something happened on Broadowler, a small crowd had gathered, but they weren't as intimidating as the group Louise had encountered the first time she had come to the estate. There was no animosity, no anger. No caged violence waiting to be let free, just the concern of friends and neighbours.

Detective Tom Bailey answered the door, pulling it open in such a way that it didn't jangle the silver bell hanging down above it. They could tell immediately by his face that he had something bad to tell them. Louise could also hear the crying coming from within the house, so she knew immediately what had happened.

'Who told them?'

'One of the daughter's friends' parents phoned them a few

minutes ago. Mrs Jackson answered it before I could stop her,' Bailey said. 'Sorry.'

'Not your fault, Tom,' Louise said.

She gave her feet a good wipe on the doormat and stepped fully inside. Once Hines had done the same, Bailey shut the door. This time he forgot about the chime, and it tinkled merrily above them, a surreal sign of Christmas' stealthy approach. With all that had happened in the days following the discovery of James in the graveyard of Holy Trinity Church, Christmas was the last thing anyone was thinking about. Louise certainly hadn't been thinking about it; was Karla coming to hers? Was she going to her aunt's? Were they *both* going to her aunt's, and how would that work? Did Karla even celebrate Christmas?

Not that there would be any celebration in the Jackson household this year. Probably not for many a year to come, Louise thought as she was led into the living room. There was a Christmas tree, she noted, tucked away in the corner of the room and forgotten about. No presents beneath the tree yet; it was only the nineteenth, Louise reminded herself, but it did seem that people got their decorations out earlier each year.

Mrs Jackson sat in a high-backed chair, her face buried into a handkerchief. Muffled sobs broke free, while behind her Mr Jackson slowly rubbed her back. He looked up, the tears in his eyes turning them watery. To the side, sitting on a sofa and nibbling on a biscuit, was Shirley Hanson. She gave Louise a nod but stayed quiet.

Louise was glad Shirley was already there. It would make their jobs pass a little easier, and a lot faster; something that would be best for all.

'I am so sorry,' Louise began. She knelt before Mrs Jackson and placed a hand over hers, still clutching the hankie. Mrs Jackson pulled her hand away.

Louise stood and turned to Shirley.

'Will you be staying with them?' She knew the answer but needed to say something, anything to fill the silence of the room.

'All the way,' Shirley replied with a gentle smile.

All the way.

Louise knew what that meant, though she was sure the Jacksons weren't aware. All the way – from discovery, through identification, collection of personal items and the worst, the post-mortem. That was already scheduled for tomorrow, with the initial findings due Wednesday morning. Manby had radioed that Doctor Wilkinson had been informed and would again be carrying out any potential inquest. Manby had been told about the marks beneath the tree and he was cautiously concerned, just as Louise was. This wasn't like the Willikar suicide; there was evidence here that a second party was possibly involved. But until they had more evidence, they would outwardly proceed as though this was just another suicide.

Just another suicide... was there ever such a thing?

Louise nodded her understanding and silently mouthed *thank you* back to Shirley.

'Louise?'

She turned to see Bailey in the doorway. He nodded in the direction of the hallway. 'Can I have a quick chat?'

'Of course,' she replied. 'Beth, could you stay with the Jacksons? See if there is anything they need?'

'No problem,' Hines said. She was looking brighter than she had done, and Louise suspected that she was still thankful she hadn't had to break the terrible news to another set of parents.

Louise smiled and slipped out of the room into the hallway.

Bailey had moved to the kitchen, where he stood taking a crafty cigarette at the back door while he waited for Louise to come to him. The cold chill of the day crept in through the open door and Louise shivered as she came into the kitchen.

'Shut the door and put that out, will you?' she said. 'It's cold as the Arctic in here.'

He stubbed the cigarette out on the outside wall and flicked the nub into the wet gutter, gave his feet a stamp to get rid of any dirt then came inside. The door clicked shut. The only sound they could hear now was the low drone of voices coming from the living room. It sounded like Shirley was talking, her soothing words encased in the strong twang of her Yorkshire accent.

Louise picked a glass from a nearby cabinet and ran the cold tap. Her throat was starting to prickle. She hoped she wasn't coming down with something less than a week before Christmas. The water soothed her throat as she drank.

While she did so, Bailey brought a green and purple notebook from his coat pocket and placed it on the kitchen table between them.

'What's that?' Louise asked. She rinsed the glass and put it back in the cabinet before picking up the book. 'This belonged to Wendy?'

He nodded. 'I marked the page.'

He pulled a chair out and sat down as Louise thumbed through the pages. Finally she came to the one he'd marked. A King of Hearts playing card, with a naked woman as the image, had been folded between two pages. She handed the card back with a raised eye that drew a blush from the other officer. Bailey slipped the card into a pocket and nodded to the book.

'Read it.'

She did.

I am so sorry. I know this isn't what you would want, but it is the only thing I can think to do. I just can't go on any more. Not like this, not without James. I love him. I know Mum doesn't think I know anything about love, but I do. I'm sorry Mum, but I do. What else could it be? Every thought I have is of him, everywhere I look I see him and what he would have seen.

I love him and can't believe he is gone.

We talked a lot before he died. We talked every day, because that was where our strength lay. Strength against the others. Against her. She was always in our faces no matter where we went. When we were at the

*park she'd come up and start shouting at us, calling us awful things.
Saying we were evil.*

*All we were doing was playing games and listening to music. But she
said it was the devil tempting us, and we were now his servants and
should be ashamed of ourselves. Crazy shit. Sorry Mum, I know you
don't like it when I swear, but I can't think of any other way of
saying it.*

*That was when we went to the church club. We thought we'd get away
from her there, but she still came. Got into the group through the others
and still attacked us. James didn't really see it, not at first, and then
when he did he chose to ignore it as best as he could.
And we know how well that went.*

And now I can't do it any more. I need for things to change.

*And I am so sorry for James. It wasn't fair what happened, and I wasn't
strong enough to help him.*

I can't do this any more. I have to make this right.

'Suicide note if I've ever read one,' Bailey said. 'And the fact
she was in Frampton's Folly, well, that seals it for me.'

Louise closed the book. 'What's so special about Frampton's
Folly?'

Bailey smiled. 'You don't know the story? I thought you were
raised here?'

'I was, but my aunt and uncle didn't exactly deal with the
usual local gossip. She was a teacher; he was an accountant. They
dealt with facts, not fiction, especially not the kind that you're on
about. So, what about the wood?'

Bailey ran his hand through his hair and gave a scratch to an
itch at his neck. He wore a long black coat and she could see
flecks of dandruff along the collar line and shoulders. Louise

thought about saying something but didn't want to embarrass the man.

'Frampton's Folly was originally called Frungal's Wood. No idea why, just that was the name. But back in the thirties the Frampton brothers, Chris and Daniel, decided that the wood was the perfect place to go and kill themselves. Strung themselves up, just like poor Miss Jackson. They were found three days later by a walker, all puffed up and weather ravaged. Pretty gruesome stuff, as the story goes. Ever since, the wood has been called Frampton's Folly.'

'Why's that?'

'Well,' Bailey said, all conspiratorial, leaning forward and lowering his voice, 'the story goes that Chris and Daniel both knew a young lass by the name of Sheila Daniels. And that young lass was pregnant.'

'And both lads had had sex with her, right?'

'On the regular,' Bailey said with a wink. 'But now here she was, threatening them both, because she didn't know which was the father, and she wanted one of them to do right by her and the child.'

'And because they didn't know which was the father, they decided to kill themselves? That seems a bit of a stretch.'

'The Daniel family ran Ossett, Horbury and Gawthorpe back in the day. Think a more violent version of the Krays and you're about there. I wouldn't be surprised if the Daniels "helped" them.'

'They were killed?'

'I think these days it's called "assisted suicide". Both are just as illegal as each other, but one is harder to prove than the other. Anyway, ever since then, the woods became known as Frampton's Folly. And the funny thing—'

'Nothing about this is funny,' Louise said.

'—turns out she wasn't pregnant at all. They killed themselves over nothing.'

Louise sat for a moment. 'There's a lot of that going round.'

CHAPTER
FORTY-SEVEN

WEDNESDAY, 21ST

Tuesday disappeared beneath paperwork and routine as it saw both Louise and Hines in court, giving testimony on cases they had closed a few months back. As was frustratingly usual, the bureaucratic wheels of law turned slowly but inextricably forwards towards justice. The Crown Prosecutors put together their arguments built from the ground up as a result of all the work already put in by officers and detectives like Louise and Hines. By then they had moved on, but when they were called on to provide their evidence in Court they were more than ready.

It was a wicked juggling act to master, finding the balance between active and dormant cases, making sure chains of evidence were kept, maintained and ready to go as soon as the word came down that a case was ready to be tried. In Louise's case it was a violent burglary charge; for Hines, her first ever time giving evidence in court, it was a drug-related theft. Luckily both cases were at Wakefield Crown Court and so the pair had travelled together. Louise's case was delayed and so she nipped in to lend some support to Hines. She needn't have worried;

Hines delivered her evidence clearly and confidently, answering both Prosecution and Defence questions deftly.

When Wednesday arrived, both detectives were feeling tired. The double suicides of James Willikar and Wendy Jackson weighed heavily on everyone, sapping all the atmosphere from a snappy Shop full of seasonal banter and excited hopes for the Christmas holiday to come. They would all be working across Christmas in one way or another; the shifts had been drawn at random, so it was fair, although DI Manby had tweaked them a little further, making sure he was in on most days. It was something he did every year, another reason why his wife had him in the doghouse.

It was the same with Sergeant Harolds; thirty years of working special days had taken their toll. It was only a matter of time now before the retirement paperwork came in; everyone knew it. Even Louise, who kept out of such office politics. Apparently the only person who didn't know was Harolds himself.

Louise was just finishing off yet another requisition form when Harolds came up. He was wearing a dirty Santa hat, the white fur now nothing more than grey, threadbare strands that dangled in front of his face like a ferret's tail.

'You know that came in with the drunk found kipping on the steps of the Town Hall last night, right?' she said. 'It stank of piss then and if anything, smells worse now.'

'Ho, ho, ho,' Harolds said, then handed her a slip of paper. 'Just had a call from a shop in Horbury.'

'Are you hinting for a pressie? How about some deodorant?'

'Funny bugger, no. They called to say there's a group of people stopping customers coming in their shop. Stood outside blocking the door, chanting and waving banners around.'

A weight settled on Louise, and she let out a heavy sigh. *Why can't they just leave alone? What the hell good is this?*

'What's up?'

Hines was coming back to their desks carrying two mugs of fresh tea. She lifted one arm and the packet of Jammie Dodgers she'd had nestled there fell on to the desk with a pleasing thud.

Louise was already reaching for her coat with one hand, the other taking the slip from Harolds. 'Please don't say it's who I think it is.'

'Yep,' Harolds said with a grin. He picked up the biscuits and started tearing the packet open. 'Your good friend, Catherine Hallum.'

'Oh, for fuck's sake!' Hines said, snatching the biscuits back from Harolds before he could steal them all. 'What's that bitch gone and done now?'

There were a dozen people standing outside the Green Dragon in Horbury, and Louise could tell straight away that they weren't waiting to buy something. The shop took centre spot on a small side street, nestled comfortably between a children's clothes shop called Ladybirds and a cobblers, one of the last few remaining in the area.

They stood in front of the shop, spread evenly either side of the doorway, a banner held between them blocking all access to the shop. Through the window Louise could see a few people inside, staring out with worried expressions. One of them was the owner, a pleasant chap called Gary, whom Louise had spoken to previously when she was looking for the shop that sold the black candles.

The others were either customers or family. With only four days left till Christmas and the schools now broken up, last minute presents would be getting picked, and by the looks of it, the Green Dragon was a popular place to get them.

DESTROY THE DEVIL'S DOMAIN! was written across the banner in thick red letters. It was against a bright blue backdrop, the writing jarring to look at. Again, the sign of the Church of Divine Light was in the top corner. Beneath that, in smaller white letters was written SOME RISE BY SIN AND SOME BY VIRTUE FALL.

'I recognise that one,' Hines said. 'Shakespeare.'

Louise looked at her friend. 'Really?'

'I read, you know,' Hines said. They were walking slowly towards the shop and the crowd, having parked the car further up the street. It was a small street, barely a car's width, and they didn't want to add to the congestion.

'I never said you didn't, but I thought it would be more Jackie Collins than Shakespeare. What are those idiots doing?'

Two of the protesters had lifted cartons of eggs from the bags at their feet. Before Louise or Hines could say anything, they started to throw them at the window. Loud jeers broke out as the eggs shattered on the window, their yellow yolks smearing thickly across the glass.

'Are you kidding me?' Hines said as the two detectives started to run towards the commotion. 'Pack that in!' she yelled when they got to the shop. 'Oi, you... down. Now!'

Hines grabbed the arm of the man about to throw the next egg. He wore a thin denim jacket and Louise winced as she heard the rip of fabric and the man's startled yell. The egg he had been holding fell to the floor where it shattered with a thick, wet *slop*!

'Jesus... that stinks!'

Hines took several steps back and gulped in a haggard rasp of air. Turning to the side, one hand braced against the wall of the cobbler's, she threw up.

The crowd let out a collective gasp and also took a few steps back. Louise caught that momentum and ushered them away, her arms outstretched as she slowly edged forward, pushing them back until they had cleared the entrance to the shop.

'Right. No one moves from there. Do I make myself clear?' She turned to Hines, who was still clutched over, spitting out onto the pavement. 'You okay, Beth?'

Rather than answer, Hines raised a hand and gave the thumbs up. Louise started to smile, but a clipped, arrogant voice tore through her head with the venom of a snake and twice the vindictiveness.

'You can't stop us voicing our anger against those that feed the beast,' Catherine Hallum said. She stood just behind the banner, her hair hidden beneath yet another wide-brimmed gaudy hat. She looked totally out of place, but also extremely comfortable at the same time.

'Give me a break,' Louise hissed beneath her breath before turning to Catherine. 'Mrs Hallum; I wonder if we could talk privately over here for a moment?' Louise gestured to where she was standing, just in front of the Green Dragon's main window. Peering out from within were a cluster of scared faces; all had some semblance of shock plastered to them. Louise gave them a nod before returning her attention to Catherine, the leader of the protest.

She wore a smug expression as she stepped from behind the banner, giving her friends and followers gentle pats to their shoulder as she walked past. 'Stand firm,' she said to each. 'The Lord's strength is your own.'

Hines came to stand next to Louise. Her face was pale but there was a determination in her eyes that Louise found pleasantly reassuring. 'You all right?' she asked.

Hines nodded. 'That fucking egg was fucking disgusting. I'm surprised a rotted chicken didn't tumble out of it, that thing was so long past its date. Caught me off guard, is all. I'm good.'

Louise nodded.

'And what can I do for you, Mrs Miller?' Catherine Hallum asked from behind her painted arrogance.

You can fuck right off, for a start.

'Firstly, it is Detective Constable Miller, Mrs Hallum. And I'm sure you remember Detective Constable Hines from the other day?'

Hines greeted her by spitting a great glob of phlegm into the gutter. 'Bad reaction to a bad egg,' she said in answer to Catherine's horrified gasp. 'Hi, Catherine. Good to see you again.'

'We have a perfectly legitimate right to be here considering the circumstances,' Catherine said, trying her best to regain her composure. Hines had rattled her, Louise could see that.

'And what would those circumstances be, exactly?' Hines asked. 'Far as we can see, this place had nothing to do with the tragic events of the last couple of weeks.'

'Of course, you wouldn't see; you're not of the faith,' Catherine said. Her lips pursed into a grin that gave her the appearance of a mannequin, the smile painted on to a featureless form. 'But luckily I see. We see,' she added, sweeping her arm to indicate those few people who stood with her. Louise had noted that several had wandered off now the police had arrived, leaving only the truly devout.

Louise had seen worse cults during her time in Manchester and had heard, of course, about the Jesus Army. That was her fear; that the Jesus Army was recruiting here in West Yorkshire, and more than likely, here in Ossett, under the guise of the Church of Divine Light. They ticked all the right – or more accurately, wrong – boxes. Following strict rules banning all the usual trappings of modern life: sweets, toys, TV and film. All the things Catherine was decrying in her little protests.

'And before you ask, this time we have a permit to protest.'

Catherine reached into her bag and brought out an envelope, which she gladly thrust towards Louise. 'Signed by the Chief Constable himself,' she added with another twisted grin.

Louise read through it with a heavy heart. All above board.

'But that doesn't lend itself to damaging property, so rein it in or I'll be taking you all to the cells. And this time your buddy won't be able to help you.'

Catherine smiled coldly. 'If you are referring to the unfortunate throwing of eggs, which so seems to have upset the constitution of your little friend, then you will notice that those individuals are no longer here. They were not part of our protest, and I would like to see you prove that they were. In fact, here is the sign-up sheet for our members, and if you care to speak to them all, you will see that everyone is present. And not one of them has any eggs, fresh or otherwise, on their person.'

Fuck.

Louise looked at Hines, who shrugged.

'Fine. But I want you over there and don't be blocking the pavement. That's a hazard, forcing other pedestrians onto the road to make their way around you, and will violate the conditions of your permit. Which I'm keeping hold of.'

'Is that it?' Hines asked, her anger plainly visible. 'We're not moving them on?'

'Can't. This is all legal. But we can go inside and see what the owner wants to do. If he fears things could get violent then we might be able to have the permit quashed. Right, *Catherine*... back over there and keep your lot under control.'

The sly smile on Catherine's face told Louise that this was far from over.

They had been inside the shop talking with the owners for less than five minutes when the brick came crashing through the window. With the doorway free for people to come in and out, they had decided it would be better to let them have their little protest and hopefully it would all be over before the afternoon rush came in.

There was a loud thud and the window spiderwebbed with fractures when the first brick hit. When the second was thrown, it crashed through, sending glass shards flying through the air. Louise and Hines were protected somewhat as they were standing behind a tall bookcase filled with Dungeons & Dragons books, but the owner took a shard of glass to the face.

Ten minutes later, Catherine Hallum and six members of the Church of Divine Light were arrested and placed under caution.

CHAPTER
FORTY-EIGHT

Catherine Hallum had asked to call her solicitor almost immediately upon their arrival back at Prospect Road station. Detective Sergeant Harolds had booked her in along with the other members of the protest, and while they waited for the solicitor to arrive, both detectives went to see their DI.

Manby sat behind his desk; once again his ear was glowing red pressed beneath the phone as the tinny voice of the Chief Constable could be heard. He indicated the chairs and they sat.

'Will do, Chief Constable,' Manby said, then hung up. He stared at them, the silence of the room broken only by the distant ringing of the main door bell. Finally, he looked down at the sheet of paper Harolds had dropped on his desk just as the Chief had phoned.

'Damage to private property. Endangerment of life. Assault and battery. Two charges of assault against a police officer, and one case of public nudity.' He looked up. 'Public nudity?'

'One of the protesters thought it would be funny if they mooned the uniforms as they tried to get them into the van.'

Manby started to leaf through the arrest sheets. 'And which idiot was that? I'm recognising some of these names: Davies, Hillardson, Clemens. Is that Dave Clemens, the butcher?'

'The very same, but he's not the one who mooned.'

'Who was it then?' Manby asked.

Hines shook her head, still not believing what she'd seen. Louise raised her eyebrows and sighed.

'It was only Catherine bloody Hallum.'

There was a knock at the door to Interview Room 3 and Harolds poked his head in. Louise and Hines were sitting with their backs to the door, and they didn't bother turning round. Catherine looked up from the desk where she'd been signing the belongings sheet that declared everything she had had on her person when she was arrested. Rather than sign when Harolds had booked her in, she wanted to read over it. Louise's patience was razor thin as it was, so Hines had said that was okay and they'd finish it in the room.

'Solicitor's here,' Harolds said, stepping aside and pushing the door open further. 'Mr Daniel McKensie.'

A tall man in a very expensive looking suit stepped inside. His hair was long and greasy, and he swished beside the desk leaving a trace of cologne behind him.

Louise looked up.

Hines stared in disbelief. 'The same...?'Louise nodded. 'We have something of yours,' Hines said, standing up. 'Be right back.'

She left the room, leaving a perplexed looking Catherine staring daggers at her solicitor. McKensie seemed unconcerned, simply taking a seat beside his client and opening his briefcase. He shuffled a few pages around, took out a pad of paper and a pen and put the briefcase on the floor beside him.

'Have they told you your rights?' he asked. Catherine nodded. 'And have they asked you any questions?'

'We have not, Mr McKensie,' Louise answered before Catherine could say anything. 'Your client is being charged with—'

'I have seen the supposed offences and they are laughable,' he said. 'Regardless, I am instructing you to release my client into my care, pending your full investigation and prior to any further action being brought before the court.'

'She threw a brick through the window of the Green Dragon, injuring one person and threatening the lives of several others, including myself and DC Hines.'

'Mrs Hallum argues that it was not her that threw the object but one of the agitators who had joined their legitimate and peaceful protest of an establishment that has been connected to dubious dealings that have contributed to the environment in which several suspicious deaths have taken place. A sad state of affairs though it is, tragic for the families involved, my client has a legitimate right to protest against any and all injustices she sees within her society.'

'Her society?' Louise asked, but if McKensie had heard her, he gave no sign. He put down his pen after making no notes whatsoever and picked up his briefcase once again.

'There are those who disagree with my client and would see harm come to her reputation. That is why they threw eggs at the shop, causing the police to be called, and when you arrived, falling into their little, well-devised trap, they escalated and threw the brick. No one in the legitimate protest – of whom you have all the names and addresses, as my client ensured that everyone who was taking part was recorded – no one in the legitimate protest saw my client throw anything other than a few harsh words when you and your colleague rolled up.'

'She lifted her dress and showed off, well... everything,' Louise said.

'Another legitimate form of protest, I gather. Look, Louise... Can I call you Louise?' Her stony gaze was answer enough. McKensie coughed, ran a hand through his greasy hair, and continued as if nothing had happened, switching tone as easily as flicking a light switch. 'Detective Miller. We both know this isn't going to go anywhere. You have no proof that Mrs Hallum threw the brick, no corroborating witness to say as such, and over a dozen witnesses who say that it was, in fact, a young boy who threw the brick.'

He turned to Catherine, who had stayed silent the entire time, a feat Louise thought must have taken the woman all the willpower in the world to achieve.

'We can leave now,' he said. His voice was slick and smooth, like oil on water. He was as slippery a snake as Catherine was; no wonder he used the services of someone like Helen Williams. 'I will of course make my client available should you need to talk to her again, but for now, as you won't be charging her with anything considering the circumstances and your lack of evidence, please make my client's possessions available to her.'

Louise watched as Catherine signed the paperwork to get her items back from Sergeant Harolds. She leaned against the wall further down the corridor, arms folded across her chest, the angry fire of disappointment burning through her body. McKensie stood beside Catherine, watching over her shoulder as she checked everything that Harolds handed back. They passed whispered conversation between them as well as occasional looks back at the detective watching them.

Louise waved, then turned as Hines came downstairs from the lab above.

'Got it,' she said, walking past Louise, who pushed herself off the wall and followed.

'Mr McKensie,' Hines called out. 'A word.'

The solicitor gave Hines a look that was pure sex. He steamed confidence through every pore, his blue eyes catching the dull light that fell from the station's ceiling and somehow transforming it into a dazzling glow.

'Of course, my dear,' he oozed. Hines appeared to shiver inwardly as she held out an evidence bag containing the wallet.

'Have you seen this before?' she asked.

'I have been looking everywhere for that,' he said, reaching out. Hines pulled the bag back before his fingers with their neatly cut nails could take hold.

'I just bet you have,' she replied. 'We've tried getting in touch with you for several days now. Left several messages for you at home.'

'I live with no one but my own good self,' he purred. 'Unless of course you mean my scatter-brained neighbour Mrs Aldwin? That good woman would forget her own name if it wasn't on the horrendous amount of post she gets every day. I haven't seen her since last week. I've been away... with work.'

'And where was that?' Louise asked. She had come up behind Hines and took the bag from her. 'This wallet looks expensive. If I'd lost something expensive like this, I'd have reported it. Did you?'

'Did I what?' he asked. His tone had changed. It had dropped. The sparkle had gone from his eyes as well, dulled like the rest of his demeanour. His shoulders had tensed, and Louise could see a nerve begin to blink in his jaw.

'Did you report it stolen?'

Hines nodded. 'You were in the Carpenters pub Saturday night, weren't you? Maybe you lost it there.' She turned back to Louise. 'Joe never said anything about anyone asking about a wallet.'

'Strange that.'

'Can I have my wallet back?'

The question was clipped. Forced. Angry.

'Are they done with it?' Louise asked Hines, who nodded.

'All done. Good results as well. Nice and clear. Enough for twelve points against a second print.'

McKensie looked between the two as Louise reached into the evidence bag and pulled the wallet out. 'All done? What does that mean? And what is this all over it?'

'I'm shocked,' Louise said, holding the wallet out. 'I thought someone with your experience, you know, being a solicitor and all, would recognise fingerprint dust. Your wallet is dark leather, so the lab used the white powder. They've brushed most of it off, but you might need to give it another pass. Sorry about that.'

Again, he reached for it, but Louise pulled it back before he could take it.

'Do you mind?' he said.

'I'm thinking,' Louise said. 'How do we know this is your wallet?'

'Could be anyone's,' Hines said. 'How much was in it?'

McKensie shrugged. 'I don't know. Maybe a hundred.'

Hines let out a whistle. 'A hundred. Wow. Would it surprise you that there was nothing in it, other than a library ticket and a driving licence?'

'My driving licence. My library ticket.'

'And you can confirm your address?'

'Ladies...'

At the head of the corridor, DI Manby stood watching. 'Give the man his wallet.'

Reluctantly, Louise handed it over.

Without looking, McKensie put it in his pocket.

'I would like a word if you don't mind, Inspector,' McKensie said.

Manby sighed but told Harolds to take McKensie to his office. McKensie asked if Catherine could come with him; Louise knew what was coming next but she didn't care.

Hines turned to Louise, a huge grin across her face. 'That was fun,' she said, then dropped the smile as Manby came up to them.

'What the hell was that all about?' he demanded. 'My arse is still stinging from having the Chief's foot up it right up to the ankle. What do you think will happen when his solicitor friend tells him about your petty antics?'

'You'll get the knee?' Louise asked. Hines couldn't help laughing. 'Seriously, Bill. The man is a fucking prick. Helen

Williams is missing and I'm pretty sure he knows something about it.'

'McKensie? You've got to be kidding. He golfs with the Chief. Runs a very successful practice in Leeds. Comes from the McKensie family, who have practised law for the last two hundred years.'

'And now he has Catherine Hallum as a client. How the hell can she afford someone like that?'

'Not our concern. And now I'm going to have to listen to that officious prick put in a formal complaint about you two, one that is probably linked with yet another from the Hallum woman. The Chief is not going to like that. I'll want to see you two after. Shit travels downhill and there's an avalanche heading your way.'

That said, Manby stormed off, slamming the door into the pen so hard the frosted glass in the centre quivered.

CHAPTER
FORTY-NINE

Louise and Hines followed Manby into the pen, being more careful to close the door than their boss had. The door to his office was closed but they could hear the dull murmur of voices as Daniel McKensie and Catherine Hallum complained.

Dropping into her seat, Louise pulled open a drawer and took out a Mars chocolate bar. Two swift tears and the wrapper was off, and half was in her mouth. The other she held out to Hines.

'No thanks,' she said. 'I'm still tasting that damn egg.'

'Fair 'nough,' Louise said around a mouthful of chocolate. The sugar rush was just what she needed; the day so far had been nothing but a shit show, another example of the worst of human nature. Two terrible deaths, both that looked like suicides on the outside, caused by the typical build-up of stress and teenage angst. Both fuelled by spiteful comments from Catherine Hallum and her religious zealots.

Louise shook her head. She wasn't even sure she could call them religious. What religion – what *true* religion – revelled in causing distress to others? To their community? Louise had dropped all faith when she stood in front of her parents' coffins in Holy Trinity Church, turning her back on the religion that her parents had happily followed. Her aunt was still devout and she would accompany her occasionally on the Sundays when they would visit The Lodge afterwards. And Midnight Mass at Christmas; that was a service Louise still enjoyed. She held fond memories of going for the first time when she was thirteen, staying up way past her usual bedtime, holding the orange with the candle in the centre, and dolly mixtures stuck on cocktail sticks. Quite what the religious significance to Christmas that represented was still a mystery to her, but she always felt warm and fuzzy when she remembered it.

There was nothing warm and fuzzy about Catherine Hallum.

She had known people like the Hallum woman all her life, people whose sole purpose of existence seemed to be to dictate to others how they lived their life. Snide sideways comments slipped into conversation as pleasantly as if they were discussing the weather, usually prefaced with a deft 'Now I really shouldn't be saying this, but did you hear...', and then quickly followed up by a self-deprecating 'but I wouldn't normally believe a word of it...', as if that exonerated them.

She was expert at throwing verbal social hand-grenades to cause maximum chaos, if not permanent lasting damage. That was Catherine to a fine point. A social agitator, always pushing her own agenda, her own beliefs, castigating those who spoke out, seeking those in higher positions to defend hers. Catherine had done exactly that by going to the Chief, doing her best to land Louise and Hines in trouble, but worse; trying to get Manby swept up in her verbal diarrhoea to the extent that he was now sitting in his office 'handling' the situation.

'You want a cuppa?' Hines asked from her own desk. She had taken one look at the stack of paperwork that leaned precariously on her desk and sighed.

'Yes, but not by you,' Louise replied. She got up, grabbed their mugs, and went to the kitchen, leaving a dejected Hines staring at the files and wondering just where to start.

· · ·

Louise flicked the switch and waited for the kettle to boil.

Aunt Fiona had taught her well when it came to brewing a decent cup of tea. It took all the right ingredients, mixed together in the correct sequence with just the right amount of time to let them blend together, in order to create a brew that had the ideal levels of taste, strength and heat. Just one of those three factors being out of whack ruined the whole, and all it took to get it right was the fourth unspoken ingredient: patience. Aunt Fiona said a stew time of anything less than five minutes or more than six and the whole thing was ruined. You would taste nothing but mush. Louise could remember several instances when Aunt Fiona had refused a cup of tea she had made. She'd even refused and sent back a full pot at The Lodge, a near unspoken thing. Patience was key, a lesson Louise had taken to heart. It was why Hines' brews always tasted like mush. She rushed the stew stage, thinking a quick stir was good enough.

It was the same with police work. For a case to be solved everything had to come together at just the right time, all the evidence stirred together and given time to stew until it all made sense. Until that happened, all you had was mush.

And right now, all they had was mush.

Louise looked up at the clock over the sink. Three minutes to go...

What were the ingredients Louise and Hines had brewing right now?

James Willikar dead in the graveyard of Holy Trinity Church, a potential suicide...

Evidence of sexual, and possibly violent, activity in the warehouse beside the church...

Wendy Jackson dead in Frampton's Folly, another potential suicide...

Catherine Hallum and her lot rousing up a storm of social unrest...

What were they missing?

Louise looked at the clock again. *Time's up.*

She was taking the tea bag out of the mugs when Hines came over to the kitchen. She had an excited look on her face and a folder in her hand.

'What's that?' Louise asked, spooning sugar into the mugs. Perfect or not, she needed two in her brew.

'Fingerprint results. They got held back for some reason. Thompson only just brought them down and we have a match.'

Louise stopped stirring.

'A match? Who with?'

Hines' smile was so wide it threatened to overstretch the Cheshire Cat's for its smugness.

'You're never going to believe it.'

She handed Louise the folder and waited excitedly as Louise read it.

A moment later she looked up, mouth agape.

'Well, fuck.'

CHAPTER
FIFTY

Detective Inspector Bill Manby smiled as he listened to Daniel McKensie vent about the supposed harassment his client had been subjected to. According to the solicitor, the public embarrassments outside Holy Trinity Church, and then the incident at the Green Dragon in Horbury had led to his client's reputation being besmirched, not to mention the indignity of having a police officer, and a junior one at that, questioning her in her own home.

Do people still use the word besmirched? Manby thought. *Only if they're pompous dicks*, he mentally added. Entitlement was becoming a major factor in a lot of the crimes taking place, and not just in the local area. Where once the need to survive, to put food on the table had been the major motivation in local crime, now it was the arrogant notion of 'I deserve it' that led to such crimes, and while Catherine Hallum and her lot hadn't broken any actual laws that he could see, the same entitlement had fuelled their actions.

They might not have acted illegally, but they certainly acted immorally, and as far as he was concerned, along with the vast majority of police officers under his command, that was just as bad.

'Let me stop you right there, Mr McKensie,' Manby said, holding his hand up. 'I hear what you are saying but you need to hear what I'm saying. Twice now your client has called my boss because she doesn't like it when her actions bring forth consequences. Well, tough shit – excuse my French – but that's the way it goes. You do something that brings yourself to the attention of my officers, then you can be damn sure I'm going to be standing right beside them holding them to account. And from what I've seen so far, the only person wading in the murky grey water is your client.'

Manby could feel the anger pulsing through his veins and knew his face had gone red; the heat was radiating from him in waves that matched the speeding beat of his heart. Friend of the Chief Superintendent or not, there was no way he was being pushed around in his own station.

He turned to Catherine. 'You might not have thrown the brick that smashed the glass that sliced the face of Evelyn Green, one of the owners of the shop you were harassing this morning, but you damned well created the environment for it to happen. And so far I've not seen you show any concern for those injured, and that tells me a lot about you as a person. About you both.'

McKensie stood haughtily, his chair scraping back across the floor with the screech of an injured mouse. He beckoned for Catherine to do the same, ignoring the look of shock on her face. She must have thought Manby would be compliant, bending beneath the will of his Chief Superintendent, not the defiant stonewall that now stood before her, demanding her acquiescence.

'I am sure you don't fully appreciate the seriousness of these allegations, Mr Manby,' she began, but McKensie cut her off.

'Don't bother trying to reason with the man, Mrs Hallum. It is very clear that further action needs to be taken.'

'Now look here... ' Manby said, getting to his feet, but before he could continue, there was a knock at the door and Louise stuck her head in.

'Not now, Miller,' Manby said hotly.

"Fraid it can't wait, Bill,' she said, stepping in. Hines followed and shut the door behind her. Standing in front of it, she leaned her back against the door and crossed her arms. Judging from the cat-that-got-the-cream look on her face, Manby knew something was going on. He saw the folder in Louise's hand and gave a nod to it.

'What's that?' he asked.

'The fingerprint analysis from James Willikar's case,' Louise said, passing the folder over. 'We have a match.'

Manby opened the folder and started to read. 'A match? From what? I thought...'

His voice trailed off until the room was silent. Catherine, still standing, looked from Louise to Hines by the door, to McKensie and back to Manby.

'I don't think this is something we need to be here for is it, Inspector? Come, McKensie; you can take me home.'

'You're not going anywhere, Mrs Hallum,' Manby said from behind the folder. He lowered it to look at Louise. 'Is this accurate? Has it been verified and cross checked?'

'Twice,' she replied.

'I'm sorry,' Catherine said, 'but as this clearly has nothing to do with me, I will be going. I am sure the parents of that poor boy would not want their personal business being talked about in front of strangers.'

'That's just the thing though, isn't it?' Manby said. His voice had turned to iron. 'You were very quick to start putting it around that the Willikar boy had committed the sin of suicide, weren't you? On the day you were mouthing off about the boy and those that attended the Holy Trinity Church group.'

'I was there, yes. And yes, I said what many were thinking.'

Manby shook his head. 'No. Not many. You. It was obvious you didn't care for the boy or those friends of his and we have the witnesses to prove it, including our very own Louise Miller.'

'That's right, sir,' Louise said. She had moved to stand beside

Hines, who had given her a nudge, thinking the boss hadn't seen. Manby ignored it and continued.

'Being troubled is not an excuse for others to pile on with their own baggage. What did you think it would accomplish? That they would suddenly get over whatever their issues were and act in a fashion deemed more appropriate by yourself? Did you even stop to consider what they were going through?'

Catherine's face had flushed, and when she spoke, it was in a flustered manner, as though she couldn't quite remember how speaking worked, or what words to use.

'I... well, I thought... it was just... I...'

'Save it,' Manby said. 'And sit back down.'

Catherine sat without another word.

'This is all highly questionable,' McKensie said. 'Whatever your officers have brought in, I guarantee my client is innocent.'

Manby waved the sheet of paper before the solicitor. 'What I have here is a fingerprint match to one found on the knife that was used to cut James Willikar's arm and wrist.'

The smile Manby gave was as cold as the snow that had fallen around the Willikar boy. There was to be no argument here, no offer of hope. It lacked all mercy and all compassion. It was the look a predator gave its prey before the final leap.

'That fingerprint, Mr McKensie, is yours.'

'What the hell are you talking about?' McKensie said. He wasn't as forceful with his question, Manby noted. In fact, his voice sounded as watery as his legs looked. His left had started quivering and he leaned forward to rest both hands on the chair he had been sitting in only a few minutes ago.

Beside him, Catherine looked pale. Her eyes had become as wide as saucers, and she was visibly shaking.

'Daniel?' she said. All the bravado had left her voice too, turning the shrill, bitter shrew-like tone into that of a little girl. Manby could almost feel sorry for her.

Almost.

'Daniel,' Catherine said again when the solicitor didn't reply.

'What are they talking about?' She turned to Manby, who ignored her, keeping his eyes on McKensie. 'What are you talking about? Knife... What knife? How could his fingerprints be on any knife? He wasn't there.'

McKensie took in a deep breath and slowly lowered his head.

'Shut the fuck up, you whining little *bitch*!'

He roared the last, making Catherine jump then instantly burst into tears.

Louise and Hines pushed themselves off the door and were beside McKensie in two fast strides. Louise put one hand on his shoulder while the other took hold of his right arm.

'Daniel McKensie, I am arresting you on suspicion of the murder of James Willikar between the hours of midnight on the tenth of December, 1988 and 4 am on the eleventh of December, 1988...'

If he heard the rest of what Louise said, he gave no sign. His eyes were locked on a fixed point in space only he could see.

CHAPTER
FIFTY-ONE

They were back in Interview Room 3. This time Daniel McKensie sat on the far side of the table, in the same seat Catherine Hallum had used only a short time ago. He had been left alone in the room while Hines and Louise prepared everything they would need for the interview to come.

Catherine had been taken home, driven by a uniformed officer and given strict instructions by DI Manby not to say anything about the afternoon's developments. If she had thought simply being questioned was bad for her reputation, wait until she saw what being charged with perverting the course of justice would do to her social standing, Manby had warned her. Catherine's response had been meek, apologetic and unwavering in her newly found community-focused mindset.

'We've got a print on a knife and nothing else,' Manby said as he watched Louise grab another notepad from her desk.

'We have his wallet found in a location not too far from the body, as well as blood. And Danes is checking on something else that Hines noticed that might place him at the scene. She's getting it now. It's not the perfect cuppa yet but let us give it another stir and we'll see what we can mash.'

The expression on Manby's face revealed the extent of his bewilderment. 'What?'

'Never mind,' Louise said. 'Private joke.'

While McKensie was being booked in, Hines had gone upstairs to the SOCO room, where Peter Danes had been going over the photos from the Jackson scene. All the evidence was stored there in a room ten times smaller than the one in Wakefield Central Headquarters where most of the CID evidence went before trial. Part of the Prospect Road experiment was being self-contained, and for now it all had to be done here, on a much smaller scale than everyone was used to. In time there were plans to take a stretch of land somewhere central to Ossett and build a larger station, one that could comfortably house a dozen detectives, processing lab and evidence storage as well as a potential armed response team. Gun crime was on the rise, and while it was focused mainly around the cities of Leeds and Wakefield, their outlying communities were starting to see an increase in firearms being used in robberies and home invasions.

With Danes' help, Hines had gathered everything needed, including the knife found beside James Willikar. 'And the other item?' Hines asked as Danes handed her the last of the paper-work they had generated.

'It's in there,' he said, 'though I'm not sure quite how it will help.'

'It might, it might not, but best to have it and not need it, rather than need it and not have it, which should have been your stance on things,' she said pointedly before turning away. She hadn't meant to say anything to him, hadn't meant to say anything to anybody. She hadn't meant for a lot of things to happen.

'What the hell does that mean?' he said, reaching out to grab her arm, forcing her to stop and turn back. 'Are you all right?' he asked. 'You've been a little... I don't know, off, lately. Is everything all right with you and Joe?'

'Why would you ask that?' she said. 'What happens between me and Joe is just that: between me and Joe. It has nothing to do with you. Nothing.'

One of the SOCO team gave a polite cough from behind them and they stepped aside so she could move past and head back downstairs to the kitchen. 'Break time,' Danes said.

'We broke a long time ago,' Hines said. She turned away and followed the SOCO officer down the stairs, wondering to herself if she had been referring to Danes or Joe.

McKensie refused a solicitor, despite being asked multiple times if he would like them to arrange one for him. He did accept the offer of a cuppa, and Louise asked Hines if she would make it for him. Hines, knowing perfectly well that Louise couldn't stand her cuppas, intended to make the shittiest, weakest cup of slop ever, the closest she could get to toilet water without actually resorting to scooping it up.

When she slid the cup over, she gave the solicitor a wide smile that appeared to instantly put his nerves up another level. For Louise she handed over a cup of water. Hines was content with the Polo mints she had brought in. She offered one to Louise, who declined. She put the packet in her pocket.

McKensie took a sip from his tea and grimaced, staring into the mug for a second before dropping it in the bin beside the table.

'You think you're funny.'

It was a statement, not a question. Hines said nothing and sucked on her mint.

'We found your wallet in the warehouse beside Holy Trinity Church on the morning of Sunday the eleventh, Mr McKensie,' Louise said. 'Care to tell us how it got there?'

'I thought this was supposed to be about a knife?' he said.

'We'll get to that,' Louise answered. 'The wallet first.'

McKensie's jaw tightened, a soft spasm evident in the lower left corner as he chose his words. Louise and Hines both knew this would be a tougher than usual interview; their subjects weren't usually as well versed in legal gameplay as McKensie would be. Most of the time the subjects were too busy showing off their manhood, calling them every slur in the misogynist's handbook that they could remember. Not that many of them actually read, or at least that was how they came across as they slouched in the chair, picking their nails or their teeth, or in one memorable instance, the crack of their arse.

No, Louise thought as she got ready to start the interview proper, this wouldn't be easy. But then, it wouldn't be overly complicated either. She could use his arrogance against him, she was sure of it. He would be sitting there thinking he had her over the barrel with his legal knowledge. Plus, she was a woman, and she could tell already that McKensie had little regard for the so called fairer sex.

'It's a wallet,' he said before Louise could say anything else, that arrogance she had suspected already taking charge. 'It's my wallet, as we've already established, and it was lost.'

'On the night of Saturday the tenth,' Louise said.

'It hasn't been established when it was lost,' he countered with a sneer. 'It could have been the Saturday night; it could have been during the day.'

'When was the last time you remember having it in your possession?' Louise asked.

McKensie shrugged as he wiped at a spot of dust on the hem of his trouser leg. 'I don't know... that Friday, for sure. Yes, I think it was Friday.'

Hines reached into the folder and pulled out a green slip of paper, which she handed to Louise. 'This, Mr McKensie, is a ticket from Ossett Library. Can you read the name at the top of the ticket for me please?'

She placed the ticket, still in the plastic evidence bag, in front of the solicitor. He looked down at it and ran his tongue across the inside of his mouth, pushing his lips forward in a gesture Louise could only define as contempt, then pushed it back across the table.

'It says my name.'

'And the date?' Louise asked.

'The tenth.'

'The tenth of December, correct?'

'Yes. It appears so.'

Louise smiled. 'Thank you. And what day would that have been... if you don't mind?'

McKensie let out a sigh of controlled anger that dragged on for several moments. The scent of his toothpaste rolled over the two detectives, mixing with his cologne to create a strange, sweet cloud. Everything about the man oozed success and excess; from the expensive suit he wore, no doubt a tailored affair from Carl Stuarts right here in Ossett, to the gold watch that clutched his wrist. Her uncle had one of their suits; he couldn't afford two.

'It was a Saturday, if memory serves.'

'That it was, Mr McKensie. So... we know you were in Ossett town centre on Saturday the tenth, as you took a book out. We know this because the ticket was in your wallet. Where did you go other than the library?'

He gave another shrug.

'I don't know. I was extremely busy that Saturday.'

'Would it surprise you to learn that you were in the Carpenters pub from two in the afternoon right through until just before ten? We have statements from other patrons that you were there, and that you were drinking all afternoon. Would that be fair to say?'

'I think I was in there, yes.' A little colour had risen in his cheeks, and he wiped his hand against the curve of his thigh.

'You were there,' Hines said, taking over from Louise, 'and then you went to the warehouse on Church Street.'

'I did no such thing!' he spat.

'We think you did, and we think you weren't alone. A person matching your description left the Carpenters pub at just before ten on Saturday the tenth of December in the company of a known prostitute called Helen Williams. Do you remember her?'

At the mention of Helen, McKensie's face sunk inwards, all colour disappearing faster than sluice water down a broken drain. His shoulders slumped and he appeared to droop like wilted grass.

'I do not know where you are leading with this, but I resent your insinuation that I procured the services of a common street whore.'

'Men do many things they normally wouldn't do when they have had one drink too many,' Hines said. 'Things that they come to later regret when the thrill and the beer wears off. I'm sure this wasn't the first time for you.'

'Is that what she said?' McKensie said. 'Is that what that little bitch said... that I was with her?'

'She hasn't said anything. Helen Williams seems to have dropped off the face of the planet right now. No one has seen her since Saturday the tenth. Since she was last seen with you.'

McKensie looked from Hines to Louise. 'You're being awfully quiet, dear. Are you seriously saying you think I killed a good for nothing street slut? Ridiculous, pure fantasy.'

'Seriously... no. Helen is known to go missing for a few days. She sometimes works out of Leeds centre or Wakefield. She has known friends and associates, fellow... what did he call her, Beth?'

'Street whore. Or street slut.'

'That's right. She has fellow street sluts that she works along-side in those cities, so when the desperate, drunk perverts seek them out, they know they are safe. Please,' Louise added, silencing the start of McKensie's next outburst with a wave of her hand. 'Keep your fake indignation to yourself. We know you were with her – people have said so. And again, no, we don't think you have anything to do with Helen disappearing. She'll turn up in a day or two, be back in the Carps and looking for another easy mark. Someone like you.'

McKensie's face had now gone the colour of a wounded beetroot as shock turned to anger. 'Then what the hell am I doing here?'

Louise turned to Hines. 'We arrested him, didn't we? Booked him under caution for the suspected murder of James Willikar, right?'

'Pretty sure we did.'

'And we told him that, right?'

Hines nodded.

'None of what you have talked about has anything to do with the damned Willikar boy. I'm starting to see now that Catherine was correct in her assumptions about the boy. Nothing but trouble, and nothing you have said so far has anything to do with him.'

'We're getting there, Mr McKensie. We're getting there.'

Hines reached down to the evidence bag at her feet that she'd brought in from the SOCO team. She lifted it and placed it down on the table with a solid thump.

'Let's talk shoes...'

CHAPTER
FIFTY-TWO

From inside the evidence bag, Hines brought out a light grey, dull hunk of plaster. It was rectangular in shape with two raised sections, both squashed, elongated ovals with a gap in the middle.

'This is the plaster-cast of a shoe print taken from inside the abandoned warehouse on Church Street where your wallet was found. Right next to it, in fact. Here...'

Hines put aside the plaster-cast of the shoe and drew out two colour photos from the folder, which she passed over. They were of McKensie's wallet lying amidst the debris and dust of the warehouse floor, with a clear footprint right beside them.

'The SOCO team took the cast and have identified three points that make this shoe print unique. These have been identified in the photo with the red marks, and on the cast with the yellow spots. Can you see where I'm pointing, Mr McKensie?'

He said nothing but nodded.

'There is also a tape measure beside the print in this photo which helps ID the size of the shoe as a size nine. Can you see that?' Another nod. 'And what size shoe do you wear, Mr McKensie?'

'A nine. Like most men my size.'

Louise took the photo back and slid it inside the folder. 'Funny you should mention size. Did you know that the depth of an imprint can give a good indication of the weight of the person wearing the shoe?'

McKensie straightened in his chair and gave a low cough. 'Actually, I did.'

'That's good. And I would go out on a limb here and say that you weigh around eleven stone. Eleven and a half at a push. How close am I?'

'Not that it is any of your business, but I weigh ten stone twelve.'

'Pretty damn close then. Look, let's just cut the bullshit dance, okay, because I'm tired. Hines is tired and you're looking pretty haggard as well. We know you were there. Your wallet was there. Your footprint was there. You were there.'

'You have nothing that ties me directly to being in that warehouse. A single plaster print and photograph is nothing.'

'Not without corroborating evidence, correct, and that is why this is a formal request to inspect your shoes,' Hines said, passing over the signed slip Manby had agreed to earlier when she came back down from the SOCO office. 'What's the bet that the soles of your shoe match the three unique qualifiers already identified?'

For several long minutes, McKensie said nothing. He was controlling his breathing, Louise noted, taking in long, steadying breaths as he fought to control his composure. His eyes kept darting from the plaster-cast of his shoe to the request form, to Louise and Hines and back to the plaster-cast.

Louise also said nothing and gave an under-the-table tap to Hines' leg let her know that she should stay silent too while McKensie weighed his options. This was the moment they had been working towards, the time when it would either go their way or he would stonewall them. Knowing how hard to push without breaking the subject was a skill only time and experience could master. Louise feared they might have blown it as he still hadn't said anything, but just sat there breathing in, breathing out, eyes taking them in.

'So... I was there in the warehouse. That doesn't mean I killed the Willikar boy. You're stretching.'

'Then explain how your fingerprint got on this,' Hines said. She pulled another plastic sheath from the evidence bag and put it on the table.

A black-handled knife.

'What's that?'

Louise leaned forward, both elbows on the table. 'What the fuck do you think it is? It's a fucking knife. The knife you used to kill James Willikar.'

CHAPTER
FIFTY-THREE

Daniel McKensie was almost albino in his complexion at the sight and mention of a knife. It lay between them on the table, encased in plastic with a beige tag fastened to it with blue string. Someone's spider-scratches had labelled the item with the date and time it was found, along with references to the photos Peter Danes had taken of it at the scene, its dimensions and more reference numbers that would lead to blood samples found along its edge and the reports that they had then generated.

'Found in the hand of the deceased, James Willikar,' Hines said. 'His arm had been cut from wrist to elbow at a penetrating depth of three-point-two millimetres.'

Louise slid a photo across the table. McKensie didn't pick it up, but they could both tell he had seen it. A little colour returned to his face; unfortunately, it was green. His lips pursed and his breathing quickened as he gold-fished in air.

The photo showed a close up of James Willikar's left arm, his hand palm upwards.

'As you can see, the injury started just below the thenar muscle group by the wrist. It then runs straight up the arm along the median nerve, nicking the medial artery, which resulted in James basically bleeding to death very slowly. When Wendy found him there was nothing she could do. There was nothing anyone could do.'

'I don't want to see this,' McKensie said, pushing the photo aside. 'So what? A dumb kid topped himself by slashing his arm. Not exactly unheard of, is it? I could cite about a dozen similar cases in the same time frame if I had the inclination to look into it.'

'I'm sure you will when it goes to trial. When you go to trial.'

McKensie laughed for the first time, a cold, harsh bark that echoed in the small interview room. 'You're having me on, right? This isn't going to trial. There's nothing to try. What possible motive could I have for killing the kid? And besides, his parents even said he had had suicidal thoughts before. I read it in the paper.'

Now it was Hines' turn to laugh. 'And that makes it true? I read about how a UFO was supposed to have crashed in Nottingham last year. Doesn't make it true.'

She turned to Louise. 'Though it would be pretty amazing if it was, right? Aliens walking amongst us. I love *Close Encounters*. I could see that happening.'

Louise closed her eyes and counted to three before continuing.

'Your fingerprint is on the handle. It matches the print from your wallet. You were there in the graveyard with James on the morning of Sunday the eleventh of December. You were nearby in the warehouse right next to the churchyard, and we can place James Willikar there as well.'

'It's over, Mr McKensie,' Hines said. 'We don't have to prove why you did it, just that you did. And we have all that. But if you tell us what happened, why you did it, why you cut his arm and left him to die, then it might go some way to helping you when it comes to sentencing.'

It was distasteful to offer him a deal; Louise wanted him to rot for as long as possible. Ideally she would leave him in a closed room with the parents for five minutes and a cricket bat.

Proper justice. But this was the next best thing, for everyone concerned. Getting a full confession reduced lengthy trial times when the parents would have to be put through another prolonged ordeal. Getting him to tell them what happened would offer some level of closure for the parents as well, as twisted as that sounded. Finally they would know what had happened, and the agonising pain of not knowing could be laid to rest along with their son.

But they would know what had happened, and some of those details might be equally painful.

'Footprint. Wallet. Knife,' Hines said. 'You're there. He's there. He's now dead and you're now here.'

Louise leaned forward.

'What happened?'

At first McKensie didn't say anything. Just sat on his side of the table with both hands placed palm down in front of him. Louise had arrayed their evidence before him; the plaster-cast of his shoe, his wallet. The knife. It was all there. All that was missing was the why.

And so they sat and waited for him to make the decision they needed him to. If he didn't they would charge him with the murder, take him to the cells and then have him transferred to Wakefield Prison to await his appearance before the judge and then face the long wait for trial. All that time he would be in remand; there was no way he was getting bailed for this. He would ask for a solicitor of his own and the arguments would then be laid before the judge for being released on remand, the appeal to throw the charges out and so on. The dance would truly begin, but that was for the Crown prosecution to handle. Louise knew they had their ducks in a row, whatever the fuck that meant.

All they could do was sit here and wait. The pot was brewing; all their evidence was mashed together, creating the near perfect cup of justice. They just needed to add the final ingredient, patience, and McKensie would be stewed.

Louise realised she desperately needed a fresh brew.

'It was that bitch's fault,' he said, pushing himself back from the table. 'If I hadn't gone with her, none of this would have happened.'

Hines looked at Louise. They had talked about what they would do if he started talking. Handling a confession was all about the subtle coaxing of information. Most people wanted to confess, they wanted to unburden themselves, to release the weight of their dark deeds out into the world so they could finally relax. That was most people. The arrogant ones, however, the ones who didn't think they would ever be caught, they wanted people to know how clever they'd been. How they had avoided all attention, even when their heinous acts had been carried out right beneath the noses of loved ones, or friends or work colleagues. They wanted everyone to know they had beaten the world, for a while. Got away with their evil. Unnoticed. Unseen. And now they wanted everyone to see. They wanted their evil in the bright light of day, no longer hidden in the dark shadows of their soul.

Louise wondered which type McKensie was.

Outwardly he was all smooth and successful. Nice suits, expensive car. Good job. Friends. Money. But did he have hidden tastes? Desires that no one knew about?

Was *that* why he had done what he had? Was *that* what had fuelled his evil deed?

'That fucking street slut took me to the warehouse and fucking robbed me. Eighty fucking quid. Eighty! And I'd already given her a tenner for the blow job. Fucking bitch!'

'The warehouse where we found your wallet and footprint.'

When he looked up, the anger burned through his eyes. 'Of course, the fucking warehouse.' His cheeks were red, and what Louise first took to be sweat rolled down his cheeks. It took a few moments before she realised they were tears and he was crying as he spoke. His voice still bore the venomous tang of resentment, but she could hear the bubble of tears in each word.

'We'd finished... she'd finished. She must have lifted it when she was on her knees. I didn't feel a thing, only realised when I got home.'

'Bit risky being in the warehouse, don't you think? You live just the street over.'

'I wasn't thinking, was I? I was pissed on whisky all afternoon. When she came up to me in the Carps and started running her hand over me, I thought I was well in. Didn't realise she was a whore until we were in my car headed home. Dressed all nice. Tight. I was taking her there, but when she asked what I wanted I knew her for what she was. Fucking street slut.'

'Sounds like you should have just kicked her out of the car then,' Hines said.

'Fuck that. I was rock solid and needed to unload. What was a tenner to me? I'd dropped over a hundred in the Carps and still had plenty left. But there was no fucking way I was taking a whore home to my bed. Fuck knows what she had. Didn't want her disease riddled arse dirtying my sheets up. So I turned into the warehouse. Made up a lie that I remembered I had a house guest.'

Louise gave her sleeve a pat down, smoothing a wrinkle in her jacket. 'Been there before, have you?' she asked.

'No. It was her idea. I guess she's got a few of these spots around town.'

'Why do you say that?'

'She seemed to know exactly where to go. So I park up and we go inside. Get busy. That's when those fucking kids turned up, just right after I blew in her mouth. Scared the shit out of me.'

Nice.

'James Willikar?' Hines asked. 'Who were the others?'

Now he was talking, he didn't seem to want to stop. All the waiting, all the patience had worked. Sometimes it did; sometimes it didn't. Louise was glad that this time it had.

'Only one other. A lad. Buzz-cut hair. Couldn't make him out.'

'Did you recognise him? James Willikar?'

McKensie nodded. 'Course I did. I've done work with his dad before. Gone golfing with them. Made me a lot of money, the Willikars have. And I've made them just as much. More even, what with tax issues, planning permits for the business David Willikar was working for. Must have been about ten, fifteen years we've worked together on and off.'

'And James saw you? Recognised you, didn't he?'

McKensie nodded again. The colour had faded along with his anger. He now seemed genuinely upset as he swiped at his eyes. The smooth talk had gone as well. Another layer of falsehood stripped away by his confession. It was as though he was shedding everything that had led to the awful, tragic events of that night. 'He fucking clocked me, didn't he? I didn't think he had, but I knew it when his face fell. And I ran. I ran right out of there, got in my car and drove off.'

'Did you go home?' Louise asked. McKensie shook his head.

'I was too scared. Too angry. I drove. I drove up through town, along Dewsbury Road towards the mad mile. I thought I'd hit the M1, maybe go up to Leeds and back. Cool down. Maybe he'd not recognised me. Maybe he had. I just didn't know.'

'What did it matter if he had?'

McKensie let out a laugh.

'If he'd told his dad he'd seen Mr McKensie getting a blow job in a dirty warehouse at midnight from some street slut...' The words died away, his face slack. After a moment he shook his head as he briefly gnawed at his bottom lip. 'He might be retired, but Willikar knows people. He's put me in touch with several big clients. People who pay well. People with influence. He's a bit prim though, so what do you think my chances of getting another referral from him would be? Fucking zero. Snowball in hell. I couldn't let that happen. It was worth too much money to me. Too much.'

'So what did you do?' Louise asked. They knew what he'd done, but needed to hear him say it.

McKensie leaned forward, his hands clasping his head, fingers gripping his hair so tight, Louise was worried he might start pulling it out in frenzied chunks.

'I drove back,' he said. He looked up and the two detectives could see the shame in the tears that poured from his eyes. 'I drove back, and I wish I never had.'

CHAPTER
FIFTY-FOUR

'I parked outside and went into the warehouse again. It was about an hour later. Maybe longer. I couldn't hear anything. Couldn't see anything either. I thought maybe the kids were still messing about. One of them had a bike; it must have been the other lad because I remember David Willikar saying a few weeks ago he was thinking of getting one for James for Christmas.'

At the mention of the upcoming festivities, the tears became a flood, and for the next few minutes the room was filled with the cold, empty sobs of sorrowful realisation. Louise didn't care how bad McKensie was feeling, she wanted him to experience it every day for the rest of his life. It was the least that could happen to him for what he had done, what he had stolen from the Willikar family. All those lost moments that would never come: James' graduation, going to university. His first job. Marriage. Children and grandchildren. All those lost opportunities because this sorry excuse for a man had wanted to get his dick wet but didn't want anyone to know.

It made her sick. It made her angry. It made her do her job.

Eventually, McKensie got himself back under control.

'There was nobody inside but I could smell cigarettes, so they hadn't long left. I saw the broken door they'd gone out of and went out that way. It led to the churchyard, and I went inside. I walked down the side of the church. It had started snowing by now. Nothing much, but enough so I could see their footprints. I followed them and that was when I found him. James. He was lying on a gravestone. Drunk by the looks of it.'

'Where did the knife come from?' Hines asked.

McKenzie blew his nose into the tissue and wiped his nose a few times before answering. 'I don't know. I think it was his. There was a backpack next to the gravestone so I'm guessing it was his. The knife was lying on top of it so I... I...'

The tears started once again, and he angrily swiped at them. 'Fuck. What was I thinking? I just didn't want it to get out. I couldn't afford for that to happen.'

He looked up at them, his eyes red and streaming. 'I owe someone a lot of money. I mean... *a lot*! I couldn't let this get out – it would ruin me. So I grabbed the knife and... and... oh fuck. What did I do?'

They didn't get anything else from Daniel McKensie. The stark realisation of his actions crushed him totally. Louise had seen people cry before, many times, but she had never seen someone collapse into themselves in the way McKensie did. One moment he was telling them what he had done, the next he was wailing and thrashing, clawing at his face. It would have been almost laughably Shakespearean if not for the seriousness of the situation.

It had taken two officers to pull his arms down to his sides to stop him injuring himself any further, Louise and Hines standing against the wall out of the way. DI Manby stood out in the corridor watching as medical staff were brought in. McKensie was sedated and taken down to the cells where he was now on suicide watch.

The irony of that was not lost on anyone.

What they had was enough though, and a full charge sheet

was put together. Daniel McKensie would be seen by a psychiatrist, and once his health had been determined, he would no doubt be transferred just as Louise had said.

'There were marks on the Willikar boy's right arm as though McKensie had tried to cut there as well, but obviously his will had gone by then, no doubt from seeing the blood. He'd put the knife in James' left hand but didn't realise that A – James was right-handed, and B – he'd severed the median nerve so that there was no way James could have gripped the knife to continue cutting. Autopsy shows the left arm was cut first.'

They were in Manby's office once again, hot cups of coffee for each of them steaming on the desk. It was just after five in the afternoon and the light outside had fallen. The faint glow of the streetlight directly outside the window was warming the room, throwing orange shadows over everyone.

Louise stretched her back, feeling the joints cracking as she did so. It had been a long, stressful day and she needed a bath. Karla was waiting for her call as well, and she knew they had a tough conversation ahead of them. But that could all wait, because there was one more job she had to do tonight. One that shouldn't be put off any longer.

She stood, drained the mug and put it back down.

'Do you want me to get someone else to do it?' Manby asked. 'Been a rough one as it is.' Louise shook her head.

'No, Bill. I should be the one.'

Hines stood. 'We should be the ones,' she said. 'I'll drive.'

Louise's smile hid the tears she could feel building behind her eyes.

Maureen and David Willikar were sitting in their living room when headlights splashed over the wall, briefly illuminating them in their clean glare. They had been sitting in silence. No TV was playing Coronation Street's Christmas special, no radio was spinning Christmas carols. There were no decorations on the wall, no Christmas tree in the corner. All evidence of the holiday season had been stripped from the room.

David stood as the car came to a stop in front of the house just beside his van. His face was slack, his eyes nothing but sunken wells that housed a darkness only grief and sorrow could penetrate. Beside him, Maureen sat unmoving, her face cast in the shadow thrown from the lamp on the table beside her. A cup of tea sat cold and forgotten next to it.

He walked to the window and watched as Louise and Hines got out of the car and approached the front door. Detached from the reality of what he was seeing, he stared as they came by, the younger police officer raising her hand in greeting as she saw him twitch the curtain. The doorbell rang a moment later and Maureen blinked.

'There's someone at the door,' she said.

'I'll go,' David said.

Maureen smiled but said nothing else.

When the door opened, Louise was shocked by David Willikar's appearance. Shocked but not surprised. She could remember how her own reflection had changed in the mirror following the death of her parents. She had been a lot younger than David when she had suffered her own loss, but that was the bizarre oneness of death; it was both personally unique and exactly the same for everyone who was left behind.

'Can I help you?' David asked. 'It's getting late and we haven't eaten yet.'

'Do you mind if we come inside, Mr Willikar?' Louise asked. 'We won't be long, nothing more than a few minutes, but it's very parky out and I think this is something your wife would want to hear directly from us.'

'Just a few minutes then,' he said, opening the door wide enough so that they could move inside. Both detectives took a moment to wipe their shoes on the door mat.

David drifted away, back into the living room, and the two police officers followed. Hines gave Louise a quizzical look. Louise shrugged and bit at the inside of her mouth.

Grief was such a leveller. It took everything from you, leaving you but a hollow shell, an automaton clanking through each day on auto-pilot. Not caring, not thinking. Certainly not feeling.

Or was it feeling too much that sent the brain into its fuggy spiral? Again, Louise could recall days of nothingness, of being. Surviving. Not living. Just getting through each day, each hour. Each minute.

Seconds felt like years, and years were a lifetime to comprehend. To endure.

To survive.

She was about to ask how they were doing and realised it was a wasted question. They were struggling, and why wouldn't they? Not even a fortnight had passed since their son's death, and with the silly season crushing around them, their emotions must be as jangled as Uncle Bernard's Christmas lights.

Maureen saw them come into the room and started to get out of the chair. Louise moved forward, lightly touching her arm. 'Please, Mrs Willikar. Don't get up. We won't be long.'

David moved to stand beside his wife, one hand on her shoulder.

'What can we do for you?' he asked.

Louise looked to Hines, who cleared her throat and attempted a warm and engaging smile.

'We have had a development in your son's case,' she said, then winced, probably at her use of the word 'case' to describe their son's death, Louise thought. Hines hurried on. 'There had been some elements regarding your son's death we had concerns with, and after looking closer, it became apparent that your son James did not commit suicide.'

A light flashed briefly in Maureen's eyes, there a moment then gone as she processed this information. Louise looked at

David; he stood solid. Stoic. Barely moving, though she could see a nerve twitching in his jaw.

'What do you mean?' Maureen asked. She looked up at her husband. 'What did she say? What did you say?' she asked again, getting more agitated. Louise knelt in front of her and took her hands in her own. The skin felt hot and sweaty, but there was a frailty that strangely reminded Louise of her aunt's fingers.

'Mrs Willikar, we now know that your son was murdered. He did not commit suicide.'

Maureen's fingers tightened around hers, squeezing hard as she took this in. David hadn't moved at all, but he spoke now.

'How did you find out?'

Hines caught his attention and he turned to face her, eyes hard as the grave his son had been found lying on. 'As Louise mentioned, there were some discrepancies in the scene where James was found.'

'I knew it,' Maureen was saying, staring into Louise's eyes. A smile had warmed her face. 'I knew he couldn't have done what they said he did. He wouldn't leave us like that. He wouldn't hurt us like that.'

Tears were falling down her face and Louise was surprised to find she was crying as well. 'You're right,' she said, fearful her own voice would break. 'He didn't leave you.'

'Do you know why she did it?' Mr Willikar asked, his voice low and tinged with anger.

'She?'

David looked from Hines to Louise. 'Wendy Jackson. Why did she do it?'

Now it was Hines' turn to look to Louise. Both had the same confused expression on their faces. It was Louise who spoke.

'I'm sorry, it wasn't Wendy Jackson who killed your son. It was a man I believe you know. Daniel McKensie.'

David Willikar took several steps backwards, one hand reaching out to grasp the mantelpiece.

'No.'

The single word was a cold dagger that sought a warm target.

'No,' he said again. 'That's not right. That can't be right.'

'Mr Willikar... are you all right?'

'She said. *She said!*'

Louise was now standing next to Hines. Both of them knew there was something wrong here. Something very, very, wrong.

'Who said what, Mr Willikar?' Louise asked.

'She said she killed him.'

A cold hand settled on Louise's heart.

No. Please let me be wrong.

'Mr Willikar, who said what?'

'Wendy Jackson.'

Louise turned her head and looked out of the window to where they had parked the car. Next to the police Rover was the Willikars' van. The window cleaning van.

With the ladders on the roof.

'Wendy said she'd found James on the gravestone. That she'd killed him.'

Please don't say it. Please don't.

He looked up and Louise saw the truth even before he spoke the words that sent a piercing knife through her heart.

'That's why I killed her.'

CHAPTER
FIFTY-FIVE

Louise had called DI Manby from the hallway of the Willikars'
home as Hines sat with them in the living room. Lights had been
switched on in an effort to throw as much of the darkness out as
they could. There was too much already surrounding the family,
and so much more about to descend on them.

'He's not going to run, if that's what you're worried about,'
Louise said into the phone. Sometimes Manby could be a real
idiot, she thought as she listened to his instructions. Not to leave
David alone, even to go to the bathroom. Make sure his rights
have been read to him and understood, a solicitor contacted if he
requested it. Shirley Hanson would be called and dispatched to
the address along with an ambulance to provide a health check
on Maureen Willikar, who had briefly suffered an anxiety-
induced panic attack upon hearing her husband's confession.

'Till then sit there and take notes if he speaks. It's a rather
unique situation, and having him in custody as soon as possible
is paramount, but considering the circumstances, let's just take
this gently.'

'The Chief might not like that,' Louise said. He was a stickler
for protocol and procedure, and what they were doing with
David Willikar, a man who had just confessed to the murder of a

fourteen-year-old girl, was as far from procedure as she'd ever been. The line was there, but it was extremely blurred.

'The Chief can kiss my Christmas goose,' Manby said, causing Louise to smile. 'See you in a bit.'

Louise hung up and went into the living room.

'I didn't mean to kill her,' David said as the paramedic took his blood pressure. The cuff was wound around his arm and the bulb being pumped when he spoke. It had been nearly half an hour since he had last spoken and Louise hadn't wanted to push.

Hines sat with Maureen on the sofa. From the kitchen came the familiar sounds of Shirley Hanson as she hummed to herself while making everyone a fresh pot of tea. She'd spoken briefly with Louise when she'd arrived, telling her that Maureen would need her company when her husband was taken in and charged. Anxiety attacks like the one Maureen had suffered were typical; Shirley said that she was just thankful it hadn't been even more serious. Some spouses when they heard such news, especially following an already harrowing experience such as the loss of a child, had heart attacks. Some even died on the spot.

'Like Laura Greene,' Louise had reminded the family liaison officer. Shirley nodded but said nothing. That case had been particularly stressful for her, and it was still ongoing, the children now slowly making their way through the adoption system.

'You don't need to say anything,' Louise reminded David, but he simply smiled.

'It's all right,' he said. 'I'm glad really.'

'Glad?'

'That Wendy didn't actually kill him. James liked her. Liked her a lot more than he let on, I think. And she was nice to him.'

He stopped talking and let the paramedic check his heart. He shivered when the cold metal of the stethoscope touched his skin and Louise felt another pang of sympathy for the man stab at her own heart. As the definitive example of a crime of passion, this was it. She had heard it all before, though, the excuses given to talk away a rash act that had led to injury, disability or death. Most of them were lame, barely thought through excuses, mental knee-jerks given in the hopes they would lessen what was to come.

He took my spade and never gave it back.

They wouldn't turn their music down.

She just wouldn't shut the fuck up.

That last one she'd heard more times than she could remember, especially when walking the beat in Hulme, Manchester. Usually said by a man as wide as a double doorway and twice as thick. Crappy white t-shirt stained with beer and fag ash. Blood on the knuckles and a grin on the face. *What was I supposed to do?* the follow up. *Crime of passion, love.*

Crime of passion? Passion? They didn't know the word, those beer-fuelled louts who thought with their dicks and talked with their fists. Punch first, second and third. A kick if their victim talked back. If it got as far as charges and court, their brief would talk it away as just another example of a marriage's many dips and curves, seen across the country. No, he wasn't a threat to her. No, it was an isolated incident. A crime of passion, your Honour. Nothing more. Nothing to worry about. And then they would be called back when the body was found, and it was never certain just whose corpse would be lying in the living room in a pool of blood, who would be standing over them, holding the blood-soaked knife or the dented kettle with the clump of hair stuck to the side in a sodden, red patch. *Crime of passion, your Honour.*

'All done,' the paramedic said, dragging Louise from her thoughts. She was right; there was a lake of darkness surrounding the Willikars, and for a moment, she had gone swimming.

'I'd gone to the school to get James' books. He'd left some in his locker and desk, along with a watch we'd bought him for his last birthday. I'd got them and was back at the van when she came up to me.'

They sat at the kitchen table now. The ambulance had gone, taking Maureen to the hospital to be checked out properly. She was having trouble catching her breath and they were worried about her. Shirley went with her and promised to call as soon as she had word. That left Louise and Hines with David. There was nothing more to do now but take him in officially for questioning, but he seemed ready to talk now and Louise didn't want to break the moment. Hines called Manby to let him know they'd be coming in soon.

She came back into the kitchen and David looked up. 'Any word from the hospital?' he asked. Hines shook her head.

'I was speaking to the Detective Inspector. Letting him know what was happening. Sorry.'

David smiled weakly. His hands had finally stopped shaking, which was good. He looked around the kitchen. Other than a few dirty cups – Louise promised they would wash them before they left – the place was spotless. It looked as though no one lived here; there was no rubbish waiting to be put in the bin. No stack of plates. No papers or unopened post left on the side to be read later, no cookbooks with colourful markers sticking out ready for Sunday lunch prep. It looked like a show house, not the home of a family in the run up to Christmas.

The house was silent. James had left. Maureen had left. Soon it would be David's turn, and Louise didn't think he would be coming back anytime soon. Only Maureen would eventually return to the house, and in that thought Louise saw the house swell. The absence of loved ones created huge pits of loneliness where once had been rooms filled with love. She had seen it herself; her fourteen-year-old bedroom on Wesley Street had become a huge dark hangar when she came back from the hospital.

This fucking sucks, she thought and wiped at her eye, hoping no one noticed. Hines did but didn't say anything.

'I thought she was going to do the usual. Offer her condolences, say how much she liked our son. Probably say how much she was going to miss him, how everyone was going to miss him, but she didn't. She didn't say anything like that. At least not at first.'

David took a drink of his tea, draining the cup. He seemed to consider for a moment before continuing. Whatever he thought, it brought a smile to his face.

'At first I didn't understand what she was saying. "He said please," she said. "So I helped. Like we'd talked about. I helped." I just didn't understand and then I did. She was telling me she'd helped him die. He'd tried to cut his arm but it hadn't worked and he needed her help to finish it. So she did. She held her hand over his mouth until he stopped breathing.'

He looked up and fresh tears broke from his eyes as he continued.

'But that's not what he meant, is it? When my son said "Please"? That's not what he meant.'

A stone had lodged itself in Louise's throat. Its twin was sinking her heart.

'I don't think so,' she said softly. 'I think he was asking for help.'

'But she didn't know,' David said sharply. He sat back, thrusting into the depth of the kitchen chair. It skittered back on its legs, and for a moment, Louise and Hines feared it would fall over. David tottered like that for another second then rocked the chair back down on to all four legs.

'She didn't know. She didn't know, and I didn't know, but I thought she was telling me she had killed my son, and before I knew it my hands were round her throat and I was squeezing. *Squeezing.*'

His hands were in front of him, clutched around an invisible neck.

'And then something *popped,* and she went limp. No one had seen; we were right next to my van, and the next thing I knew she was in the back, and I was driving down the lane. I was crying, I remember that. Screaming, actually. How could she have done that? How could she have killed my son? I didn't understand. *I didn't know!'*

It was a pure wave of pain that rolled out from David, sitting there in the kitchen where he had shared meals with his son for fourteen years, where they had played Subbuteo on rainy Sunday afternoons. Where they had held birthday and Christmas parties. Louise could feel it wash over her, almost a wall of heat as he continued to tell them what had happened that awful Monday.

'All I could think to do was try and make it look like another... another suicide. So I did. I parked by the wood, got the ladder set up and carried her from the van. Tied her coat around her neck and the branch and...'

His head dropped again, and David Willikar didn't say another word until he was taken before the Magistrate's Court in Leeds to answer to the charge of the tragic murder of Wendy Jackson.

CHAPTER
FIFTY-SIX

SATURDAY, 24TH, CHRISTMAS EVE

The Lodge's restaurant was full.

Christmas music fell from hidden speakers, coating the diners with saccharine songs about dancing Santas, randy reindeers and sugar-coated snowy wonderlands as they ate. Louise thought seasonal music was the true work of the devil, along with that panpipe shit they played in the lifts of multi-floor department stores like the Co-op in town, or C&A in Leeds. She was sure it was designed to drive shoppers mad, so they stumbled around and bought the next thing they saw.

'How's your turkey?'

Louise turned to her aunt, who was spooning up a forkful of cheese-coated mash. The Christmas early bird special was a huge favourite on Christmas Eve and had become somewhat of a tradition for her surrogate parents. Evening dinner at The Lodge followed by Midnight Mass service at Holy Trinity Church. She had agreed to go long before she had been dragged into the tragic, complex case of James Willikar and Wendy Jackson.

Word had already started to spread throughout the town

about what had happened, the gossip mill winding on and on, overjoyed at the lusciousness of it all. Sex, money and murder.

Surprisingly, none of the rumours were coming from the usual suspect. Catherine Hallum had been noticeably silent on the whole affair. In fact, she hadn't been seen since leaving the station following her interview, packing up and going abroad for a Christmas holiday with her husband. Somewhere nice and hot. Somewhere where her own involvement in what had transpired could be safely ignored. That her own solicitor had killed James was perfect fodder, and Louise had hoped she could have seen her just one more time. It wouldn't have been a piece of her mind that the detective would have given; it would have been the whole damn thing. For several days certain sections of the town had been fired up by her damning rhetoric, and Louise was certain it had contributed to everything that happened afterwards.

'Louise, dear? Are you all right?'

That's what Bill Manby had asked when they were in the office together. She wasn't all right. She was tired. Really tired.

Manby had warned her this might happen. When they'd returned to the station with David Willikar, after handing him over to Sergeant Harolds to book in, Manby had called her into the office.

He'd pointed to a chair, and she'd sat. For a few moments he'd said nothing, then he'd pulled open a drawer and taken out a half bottle of bourbon. With no glasses, he'd taken two paper cups from the sideboard where he always kept a jug of water and poured them each three fingers. He handed one over to Louise, who took it without question.

'Tough one,' he'd said after taking a nip. Louise had nodded. 'Heart breaking, really.'

She didn't trust herself to speak. Not yet.

'Going to be raw for you awhile this,' Manby said. 'Going to be tough. Those cases where there doesn't seem to be any real "winner" – those are the hardest.'

'How can anyone win this?' she'd asked. Manby heard the anger in her voice; Louise felt it. 'Two kids killed. One by a greedy, selfish animal; the other by a distraught father acting on bad information. Two families ruined, over what?'

'You got the ones responsible, Louise. That's all you can do. Catch the bastards. And you did that. It's not clean, it's far from fucking perfect, but you did it. But it's going to be tough. It'll eat at you for a bit. Tire you out as you roll it around in your head. Best advice I can give – speak to someone about it. Family, friend, boyfriend. Girlfriend...'

She'd looked up then. Manby was smiling at her.

'How is Karla?' he'd asked.

'Everything all right?'

Uncle Bernard was walking back with a tray of drinks. Beside him was Karla Hayes, her own hands full with another plate of food in one hand, a tall champagne glass in the other. She wore a long black dress that plunged at the neckline to what Aunt Fiona would call a 'respectable level'. Silver glitter speckled the dress, and wrapped across her shoulders was a silver shawl. The dress clung to her legs, stopping just above the ankle clasp of her new shoes, bought especially for this occasion.

'This food is gorgeous,' she said, taking a seat next to Louise. She leaned in and gave her a peck on the cheek. 'How come you've never brought me here before?'

'Have you seen the prices?' Louise said, then offered a faint smile. She reached over and took Karla's hand.

'I'm glad you're here,' she said.

Karla's smile was enough to push the darkness away at least for a moment.

CHAPTER FIFTY-SEVEN

The Carpenters was full.

Elizabeth Hines stood at the far end of the bar and sipped on a tall glass of something that Joe had called a Winter Wonderbang. Extremely alcoholic, it stung her lips as soon as it touched. She put the glass down and picked up her lager and black instead. Joe might be a good bartender, but he was lousy at making cocktails.

'Fairy Tale of New York' played for the thousandth time over the Carps' speakers, accompanied by the drunken warblings of the pub's patrons. Glasses were waved in the air, the contents swishing over the sides to fall to the already soaked carpet, adding to the years of spilled drinks. Gold, red and silver tinsel hung down in tattered strips, and fake snow had been scattered all about the pub to add to the seasonal look. Small plastic Christmas trees had been placed on each of the tables. Of the few that remained, most had dead cigarettes stuffed into their fake boughs.

Hines watched as Joe flirted with a girl dressed in the sluttiest Santa outfit she had ever seen. Not much was left to the imagination, and she knew Joe's was particularly active. She knew it was over between them. As soon as the test had come back negative she had known she had narrowly avoided a huge mistake, one that would have meant being locked into a relationship with this huge man-child. It would have also had devastating consequences for her career, one that she loved, and she was good at.

'Hey, copper. Spare a copper?'

Hines turned and stared into the beaming face of Scruffy Pete, only this time he wasn't so scruffy. Gone was the dirty green parka he always wore. Instead, he had on what appeared to be a featureless funeral suit. His hair had been combed back and there was an almost pleasant whiff of aftershave.

'Pete. Merry Christmas!' Before she thought about it, Hines reached out and gave Pete Williams a hug. He looked shocked; she suspected that no one had hugged him for a long time.

'Same to you. Still not heard anything from Helen,' he said. 'You think she's all right?'

'I hope so,' Hines said. 'You want another?' she asked, nodding to his empty glass.

'Thought you'd never ask.'

A groan rang out as Cliff Richard started singing about mistletoe and wine. Hines turned to the bar.

Joe was leaning forward and whispering something. Sexy Santa giggled and everything jiggled.

Hines handed Pete her almost full glass, which he happily accepted. Without looking back, she walked out of the pub, leaving behind the faint drunken singing of the customers, and a man she had once thought she loved.

Strangers all.

CHAPTER
FIFTY-EIGHT

Holy Trinity Church was full.

Louise sat next to Karla, who in turn was sitting next to Aunt Fiona. The pair had hit it off over dinner, with the two talking about the psychology of children and the effect it had on their education, topics the two women were experts in.

And now they were at Midnight Mass. Uncle Bernard had dropped them off; his Christmas Eve duties did not extend to going to church. Instead, he would be at home, listening to Mozart's violin Sonata No. 26 in B-Flat Major, as he did every Christmas, while reading a Tom Clancy novel, sipping on a whisky and eating a mince pie or three.

It was warmer in the church than the last time she had been here. Had it only been two weeks since this had all begun? She looked into the aisle, to where Wendy Jackson had come staggering in, all covered in the blood of James Willikar, who lay in the churchyard. Again, the questions came unbidden: had she missed something? Could she have prevented the events to come if she had only looked a little harder? Asked more questions?

The organ started and everyone stood.

She held the orange with the candle in the centre and the

dolly mixtures on cocktail sticks and joined in the singing as the choir began to make their procession out. She was thankful this was over. She was tired. Really tired.

The choir shuffled towards her, moving slowly as they sang 'O Little Town of Bethlehem'. At the head, Marcus Riley carried the large cross of Holy Trinity. Around his neck was the red ribbon of the chorister's medal. Behind him, the rest of the choir walked slowly, psalm books held before them. One or two of the older ones carried orange-candles similar to the one Louise now held. Theirs didn't have dolly mixtures, she noted.

And then she paused.

In the choir, walking towards the rear was a face she recognised.

Ian Neal Peterson.

Over the last few days his name had come up once or twice when they considered who could have been with James in the warehouse. Every time, Ian's name was mentioned. Even Catherine Hallum had talked about him. He had been at the protest in Horbury, although he wasn't an official part of the Church of Divine Light.

Louise had wanted to speak to him, but Manby had stopped that. No evidence tying him to the warehouse, no need to question him.

But Louise could bet he was the one who had stolen the bike. The prints in the dust hadn't been deep enough to take a plaster of like they had with McKensie's shoe, but she was sure they were the same.

What does he know?

Ian saw her looking and smiled as he passed her by, his voice rising in tone and power as though a sudden surge of confidence rode through him.

Karla gave her a nudge and mouthed, 'Are you all right?' Louise nodded.

She was fine.

But she was going to be keeping a close eye on Ian Peterson from now on. Reaching down she plucked a dolly mixture from the stick and popped it in her mouth.

A very close eye.

CHAPTER
FIFTY-NINE

SUNDAY, 25TH, CHRISTMAS DAY

Her bed was full.

Louise had woken just after four in the morning. There had been no nightmare this time to pluck her from her sleep. There was no crushing weight on top of her, pushing her into the bed as cold fingers of fear clutched at her chest. For the first time she could remember, Louise had just simply woken up.

She looked at Tom at the foot of the bed. He was snoring, curled up on the Star Wars blanket Karla had bought him. He gave a twitch, chasing something in his dreams, and she sat up so she could soothe him with a gentle stroke down his back. His back paw gave a kick and he settled, his purr growing louder for a few moments under her touch.

The bed jostled slightly as Karla Hayes rolled over in her sleep. Louise looked down and stroked her hair as gently as she had stroked Tom's fur. Lying back down, Louise snuggled into Karla's back, wrapping her arms around her. She kissed her neck, the scent of her perfume still faint, mixing with her own.

Louise smiled as the memory of their lovemaking rolled back

over her. She could still feel Karla in her arms, taste her on her lips.

Closing her eyes, her face pressed against Karla's shoulder, Louise Miller went back to sleep.

EPILOGUE

His soul was empty.

Ian Neal Peterson opened his present to himself.

A small shoebox he kept in a very special place known only to him sat on his bed. The door was shut. The house was silent. He lifted the lid, dropping it to one side, and took out the scrap of fabric he had taken from the woman in the warehouse.

Lifting it to his face he inhaled deeply.

He could still smell her.

He had visited her after the service, going back to the other warehouse and the room that led to the basement where he had moved her after dealing with James.

Thinking of James got him angry. James, the one who had everything. The one who had a family who cared. Who had a girlfriend who loved him. James. The one who had ruined everything.

All it had taken was a gentle tap with the rock and then he'd put him on the grave. He'd taken his knife out and was about to see what his insides looked like when the weird pervert had come back and disturbed him. He'd only had time to duck out of sight, dashing quickly to the steps to the basement of the church.

Only when he got there did he realise that he'd left his knife.

Then he watched as the man took the knife and cut James. He could see the blood start to roll out over his skin. Not wanting to be caught, he had snuck away, going back to the warehouse where the woman was.

He'd known about the basement for some time, stumbling across it when he was chasing one of the small dogs that roamed the streets from time to time. He'd watched. He'd learned, and so that was where he'd taken her.

He hadn't been able to see what James' insides looked like because he'd been disturbed.

And no one was looking for the woman.

When he had shown off his new prize, he'd been rewarded with the promise of learning more. Together.

Ian Neal Peterson sniffed the scrap of panties again and shivered.

Soon...

Louise Miller will return in *Cut and Shut*.
Read on for a thrilling extract.

ACKNOWLEDGMENTS

I'd once again like to thank Sue Davison, my editor, for her amazing work on this book and the first, *Dirty Little Secret*. Her notes and comments made sure that the book didn't walk out into public stark naked. Any mistakes are all mine.

I'd also like to thank the following people for their kind words of encouragement and support: Lin Anderson, Peter James and M.W Craven. Before writing my first crime novel, I devoured yours to learn how to do it, and all were generous with their comments and support when this hopeful writer reached out.

Lastly, for their belief, confidence, and generosity of time, I would like to thank my publishers, Adrian and Rebecca. Working with you is a joy, and your insights and knowledge have helped shape my books into what the reader now holds.

JONATHAN PEACE

ABOUT THE AUTHOR

Jonathan Peace is a husband, cat-dad and author of the Louise Miller novels. He is a member of the Crime Writers' Association and is just about to complete his BA in Creative and Professional Writing at the University of Derby.

Jonathan now writes the Louise Miller series of psychological crime thrillers set in a fictionalised version of his hometown of Ossett, West Yorkshire. He has recently written the third in the series and while researching the fourth book, will write a stand-alone suspense novel called *The Groundskeeper*.

To find out more, visit Jonathan's website, where you can sign up to his monthly newsletter, or follow him on Twitter or Facebook.

Website: www.jpwritescrime.com
Twitter: @JPwritescrime
Facebook: JPwritescrime

THE LOUISE MILLER NOVELS

One Night in Manchester (short story prequel)
Dirty Little Secret
From Sorrow's Hold
Cut and Shut

ONE NIGHT IN MANCHESTER

Jonathan Peace has also written a short story prequel to the Louise Miller novels which is free to subscribers to his website www.jpwritescrime.com.

WPC Louise Miller ha been pulled from her usual beat n the notorious Hulme estate into the city centre where a string of murders has led the police to believe a new serial killer is on the prowl.

As the night stretches on, what starts as a drunken dispute outside a nightclub turns into a nightmarish situation, one that will have lingering effects on Louise, and bring great change to her life.

CUT AND SHUT

Louise Miller returns in 2023 in *Cut and Shut*

June, 1989
Amidst a growing atmosphere of racial tension in the area, WDCs Louise Miller and Elizabeth Hines investigate a tragic car crash which has left three people dead.

As their investigations deepen, they discover ties between a local garage and a BNP group in Dewsbury, but the racial tensions mask an even worse crime, one that has devastating consequences for the Ossett CID team.

Here follows a taster…

Women are the twin halves of men.
The Prophet of Islam

PROLOGUE

SATURDAY, 24TH

She could hear him mumbling to himself somewhere in the darkness.

His words were lost within the ringing that pulsed in her ears; the place he had struck her throbbed painfully and when she focused on it, the pain only intensified. Thoughts rolled around in her head, jumbled together. The rally, people pushing close. Shouting, and then strong hands grabbing her. Something hard hitting her head. Blackness that closed all around her. The screams and the shouts had drifted away as she floated in the darkness.

Something crashed, a metallic clash that echoed through her head with the stabbing pulse of hot needles.

He cried out, the words a non-sensical mush that ended with a heavy thud and a wet slap. Another voice cried out in pain, the low murmur of angry whispers cutting them off. She could feel four hot lines on her face where she had been slapped into silence when she had been taken, snatched from the crowd before her friends could get to her.

The fog in her head lifted slightly and her stomach rolled. If she hadn't been bound to the table with thick straps of leather she would have turned to the side to vomit. Four of them; two across her legs, another two across her chest. Each one was secured in the centre with a silver buckle, that too secured with a small gold padlock, the kind she used on her locker back at the office. Not that that had stopped them from getting inside. Leaving her "jokey" messages and gifts.

She thought about calling out, but knew that would only alert whoever had grabbed her that she was awake once more. If she had any chance of getting away, it would be now when he was preoccupied, and the last thing she needed to do was give him any indication she was awake.

Her wrists wiggled just enough that she could move her hand fractionally. The straps covered her forearms, the sleeves of her jacket bunched up beneath the elbow to reveal the soft skin of her arms. Several long cuts ran across in jagged streams, the blood already hardened into a crisp shell, the result of the scuffle in the marketplace.

It was starting to come back as the fog lifted; the BNP protest in Dewsbury town centre which she'd attended. The lines of Police with their batons and their shields. The cries for white justice. And then it all went to shit and everyone was being pushed back. The call came and they all fled back towards Saville Town.

The fog fell again, drifting across her mind to the pulsing beat of her headache. Still she fought on, fought to stay awake; she fought to not close her eyes again for fear she would never open them again. She could slip her arms side to side. Maybe only a couple of inches but it was enough to give her hope. If she moved enough times, perhaps she could loosen the straps and slip her arms out one strap at a time.

She tried to look down and then realised she couldn't move her head further than a slight nod. Another strap crossed her forehead, her hair pulled back tightly beneath her head. He'd taken her hair scrunchie, letting her hair free but had bunched it under her head like a purple pillow.

Another crash came from the darkness followed by the heavy tread of footsteps on a metal floor. Two sets of them judging by the delayed echo, she thought.

So there were definitely two people. Not one.

'You've not given us much time,' a voice said with a York-shire accent so thick it was almost cliched. 'Going to have to work fast.'

'Yes, dad,' was the reply.

Dad?

She flinched as a sudden bright light exploded all around her. She closed her eyes under the harsh glare.

'She's awake.'

Rough hands grabbed her face, pinching her cheeks tight. A foetid breath of air washed over her face and she retched as the scent filled her nostrils. Heat spread across her face as the slap rocked her head. The leather strap around her forehead caught and she jerked still.

'Open your eyes!' The voice roared directly above her and she couldn't help but follow the command. She winced as she found herself looking into her own face as a rounded mirror was wheeled into place beside her, its oval casing hovering a few feet above her. She gasped when she saw the swelling of her left eye and the blood that still ran from the split lower lip.

A shadow moved beside her, the metal squeal of rusty wheels as a tall tray was manoeuvred into place. It was the kind of tool tray that belonged in a garage, except instead of wrenches and spanners, she could see wicked looking knives with curved blades and jagged teeth. A set of pliers, the grips dark with old blood lay beside a compact saw.

'Oh Jesus,' she said when the realisation of where she was and what was about to happen sank in. 'Jesus fucking Christ, no.'

She started to thrash on the table, urgent need overwhelming conscious thought. She heaved against her bonds, pushed them as far forward as she could.

Another form appeared to her side and a small hand pressed against her shoulder. She couldn't make out their face but she could hear their voice; soft and cowed, it trembled as they spoke.

'Lie back,' they said.

'Grab her shoulders,' the other voice ordered.

A gloved hand reached to the tray and took up a thin bladed scalpel. The tip had been broken off at some point leaving a craggy disjointed edge. It caught the light from the mirror overhead, the sparkle reflecting in her fear-filled eyes.

Another gloved hand came down and pushed her skirt up, exposing her legs. 'Nice,' the voice whispered. 'Very nice.' She could hear the pleasure in his words. Even worse, she could feel his excitement as he pressed his groin against her trapped arm.

Two more hands came from overhead and pushed her shoulders down, holding her tight. She tried to look at this new person but all she could see was a silhouetted shape against the darkness. 'It's better if you don't struggle too much.'

'You don't have to do this,' she said, knowing it was useless but trying anyway.

'Yes I do,' he said, pressing the blade against the exposed skin at the top of her thigh.

When the blade bit into her flesh, she cried out in pain.

When he started to cut, she screamed.

PART ONE: SHUT

Six days earlier…

CHAPTER
ONE

Sunday, 18th

'It'll be fun.'

That's what Steve had said and in the warm embrace of the pub, the idea certainly held its charm. Steal a car. One of the expensive Paki ones down by the cricket field. 'Teach 'em a lesson. Show 'em who's boss,' he said, grinning like a loon.

Steve had said a lot of things over the course of the six hours they'd been drinking, a lot of it aimed at the Asian's who lived in the area. Harsh things, nasty things that left a cold feeling in Luke's stomach and an ever-growing sense of dread. Something was coming, that was certain. They'd all heard the rumours, they'd all dropped a few of their own. The Muslims were taking over. Their shops were sprouting everywhere, filled with a thousand variations of rice and hundreds more of curry powders and exotic spices. They stank of it, a sweet tang that reminded Luke of cold sweat. It made him sick. Made a lot of his friends sick. Friends like Steve who was still going on about stealing a car.

Luke took a long pull of his pint and let Steve waffle on.

'They always park on the curb just opposite the cricket ground. Looks like a fucking Paki convention with their beaded seats. Stinks like one too. I say we nick one, take it for a spin then torch it.'

He didn't keep his voice down. Everyone in the pub felt the same way Steve did, though perhaps not as strong, Luke thought as he caught the eye of another drinker. The man turned away, eyes moving back to the young blonde with the big tits beside him. Yes, the Pakis were everywhere, infesting the streets with their weird ways and even weirder food. And when they talked, fucking hell it was like listening to someone having a fucking stroke.

The parents of the white kids were not having it. Talk was they were pulling their kids from the schools until something was done about it. Action, not just talk.

Well, Steve wasn't just talk, was he? Steve got shit done.

It had been Steve who had introduced Luke to the local chapter of the British National Party and then to their pub here on the outskirts of Saville Town. It was nothing but a short walk to the cricket ground. And it wasn't as though he were suggesting throwing a few bricks through windows or, worse, something lit. He'd heard rumours about the strong possibility of someone planning such a thing. Luke didn't like the Pakis or the Asians or the Muslims, but he didn't think he wanted to see anyone hurt. All they had to do was go somewhere else and there wouldn't be any trouble. Go back to where they came from. Fuck, if he had the chance of moving to warmer climates he'd fucking jump at it. So what if the women had to cover their faces; some of the birds round here could do with covering up their mugs.

Instead, he was stuck here, working the rail track four nights a week for little more than pocket money while these bastards got all the handouts and were treated like fucking royalty.

Well fuck that!

'Fuck that,' he said, slamming his empty glass onto the table. 'Let's fucking do it!'

. . .

The car was right where Steve said it would be. While he and Luke watched either side of the road, Kevin got to work. It was just after ten at night and the road was quiet. The houses that sat just behind the cricket ground were dark; only one had a light on in the upper floor and there was no way they could be seen, tucked away behind a row of trees. In thirty seconds he had the door open. In a minute he had the engine running.

'Hop in, gents,' he called out.

Steve got in the front seat, ripping out the beads and throwing them to the ground before sitting down. Kevin did the same. Luke got in the back.

'Jesus, it fucking stinks!' Steve cranked down a window as the car began to move. Gunning the engine, Kevin pulled on the handbrake and spun the car around, dead centre of the road. Smoke blew out from the rear tires, the squeal as the rubber bit into the road, seeking traction loud in the cold silence of the night.

Thirty seconds later and they were off, speeding down Saville Road back towards Dewsbury town centre, all three of them whooping with delight.

The car roared across the bridge spanning the river Calder, its dark surface reflecting the waxing crescent of the moon. The sky was an oily black, the stars trying their best to peak out from behind heavy clouds that drifted to their own tune. Reaching the end of Saville Road, Kevin made a hard right up Railway Street and then another onto Wakefield Road.

'Where we going?' Luke called out from the back seat, his voice raised above the roaring wind coming through the open window.

'We get to the Mad Mile we can get onto the M1,' Steve said from the passenger seat. Kevin grunted a reply, his concentration switching between the road and the bright red warning light that was starting to flash intermittently on the dashboard. He wasn't a hundred percent sure what it meant, but judging how the car was starting to growl he was pretty sure the engine was overheating. There was also a vibration starting to grow in the left wheel, a gentle wobble that he had to correct by oversteering to the right. It felt like the damn thing was coming loose, but that was impossible.

'I'm not sure we can make it to the motorway,' he said through gritted teeth. They were on Wakefield Road, heading through Earlsheaton so fast everything was becoming a streaky blur. The stone-faced houses that lined either side of the road were stained orange in the newly fired-up streetlights. A few people walked on the pavement, presumably heading back from the local. Steve was sure he saw one of them carrying a pool cue. He wore short sleeves; the night air still held a trace of the days heat, though the tattoos that ran down the length of his bare arms suggested he didn't feel the cold.

The car lurched violently to the left, the front passenger wheel barking up the curb to briefly run along the pavement. Kevin managed to yank the steering wheel in time to avoid hitting a streetlamp. Everyone bounced as the wheel bit into the road once more.

'Jesus, man! Who the fuck taught you to drive… Stevie-fuck-ing-Wonder?'

'Shut the fuck up,' Kevin bit back just as the steering wheel ripped itself from Kevin's hands. The vibration became an earthquake beneath his fingers.

'What the fuck?' he said as the car jostled to the left, the rear underside striking the road at ninety-four miles an hour. They had just made the turn around the roundabout, and were dashing under the overpass and onto the dual carriageway that led to the M1 when sparks illuminated the inside of the car, throwing the occupants into momentary shades of red and gold. They all bounced as the left rear dipped suddenly and the car was filled with the shriek of tearing metal.

As the front half of the stolen car spun right, crushing into the barrier that separated the two carriageways, the rear end tore away, catapulted further down the road by inertia and momentum. In the back seat, Luke screamed as blood gushed from the stump of his ruined left leg. It had been caught under Kevin's seat, his foot jammed when the car ripped in two. As the shattered edge of the car bit into the road, it sent more sparks exploding in a cascade of orange and yellow fire. The ruptured fuel line bled petrol and the sparks ignited it with a sound like a dragon clearing its throat.

The fire rushed into the metal box, engulfing Luke whose screams quickly died as the flames rushed down his throat. The back half of the car careened into the grassy bank of the carriageway, its steep incline trapping the wreckage. The grass quickly caught fire and burned brightly.

The front of the car with its two passengers hit the central barrier and crushed the engine block, shattering the legs of both men and trapping them as glass and metal continued to rain down around them.

Oil and petrol bled out onto the road and for those shocked first moments, the only sound that could be heard was the writhing growl of the engine and the screams of the two men trapped in the burning car.

HOBECK BOOKS – THE HOME OF GREAT STORIES

We hope you've enjoyed reading this novel by Jonathan Peace. To keep up to date on Jonathan's fiction writing please subscribe to his website: **www.jpwritescrime.com**.

Hobeck Books offers a number of short stories and novellas, free for subscribers in the compilation *Crime Bites*.

- *Echo Rock* by Robert Daws
- *Old Dogs, Old Tricks* by AB Morgan

- *The Silence of the Rabbit* by Wendy Turbin
- *Never Mind the Baubles: An Anthology of Twisted Winter Tales* by the Hobeck Team (including many of the Hobeck authors and Hobeck's two publishers)
- *The Clarice Cliff Vase* by Linda Huber
- *Here She Lies* by Kerena Swan
- *The Macnab Principle* by R.D. Nixon
- *Fatal Beginnings* by Brian Price
- *A Defining Moment* by Lin Le Versha
- *Saviour* by Jennie Ensor

Also please visit the Hobeck Books website for details of our other superb authors and their books, and if you would like to get in touch, we would love to hear from you.

Hobeck Books also presents a weekly podcast, the Hobcast, where founders Adrian Hobart and Rebecca Collins discuss all things book related, key issues from each week, including the ups and downs of running a creative business. Each episode includes an interview with one of the people who make Hobeck possible: the editors, the authors, the cover designers. These are the people who help Hobeck bring great stories to life. Without them, Hobeck wouldn't exist. The Hobcast can be listened to from all the usual platforms but it can also be found on the Hobeck website: **www.hobeck.net/hobcast**.

CPSIA information can be obtained
at www.ICGtesting.com
Printed in the USA
LVHW041659210622
721800LV00003B/76

9 781913 793753